The Uncollected Cases
of Sherlock Holmes

Geoffrey Finch

Hardcover ISBN 978-1-78705-992-4
Paperback ISBN 978-1-78705-949-8
ePub ISBN 978-1-78705-950-4
PDF ISBN 978-1-78705-951-1

Published by MX Publishing
335 Princess Park Manor, Royal Drive,
London, N11 3GX
www.mxpublishing.com

Cover design by Brian Belanger

Contents: Pages

The Sicilian Defence   1

The Pike at Saltmarsh   39

The Great Game   79

The Last Highwayman   116

The Cathedral Cat   158

The Missing Heir   201

The Archaeopteryx   248

The Dunwich Ghost   289

For Lily, Annabelle, Ruby and James

Acknowledgements

I have been fortunate in receiving encouragement and advice from a number of friends and family in writing these stories, and should particularly like to thank Jacqueline Banerjee, Pat and Geraldine McHugh, Glen and Sharon Bomstad, and Amy Barker for their diligence and patience in reading my work.

I owe a considerable debt to Nick Cardillo, author of *The feats of Sherlock Holmes* and *The Improbable Casebook of Sherlock Holmes* (with David Marcum), for his invaluable guidance in the preparation of the manuscript. Any remaining errors are entirely my own.

Thanks also to all at MX for their assistance in the publication of my book.

Finally, a huge thank you to Marion, my wife, for her inspiration, critical advice and constant support throughout.

Foreword

I began writing these stories during the recent lockdowns as an amusement for my grandchildren, in particular, Lily, whose tale of injustice at her local school prompted me to try responding in the style of Conan Doyle. It was a style I quickly found congenial, and like many things which begin casually, the project soon outgrew its origins until I had an entire volume on my hands, which I now hope is worthy of a wider audience.

This is my first attempt at literary pastiche, and whilst inhabiting the style of another writer has its rewards, it has not been without a sense of wearing borrowed clothes. Like every pasticheur, however, my hope has been that I have added something to what I have borrowed, and that by putting Doyle's characters in fresh and unique situations, I have enabled them to remain vivid and alive for a contemporary readership.

[Sherlock Holmes]……

"whom I shall ever regard as the best and wisest man whom I have ever known"

(The Final Problem)

The Sicilian Defence

It was in the spring of 1895 that Holmes and I first made the acquaintance of Major John Bartholomew, a meeting which was to lead to what Holmes later referred to as "one of the darkest and most perturbing cases" of his career. Winter had been distinguished by a dearth of criminal activity, and I had become accustomed to Holmes's outbursts as he flung down the morning newspaper,

"The London criminal is a very dull fellow, Watson. One could be forgiven for thinking the earth had swallowed him up."

"An event which Scotland Yard must pray for daily," I replied.

"Their interest is merely professional. Mine is scientific. I must have materials to practise on."

"Is there nothing at all?"

"An outbreak of cat kidnapping in Fulham, which the Courier has the temerity to put on the front page."

He got up wearily and went to his room, closing the door firmly, a sign I had come to know well over the past weeks. The habit was becoming more regular. It was evident in the pallor of his skin and the dilation of his pupils. I had made up my mind to speak to him, though I knew from experience he would take little heed. And in any case, I was preoccupied with concerns of my own. I had lately lost more than I could comfortably afford on "the sport of kings," and my small army pension now seemed smaller still. In addition to which, an unusually wet spell in January, aggravated my wound, robbing me of sleep. I have thought much of late how my brief military career, distinguished only by the receipt of a Jezail bullet has shaped my life – the meeting with Holmes, the struggle to be well, the struggle to be solvent. It is a strange, and not unwelcome, mercy that hides the future from us. As for my wound, an article in the Cornhill Magazine extolling the merits of exercise had recently appeared and I determined to follow its advice by walking five miles every morning, a routine which did not go unnoticed by Holmes.

"Your fascination for fresh air is becoming positively fanatical, Watson. You should have remained in the army."

"You forget that I was invalided out."

"Indeed. The recommendation as I recall was for rest and recuperation."

However, even he could not help but notice the change in my demeanour. After only a few days I began to feel more energetic. The doldrums of the past months started to recede, and I found myself sleeping more soundly at night. Even so, I could not persuade Holmes to accompany me.

"It is mental, not physical, exercise, which I require," he said.

One morning, in early March, I returned from my walk a little later than usual and found Holmes pacing round the room, smoking furiously.

"Where the devil have you been, Watson?" he broke out.

"Where I have been every morning, for the past two months."

He waved his hand dismissively. "No matter. What do you make of that?" He pointed to a piece of paper on the table. Beside it was an envelope. I looked at him again. Gone was the lassitude and dullness which had lately been his constant companions. He was alert and eager-eyed.

"You have a case, Holmes," I said.

He smiled and snapped his fingers. "I think I have. It came today just after you left. Read it."

I picked up the paper. It was pale cream, with one careful fold exactly in the middle and an address in Surrey embossed at the top.

"Handmade," Holmes said. "There's only one stationer in London that produces paper of such quality. Allsop's in Bond Street."

"Expensive tastes," I replied. "The sender is clearly a person of some importance."

"Or some pretension. Observe the handwriting."

I looked at the simple black script. Three lines of thickly formed letters, unevenly spaced.

"That is not an educated hand," Holmes said. "It is bold and confident but lacks flourish. The writer has used a dip pen. The broad nib is unmistakable. The fountain pen has a finer point to it and the ink flows more evenly."

"A simple fellow, then. A military man perhaps."

"Excellent Watson. I believe you are on the right track. And what of the message?"

I read it out: "*Dear Mr. Holmes, I must see you on a matter of some urgency. I will call on you this evening, if convenient, John Bartholomew.* Blunt and forthright, I should say. He doesn't stand on ceremony. Is there anything else to be gleaned from it?"

I looked pointedly at Holmes.

"No, nothing Watson. I believe you have wrung the missive dry."

I raised my eyebrows. "Really?"

"There are a few minor points," he said carelessly. "Our correspondent walks with a limp, has married above his station, and plays chess."

I burst out laughing. "You can't possibly have discovered that from this letter," I protested.

"Of course not. It's all in there, or most of it," he replied, tossing a volume of Baker's *Military Register* on the table.

"That is unworthy of you Holmes."

"You must allow me my small joke, Watson," he said, smiling. "You are constantly depicting me in your lurid narratives as some sort of magician. I am apparently capable of deducing that a man has two cats and lives in a basement with no heating, merely by examining his walking stick. What an absurdity."

"Readers require entertainment," I replied slightly nettled. "They are not interested in dry exercises in logical reasoning. I simply embellish the accounts a little. That is all."

"And in so doing, destroy any credibility my methods of detection have."

This was an old bone of contention between us and one which I saw it was pointless to pursue. But despite his disdain for my accounts, I knew he was not displeased by the attention they brought him. Why else would John Bartholomew have sought him out?

"You were correct in your suggestion that Bartholomew is a military man," he continued. "Major Bartholomew served in the Lancashire Fusiliers. He was badly wounded in the thigh in the Sudan."

"Thus the limp," I said.

He nodded. "Any man with such an injury must find his walking affected."

"And what of marrying above his station? I am sure the *Register* would not venture to comment on the circumstances of his marriage."

Holmes pointed to the letter. "Smell the paper, Watson."

I put my face close to the sheet and sniffed. There was the most delicate aroma of vanilla. "Exquisite. What is it?"

"Tahitian vanilla. One of the most expensive perfumes in the world. I have only smelt it once before and that was on a countess. She wore it the day she was hanged for murdering her husband. Remarkable woman."

4

"You are surely not suggesting the Major wears perfume, Holmes?"

He let out a roar. "I think not, though one cannot exclude the possibility altogether. No! He has used his wife's notepaper. The expensive tastes are hers. A woman does not acquire such tastes overnight. Not if she is the wife of a humble Major."

"And the chess?" I asked.

He motioned to the envelope. "There is more."

I picked up the envelope, which had Holmes's name written on it in the same sprawling handwriting and felt inside. My fingers touched a small wooden object. I withdrew it carefully and held it up to the light.

"A chess piece," I said. "What on earth does it mean?" I tipped the envelope up hoping to find an accompanying explanation. But there was none.

"Precisely. A black pawn. From a Staunton chess set if I am not mistaken. It's commonly used in matches. As to its significance, we shall have to wait for our visitor to enlighten us. I'm surprised that you haven't heard of him, Watson. Before the Sudan, the Major was in Afghanistan."

"It's a big place, Holmes. Almost three times the size of the United Kingdom. And my time there was very short-lived. But one thing is clear. If the Major served in the Sudan against the Mahdists, he will not be consulting you about a trivial matter."

The clock had just struck seven when a loud knock from below, followed by the scurrying feet of Mrs. Hudson, told us that our visitor had arrived. We had just finished a light supper of baked fish and apricots and had begun smoking.

"A gentleman to see you, Mr. Holmes," announced Mrs. Hudson, ushering in a heavily built man leaning on a stick.

"Holmes rose from his chair. "Thank you, Mrs. Hudson. Major Bartholomew, I presume."

The man looked momentarily startled. "I no longer use that title, sir. I am surprised to hear it on your lips."

"I have spent the afternoon perusing the archives of the *Military Register*, in which you have an honourable mention. My friend and associate, Dr. Watson, is also a military man. You are among friends here. Please be seated and tell us how I can be of assistance?"

The Major sat down in a chair, conveniently placed by Holmes, midway between us. Despite his injury, he had a strong and vigorous appearance, a man more used to action than reflection, I surmised. I judged him to be in his mid-forties, though his lined and careworn face suggested another ten years.

"You call me a military man, Mr. Holmes, and so I was, but it has been my misfortune to incur the contempt of those I considered my comrades."

I looked across at Holmes and saw an unmistakable gleam in his eyes. "I am sorry to hear that, Major," he said. "By all accounts, you served honourably in the Sudan and were wounded in defence of your country."

Bartholomew let out a derisory snort. "That wound has been the source of my misfortunes, and what I find most hard to bear, those of my wife too."

"How so?" Holmes exclaimed.

"Because it was not honourably gained."

"You must tell me all. Be absolutely frank with me, Major. It is the one thing I demand of my clients."

Bartholomew looked apprehensively over at me.

"You can trust in Dr. Watson's complete discretion," Holmes said. "As indeed, you can mine."

The Major nodded. "Very well. I should explain that I come from a family with a long history of military service, stretching back to the Napoleonic wars. I was brought up from a young boy to believe that courage, discipline, and sacrifice were the important things, and I expected to spend my life in service to the Empire."

"A noble ambition," I commented.

Holmes smiled thinly. I knew very well his opinion of military life. It would be difficult to find anyone less inclined to follow orders. "Indeed," he said. "And what prevented you from fulfilling such a worthy goal."

"I fell in love," replied Bartholomew.

"As far as I am aware, the military has not yet embraced celibacy," Holmes said. "It is still possible to continue the even more noble art of procreation."

"With a Sudanese woman."

"That is certainly uncommon," I put in. "Though not unheard of."

"Yes," Bartholomew replied. "But in this case, the lady in question was the daughter of a wealthy sheikh who was friendly to the British."

"Your feelings were returned, I take it?" Holmes asked.

"Indeed. I had been assigned to guard her and her entourage from the rebels who were rumoured to be massing in the desert for a final assault on the Red Sea ports. We were immediately drawn to each other. I cannot explain it, Mr Holmes. It was beyond anything I have ever felt before."

"Quite," said Holmes briskly. "And the outcome was an attachment?"

"Yes, but unknown to us, we were observed. I was summoned before the Colonel and immediately relieved of my duties. The sheikh, however, was not so easily satisfied. He said I had dishonoured his daughter, the penalty for which in his country was death. The Colonel was not about to submit me to such a fate, but he said that without further retribution the sheikh might very well punish his daughter. The day afterwards, the rebel attack on the main port began, and I was sent to defend the city. It was a fierce and bloody campaign."

"But you were victorious," I said.

Bartholomew grunted. "Eventually, though the carnage was terrible. But it gave me the chance to reflect on my situation and that of Isabella, whom I had put in danger. I decided then that I would not survive the encounter."

"You determined to take your own life?" said Holmes.

"In a manner of speaking. I thought if I were killed the sheikh might see it as a form of justice and be merciful to his daughter. There was a part of the fortress which had been subject to sniper fire. Many men had lost their lives defending it. One night the Colonel asked for a volunteer to stand on sentry duty. Two of us stepped forward. A lower-ranking officer and myself. It was usual in such circumstances for the subordinate to be chosen but the Colonel turned to me. I saw a look of recognition in his face as he nodded in my direction. We understood each other very well. The night was clear, hardly a cloud in the sky, with a full moon. The advice was always to expose oneself as little as possible and keep below the parapet. I waited until the moon was at its height and stepped clear of the stone turrets. There was nothing at first. Then six shots rang out in quick succession, smashing into the stone pillars. The last one hit me just above the right thigh. I fell to the ground, bleeding heavily, and passed out. When I came to hours later, I was in a makeshift field hospital with the Colonel standing over me. It was evident from his expression that he was disappointed."

"Your death would have got him out of a tricky situation," I commented.

"Exactly, but he reasoned that as many thought I had died, it might be convenient to encourage that belief. A few days later there was a funeral for the victims of the action and my name was read out with the rest. Meanwhile, arrangements were made to ship me home secretly. It seemed for a while that the danger was over. The sheikh's demands for my death stopped and things returned to normal. But then two days before I was due to leave, Isabella turned up at our camp. She had been badly beaten and her clothes were torn. She was also clearly with child. It seems her father had been prepared to forgive her until her situation became evident. She was flogged and thrown out."

"And she returned to England with you?" Holmes asked.

"Yes. We were married privately by an army chaplain and came back together where we have lived quietly ever since."

"And the child?" I enquired.

"Isabella miscarried and we have not been blessed with any more children."

"This is all most affecting," Holmes said, knocking out the remains of his pipe into his slipper. "But I am yet to see how I can be of service to you."

"It is very simple," Bartholomew replied. "We have lately been subject to threats and abuse. I fear for my wife's safety, Mr. Holmes."

"What form do they take?" Holmes asked.

"In the beginning, it was letters sent anonymously warning us of 'consequences' should we choose to remain in England."

"You showed them to the police?"

"Yes. They considered them the product of someone in the neighbourhood annoyed at the presence of a foreigner in the area, particularly from a country with which we were at war and advised me to ignore them."

"Do you still have the letters?"

"No, I destroyed them."

Holmes gave a sigh of annoyance. "That is a pity, Major. But I take it that matters did not stop there?"

Bartholomew shook his head. "Things started disappearing from the house. Nothing valuable, a bag of candles, my cigar case, a box of handkerchiefs. I thought at first that I had simply misplaced them, but my wife noticed it too."

"What servants do you have in the house?" enquired Holmes.

"Just three. A local girl from the village, who is our maid, and a housekeeper and her husband, who live in. But I do not doubt their honesty."

"All the same, petty pilfering among servants is not an uncommon occurrence, I'm afraid."

"But commonplace thieves usually confine themselves to taking things, Mr. Holmes. They do not return them."

We looked at Bartholomew in surprise.

"A few days later, the items reappeared in the same place, undamaged and with nothing missing," he said.

"You mean the thief simply borrowed them?" I exclaimed.

"It would seem so."

"How long have these mysterious reappearances been occurring?" Holmes asked

"For several months."

"And yet you have only come to consult me now. Why?"

"Because yesterday things became more serious. I have a dog, a Pyrenean mountain dog, which is devoted to me, and I to him.

Yesterday morning I came down to breakfast and found him lying dead just outside the rear door. He had been poisoned."

"You are sure that was the cause of death?" Holmes asked.

"Yes, there was froth around his mouth and no sign of injury."

"I suppose it is just possible he was foraging for food and ate something," said Holmes.

"That is not all," Bartholomew went on. "By his head, I found the chess piece which I sent you."

"The black pawn?"

"Yes."

"What significance do you attach to that?" Holmes asked.

"That whoever killed my dog knows me. I have been a keen chess player since my youth, though I have not played competitively for several years."

"I see," said Holmes. "Is the choice of piece significant?"

"All my notable wins were with black," replied Bartholomew. "I was an exponent of the Sicilian Defence. You are familiar with the opening move Mr. Holmes?"

"Pawn to c5 as I recall."

"Yes, white is expecting pawn to e5 and is thrown off-guard. I learned the strategy from Howard Staunton."

"Whoever has done this has a macabre sense of humour," I said.

"He also has revealed something about himself. Our opponent is not quite so anonymous as before," Holmes commented

"Perhaps not," replied Bartholomew. "But it has greatly alarmed my wife. Isabella has suffered badly from her nerves since coming to England."

"I am sorry to hear that," I said. "I would be happy to offer my services."

"Thank you, Dr. Watson. Isabella has a consultant in London whom she sees and who has prescribed medication."

"Tell me, Major. Would you consider yourself a wealthy man?" Holmes asked setting light to a fresh pipe of tobacco.

Bartholomew looked startled by the question and hesitated before answering. "Not in the slightest," he replied eventually. "I have my army pension which allows us to live modestly, though I sometimes feel my wife misses the luxuries of her former life. But she has never complained. However, I was fortunate about a year ago to come into a legacy from a distant relative. It is paid in the form of an annuity and allows us to live with more ease."

Holmes got to his feet. A sign he had learned all he could from the interview. "Thank you, Major," he said, holding out his hand. "I shall do what I can to help you and your wife. But I advise you to be on your guard. Our opponent has raised the stakes by this latest move and has shown that he is in earnest. Dr. Watson and I will visit you next week if that is convenient."

"Goodbye, Mr. Holmes. It's a relief to me to know you will investigate," Bartholomew said.

When the Major had departed, I looked at Holmes. He was standing by the window observing Bartholomew depart in a hansom cab.

"A fine fellow," I said.

"And a deeply troubled one," Holmes replied. "I fear he has made a powerful enemy."

"You think there is more to this than the malice of a disgruntled neighbour?"

"I do, and so does Bartholomew. I could see it in his eyes. I believe he knows more."

"But apart from the dog, all the incidents have been petty annoyances. Even the robberies were not actual thefts. The items seem to have been taken at random."

"But there was one striking thing about them. They were all containers of some kind, boxes and bags."

I looked blankly at him.

"The thief was looking for something. He removed them to search them without the threat of being discovered."

"But why return them?"

"To avoid the involvement of the police. Ostensibly no crime was committed."

Holmes spent the next few days traversing the streets of London. He went out immediately after breakfast and did not return until early evening. All questions about what he was doing were met with an airy dismissal.

"I have a few lines of enquiry. But you know my methods, Watson. I never theorise in advance of the facts."

It was the following Saturday before we could arrange our visit to Major Bartholomew. We boarded the 9.45 from Waterloo and were soon deep in the Surrey countryside. Holmes was silent for most of the journey. The sight of green fields and wooded valleys seemed to induce a state of inertia in him. When I remarked on the beauty of the scenes passing before us he merely nodded and said,

"Quite so, but they are devoid of people."

"You mean they are devoid of crime," I replied.

"That is a common illusion. The most beautiful places frequently conceal the worst crimes. I mean they are devoid of action."

"But that is their chief virtue. You won't deny the power of nature."

"Not for others, perhaps. But for myself, I do. The chief virtue of the countryside, as you put it, is to make me long for the city."

I laughed. "That is heresy, Holmes. You are saying it merely to be controversial."

Shortly before midday, we arrived at our destination, the small village of Bardford End. Waiting for us was a horse-drawn wagon which took us the two-mile journey to the gates of a rambling old house that had clearly seen better days. At some time in its past, it must have served as a farmhouse. The sign "Marsh Farm," and the litter of outbuildings announced as much. There is a melancholy about buildings which have fallen into disuse or which have been converted to some other use, a hint of something richer now vanished. But as we approached it, we saw that it was a bustle of activity. The outbuildings were swarming with policemen shouting noisily, and in the middle directing this cacophony was Inspector Mallory of Scotland Yard. He looked up in surprise as we approached.

"You're quick off the mark and no mistake," he said to Holmes. "How did you hear about this?"

"You have the advantage of me, Inspector," Holmes replied "We have heard nothing. What has happened here?"

"Mrs. Bartholomew was abducted last night? Two men broke in and seized her."

"And what about the Major?" I put in.

"He was injured. He's upstairs now, still unconscious. But if you didn't know about it why are you here?"

"Bartholomew is a client of mine," Holmes replied. "I have been assisting him with a small matter."

"Well, now that you're here I suppose you'll want to poke about in your usual fashion. I don't mind as long as you don't get in the way of my officers."

Inspector Mallory was new to the Yard. A pert young man from the provinces, bristling with ambition, who had been promoted for solving a local murder a year ago. He considered Holmes's powers overrated and wasn't shy of saying so.

"Never fear, Inspector. I am not here to steal your thunder. Anything I discover will be at your service," replied Holmes disarmingly.

Mallory nodded. "All right then. We understand one another," he said.

We watched as he walked off, barking instructions at his men.

"That young man would be better if he did more poking, and less strutting, about," commented Holmes. "Let's go into the house and see what we can make of this mayhem."

We went through the open door into a large hall. To the right was the drawing-room, an elegant though sparsely furnished room with a faded divan and a cluster of chairs of different sizes around an open fireplace. Seated on the divan was a stout lady weeping quietly, being comforted by a burly man in a gaberdine coat, who looked more used to being outdoors than in. These I guessed were the housekeeper and her husband. On a small chair to the side of the fireplace sat a pale young girl staring anxiously at her feet, evidently the maid. Holmes nodded to the constable standing guard over this forlorn cameo.

"I am Sherlock Holmes," he said, addressing the housekeeper. "And this is my companion, Dr. Watson. We are here to assist the police in their enquiries."

The lady looked up at Holmes her face visibly brightening at the mention of his name and the sound of his voice.

"Oh, Mr. Holmes it's a blessing you're here. The police are all very well, I'm sure, but they're not like you."

Holmes smiled appreciatively.

"And Doctor Watson too," she went on. "Such wonderful stories."

"Quite," replied Holmes his smile vanishing. "I will do what I can. You are Mrs. Bartholomew's housekeeper, I take it."

"Yes, Ellen Hodge. This is my husband, Thomas. That's Mary over there, the mistress's maid."

Holmes nodded. "What has happened here? Who can tell me?"

Mr. Hodge cleared his throat. "The mistress has been took and the master near murdered," he said.

"How was this discovered?" Holmes asked. "Tell me everything from the beginning."

"About midnight I was just closing the house for the night and Mary come running in from the courtyard. She said she'd seen two men lurking about near the bushes."

Holmes held up his hand. "Can you describe these men, Mary?"

The maid looked flustered at being suddenly the centre of attention.

"Take your time," Holmes said.

"It was very dark, sir. They were looking through that window there." She pointed to a small window in the corner of the room. "And they were talking to each other."

"Did you hear what they were saying?" I asked

She shook her head. "It was all gobbledygook."

"What did you do when Mary told you this?" Holmes enquired, turning to Hodge.

"I told her to make haste and fetch the constable. Then I went outside to see for myself, but there was no one about. I searched the outbuildings and then went back to the house. I come into the hall and heard this cry from the landing. There were two men on the stairs.

One of them was carrying the mistress and had his hand over her mouth. The other one had a pistol and told me to stand off or I'd regret it. They was both black as the ace of spades. There wasn't nothing I could do so I let them pass and ran up to see the master. He was lying as he is now, still as death with a gash in the side of his head."

"How did they get in," Holmes asked

"There's a window at the back. It's been forced," said the housekeeper.

"And what of you? Did you hear nothing of this?"

"Not a whisper. I sleep like a baby Mr. Holmes. The first I knew was when Thomas came and told me."

Holmes got to his feet. "Come Watson. Let us do a little poking about as Mallory calls it. Thank you for your help." Holmes glanced over at the policeman. "I think they can all return to their duties for now, constable."

We made our way upstairs to the bedroom, where the crime had occurred. It was a modest-sized room dominated by a large double bed. The Major lay on his left side as if in a deep sleep, a trickle of blood over his right ear the only sign that anything was amiss. At the foot of the bed sat a nurse. She made to get up as we entered but Holmes motioned to her to sit still. He got out a magnifying glass and began examining the Major's wound closely. The nurse stirred.

"It is all right, I shall not disturb the dressing," he said. "I merely want to establish the angle of the blow." He paused and made some notes in a pocketbook. "He was struck from behind. Do you agree Watson?"

I looked at the blood-soaked bandage which had stanched the wound. "Yes, the blood is thicker at the back, towards the crown."

"He was struck whilst sleeping," Holmes said. "The attacker did not want to run the risk of him waking up and preventing the abduction."

"A cowardly blow. A little harder and it would have been a case of murder."

"That is still a possibility," Holmes replied. "We have yet to find his wife."

He bent closer to the pillows and began sniffing on the other side of the bed.

"Chloroform," he said. "She was sedated."

"And why not the husband as well?" I asked.

"It takes time to work," he replied. "Sedating a man of the Major's build would be no easy task."

"It may be some time before he fully regains consciousness," I said. "There is the possibility of permanent damage."

We left the room and went downstairs to the back of the house. A passage led to a small parlour with a window looking out onto the garden. Its use as a storeroom was evident from the assorted garden implements which lay around. The lower part of the sash had been pushed up with considerable force, shattering the metal lock.

"This has been done with a strong lever," said Holmes. "Our intruders came prepared." He got down on his hands and knees examining the floorboards.

"Curious. It rained quite heavily yesterday yet the boards are clean. Are we to suppose they removed their shoes, like good house guests? Let's see if we have better fortune outside."

We returned to the hall and out through the main entrance. Mallory and his men were still scouring the outbuildings and paid us scant attention as we skirted the house. All around lay the imprint of heavy police boots. Holmes let out a sigh of exasperation.

18

"We might as well have let a herd of elephants loose. My talents are wasted here, Watson."

We picked our way through some shrubs immediately underneath the rear window and Holmes crouched down for every bit like a hunter tracking the spoor of an animal. Eventually, he let out a cry of success.

"See here Watson. Two sets of prints. One set is deeper underneath the sill. This is the fellow who forced the lock."

He took out his magnifying glass and peered intensely at the prints. "Both sets are exactly the same size and shape."

"So the men were of the same build?" I said.

"Not exactly," Holmes replied. "Look at the heel of the right shoe of the first set. It has the same worn outer edge as its partner in the other set. And there's a stud missing in the left shoe of both sets."

I bent down and saw that he was right. Both sets were identical. I glanced up at Holmes who was smiling at my bewilderment.

"It's simple Watson," he said. "We have one set of prints made twice."

"But there were two men. The maid and the housekeeper's husband both agree on that," I replied.

"They do. And as yet I have no explanation. But we have seen all there is to see here. Let us continue our circuit."

We made our way round to the front of the house, passing as we did so the servants' quarters. The housekeeper was busy hanging out some washing and called out to us as we approached.

"Good morning, sirs. Do you know yet who has done this dreadful thing?"

"We have made some progress," I replied.

"God be praised. The master and mistress didn't deserve such wickedness."

"You are fond of your mistress?" Holmes asked.

"Indeed, I am sir. Such a dear sweet creature."

"Would you say she was happy here?"

She hesitated. "She loved the Major, but she missed her home something terrible. She was forever talking about it. The beautiful mountains, the blue skies. Master bought her some plants to remind her of her it. Very exotic they were. She loved tending them."

"Where are they now," I asked.

"Over there," she pointed in the direction of a large greenhouse some hundred yards away from the house.

"Thank you, Mrs. Hodge. Watson and I will stroll in that direction. By the way, has anything gone missing from your larder recently?"

"It's funny you should say that," she replied. "A few things have disappeared during the past week. Some chicken, a ham pie and some milk. I'm afraid Mary is given to taking food. Her mother is very poorly and has three children to feed so I haven't liked to say anything."

"What was all that about?" I asked as we walked towards the greenhouse.

"Just a line of enquiry," Holmes replied.

The sun was high in the sky as we opened the door to the greenhouse and went in. Inside we were greeted with a display of colour that I have not seen outside of the Royal Botanic Gardens at Kew. Wonderful blue irises, their heads spread-eagled like giant hands, deep red poppies the size of footballs and cacti of every shape and dimension.

"Amazing!" Holmes said. "Who could have imagined such splendour in the heart of Surrey?"

"This is the work of a talented gardener, Holmes."

We wandered down the main aisle marvelling at each new specimen. Occasionally, Holmes would take out his magnifying glass and look more closely at a particularly striking formation of petals and stamens.

"This would convert the most ardent non-believer," he said. "How is it possible to deny the existence of a creator?"

I reminded him of his earlier dismissive comments about the power of nature.

He smiled. "I believe, for once, Watson, you may be right. Let us hope at any rate that it brought some consolation to Mrs. Bartholomew, forlorn amid the alien greenery of Surrey."

Outside we paused to take stock of our situation. It was now mid-afternoon, and we should have to hurry to get the last train back to London.

"We have done as much as we can for the moment," Holmes said. "Baker Street and one of Mrs. Hudson's fine pies beckons. We'll return tomorrow."

I desisted from asking him whether he thought we should find Mrs. Bartholomew alive. The melancholy alternative was too unthinkable to contemplate.

Crossing the courtyard of the house we were met by Inspector Mallory looking unusually pleased with himself.

"Have you found anything interesting gentlemen?"

Holmes waved his hand airily. "A few small things but nothing definitive."

"I thought not," Mallory replied. "My men have been over everything with a fine toothcomb."

"Yes, we saw plenty of evidence of that," said Holmes grimly.

"I'm sure we will find the lady soon," continued Mallory. "But in the meantime, we have the weapon used to attack Mr. Bartholomew."

21

"You have found the poker?" Holmes said. "Well done."

The inspector's face fell. "You knew?"

"It was the one implement missing from the companion set in the bedroom. There was a very obvious space for it. Brush, tongs, scuttle, but no poker. It is the object I would seize were I intending to render someone unconscious. You found it in one of the outbuildings?"

"Yes."

"Just so."

An hour or so later we sat opposite each other in an otherwise empty compartment speeding to London, smiling broadly at each other.

"A small victory, Watson. But pleasurable nonetheless."

"True," I replied, "but there are bigger mysteries to this case than the whereabouts of the poker. I am still not clear why anyone would want to abduct Mrs. Bartholomew in the first place. Presuming the two men were employed by the sheikh why would he go to the trouble of abducting a wayward daughter whom he had already turned out of his house?"

Holmes drew deeply on his pipe and blew a cloud of smoke into the carriage. "You remember that I spent several days researching this case before coming down here?"

"Yes," I replied. "I also remember that you would tell me nothing of what you were about."

He waved the smoke away and laughed. "Well, I will tell you now. The sheikh, or to give him his full title, 'His Highness Sheikh Wadi El Halifa' is one of the richest men in the Sudan. His wealth comes principally from a large diamond mine which he owns."

"So Mrs. Bartholomew was sacrificing a life of considerable luxury in her attachment to the Major?"

"Yes, though being a woman of great resourcefulness as well as courage she had devised her own solution. Let us suppose that when the sheikh expelled her from his home that she did not leave empty-handed. She could easily have hidden some gems about her person. In all probability she had them sewn into one of her garments."

"But if so, why did she not tell the Major? He was her husband."

"She could not be sure of his reaction. He is after all an honourable man and may not have approved of her stealing from her father. Besides, with his own modest means, he would not have liked to think himself indebted to his wife's greater wealth. At all events, she decided to keep the knowledge to herself."

"But how can you possibly know all this? It is pure speculation."

"You know my methods, Watson. Follow the facts and then build a hypothesis. You recall the Major telling us his wife suffered with her nerves and was accustomed to visiting a consultant in London?"

"Indeed, though the picture you paint of her hardly suggests a nervous disposition."

"Precisely. I made it my business to visit every medical consultant in Harley Street."

I blew out my cheeks in surprise. "Medical information is confidential Holmes. How could you hope to find out anything?"

He smiled. "A little bit of pretence can go a long way. I simply presented myself to the receptionist at each establishment as Mr Bartholomew and said my wife had lost her purse and thought she might have left it behind when she came for her appointment. They looked through their records and politely informed me that there was no Mrs Bartholomew on their books. It took me the whole day but at the end of it I was convinced that the lady had another reason for wishing to be in London."

"Did you consider the possibility of a liaison?"

"I confess that I did, though I didn't think it likely. Her visits to London were very infrequent. It would be a very tardy lover who would be content with such a cavalier arrangement. Besides she was in a foreign country and hardly knew anyone. It was more likely that she came to London to conduct some business. You have probably never had reason to visit Hatton Garden, Watson."

"No, though I know it by reputation."

"It shares with Amsterdam the reputation of being the world centre of the diamond trade. Everyone knows everyone else there. It's completely unlike the medical world. I had no sooner described Mrs. Bartholomew to the jewellers there than they nodded their heads. Over the course of the past year, she has been to Hatton Garden on four separate occasions and sold several cut diamonds of considerable value."

"But this is to exchange one problem for another," I said. "If she could not explain to her husband possessing a fortune in diamonds, how could she explain having an equivalent amount in cash?"

"Put yourself in her situation," Holmes replied. "You have a large amount of money which you wish to be at the disposal of your husband without him knowing how you came by it. What is the best way of accomplishing that?"

I thought for a moment. The solution, when it came, was obvious. There were but two possible ways of managing this. One was a large win at the gaming table, something which was hardly conceivable in the lady's case. And the other was a legacy.

"The Major's legacy," I burst out. "Of course!"

"Exactly," Holmes replied. "He said it was from a distant relative whose existence he had not been aware of. What's more, it was in the form of an annuity. Regular payments were made every year. A very unusual form for a legacy wouldn't you say?"

"I must say Holmes that my admiration for the lady grows by the minute."

"Indeed, though unfortunately, the venture carries a risk. The international diamond world is a small one. Sooner or later the transactions were bound to reach the ear of her father. Diamonds of quality are unique objects. He would recognise his own property."

"And send emissaries to reclaim what was left."

"Yes," Holmes said "and possibly punish her too. The sheikh is by all accounts a vengeful man. There is one hopeful sign, though. They did not kill the Major. I would have expected them to."

"I am not so sanguine. That blow could yet prove fatal."

Holmes nodded. "Let us hope not Watson."

We passed the rest of the journey in silence pondering the unlikelihood of the case having a good outcome. Even the excellent dinner which Mrs Hudson had prepared for us on our return failed to revive our spirits and we retired to bed discontented with ourselves and with the world.

The next day saw us returning to Bardford End by the first available train. Alighting at the station we were soon at the front door of the farmhouse. The housekeeper answered the bell looking flustered and excited all at once.

"Mr. Holmes," she burst out. "The police have got them."

"Got who?" Holmes asked.

"The men that took the mistress. And the master's recovered. He's sitting up in bed as well as ever. God be praised."

"Excellent news," said Holmes.

"And what of your mistress. Has she been found?" I asked.

"No. But the inspector says it won't be long. He's upstairs now with the master."

She took us upstairs and announced us to the Major who was sitting bolt upright as if to attention, drinking a cup of tea. Though pale and bandaged he looked none the worse for the attack. By his side stood Mallory who had evidently been narrating the events of the night.

"Good morning gentlemen," he said as we entered the room. "You have heard the news?"

"Indeed. Congratulations, Inspector. You have done well," Holmes replied.

"Just simple police work. Nothing fancy," Mallory said.

"Perhaps so," put in the Major lowering his cup. "But I am enormously grateful to you and your men."

Mallory nodded, smiling broadly.

"How did you find them?" I asked. "Were they close by?"

"We did a sweep of the area and found them just five miles distant, staying in a lodging house. They came quietly enough."

"Are you sure they are the men who broke in?" asked Holmes.

"The maid and the housekeeper's husband have both identified them as the men they saw."

"And what do they have to say for themselves?" Holmes continued.

"Precious little," Mallory replied. "Their English is poor, and we've had to employ an interpreter. But they don't deny seeking out Mrs. Bartholomew. They are servants of the sheikh sent here to recover his property."

"That is the most puzzling aspect of this business," said the Major. "We do not possess any property of the sheikh's."

"Perhaps you don't Major, but it appears your wife does," said Mallory.

Bartholomew shook his head. "How can that be?" He asked.

Holmes signalled to Mallory. "If you will allow me, Inspector." He turned to the Major.

"When your wife was expelled from her father's house, she brought with her some diamonds."

Bartholomew looked startled, "She said nothing of this to me?"

"She did not wish to alarm you, Major. But she did it for both of you and was thinking of your future together."

"Holmes is right," put in Mallory. "Though I've no idea how the devil he knows."

"Just simple detective work, Inspector," Holmes replied smiling.

"But what of the lady," I asked. "Is she safe?"

"At the moment they are denying any involvement in the abduction, though they're guilty right enough. We found a gun amongst their things. It has been made clear to them that if any harm comes to your wife, Major, they will hang. I have no doubt we will break them soon. In the meantime, I am removing my officers from the farm. There is no longer any danger to you, and we are searching farther afield for your wife."

The inspector reached over and shook the Major's hand who thanked him again for his diligence in pursuing the case. When he had gone, the major turned to Holmes,

"I am very sorry to have troubled you with this case, Mr. Holmes. You are a busy man, and I clearly should have had more confidence in the police."

Holmes waved his hand after his usual fashion. "Do not give it another thought, Major. Watson and I are pleased that matters seem to be reaching a satisfactory conclusion."

"Nevertheless, I know your time is of value so please do accept this from me."

He stretched out his hand to Holmes with a cheque clearly visible between his fingers.

Holmes shook his head. "No, Major. It is a principle with me never to accept remuneration where I have not been successful. Consulting detectives also have their honour."

We left the house in a sombre mood, and I fancied my friend a little downcast at not being able to play a more important part in the case.

"Perhaps we underestimated the talents of Inspector Mallory," I said.

"Perhaps so," Holmes replied. "At all events, we are finished here for the moment."

We boarded the train back to Waterloo each busied with his own thoughts about the case. So preoccupied was I that I took no notice of Holmes getting to his feet and looking out of the carriage window.

"We are approaching Pincher's Halt," he said. "Our first stop."

"What of it?" I replied. I had never known him to resort to a running commentary on our journey before.

"I must alight here," he said.

I looked up in alarm. "Whatever for Holmes?"

"There is unfinished business to attend to," he replied. "The Major's wife remains in danger."

"In that case, I shall certainly accompany you," I said.

Holmes shook his head. "No, old friend. You must continue to Baker Street. All must seem perfectly normal. But I would be grateful for your revolver. I know you always carry it with you."

"Holmes!" I protested. "If there is danger then I must go with you."

"It is merely a precaution. That is all. Were I in any real danger you know there is no one else I would rather have by my side."

He had evidently made up his mind about his course of action and I knew it would be fruitless for me to try to dissuade him. The train stopped at the Halt, and he got out of the carriage.

"Be careful!" I called out to him as we pulled away.

He turned and waved. "I shall be back by breakfast time. Tell Mrs. Hudson I will have the kippers."

I spent the remainder of that train journey in a state of high anxiety. That Holmes was exposing himself to great danger was clear to me. Why else would he ask for my revolver? I blamed myself for letting him go so easily, alternately imagining insisting on accompanying him and accepting my powerlessness in the face of his determination. I had never in the course of our entire friendship been able to impose my will on his. That was always his prerogative.

I arrived at Baker Street late in the afternoon, having decided to walk the few miles from Waterloo to clear my head. Mrs. Hudson opened the door to me and asked where Holmes was. I explained as best I could but, from the look of concern which crossed her face, my unease must have been all too plain. She prepared an early supper for me which I successfully pushed about the plate for five minutes and then spent the rest of the evening with whisky and tobacco for company. At some point, I must have fallen asleep because I awoke with a start and a raging headache to hear Mrs. Hudson knocking at the door. I looked at the clock. It was nine in the morning.

"Look at the state of you, Doctor," she chided. "You'd best tidy yourself up. There's a telegram from Mr. Holmes for you."

I took the slip of paper and opened it. "Developments." It read simply. "Back soon. Tell Mallory to call. Holmes."

I cursed silently. Why the devil did he have to be so cryptic? Then I collected myself. "Developments" was invariably a positive word in Holmes's lexicon. It usually meant he had discovered something. I dashed off a note to Mallory telling him Holmes had something important to relay and asking him to call round as soon as he could. Then I shaved and changed my attire.

Inspector Mallory arrived about an hour later, clearly not pleased at being summoned by Holmes, and even less so to discover that he was not there.

"I hope I'm not here on a fool's errand," he said. "I have work to do."

I offered him tea and some of the breakfast which Mrs. Hudson had brought in, but he waved both away and passed the time by drumming his fingers loudly on the table. He was on the point of leaving when Holmes burst into the room. I could see straightaway from his drawn face and grave expression that it had been a difficult night. He sat down heavily and began gulping a cup of tea I had just poured. I noticed then that his right hand was bandaged.

"You've been hurt!" I cried.

"It's nothing, a scratch that's all," he replied. "This is a darker case than we could have imagined Watson."

"I was told that you have something of importance to tell me," said Mallory. "I would be obliged to hear it and I shall be on my way."

"I'm afraid Dr. Watson is in the habit of embroidering my messages," Holmes said.

"Mallory got to his feet. "I thought as much. You've found yourself out of your depth at last as I knew you would."

"Don't rush away, Inspector," replied Holmes. "Stay and share the excellent breakfast Mrs. Hudson has prepared."

"I have already breakfasted, and I have things to do." He nodded to us both and made towards the door.

"If you must go," said Holmes. "At least take this with you." He held out a sealed package to the inspector. "Bartholomew said you would know what to do with the contents."

Mallory hesitated and took the package from Holmes reluctantly.

"What is it?" he asked.

"Open it and see, Inspector."

Mallory tore off the seal and upended the package on the table. Out poured a stream of translucent crystals. We stared, astounded.

"My God!" said Mallory. "You found them."

I looked up and saw Holmes grinning broadly. The lethargy and air of defeat had vanished. And so too had the bandage. Despite myself, I burst out laughing.

"Forgive me, Inspector. Watson will tell you that I have a fondness for the theatre."

"You are incorrigible Holmes," I said. "How on earth did you find them? And what about the Major's wife?"

"She is well and safely restored to her husband. I shall tell you all, but I must eat first. The night air has sharpened my appetite."

He helped himself to several kippers and would answer no more questions for fully fifteen minutes. After which he lit a pipe and drew deeply.

"When I left you, Watson, I had no clear plan of how to proceed. I believed the diamonds to be still at the farm, as I did Mrs. Bartholomew."

"But we searched the farm and the outbuildings thoroughly," said Mallory.

"I have no doubt of it, and no blame attaches to you, Inspector, but this deed has been planned for a long time and the hiding place was well concealed. It might never have been found. I surmised that in order to find the Major's wife and the jewels, it was necessary to wait for our quarry to reveal himself. This would only happen when he considered himself safe from discovery. I returned to the farm just as the last of your men was leaving, Inspector, and cast around for somewhere to hide. A little way outside the greenhouse there is a scattering of trees. I settled behind the largest of them and waited for it to grow dark."

"But why there?" I asked. "There can only be a limited view of the farm from the greenhouse."

"Because it was not the farmhouse I intended to watch," Holmes replied. "Imagine yourself in Mrs. Bartholomew's position. You have a quantity of valuable diamonds to hide. But where to conceal them so that no one could possibly hope to find them? Anywhere in the house is bound to be vulnerable. Besides you need to have access to them without anybody seeing. There must be above a thousand plants in the greenhouse. Even if a thief guessed where they were it would take months to find the exact location."

"And being a keen gardener, the lady would have every reason to be in the greenhouse whenever she wished," I put in.

"Exactly. We are dealing with an astute woman Watson. The one thing I was not sure of was how long I would have to wait. If, as I supposed, the Major's wife had been abducted in order to persuade her to reveal the whereabouts of the jewels, it was conceivable that she might hold out for some time. But I reasoned that although she might risk her own safety, she would not want to risk that of her husband. I remained in hiding for several hours and was beginning to think I might have to stay a second night when about three in the morning I saw a shadow slip from the side of the farm and move silently towards the greenhouse. I recognised it immediately as Hodge, the housekeeper's husband. He opened the door and moved quickly inside. Once I was sure I could not be seen I moved to the side of the greenhouse and looked through one of the glass panes. He had a lantern with him which made it easier to follow his movements. You may remember Watson that there is a dwarf date palm in the centre of the building."

"Indeed," I replied. "A magnificent specimen."

"Just so," Holmes went on. "He had stopped there and was busy digging in the earth at the side of the plant. After about a quarter of an hour, he scooped something up and started retracing his steps to the entrance. This was my chance. As he emerged from the greenhouse, I clapped the revolver against his head and informed him not to move or I would gladly put a bullet through him. The cold steel against his neck made it plain that I was in earnest."

"You took a risk," said Mallory. "He might have been armed. You should have followed him and reported the matter to us."

"It has always been my motto to strike while the iron is hot, Inspector. I had him at my mercy. He tried to bluster it out for a few minutes and pretend he was just locking the premises for the night, but I seized the pouch he was holding and said I knew everything and that unless he cooperated, he would spend the rest of his life behind bars."

"The housekeeper's husband?" I said in amazement. "Was he acting alone?"

"I am satisfied that he was."

"But how could he hope to get away with it?" I asked. "Did he intend to kill the lady?"

"No, though I am sure he is capable of it. Having recovered the diamonds it was his intention to vanish abroad leaving behind a note with instructions on how to find the Major's wife. And he very nearly succeeded. I suspect that 'Hodge' is one of a number of aliases that he has used over the years."

"But what of the two men I've arrested?" Asked Mallory. "Am I to understand they played no part in this whatsoever?"

"Their part was crucial," replied Holmes. "Though it was played unwittingly. Hodge had formed his plan some time ago but was waiting for the right time to execute it. He must have seen Mrs. Bartholomew in the house with the jewels on one occasion. Perhaps she was sorting some out to take up to London. At any event, he was not quick enough to see where she replaced them but naturally assumed they were concealed around the house. He began a campaign of anonymous letters intending to lay a false trail for the theft he planned. But unfortunately for him, no amount of searching revealed their hiding place. And then he realised that the Major's wife had begun selling some of the jewels. This must have alarmed him. His one chance of acquiring a fortune was disappearing. It was then he began to plan her abduction. He knew of an underground cellar in one of the outbuildings which could serve as a temporary prison where the lady could be held. He had access to the larder and could aim to keep her alive there for quite a while until she submitted."

"That explains your question about the missing food to the housekeeper," I said.

Holmes nodded. "Yes, although her reply was not definitive. There were two problems with Hodge's plan, however. The first was the Major's dog. It would be certain to defend the Major and his wife from any attack. The solution to that was simply to kill it. You remember my concerns at that event Watson. I feared that it heralded something more significant. More problematic though was how to avoid suspicion for the crime. He could not be certain the police would connect it with the sender of the anonymous letters. But then came the opportunity he was waiting for. Quite by chance, two men were seen by the maid hovering about the outside of the house. The emissaries of the sheikh. It must have seemed like a miracle to him. He sent the maid for the police and then went outside and chased the men off. Once the coast was clear he continued upstairs to where the Major and his wife were sleeping. He first made sure of the Major by attacking him with the poker and then chloroformed the lady sufficiently to render her unable to resist. He carried her downstairs to the outbuildings and placed her in the cellar. It was then that he made his first mistake. He decided to throw us off the scent by forcing the back window and reproducing two sets of footprints on the ground outside. Unfortunately, he had only one set of boots and little time to make the prints. The consequence, of course, was the conundrum of two people apparently using the same pair of boots."

"You said that was Hodges's first mistake," I said. "What was his second?"

"You recall he told us that when he confronted the men on the stairs, one of them pointed a revolver at him and told him to 'stand off or I'd regret it'. Yet the men Mallory arrested could hardly speak English let alone use London slang. I suspected then that Hodge had fabricated the encounter."

Holmes sat back in his chair, and I saw for the first time how exhausted he was. The night's adventures had taken their toll. As for Mallory, he had his head in his hands and looked thoroughly shaken.

"I can't deny feeling vexed at what I have just heard, but you are to be congratulated. It's as fine a piece of detective work as I've come across," he said.

"Thank you, Inspector."

"All the same, I shall be a laughing-stock down at the station."

"No, no. I do not wish my name to be associated with the case at all. This is your success, not mine."

35

Mallory was taken aback by this concession from Holmes. "That is extraordinarily generous of you Mr. Holmes, though I can't see what I have done to merit it."

"Watson will tell you that public acclaim has never been my object. I am quite content for others to receive that. My reward is the opportunity to exercise my powers of deductive reasoning. There is one thing in which I have not succeeded, however. I cannot deliver Hodge into your custody. I was forced to strike a bargain with him. His freedom in exchange for Mrs. Bartholomew's."

Mallory's face looked downcast. "That's a pity," he said. "I would have liked to see Hodge face justice."

"I am sure he will eventually," replied Holmes. "He is a man for whom crime is a career. He will cross our path again."

After the inspector had gone, I looked keenly at Holmes.

"Was that the only reason you let Hodge go? You would not ordinarily let such a villain escape justice."

He shook his head. "I am not convinced the Bartholomews are out of danger, Watson. It would have meant a lengthy court case and endless publicity for them. The sheikh now knows that the army deceived him and that the Major did not perish in the Sudan. That is why I have recommended he return the remainder of the diamonds. Maybe the sheikh's pride will be assuaged. In the meantime, I have suggested he leave England and seek refuge somewhere less public for himself and his wife."

"There is still one mystery unsolved," I said. "The black pawn. You have not explained that."

Holmes laughed. "The Sicilian Defence. There is no mystery about that at all. It has absolutely no bearing on the case." He paused, relishing my puzzled look. "It was an invention of the Major. He confessed it to me."

"The Major? What in God's name for?"

"He was concerned that I might think the case too mundane and not take it. He knew from your stories of my liking for the bizarre so he added it hoping to catch my interest."

"So you have me to thank for it?"

"Indeed, and if you ever write about this you have a ready-made title."

"The Sicilian Defence. It has a ring to it. But you should get some rest old friend. You look exhausted."

He nodded. "And later perhaps some dinner at the Dorchester and then Louis Blanchard is playing the Beethoven quartets at the Wigmore Hall."

I raised my eyebrows. "The Dorchester is a trifle expensive Holmes."

"I have the Major's cheque," he replied flourishing a piece of paper aloft.

It was a year later. Holmes's consultancy work had grown to the point where he could pick and choose his cases, and my finances were in a healthier state as well. This was generally a happier and more settled time for both of us. I was busy reading the sports pages of *The Times* and humming quietly to myself. Holmes looked across at me.

"How much have you won this time?" he enquired.

"Your reasoning Holmes?"

"Apart from your tuneless humming, the only time I have ever seen you slap your thigh so vigorously is when you have indulged your addiction successfully."

"You will not believe this. I placed £10 on a rank outsider which romped home at 20 to 1. A cool £200."

"Perhaps you will now abandon this ridiculous habit while you are in credit."

"I intend to Holmes. I am cured completely."

He gave out a rueful laugh. "Until the next time. But if you have finished with the paper, you can pass it over."

I passed it to him and settled down for the first smoke of the day. I was just putting a match to my pipe when I saw Holmes drop the paper, get up and cross to the cabinet.

"What is it?" I asked.

He pointed to the paper. "Second page, top right. Read it."

I picked up the paper and did as he said. There, underneath a piece about the uncommonly hot weather we had been having, I read:

"Mysterious death of English Major in the Dolomites. Major Bartholomew, late of the Lancashire Fusiliers was found lifeless yesterday at the bottom of a crevasse near Belluno. Friends were alarmed when he did not return from his usual evening walk in the hills near his home. It is believed he missed his footing and stumbled in the twilight. His walking stick was found shattered by his side."

I looked over at Holmes. "It could have been an accident," I said. "The light was poor and I daresay it's not the safest place to go walking."

"The stick Watson! The stick! It would not have broken like that merely from a fall. He was fighting for his life. People may talk of the long arm of the law, but the arm of revenge is longer."

He opened the draw of the cabinet. "Where is it, Watson?"

"No Holmes, please."

"You have your addiction and I have mine."

He crossed into his room and closed the door. I waited, expecting to hear the long groan which usually accompanied the insertion of the needle. But then I heard, softly at first and gradually getting louder, the soaring sound of the adagio from Mozart's fifth violin concerto.

The Pike at Saltmarsh

It is entirely possible that Holmes and I would never have become involved in the case of the Saltmarsh Pike were it not for our mutual love of tobacco. It was clear from our first meeting some years before that Holmes was, like myself, a habitual smoker.

"I have only one requirement of any house share," he said. "That you never complain of my smoking."

This was a stipulation with which I readily concurred, and it was never a source of disharmony between us. I cannot say as much for Mrs. Hudson, however, whose Scottish sense of uprightness was frequently appalled at Holmes's excesses. It was not uncommon, when he was working on a case, for him to smoke the entire night only to begin again straight after breakfast. One day, after a particularly lengthy case, she took me aside and asked me if I might intercede with him to moderate his smoking.

"It's not for myself, you mind," she said. "But my sister has a weak chest and whenever she visits, she is ill for a week."

I promised to do what I could, though I held out little hope of success. Holmes did not take kindly to advice of any kind and was likely to be scornful of Mrs. Hudson's Presbyterian sensibilities, as he was wont to term them. But I reflected that if I could not persuade him to smoke less, I could perhaps persuade him to smoke differently. Despite his extensive scientific knowledge of the different varieties of tobacco, Holmes's own tastes were quite rudimentary. His preference was for the strongest sorts, in particular "Old London Shag," a favourite of sailors and dockers which produced an odour not dissimilar to that of rotting compost. Equally concerning was his habit of keeping the dottels from each day's smoke and using them the following morning, a practice which made even me throw open our drawing-room windows.

I had of late encountered a new tobacconist in the Strand. Holmes had been toying with purchasing another pipe for some time, and my hope was that I could lure him there under the guise of looking at the new porcelain pipes from Holland. He responded to my suggestion that we visit together with alacrity and the following day saw us surveying the many delights the shop had to offer. The owner, a seasoned smoker himself, was an experienced blender of tobacco leaves from the Old and New Worlds. I had visited the day before and he had introduced me to a handmade variety called Balkan Relish, a mixture of Russian latakia leaf with American virginia. As soon as I tried it, I knew it would appeal to Holmes. Accordingly, after he had chosen a pipe, a small briar with a curved stem, the owner invited him to break it in with a sample. I watched as he filled the bowl carefully and set light to the mixture. He drew deeply on it, and I saw his eyes settle contentedly as the flavour filled his mouth and nostrils. He blew the smoke out in a steady stream and turned and looked at me.

"Well done, Watson. You can tell Mrs. Hudson you have succeeded in your task."

So it was that one morning in midsummer, we were enjoying the first pipe of the day when Mrs. Hudson knocked on the door. We had reached that moment when the red coal of the tobacco has subsided to a dull ember and the pipe seems to be slumbering, when the merest pull is enough to bring it to life and flood the senses. It is enough to say that we were both sublimely pleased with ourselves and with the world.

"There is a man at the door who insists on seeing you Mr. Holmes," Mrs. Hudson announced. It was evident from her tone that she did not hold the caller in high regard.

"I thought he was the fishmonger come about his bill," she went on. "I said you are not in the habit of seeing anyone without an appointment. Shall I send him away?"

"No, no, Mrs. Hudson. Watson and I are not engaged this morning. Let us hear what he has to say."

"Very well," she replied, backing out of the room.

"And please arrange for some refreshment for our visitor," called out Holmes.

This was met with an audible grunt from her retreating figure.

"I am afraid, Watson, I am not gentleman enough for Mrs. Hudson," Holmes said. "I am a constant disappointment."

I laughed. "Nonsense. You know full well she is one of your greatest admirers. She is continually praising the stories."

Holmes snorted in response to this. "I rather think that makes her your admirer, not mine."

A few seconds later, Mrs. Hudson reappeared followed by a weather-beaten man dressed in corduroy trousers and clutching a cap. "This is Jacob Duffy," she said.

"You are welcome Mr. Duffy," said Holmes. "I am Sherlock Holmes, and this is my friend and associate, Dr. Watson. Please be seated and let us know how we can assist you."

"Thankee gentlemen," replied our visitor. "I'm sorry to be troubling you. I know you are busy gentlemen."

Holmes waved his arm, "It is always a pleasure to meet someone from Lincolnshire." He turned to me. "The short vowels, Watson. Unmistakable."

Duffy shook his head, "You're right enough. Born and bred. I keep the Pike at Saltmarsh, nigh on two score year now."

"A publican!" cried Holmes. "Excellent profession. I sometimes think it would have suited me if I had not become a consulting detective."

I let out a roar. "Then you would have had even fewer clients than you do now," I said.

"That is cruel of you, Watson."

"No gentlemen, you mistake me," Duffy said. "I am not a publican."

"Is the Pike not a public house?" enquired Holmes.

"No sir, it's a turnpike."

Light dawned on us simultaneously. "A turnpike! But I thought they were closed years ago," I said.

"Most were, sir. But a few remain. Saltmarsh turnpike is one of the last and it won't be there much longer."

"And you live there with your family?" Holmes asked.

"I did sir, but my son left three year ago. He never took to the life. Gone to America so I've heard. I shall most likely never see him again. My wife died last year."

I looked at Holmes.

"You must excuse our levity, Mr. Duffy," he said. Dr. Watson and I are in unusually good spirits this morning. But I see you are in earnest. Please continue. I am all attention."

Duffy coughed nervously. "Well sir, it's like this. The toll house is out on the saltmarsh where an old drovers' road cuts across the fen. It's been a byway for centuries. It's a lonely life but I like it there, until recently."

"What has happened to disturb you?" I asked

"I'm being watched, gentlemen."

"Watched?" said Holmes. "By whom?"

"That I don't know, Mr. Holmes. I never seen him."

"But then how can you be sure you are being watched?"

"I hear him, sometimes of a night. A movement in the reeds, a cough, a footstep."

"Mr. Duffy," I said. "Such noises are probably just the wind. You mustn't let your imagination run away with you."

"I know what you're thinking, sir," he replied. "But I know every sight and sound in the marsh and these sounds are not natural."

"And you think this person wishes you harm?" asked Holmes.

Duffy laughed grimly, "There's plenty that do. They say as the toll restricts trade. Six month ago the Pike over at Ringmer were attacked and the keeper injured."

"Have you reported your concerns to the police?" I asked.

He nodded, "I have, but they say they can't do nothing until a crime has been committed."

Holmes shook his head, "I'm not sure we can do any better, Mr. Duffy. There is little here for me to investigate."

"Then there's the flowers," said Duffy.

"Flowers?" Holmes queried.

"Yes sir. Close by the toll house there's a headstone. There was a drowning in the fen ten year ago. Every few weeks for the past four months a woman leaves flowers by it."

"Presumably some relative," I said. "Still grieving for her loss."

"But a couple of days later they're gone," Duffy said.

"You mean someone is stealing the flowers?" Holmes put in.

"Seems so, sir, yes."

"But you never catch sight of him, or her?"

"No. It happens in the night," Duffy replied.

I exchanged glances with Holmes. "That is odd," I said.

"Indeed," he replied. "But hardly a major crime."

"I have examined the flowers, Mr. Holmes," Duffy went on.

"And what have you discovered?"

"The bunches always have three different kinds of flowers with the same colours, red, blue and white. Sometimes there are more of one kind than another. I have counted them and set down the dates when they were left."

Duffy handed a piece of paper to Holmes. I saw a gleam in Holmes's eye.

"You are to be commended Mr. Duffy," he said. "I fear Dr. Watson is right that I would not have made a good publican but you, sir, would have made an excellent consulting detective."

"Counting is my hobby, Mr. Holmes. I've made a record of every horse and cart that has passed through the toll these past twenty year. I know what they were carrying and how much was paid."

Holmes nodded. "I cannot promise anything, but we may be able to help you. I ask you to do one thing for me, let me know immediately if more flowers are laid."

Duffy hesitated. "I am not a rich man, sir."

Holmes held up his hand. "Do not concern yourself about that Mr. Duffy. If I decide to take a case, it is solely because of its merits and not the wealth of the client."

Once our visitor had gone, I turned to Holmes, "Do you think there is something in this?"

"Very possibly," he replied. "There are two salient features of these flowers. Firstly, whoever takes them is plainly not intent on an act of vandalism, otherwise they would merely be cast aside. And secondly, the removal of them does not deter the woman from laying more, which would suggest there is some purpose here other than a simple memorial. I am inclined to think the flowers are some form of communication. The differing proportions of flowers and colours would suggest as much. But of what we cannot yet know."

"At any event, Duffy is clearly worried, though I am still of the opinion that the loneliness of his life and the barrenness of his surroundings might explain much of his present nervousness. He has only recently lost his wife."

"Indeed, Watson," Holmes replied. "It is a melancholy fact that Lincolnshire has a higher incidence of madness and suicide than any county in England. Nevertheless, our visitor struck me as remarkably sane."

I smiled. "That's because you share his passion for counting."

"Perhaps so. But in the meantime, you would oblige me by finding out what there is to know about turnpikes. I intend to smoke another pipe of this excellent tobacco you have persuaded me to buy."

I spent the rest of the day doing as he bid me, though the task did not prove particularly enlightening. The history of turnpikes is by any reckoning a dry and dusty subject. Essentially, a means of exacting a toll on travellers for the upkeep and maintenance of roads, they were from the beginning a source of annoyance to the travelling public, and violent protests of the kind mentioned by Jacob Duffy were not uncommon. They sank into disuse with the spread of the railway system and now these once plentiful sights were a rarity. In short, our client belonged to a dying breed of men who faced a difficult future.

It was about a week later. Holmes and I had just finished breakfast when Mrs. Hudson came in with a telegram. It was from Jacob Duffy and said simply, "Flowers left this morning."

"Come, Watson," Holmes cried out. "If we hurry, we can just catch the midday train from Liverpool Street."

We boarded the train to Stamford with a few minutes to spare clutching a pair of hastily packed Gladstones and settled into an empty first-class apartment.

"Let's hope the weather stays fine," Holmes said. "I fear we may be spending a considerable time out of doors."

We arrived at Stamford shortly after 2 p.m. and changed to a branch line. A further hour brought us to the small fenland village of Saltmarsh where we alighted and made our way to The Lazy Fox in the centre of the village. It had once been a large coaching inn accommodating travellers along the Great North Road, but since the coming of the railways had dwindled to a dilapidated and insignificant looking tavern. We had wired ahead to secure rooms, though at first sight it hardly seemed necessary. The landlord, a large genial man, welcomed us and enquired where we were going. He seemed surprised at our answer.

"Old Jacob's place out on the fen!" He exclaimed. "You'll be wanting the pony and trap. It's a fair step from here."

"Do you know Mr. Duffy well?" I enquired.

"These past forty year," he replied. "More since his wife died. He likes a drink, if you get my meaning."

"The turnpike is due to close soon I gather?" Holmes said.

"Ay. The lease is up in a couple of months. There's few'll be sad to see it go."

It was a short journey to the turnpike by trap down a rough track that crossed a landscape of dykes, ditches, and reeds with the occasional stunted tree or hedge as far as the eye could see.

"This probably hasn't changed much in a thousand years," I said.

"Not since Roman times," Holmes replied.

"It's a trifle depressing. I think I would find it difficult to maintain my sanity here."

"Without cultivation there can be little progress," Holmes commented. "And without progress, the mind has little with which to occupy itself."

After about twenty minutes, we arrived at a small building with a sign indicating it to be the toll house. At its side was a large, hinged gate with a tariff of fares attached: 2 shillings for a coach and horses, ten pence for a flock of sheep, and threepence for a single rider. We were set down at the gate, and Duffy came out of his house to greet us.

"Welcome gentlemen. I have some refreshment waiting," he said.

"Most kind," replied Holmes. "Watson and I have been remarking on the singular nature of the landscape."

"Ay 'empty' most people call it," Duffy said. "But put me down anywhere and I'd know where I was right enough."

Holmes pointed towards a large stone rectangle at the rear of the house, a few metres into the fen. "That's the headstone, I presume though I can't see any flowers."

"They're behind the stone, just out of sight from here," Duffy answered.

We walked over to the memorial. It was a slab of granite containing a simple engraving: *"Sacred to the memory of Anne Wells who perished near here, 1875."* Round the back of the stone was a hand-tied bunch of flowers, red, blue, and white.

"Clearly not meant for the common gaze," commented Holmes.

"There's ten red, seven blue, and four white," said Duffy. "They'll most likely be took this evening, after dark."

"The flowers were laid this morning?"

"Yes, at first light. I was feeding my chickens when she come by. She seemed in a hurry and her bonnet slipped off as she bent down. She had a small cap on underneath."

"Of the kind that maid's wear?" I asked.

"Yes," he replied.

"A servant, Holmes," I said.

"It would seem so. Visiting before anyone would miss her. You have been most observant, Mr. Duffy. It is now up to Dr. Watson and me."

We made our way inside the toll house, a plain whitewashed building of bare walls, stone floors, and simple furnishings. Duffy supplied us with local ale and oatcakes and apologised for not being able to accommodate us. Holmes waved his hand.

"Watson and I are terrible guests. We will be perfectly comfortable at the inn."

After a couple of hours, it began to grow dusk. Holmes turned to me.

"We should begin our vigil. We have not travelled all this way to let the fox escape us."

We went outside and concealed ourselves behind a bank at the side of the toll road, about 50 yards from the headstone, and waited. There was a faint breeze ruffling the reeds and overhead the clouds had formed a solid phalanx. I looked at Holmes and saw the same thought forming in his mind. It had better not rain. We took turns watching, and the hours ticked by till about midnight when Holmes shook me gently and held a finger to his lips. I turned to follow his gaze and saw someone approaching the stone. He was tall and walked with a loping gait. He glanced up before bending down to pick up the flowers and I caught sight of a bearded figure in a long gaberdine coat and a sou'wester.

Once he had the flowers, he retreated quickly back into the fen. We set off in pursuit trying to keep a healthy distance but anxious not to lose him. The possibility of going astray in that wilderness was not to be contemplated. Behind the headstone lay a small track, probably the run of some animal, which led into the heart of the fen. It was this path which the man was evidently following. We could hear him up ahead, brushing against the reeds, his heavy tread squelching in the soft mud. After half an hour, we were panting with the exertion and becoming visibly exhausted. I was on the point of telling Holmes to continue without me if he were able when the fen opened out and we saw a broad grassy expanse. Up ahead, the object of our pursuit had paused before a large wooden caravan. A few yards behind it, a large horse, tethered to a tree stump, was busy grazing. The man looked around briefly and climbed into the van.

"What do we do now Holmes?" I asked.

"Wait," he replied. "This man is just a courier."

After a further half-hour, the man came down the steps from the caravan still holding the flowers and set off in the opposite direction. Fortunately, the going was now much easier. The ground became firmer, and the reeds gave way to rough grass. But with little cover to conceal our pursuit we were forced to drop further back. Eventually, we emerged onto a dirt road. In front of us was a crossroads with a signpost. As we watched, the man laid the flowers at the side of the post and disappeared back into the wilderness. I looked at Holmes. This was plainly not the end of the trail.

"Someone has gone to a lot of trouble to avoid exposing themselves," he said. "Whatever enterprise is afoot, it is no small matter."

"At least we have something to keep us warm," I replied. I reached inside my coat pocket and passed him a small bottle.

"Whisky! You never cease to amaze me, Watson."

We settled down at the side of the road and wrapped our coats round us. Above us, the clouds began to disperse, and the night sky lit up the landscape. The hours passed and we dozed a little in turns till about five o'clock, when we saw the first hint of sunrise and heard the accompanying sound of birdsong. I began to stretch but immediately felt Holmes's arm restraining me.

"Ssh," he said. "Listen!"

In the distance, I could hear the faint sound of hooves striking the ground and the creaking of wood. After a few moments, a horse and cart appeared coming up the road from behind us. Reaching the crossroads, it stopped, and the driver got down and picked up the flowers. We saw him count them before putting them into the cart and driving back down the road. Holmes watched the cart until it disappeared in the distance.

"Most disappointing," he said. "There's no point in trying to follow on foot. We might as well return to the village."

The signpost indicated that Saltmarsh village was three miles to the east of us and we set off feeling not a little frustrated that our night-time adventure had not yielded more. We were no further forward in knowing who the flowers were intended for nor what their significance was, though, as Holmes pointed out, it was clear there was more at stake here than a simple romantic assignation, a possibility which had been uppermost in my mind, at least. We arrived at The Lazy Fox just as the village clock was striking six and went straight to our beds. It is often said that the sweetest sleep is that which is unanticipated. So grateful was I to be in my bed at last that I slept soundly until ten o'clock. I washed and shaved and went down to the inn parlour feeling more refreshed than expected. Holmes was already there, wreathed in smoke and studying the newspaper.

"What a marvel modern transport is, Watson. The landlord gets *The Times*. A day late, but civilisation is within reach even here."

"I'm not sure one can equate *The Times* with civilisation," I replied. "Though I'm impressed by your ability to command breakfast at such an hour." I stared at the remnants of what had obviously been a substantial plate of eggs and bacon. At that moment the landlord came in with a plate for me. Holmes smiled, "You have not been forgotten, Watson."

I sat down and he resumed his perusal of the paper.

"Inspector Mallory will be busy for the next few weeks, I fear," he said with ill-concealed satisfaction.

"Has there been an outbreak of crime in your absence?"

He laughed and pointed to a column on page three. It was a story about an increase in the forging of banknotes in London and a warning to the public to be on the lookout for counterfeit £5 notes.

"Counterfeiting is the least rewarding of crimes to investigate," he said. "The general public is unaware of it and tracking down the source is a thankless task. One might as well try to find the source of the influenza. Twenty per cent of all coinage is counterfeit, Watson."

"As much as that?"

"I fancy were we to examine the contents of our pockets we should find some doubtful tender."

"I'll take your plates away gentlemen if you've finished with them," said the landlord coming into the parlour.

"Thank you," I said. "That was excellent. My friend and I came across a gipsy caravan yesterday, parked up not far from the turnpike. The owner seemed an odd-looking fellow."

The landlord grinned. "That'll be Trinny. He's been a reg'lar here for the past year. Makes a few bob mending folks' pots and pans. Don't say much. They say he's not right in the head, but I reckon he's just a bit simple. Harmless enough."

"Well," said Holmes, after the landlord had returned to the kitchen. "Simple he may be, but he certainly knows his way about the fen."

I filled my pipe and put a match to the mixture. The smoke coiled lazily upwards.

"We seem to have made little progress, Holmes," I said. "Have you formed any theories?"

"Several, though they are at too early a stage to warrant mentioning. But some things are clear. Firstly, the woman is not the originator of whatever message the flowers contain and Trinny is not the recipient of it. They are both intermediaries. Secondly, although the headstone is the site of the drop, it is incidental to the matter in hand as is also, I believe, the turnpike itself. Whoever is behind this has taken care that each link in the chain is quite separate. I doubt that any of the parties are known to each other."

"But what of the flowers themselves? What is the significance of the differing amounts and colours?"

"I have made some headway, though more information is necessary to complete the process. It is a reasonable supposition that we are dealing with some form of code. The question is what could it relate to? Consider the sequences Duffy has noted."

He pointed to a sheet of paper on the table with a series of figures and dates attached.

"The number of blue flowers is remarkably regular, increasing by just one each time. In March it is 3, in April 4 and so on up to the latest which is 7. The most obvious conclusion is that the number of blue flowers correlates to the current month. It is likely then that either the white or the red indicate a particular day of the month. In the recent bunch, there were ten red and four white. Since yesterday was the 5th of July, it is more than likely that the red flowers give us the day."

"So the flowers are notifying the receiver of a date, sometime in the current month," I said.

"Yes, though for what purpose remains obscure."

"And what of the white flowers, do they indicate the time of day, 4 o'clock, 5 o'clock?

"Possibly," Holmes replied. "Though I suspect there is a piece of the jigsaw missing in respect to that."

"Presumably, then we can expect something of importance to occur on the 10th of this month?"

He nodded. "And all we know is that it is a frequent occurrence."

"A series of burglaries perhaps," I suggested.

"There have been no reports of any in this area."

"What then?" I asked

He shrugged his shoulders and glanced through the parlour window. "It is a fine morning, Watson. Let us hire the landlord's pony and trap and return to where the flowers were left. Whoever collected them must live locally."

An hour later saw us back at the crossroads close to where we had waited the previous evening. It looked different in daylight, more desolate and remote. All around us stretched the flat and featureless terrain of the fens. But there is something hopeful about a meeting of roads, especially when accompanied by a signpost. Everywhere leads somewhere. And in our present predicament, there was at least the possibility that by retracing the path the cart had taken, we might come across some clue as to the final destination of the flowers.

We set off down the road, passing our hiding place which seemed remarkably shorn of cover. I observed to Holmes that we had been fortunate not to be discovered.

"Indeed. Had the hour been any later we would have been," he replied.

After a few miles, the landscape began to change. Marsh and moorland gave way to fields and hedgerows with the occasional flurry of trees. The first establishment we came to was a farm with cattle grazing in the water meadows. Outside, a board advertised eggs and milk for sale. We stopped on the pretence of purchasing some eggs and were served by a buxom lady whose pleasure at having visitors, even of the buying kind, was evident from her extreme reluctance to let us leave. Eventually, the sound of her husband calling for assistance gave us the opportunity to make our excuses.

"You can see why I have never married," Holmes said. "Can you imagine such volubility at breakfast?"

I shook my head at his misogyny. Although he was unfailingly courteous to women, I had always suspected that his politeness served as a means of keeping them at bay.

A mile or so further we came to a stable where horses could be hired, and riding lessons given. We drove into the yard and breathed in the heady aroma of hay and horse dung, both of which were liberally spread around. We stopped and admired a particularly fine black stallion standing rather haughtily as its rider dismounted.

"Noble creatures, don't you think?" I said to Holmes.

"Indeed. Had we more time we could do worse than hire a couple of cobs for an hour or so."

A man came out of the stables and asked in a friendly manner if he could be of assistance to which we replied by complimenting him on his horses and enquiring about the cost of hire. As we drove away, I couldn't help remarking to Holmes that we had spent a very pleasant afternoon roaming about the countryside but had accomplished nothing material to the case. He nodded and we agreed to try one more establishment and then return to The Lazy Fox.

Our last call was about ten minutes' drive from the stables. Our attention was first attracted to it by the constant noise of dogs barking and as we came closer, we saw that it consisted of a series of cages set back from the road at the side of which lay a modest-sized building with a small driveway. A sign outside informed us that this was Blake Hall Kennels where canines of all varieties could be boarded. We pulled into the drive behind a cart and got out with the intention of asking the way to Saltmarsh village. As we did so, a man came round the side of the building with a German shepherd on a lead. We bid the man good afternoon and Holmes explained that we had lost our way and would be grateful for directions to the village. The man surveyed us closely and said we needed to go back a mile and take the turning on the left. We thanked him, got back in the trap, and left.

Once clear of the property I looked meaningfully at Holmes and saw that he was thinking the same as me.

"That cart looks very similar to the one we saw last night," I said.

"Yes, and the shepherd is clearly not being kept as a pet," he replied.

"Did you notice the man's hand as he was directing us?" I went on. "It was practically black around the fingernails."

"That was ink, Watson."

"Ink?"

"Printer's ink. It is extraordinarily difficult to get off. I think we may have stumbled across the missing piece of our puzzle."

We arrived back at the inn by late afternoon, by which time the previous night's escapade had finally caught up with us and we were both extremely tired. After a light dinner, we agreed on an early night and went to our rooms. It was fortunate that we did so because at around six in the morning, Holmes came into my room in his dressing-gown clutching a note.

"Read that," he said, thrusting it into my hand. "The landlord just gave it to me. It's from Mallory."

I took the note. It was brief and to the point: *"Understand you are in the locality, Holmes. Would value your help with a drowning in Stamford. Come as soon as is convenient. Mallory."*

"Mrs. Hudson must have told him we were here," Holmes said.

"A bit of a coincidence," I remarked.

55

"Indeed."

"I wonder what help he has in mind."

Since the affair at Major Bartholomew's the previous year, Inspector Mallory had called on Holmes's services twice and now seemed to regard him as an unofficial member of the Yard.

"Let us hope it is worth missing breakfast for," Holmes replied. "There is a train in half an hour."

We arrived in Stamford just after 7 o'clock. The day was overcast, and rain looked likely as we alighted from the carriage and made our way through the centre of the town to the scene of the incident. Included with Mallory's message was a hand-drawn map with directions to the River Welland. A little way along the south bank we came to a small tent around which stood several police officers. As we approached, Mallory walked to meet us.

"Thank you, gentlemen," he began. "It's a sad business. It seems to be a case of suicide, but I would be grateful for your opinion, Holmes."

Holmes nodded. "Who is the unfortunate person?"

"A young woman, in her twenties. She was found in the water this morning. She had a quantity of stones in her pocket."

"No accident then?" I said.

Mallory shook his head.

"May we see the body?" Holmes asked.

"Yes. Come this way," Mallory replied.

We followed him into the tent. Laid on her back with her head to one side as if in a profound sleep was the slender figure of a finely featured young girl, dressed in a fashionable outdoor cape and a black satin skirt.

"A lady of some quality," I said.

Holmes shook his head. "Look at her hands, Watson."

I knelt down and examined her hands more closely. The backs were chapped around the knuckles and the fingernails had been bitten down.

"She is in service somewhere," Holmes said.

"But her clothes!" I protested.

"They are not the clothes she normally wears," he replied.

He turned to Mallory. "Have you examined the body for any sign of violence?"

"There is some contusion at the side of her neck but nothing that might explain her death," Mallory said.

Holmes sighed. "Watson, be so good as to examine her. We will wait outside."

They left me in the tent, and I carried out as thorough an examination as the circumstances would allow. After about half an hour I called Holmes and Mallory back in.

"There are no obvious signs of foul play but one thing I can tell you is that the girl was pregnant. About two months I would say."

Mallory gave a nod of satisfaction. "I think we have our motive gentlemen. It's a common enough story. A servant girl is seduced by a wealthy man and kills herself when the consequences of the liaison become apparent."

"And the marks on the neck, Watson?" Holmes enquired.

"There is some chafing on either side but nothing to say what caused it and there is no real injury," I replied.

Holmes withdrew his magnifying glass and bent low over the body.

"They are marks from the index finger and thumb of someone with a remarkably large left hand." He put his own hand round the back of the girl's neck. "My hand is larger than average and even so, it will not reach."

"But she has not been strangled, Holmes," Mallory protested.

"No, she has been held face down under the water until she drowned," he said. "That explains why the front of her apparel is more soiled than the back. The drowning was then made to look like suicide."

"So, we have a killer at large!" Mallory replied with thinly disguised annoyance.

"Yes, though if you will take my advice, I suggest you keep that knowledge to ourselves. As far as the general public are concerned this may remain a suicide for the time being. Our chances of apprehending the person responsible will be much greater if he thinks himself safe."

"The problem is, Holmes, that I do not have the resources at present to carry out a proper investigation. You have read of the outbreak of counterfeiting in London?"

Holmes nodded. "If you will allow me, Watson and I would be happy to investigate this for you. As you see, we are already in the area and have the time at our disposal."

A look of relief passed over the inspector's face. "It's highly irregular, but in the circumstances, it would be extremely helpful. I know I can rely on you."

"Do you know who the girl is?" Holmes asked.

"Emily Thornberry. There was a name tag sewn into her cape. And we found a return train ticket in her pocket."

"Where to?" I enquired.

"Saltmarsh," replied the inspector.

"Your thoughts Holmes?" I said, as a few minutes later, we sat in the railway carriage on our way back to the village.

"I am thinking that this case gets darker by the hour."

"You believe Emily Thornberry and the woman who leaves the flowers are one and the same?"

"I have little doubt of it. I fear she got caught up in something larger than she imagined and paid the price."

"So very young. And the baby too," I said.

"There is wickedness everywhere under the sun, Watson."

We arrived back at The Lazy Fox around midday and immediately asked the landlord about the girl. As we expected, he knew her well, as he did everyone in the area

"Emily, ay. A friendly young lass. She's often in the village getting things for the old manor house."

"And where is that?" Holmes enquired.

"Not far from here. It's on the way to the turnpike."

The rain which had been threatening had already set in as we drove away from the village. We were snug enough in our waterproofs and sou'westers but even so were glad after about five minutes to see the manor house appear, set back from the road down a short drive. A middle-aged woman in a pale pink pinafore and clutching a rolling pin answered the door. She seemed surprised to see us.

"I'm sorry gentlemen," she began. "You've caught me in the middle of rolling my pastry. The maid was supposed to do it, but the naughty girl has disappeared."

"May we come in?" asked Holmes. "It is your maid we have come about."

She showed us into the drawing-room, a large comfortable room which smelt of leather and oak furniture.

"I'd best get my husband," she said. "Please sit yourself down."

After a few minutes, she reappeared accompanied by a portly gentleman with a florid countenance who regarded us with an air of bewilderment. Holmes quickly introduced us and explained that we had some unfortunate news about their maid.

A look of fear crossed the woman's face. "Emily! What's she been and done now?" she said. "I know she can be a bit wilful, but she's a good girl really."

In as few words as possible Holmes explained that there had been an accident involving Emily and she had been found in the river at Stamford. They both stared at Holmes, dumbfounded.

"But that's impossible," said the man. "She only went there yesterday, and she was all right then."

"Did she say why she was going there?" I asked.

"To visit her mother," replied the man. "She's been poorly for some time but yesterday she took a turn for the worse. Emily asked if she could go, and we said yes, providing she was back first thing this morning."

"What sort of accident?" asked the woman. "She's going to be all right, isn't she?"

"I'm very sorry," I said. "But Emily has drowned."

"Good God!" said the man. "I can't believe it."

The woman covered her face with her pinafore and sobbed quietly.

"How did it happen?" she asked eventually.

"The police are trying to establish that," Holmes replied. "And we are assisting them. If you wouldn't mind, perhaps we could ask you a few questions."

She nodded and grasped her husband's hand.

"How long has your maid been working for you?" Holmes asked.

"About a year," said the woman. "Though she's much more than a maid. She helps out with the cooking as well as the cleaning.

And she's done marvels with my cottage garden. Real green fingers. She always does the flower displays around the house."

"Has she any relatives," I asked.

"Just her mother in Stamford. She's quite elderly so we allow her to visit every Sunday evening. She'll be devastated at the news, poor thing."

"You know the lady?"

"No, but we have her address." She reached in her bag and passed me a piece of paper.

I thanked her and Holmes turned to her husband.

"I noticed several barns at the rear of the house. Are you engaged in business of some kind?"

"We are brewers, Mr Holmes. It's a family business. The barns are where we dry the hops prepare the malt and ferment the beer."

"I see," said Holmes. And how many men do you employ?"

"Just three. We manage it between us."

"Have you something planned for the 10th of this month?"

"Yes, we have, though I don't know how you heard of it. Every few weeks during spring and summer we take our beer round to the local fairs and markets. We're usually away for a few days."

"All of you?"

"Yes, except for Emily. She stays and looks after the house. We shall have to cancel the trip this time."

"Please don't do that," said Holmes. "I can't explain why at the moment. But it's important that you continue to do everything you had planned and let everyone know this. It would help also if you did not say anything about our visit."

"Very well Mr. Holmes. We will do as you ask."

"Thank you. You have been most helpful. May Dr. Watson and I see Emily's room before we leave?"

"Yes," said the woman. "If you'd like to come this way." She got up and we followed her out into the hall. Holmes paused suddenly in the doorway.

"One last thing," he said, turning to her husband. "Do you by any chance take *The Times*?"

"As a matter of fact, I do," the man answered.

"Excellent!" Holmes replied.

The maid's room was at the top of the house, under the eaves. It was scarcely larger than a closet and consisted chiefly of a bed, a chest of drawers, and a small wardrobe. Surveying the spartan interior, the plain walls, single gas lamp, and rush mat, it was difficult not to feel again the sadness of her short life.

"This is a room to sleep in, Holmes, and little else," I said.

He nodded. "Yet there must be some trace of her."

The wardrobe contained two changes of her servant's outfit and an assortment of shoes. Beside the bed, a tiny table had a prayer book and a small piece of embroidery with her name stitched in flowers. Holmes held the prayer book by the spine and shook it and a piece of paper floated to the floor. I picked it up. On it was written in immaculate flowing handwriting a sonnet by Elizabeth Barrett Browning, "How do I love thee, let me count the ways." Holmes took it from me and placed it carefully in his wallet.

"We may have need of this," he said.

We searched through the chest of drawers, raking through her linen in silence.

"What are we looking for?" I asked.

"The key to understanding her," he replied. "A young woman's life has been brutally cut short. I'm convinced the answer is here somewhere."

He looked around shaking his head in frustration.

"The mattress, Watson," he said. "That is the only place in this room where one might hide something."

He bent down, took hold of the bedding, and pulled the mattress clear of the frame. Underneath, pressed against the wooden slats was a small envelope. Holmes picked it up and shook the contents onto the bed. A dozen £5 banknotes cascaded over the sheets.

"Voilá," Holmes exclaimed gleefully. He picked one up and began examining it closely through his magnifying glass.

"These are of the highest quality, Watson. The workmanship is exquisite."

"But forgeries?"

"Undoubtedly. See if you can tell the difference."

He took a genuine note from his wallet and handed it to me along with one of the counterfeit ones. I borrowed his magnifying glass and examined them closely.

"The genuine one is printed on slightly heavier paper," I said.

"Paper quality is a problem for all counterfeiters," he replied. "The paper used by the Bank of England comes from a single source which is not available commercially, though the difference is only apparent if you have them side by side. Anything else?"

I shook my head. "No, they look identical to me."

"Look at the engraving of Britannia in the top left-hand corner. All banknotes carry it. Then look at the counterfeit version."

"The genuine one has a beehive at the side of her throne which isn't in the forgery," I said.

"Capital, Watson. The beehive is meant to symbolise industry. It's produced by a method of engraving which is hard to reproduce. The forgers have counted on no one noticing."

"I can see why," I replied. "But what are these notes doing in the maid's bedroom?"

"This is one of those cases where we have come across separate parts of the puzzle which are only now just beginning to fit together. The significance of the flowers, for instance, is clear. The red ones indicate the day on which the property is going to be empty and the blue ones the month, while the white ones tell us the amount of time it will be empty. We know that from July 10th to July 14th no one apart from the maid will be here."

"But what use could the counterfeiters make of that?"

"The barns, Watson! Counterfeiting is a complex process with many stages, as is brewing. It requires heat, ventilation, and access to water, not to mention complete seclusion, all of which are available here. It would be a simple matter to bring the equipment by cart and remove it afterwards."

"With the maid acting as lookout and providing access."

"Yes, most probably with duplicate keys."

"We should inform Inspector Mallory. He needs to raid Blake Hall Kennels before it's too late."

"I have considered that Watson, but we can afford to wait a little longer. The men may well have heard about Miss Thornberry's death, but they have no reason to know who she is or what part she has played. Remember that whoever has masterminded this crime has been careful to keep all the pieces separate. Besides, there is a bigger prize at stake. Capturing a few counterfeiters is one thing, but as long as the plates which produced these notes remain in circulation a forger can set up again anywhere in the country. We must find them and when we do, we shall have found Emily's killer."

"Why do you think she was killed?" I asked.

"Because she became a threat to the operation. Let us suppose she was groomed for the task she was required to perform. The poem she copied out suggests an attachment of some kind. Her lover showered her with money, albeit not genuine, and may well have promised marriage but he used his influence with her to help him gain access to the barns. He probably said that he and his friends fancied some of the kegs which she may well have considered her due. By all accounts, her employers were rather demanding."

"Much more than a maid!"

"Quite. Two mornings ago, she took the flowers as instructed and laid them by the headstone. But when she got back, she saw *The Times* open on the drawing-room table. Perhaps she meant to tidy it away, but in any event, her eye fell on the story about counterfeit £5 notes in London and she became suspicious. Stealing a few kegs of beer is one thing, but counterfeiting is a hanging offence. She made up a story about her mother's deteriorating health and got permission to travel to Stamford. Once there she presumably confronted her lover and told him it had to stop. It may well have been then that he learnt she was pregnant. She had now, of course, become a liability. He persuaded her to go for a walk along the river to talk it over and then killed her."

"And we have absolutely no idea who he is," I said.

Holmes shook his head. "I was hoping for some clue in her room, but there was nothing. Which is why we must return to Stamford tomorrow and try to retrace her steps."

The next day we set off early from Saltmarsh. It was fine and bright after the wet weather of the previous day, and we were both in better spirits, although the melancholy nature of our task still hung over us. Over dinner at The Lazy Fox the evening before we had decided on our strategy for the day. To appear as ourselves would immediately arouse suspicion and be at odds with the story which the police had allowed to circulate about Miss Thornberry's death. We settled on presenting ourselves as officials from the coroner's office gathering evidence for the inquest which would naturally follow any sudden demise.

Arriving in the town we headed first for the address of Emily's mother, a house in a quiet back street, one of a series of small impeccably respectable Georgian residences.

"At least the house exists," I said.

He nodded, "Though I do not have high expectations of the mother, Watson."

We knocked on the door and an elderly gentleman in a frayed tweed suit answered it. Holmes enquired whether a Mrs. Thornberry lived there.

"She did," he replied. "Up until six months ago."

"Has she moved?" asked Holmes.

"No, she died. I believe there is a daughter somewhere near, but I don't have an address."

We thanked him and walked back down the street.

"It's good to know she wasn't entirely fictional," I said.

"Indeed. We can assume that the visits since the mother's death were to see her lover. The question is, where did she go?"

After some consideration, we determined on a trawl of the guesthouses and hotels in the town on the assumption that they were often the venue for liaisons, certainly of the illicit variety. The town offered a fair sprinkling of these, and we spent the rest of the morning visiting them. At each, we asked to see the register, gave a description of the maid, and enquired whether anyone had seen her. But to all intents and purposes, she might as well have been invisible. It appeared no one had any information at all. At last, we were left with The George Hotel, the largest and finest hotel by far Stamford had to offer. I looked sceptically at Holmes.

"It's rather grand and expensive for a maid, Holmes."

"But remember her clothes, Watson. She was in disguise. And where else to avoid being noticed but in a large and bustling hotel. It is worth trying."

We approached the desk and asked the clerk if we could see the manager. He disappeared briefly and then bid us follow him. We were led into a large office with a smartly dressed man sitting behind a desk. A silver nameplate announced him to be Simon de Vere, general manager of the hotel. He welcomed us and asked how he could be of assistance. Holmes explained the purpose of our visit and I saw a flicker of surprise cross the manager's face.

"But I gathered from this morning's newspaper that the police considered the poor girl's death suicide."

"Precisely so," Holmes replied. "There is no question about that. The police have completed their investigation. But there will naturally be an inquest. It's purely routine. The coroner will try to establish what is known about why Miss Thornberry took her own life, though in this case, it is fairly obvious. Is there any possibility she might have been staying at the hotel?"

The manager rang a bell on his desk. The clerk appeared and was instructed to fetch the register.

"There's no one of that name registered here for the day in question," the manager said, leafing through the large leather-bound volume which the clerk had brought in. "See for yourself gentlemen."

He turned the register round and pushed it across the desk towards us. Holmes looked at the open page and traced the names with his finger. As he did so he was caught by a sudden fit of coughing. His face began to go crimson, and I was momentarily alarmed. "Water," he said in a croaky voice. The manager leapt up and went into the corridor calling for the clerk to bring a glass of water. Immediately, Holmes reached inside his coat pocket and produced a piece of paper which he put alongside the entries in the register. I saw the gleam in his eye which I well knew was a sign of success. A few seconds later the manager appeared with a glass of water which he handed to Holmes.

"Thank you," said Holmes sipping the water. "I'm afraid I suffer from hay fever during the summer months. Most unfortunate. I think we are finished here, Mr de Vere. Miss Thornberry appears to have had no connection with the hotel. We thought it unlikely of a simple maid. We'll take up no more of your time. Good day, sir."

The manager showed us to the door, apologising that he could be of no further help. Holmes said he should not concern himself and it was quite often the case in matters of sudden death that no more could be discovered. At least we could now return to the coroner's office and close the file.

When we were at a safe distance from the hotel Holmes looked triumphantly at me.

"She stayed there under an assumed name, Watson. The handwriting was unmistakable. I used the sample from the Browning poem. Not only that, she has stayed there on several occasions in the past."

"Excellent Holmes, but there is still the question of whom she met there."

He snapped his fingers, "You did not observe the manager when he handed me the glass of water?"

"I was more concerned with your fit of coughing. It looked alarmingly convincing."

"As it was meant to. But de Vere is left-handed. What is more, the size of his hand is considerably larger than average. And there was ink underneath the nail of his middle finger with reddening around the others where something had been scrubbed off. We have him, Watson! We must return to Baker Street immediately."

Some four hours later we were relaxing in our lodgings having sent a message to the landlord of The Lazy Fox saying we had been called back to London urgently and requesting our luggage to be forwarded. Inspector Mallory had arrived soon after us and was busy telling us about the manager of The George Hotel.

"Your hunch about de Vere was right, Mr. Holmes."

I looked across at Holmes and saw him wince at the word "hunch".

"We did a background check on him as soon as I got your telegram," the inspector went on. 'de Vere' is an alias. His real name is Robert Jennings. He's been linked with a series of financial crimes in the north of England, but so far there has been insufficient evidence to prosecute him."

"As there still is, Inspector," Holmes replied. "We have no evidence to arrest him for anything at present."

"What do you suggest then?" I asked. "We cannot allow him to escape."

"That we do nothing for the moment. In three days' time, the manor house and barns will be empty again. We have to hope that de Vere and his gang are brave enough and greedy enough to continue counterfeiting."

"It's very risky," Mallory said. "If they get wind of anything they could disappear overnight, and it would be the devil's own job to find them again."

"It's a gamble, Mallory. But think of the prize. The lot of them in one fell swoop."

The inspector hesitated but Holmes had judged his man correctly. Mallory had lost none of his youthful ambition, and even he could see the personal as well as professional credit of what Holmes was proposing.

"How do we do we carry it off then?" He said at last.

"Choose six of your best officers, Mallory. We want men who have the discipline to stay concealed for many hours. The owners will leave the property early on the morning of the 10th. Your men must be in place the night before. The gang may well send someone to reconnoitre the grounds to make sure it is safe. If they come it will probably be the next night. I expect de Vere to arrive separately with the plates. He will wait until his men are in the barns. No one is to move a muscle until the entire gang is present and has started working."

"And what of you and Dr. Watson?" the inspector asked.

"We will be in the house with the curtains drawn. When everything is in place, I will signal with a lamp for the action to begin."

"Very well," Mallory replied. "I'm not happy about this but I suppose we have to try it."

Holmes nodded. "One last thing, Inspector. Make sure your officers are armed. These are desperate men. They know they face the gallows if caught."

On the morning of July 10th Holmes and I were ensconced in the manor house with the outer doors locked and the house completely blacked out. We had arrived the previous evening and made ourselves comfortable in the drawing-room whilst the owners prepared to leave. They had been told as little as possible about the operation and at about six in the morning they departed as instructed with their carts laden. We had nothing to do now but wait and keep our movements to a minimum. At about midday, we heard the tread of someone outside. A few minutes later there was the sound of a door being rattled, followed soon after by another.

"That's promising," whispered Holmes. "They're making sure the coast is clear. Let's hope Mallory's men stay hidden."

The hours passed slowly, and we were aware of the light fading outside and the wind stirring in the trees. It was possible the gang might not come the first night in which case we would be in for a long wait. But around 2 a.m. we heard the sound of carts on the rough track outside and men's voices, low and muted. They made their way round the side of the house to the barns at the rear. We could hear the sound of padlocks being rattled and undone and then silence.

"They must be inside by now. But they will have left someone on guard," Holmes said. "All we are waiting for now is de Vere to show up."

We peered through a crack in a curtain at the back of the house. The carts had been unladen and the horses were silently chewing the grass. Suddenly Holmes stiffened.

"He's here, look."

To the left of the house, I could make out a dark shape moving slowly in the direction of the middle barn. It stopped momentarily and we heard a whistle answered a few seconds later by another whistle. The figure began moving cautiously again and was about to enter the barn when it stopped again.

"Damnation!" said Holmes. "One of Mallory's men has shown himself."

The man turned immediately and ran swiftly back towards the road. As he did so we heard the sound of a police whistle and men suddenly appeared from every direction accompanied by the sound of gunshots.

"Quick," said Holmes. "de Vere must not escape."

He unbolted the front door and we raced across the road in the direction de Vere had taken. In the distance his figure was just discernible, disappearing into the fen. Holmes was quicker than me and reached the fen first. It was impossible in the darkness to see any kind of track, but we followed as best we could the trail of trodden down reeds and sedge he had blundered through in his desperation to escape. The breeze had begun to pick up and I caught the unmistakable smell of rain. Holmes was ahead of me now. I could hear him splashing through the miry expanse of water holes and tuberous thickets at the heart of the fen. My progress had slowed right down, and I started slipping against the roots and outgrowths which clutched at my feet like so many hands. And then the lightning started. The first flash took me by surprise, irradiating the landscape with a sudden brilliance. It was followed soon afterwards by a fierce detonation, as though I had stepped on a mine, and the first drops of solid, penetrating rain.

I could hear Holmes shouting and guessed he'd caught up with de Vere. I shouted back and forced my way blindly on until the maze began to clear and I saw them fighting on the edge of a muddy pool. Holmes had de Vere round the waist, but he was clearly exhausted, and his grip was slipping. As I watched, de Vere struggled free and pushed Holmes backwards but as he did so his feet went from under him, and they both fell heavily into the pool.

I cried out to Holmes but by the time I got there they had both disappeared beneath the water. I threw myself down and reached out for Holmes's coat, but the strength had gone from my limbs, and I couldn't hold him. Suddenly an arm pushed me aside and a tall figure dressed in a long gaberdine bent down and grabbed Holmes pulling him clear. I could see him struggling, but he was held firmly like a doll in the hands of a giant. Then he turned and reached for de Vere, but he had slipped too far beneath the water and there was no sign of him. Holmes lay gasping for breath on the ground. I leant over him, and he pulled me towards him.

"I have them," he said triumphantly. "I have the plates." Then he lost consciousness.

Trinny picked Holmes up, cradling him like an infant, and we walked a mile or so to his caravan, parked close by. There he made Holmes comfortable in a small bed and once I was sure he was safe I went back to the manor house. Inside, Mallory and his officers were in a jubilant mood. The entire gang had been captured with only minor injuries and were now on their way to Stamford Jail. I told them briefly about the fate of de Vere and Holmes's fortunate escape and Mallory said he considered this Holmes's greatest triumph. As for me, I decided to return to The Lazy Fox and visit Holmes again the following day.

The next morning, I rose early and made my way by pony and trap from the inn to Trinny's caravan. I could see immediately that Holmes was not well. He lay in a fever, by turns sweating and shivering. We tended him as best we could, and Trinny fed him soup and bread. Two days he lay while the fever ran its course and he alternated between mumbling incoherently and shouting. Finally, on the third day, the fever left him and when I arrived from the inn, I found him sitting up and eating a bowl of fresh eel prepared by Trinny.

"Watson," he said. "I have an errand which I would be exceedingly grateful if you would undertake for me."

"Willingly, Holmes," I replied.

"Take this parcel to the Bank of England and ask to see the governor. You must give it into his hands only along with this note which I have written. Then return as quickly as you can. Don't stop to visit Baker Street."

I laughed. "That is not possible. Mrs. Hudson is very anxious for news and besides, I must get some fresh clothing for you. To be quite frank, Holmes, you are in need of a good wash."

"Very well," he replied. "If you must. But don't tarry longer than necessary."

73

I returned to London to carry out Holmes's bidding as quickly as I could, though not as quickly as he would have wished. I was determined to spend some time at Baker Street reassuring Mrs. Hudson whom I knew to be extremely worried about Holmes. Gaining access to the governor of the Bank of England was also not as straightforward as Holmes seemed to think. It involved satisfying the scrutiny of several secretaries and minor officials. Fortunately, however, Holmes was well enough known at the bank for the governor to agree to see me briefly between a business lunch and a business dinner. He was delighted with the package I gave him, and his manner changed sufficiently for him to invite me to dinner, but I declined, saying I was on strict instructions from Holmes to return immediately. In a little over twenty-four hours, I was back at the caravan where I found Holmes sitting outside dressed and evidently his old self again.

"I have become quite enamoured of the gipsy life, Watson," he said expansively. "There is positively everything a man could want. I have bathed in a stream nearby and breakfasted on fresh eggs from Trinny's hens. My clothing has even been washed and dried. What could be more civilised?"

"A copy of *The Times*?" I replied.

He laughed. "That publication is overrated." His gaze fell on an envelope I was carrying. "But I see you have something for me"

I handed it to him, and he opened it eagerly.

"Excellent!" He exclaimed. "Just as I hoped." He jumped to his feet. "There is one final duty to be performed and then we can return together to Baker Street."

"What duty is that?" I asked.

"I have unfinished business with my client," he replied.

It was a short journey to the toll house by trap. Holmes insisted on Trinny accompanying us. "I am not yet back to full strength," he said. We found Jacob Duffy busy packing some of his belongings into a large chest. He had been informed his lease would expire at the end of the month and he would be required to leave the premises. We commiserated with him on the harshness of this announcement, but he refused to dwell on it and invited us in for some refreshment. Inside, Holmes said how pleased he was that Jacob had sought his help and that he could now say the case was closed.

"You were indeed right in thinking you were being watched," he said. "And the person who was watching you stands before you now." He pointed to Trinny.

"Trinny?" Duffy exclaimed. "I don't understand. Why ever would he be watching me?"

"Because his name is not Trinny, but Benjamin," Holmes replied.

Duffy looked incredulous, "Benjamin?"

"You must imagine him without his beard and long hair and three years younger."

Trinny took a step nearer Jacob. "It's true, father."

Duffy's legs began to wobble, and he sank heavily into a chair.

"You should not have sprung this on him, Holmes," I protested. "It is too much."

"No, no," Duffy said. "I'll be all right."

"Forgive me, Mr. Duffy. I have no wish to distress you. But this is indeed your son. How and why, he will explain to you when Watson and I have gone. But before we do I have one more thing to give you."

He handed him a piece of paper which I saw was a banker's draft for a significant sum.

"The Bank of England pays a reward to anyone seizing counterfeit plates. The governor has decided that the reward is due to you. Had you not brought this case to my attention these plates might never have been recovered."

Duffy shook his head, "But begging your pardon, sir, that's not right. The reward should be yours."

"I was merely following my profession, for which the bank has agreed to pay me. You, on the other hand, performed a service to the community."

"But what will I do with it?" Duffy said.

Holmes laughed. "Buy a house where you and your son can live. And if you will take my advice, move into the village. Isolation is all very well, but remember your Bible, Mr. Duffy, 'it is not good for man to live alone'."

"How the devil did you know Trinny was the old man's son?" I asked Holmes as we sat in the pony and trap returning us to The Lazy Fox.

"It's impossible to spend three days in someone's company without learning a lot about them."

"But how did you get him to talk? He's as silent as the grave."

"That, Watson, is the root of the problem. Duffy's son has a speech impediment. He was probably born with it. The condition was studied some years ago by a Frenchman, Paul Broca. He can understand language perfectly but has difficulty producing it. His speech is slow and effortful."

"Not a condition which would endear him to others."

"Precisely. He was bullied at school by the boys and mercilessly mocked by his teachers. When he became a teenager, he left school to help his father at the toll, but travellers became annoyed by what they perceived as his stupidity. Eventually, he decided to run away. Someone must have heard him mention America, which is why Duffy thought he'd gone there, though there was never any possibility of that. But he was good with his hands and picked up a job as an itinerant tinker. A year ago, he heard that his mother had died and became concerned about his father living alone on the fen. So he returned to the area but felt too ashamed to speak to him."

"This is all very well, Holmes, but he is still guilty of assisting the counterfeiters," I said.

"I'm convinced he didn't understand what he was involved in. Besides, the police know nothing of his involvement, and I have no intention of enlightening them. As for myself, I shall forever be in his debt."

We had been back about a week from Lincolnshire when I returned to our lodgings from visiting an old patient of mine and found Holmes smoking in the drawing-room.

"Holmes, what does this mean?" I asked.

He looked up from the newspaper he was reading.

"I'm afraid we shall not be seeing much of Mallory in future. His success in the counterfeiting case has earned him a promotion to superintendent. No doubt we shall have to get used to another young blood from the provinces."

"You know what I'm referring to. Why are you smoking Old London Shag?"

"Balkan Relish is very fine Watson, but it is a Sunday-best tobacco. I need something for every day."

"But what shall I tell Mrs. Hudson. I promised her you would not smoke it again."

"I have a solution to that. If she will let us know when her sister is coming, I will undertake not to smoke it during her visit."

"And the dottels," I asked.

"There you are victorious Watson. Only new tobacco from now on. You will have no need to inflict so much fresh air on us in future."

The Great Game

"This is insupportable," said Holmes, laying down his knife and fork. "What has possessed Mrs. Hudson to inflict curried meat on us every evening this week?"

"I'm afraid it's that time of year Holmes," I replied.

"Maybe so, but there is a limit to how much cold meat and potatoes a rational person can be expected to consume."

"Let me speak to her."

I considered it better for me to voice our discontent. Holmes was likely to be too direct and send our landlady into a state of utter dejection. We both knew, of course, what the problem was. Every year when the circus came to Regents Park, it was the same.

Mrs. Hudson was in every respect an excellent woman. A person of strict standards she was fastidious in carrying out her duties and responsibilities whilst nevertheless tolerating our irregular hours and general untidiness. But the arrival of the circus in the neighbourhood of north London produced a marked change in her demeanour. Her early childhood had been spent in a very religious household in Scotland where her father was an elder at the local kirk and where the attitude toward public entertainments was generally disapproving. The one exception to this life of rigid conformity was her annual visit to the circus.

"It was the only treat my father would allow us," she explained to me one day. "Before his conversion, he was a performer, and he always retained a fondness for the profession."

As a consequence, every September, when the evenings began to draw in and the touring circus paid its last visit of the season, she became unusually excitable. Together with her sister, she waited in the crowds watching the parade of animals, performers, and highly coloured caravans around the park. When the performances started, she went to as many as she could afford and her casual conversation as she tidied our rooms and served our breakfast was full of the delights of the previous evening. Holmes would inevitably throw me a despairing look before retreating to his room.

"I sometimes think her father did a great disservice to mankind in taking her to the circus, Watson," he complained one morning. "If the apocalypse were to overtake us all, she would still be talking of it."

"Well, it will be gone in a week's time," I replied.

"So will my sanity," he said gloomily.

But it was the decline in culinary standards which was arguably the most noticeable consequence of Mrs. Hudson's addiction. She was a proficient and imaginative cook whose talents would not have been out of place in the Savoy. But once the circus season was underway, the same cold food appeared with relentless monotony. After five nights of this, it was agreed between us that I would raise the matter with her when she came to clear away our plates.

Mrs. Hudson eventually appeared about 10 o'clock that evening, but it was apparent straightaway from her manner that all was not well. Instead of her usual animation, she was subdued and distracted. I wondered if Holmes had already spoken to her. I looked at him, but he shook his head.

"Are you quite well Mrs. Hudson?" I said. "You don't seem yourself this evening."

"I'm perfectly well, thank you, Doctor," she replied picking up the plates.

"How was the performance?" Holmes asked. "Was it as good as usual?"

She hesitated before answering. "It was fine, thank you. Will there be anything else?"

"No," Holmes replied.

"Was the dinner to your liking?" she asked.

"Perfectly," he said. "But please sit for a moment. There is something Watson wishes to ask you."

Mrs. Hudson remained still for a moment and then to our utter amazement she burst into tears.

"Watson!" Holmes cried. "A glass of brandy. Sit down, dear lady."

"I'm sorry, sirs," she said. "I'll be all right in a moment."

I passed her the brandy, which she was going to refuse, but I insisted on her taking it.

"It will help calm your nerves," I said. "What has happened to distress you?"

She steadied herself and her breathing gradually became more regular.

"The 'Flying Farini' fell tonight," she said. "At the end of the show."

"Fell! Was he badly hurt?" I asked.

"He's dead, Doctor," she said and started sobbing again.

"He was crossing the arena, 100 feet up, blindfolded, and without a safety net. It's the climax of the show," she continued.

"Sergei Farini!" exclaimed Holmes. "He crossed Niagara Falls only last year. Amazing man."

Mrs. Hudson nodded. "I've seen him perform it many times. He got to the other side and was on his way back. He stopped in the centre of the rope. We thought he was doing it for effect. But then he started swaying and seemed to miss his footing. He dropped like a stone, Mr. Holmes. I can see it now!"

"You have witnessed something appalling," Holmes said. "For which the best remedy is rest."

"Holmes is right. I'll give you a sedative. It will help you sleep."

"Thank you, Doctor," she replied more calmly. "What was it you wished to ask me?"

"It is of no consequence," Holmes said. "Simply if we might have dinner a little earlier next week."

Once she had gone, I turned to Holmes. "She will be in shock for several days. We should send for her sister."

He nodded. "I've seen him perform Watson. He was fearless. Most men run from the threat of death. Farini ran towards it."

"It's a risk of the profession, I suppose."

"Indeed, and yet they mostly die in their beds."

"Are you suggesting this was not accidental?"

"No, but Scotland Yard will undoubtedly have to investigate."

The papers next morning were full of Farini's death with eyewitness accounts of his fall and speculations about why he slipped. Despite the severity of the accident, he did not die immediately but remained semi-conscious for an hour before succumbing to his injuries. Inspector George Taylor was quoted as saying that Farini had been suffering from a head cold at the time and had been advised not to do the final performance. We decided it was better Mrs. Hudson did not see the papers at present, but to our surprise she was up and about even earlier than usual and responded briskly to our enquiries about her well-being.

"Thank you, gentlemen, for your concern," she said. "But there's a mountain of things to be done, and I can't be lying in bed."

I was about to remonstrate with her when she handed Holmes a note.

"This came a few minutes ago for you Mr. Holmes."

"Thank you," he replied, opening it hastily. "It's from Mycroft. He wishes to see us at the Diogenes Club on an urgent matter."

I raised my eyebrows. Holmes had not had a summons from his brother since the attempt by a foreign power to steal the Crown Jewels, a year before, a case of such national importance that we were still sworn to secrecy.

"Let us find out what he wants Watson. He has used official notepaper and sealed it with the Diogenes Club seal."

We hailed a hansom and within ten minutes were in Pall Mall, outside the club headquarters. The anonymous grey brick of the building betrayed nothing of its real importance. There was little that went on around the world in which the Diogenes Club did not have a hand.

"Apart from Downing Street, Watson, this is probably the most powerful place in the country," Holmes said. "And yet very few people are aware of its existence."

Inside the building, an official asked us our business whereupon Holmes flourished the note from Mycroft, and we were immediately ushered into the Stranger's Room, where we found him waiting for us, ensconced in an upholstered armchair, surrounded by a sea of papers and cradling a glass

"Good of you to come Sherlock, and Dr. Watson," he said, waving us to a couple of chairs. "Can I get you anything, gentlemen? The club has some very fine madeira?"

"No thank you," Holmes replied. "Your note said this was urgent."

"Always the same, Sherlock. Never one to let pleasure get in the way of business."

"Isn't that why you sent for me?"

"Indeed. Your energy is admirable, dear brother, if a trifle exhausting. But you are right. I did not use the word 'urgent' lightly. It goes without saying that what passes between us in this room is absolutely confidential."

"Naturally," Holmes said.

"And Dr. Watson?"

"Of course," I replied.

"It will shortly be announced that the Emir of Afghanistan will be sending a delegation to Britain. It will be led by a cousin of his, the Nawab of Baradhur. The Nawab is coming to sign a protocol which will ensure continued British influence in the region. In return, we have promised to increase our military support against the Emir's enemies."

"Enemies?" Holmes queried.

"The Russians, dear boy."

"Ah, the great game!"

"Precisely. Control over Afghanistan will cut off the route to India which we know the Tsar has designs upon. India is the jewel in the British crown, Sherlock. It must be protected at all costs."

"And does the Emir know we have no actual interest in his country at all?" Holmes asked.

"He is a man of the world," replied Mycroft. "He knows that he holds the balance between two great powers and will seek to gain as much advantage from that as he can."

"And how can Watson and I be of assistance?" Holmes enquired. "I'm assuming that is why we have been summoned."

Mycroft leaned closer in his chair and his voice became graver. "We have it on very good authority that the Russians have recently sent one of their agents into Britain."

"Which one?" Holmes asked.

"Todorov."

I saw a shadow cross Holmes's face.

"Who is he?" I asked.

"He is an assassin," Holmes replied. "Undoubtedly Russia's top agent, responsible for at least ten assassinations, though he has never been caught and virtually nothing is known about him."

"Exactly so," echoed Mycroft. "There can be little doubt that his target is the Nawab. If he succeeds, all hope of the protocol being signed will be lost. If we can't defend the Emir's emissary, how can we be trusted to defend his country?"

"Presumably, the itinerary for his visit has been kept secret?" Holmes said.

"Yes, though we cannot answer for all the members of the Nawab's entourage. He is not a popular figure, even in his own country."

"What measures have been taken to protect him whilst he is here?"

"The usual things, Sherlock. Blanket security wherever he goes. Only invited guests at the various functions he will attend. No one allowed within ten feet who has not been vetted. But there is one item we cannot fully control, which is why you and Dr. Watson are here this morning."

Holmes and I exchanged glances and I read in his look the same sense of foreboding.

"The Nawab is a passionate admirer of the circus," Mycroft continued. "And wishes to attend a performance during his visit. It has been pointed out to him that we cannot guarantee his safety, but he is insistent on attending."

"You are aware, of course, of the death of Farini yesterday evening," Holmes said.

"Yes, it may well be a simple accident. We all know these things happen in such professions. But I need you to investigate it, Sherlock. It has occurred uncomfortably close to the Nawab's visit. I take it you have nothing much on at the moment?"

"There are a few lines of enquiry I am pursuing on behalf of my clients," Holmes replied.

"I thought as much," said Mycroft. "You must drop everything and focus all your powers on this. If Todorov is active he must be found and stopped, by any means whatsoever. You understand?"

"Perfectly. Have you informed Inspector Taylor of our involvement in the case?"

"Yes, he is expecting to meet with you today."

Very well," Holmes said. "Watson and I will do what we can."

We got up and turned to go. As we did so, Mycroft also rose from his chair.

"Be careful Sherlock. Todorov is a dangerous man. If he is active and thinks you are standing in his way, he won't hesitate to kill you, and Watson too."

Holmes smiled. "Thank you, Mycroft. Watson and I have a few games of our own which we can play."

Once outside, Holmes put his hand on my arm. I knew exactly what he intended to say. But I spoke first.

"No, Holmes. I am not letting you investigate this on your own. Don't even consider it."

"But I know this man, Watson. Mycroft is right. I cannot ask you to put your life at risk."

"You don't need to," I replied. "You never need to."

He looked at me for a few seconds and then stretched out his hand. "Thank you, Watson. I knew I could count on you."

It was a short drive to Regent's Park. The day was sunny and bright and despite our errand, our spirits rose as we gazed on the litter of brightly coloured tents and caravans which met our eyes. It seemed as though an army were encamped before us, and I tried to imagine how it must have appeared to our landlady when she saw it for the very first time as a young impressionable girl. At the centre of this colourful scrum was a large marquee where the performances took place. We went inside and made our way towards a knot of people standing around a small cordoned-off area. One of the group detached himself and approached us.

"Thank you for coming, gentleman," he said. "I'm George Taylor."

The inspector was a tall man in early middle age with a soft West Country accent. He had an open countenance and addressed us in a warm friendly manner. I thought briefly of our first encounter with his predecessor, Inspector, now Superintendent, Mallory, and reflected on how much Holmes's reputation had risen since those early days.

"The superintendent has told me a lot about you, Mr. Holmes. I'm very pleased to make your acquaintance."

"Quite so," Holmes replied briskly. "And who are these other people?"

"These three are fellow officers," he said, indicating three men in uniform. "And the gentleman and lady here are the ringmaster, Gilbert Johnson and his wife, who manage the circus."

Holmes pointed at a patch of ground stained a dark rusty colour. "This is where Farini fell, I presume."

"Yes, those two wooden ledges about 100 feet above you are the landing stages which he was walking between."

We stared up into the gloom at the top of the tent. Even in daylight, it seemed incredibly dangerous. But blindfolded, under the glare of artificial light and without a safety net, the feat looked impossible

Holmes turned to the ringmaster. "I understand Mr. Farini was not entirely well before the performance."

"That's right," Johnson replied. "He was complaining of a head cold. But he insisted on performing."

"He must have been aware of the extra risk. Why would he have been so determined?"

The ringmaster shrugged his shoulders. "I can't say. I advised him against it."

"He was a professional, Mr. Holmes," his wife added. "They have a duty to their public."

Holmes smiled briefly, "I imagine he was paid extra for this feat. It was after all the climax to the show and carried a significant risk of death."

The ringmaster hesitated. "We paid him a little extra, yes."

"So, if he had not performed, he would have forfeited it?"

"We cannot afford to pay our performers if they do not go on. They all know that," Johnson replied.

"Of course," Holmes continued. "Did he suggest performing the act but with a safety net?"

"No," put in his wife. "Farini was a vain man. He had an invincible belief in his own ability. He'd performed it countless times before."

"Thank you," Holmes replied. "You have been most helpful. Can Watson and I see the things Farini was using yesterday evening, Inspector?"

"Yes, Mr. Holmes. I've got them over here. No one has been allowed to touch them."

"Excellent!"

The inspector led the way to a small tent just outside the marquee and signalled to the officer outside to let us through. Inside, laid out on a trestle table were a length of coiled rope, a long wooden balancing pole, two thin leather-soled shoes, a body costume, and a bandana. Holmes spent a good hour examining the rope and the pole before pronouncing them both sound.

"There are no obvious signs either has been tampered with. The quality of the rope is first-rate."

Taylor nodded. "It was made by Outhwaites, a Yorkshire firm. I had one of their representatives inspect it earlier."

"You continue to impress, Inspector. Let us see if there is anything to be made of the costume."

Holmes withdrew his magnifying glass and scrutinised the costume and shoes closely, arriving at last at the blindfold.

"It was a favourite of Farini's," commented the inspector. "He always used the same bandana."

"High wire performers are notoriously superstitious," said Holmes, holding the cloth close to his eyes. "Understandably so." He paused for a moment and then passed the bandana to me. "Smell that Watson and tell me I am not mistaken." I took the cloth and did as he asked.

"Well?" he asked.

I nodded. "It's very faint," I replied. "But I would say it's marijuana."

The inspector looked perplexed. "I don't understand gentlemen. Are you saying Farini had been taking drugs?"

"No," Holmes replied. "The blindfold has been impregnated with the drug. Marijuana can be absorbed through the skin. The sweat from Farini's brow would have aided absorption into his bloodstream. Whoever did this, intended to kill him."

"Marijuana is a mind-altering drug, Inspector," I explained. "It affects the senses and can disorient the user."

"But wouldn't Farini have smelt it when he put it on?" Taylor said.

"Don't forget he had a head cold," Holmes replied. "The drug takes about fifteen minutes to become effective, which is why he was able to complete the first crossing. He would not have known anything was wrong until it was too late."

"You think Farini was murdered?" the inspector said incredulously.

"Yes, I do. But by whom and why are things we have yet to discover."

"Well, this changes things and no mistake."

"Indeed," replied Holmes. What do we know about Farini?"

Taylor leafed through his notebook. "Sergei Farini, born about 30 years ago in Siberia of Italian parents."

"He was Russian!" I exclaimed.

"Became a tight-rope performer at 15 and joined the present circus three years ago," the inspector continued. "There are no known dependants."

"Is there nothing else about him at all?" Holmes asked.

"We did find some markings on his right wrist when we examined the body," Taylor replied. "A number with six digits had been burnt into the skin."

"And your conclusion?"

"Possibly a prison number, Mr. Holmes. Some countries brand their prisoners."

"Indeed, particularly if their crimes are political. What about his caravan? Was anything found there?"

The inspector shook his head. "Nothing out of the ordinary."

"Well, let us look again," Holmes said. "You were not seeking a motive for murder."

Farini's caravan was one of the largest on the site. In bold blue and white stripes, it stood out dramatically from the rest. I recalled what Mrs. Johnson had said about Farini's vanity. Inside, there was clear evidence of his profession with an assortment of costumes and several testimonials on the walls from previous employers. Prominently displayed above a mantelpiece was a framed cutting from *The New York Times* describing his crossing of Niagara Falls the previous year. We spent about an hour looking through drawers and boxes in the hope of learning something about the man who had met such a violent death the night before. But there was nothing.

"There is nothing personal here, Holmes," I said. "No letters, pictures, keepsakes, memorabilia. How can someone leave so little?"

"We're looking at what we are meant to see," he replied. "If you had something important to conceal, but within reach, where would you choose?"

My gaze turned to the framed cutting. "Probably there," I said. "It seems the most obvious place."

He reached up, took down the cutting, and turned it round. On the back, taped to the inside of the frame was a small notebook.

"Bravo Watson! You reasoned from first principles."

Holmes undid the tape and flicked through the pages.

"What is it?" asked the inspector.

"A motive!" Holmes replied triumphantly. "See for yourself."

91

We looked at the narrowly lined pages. There was a series of initials on each with amounts of money against them and dates.

"It's some sort of receipt book," said the inspector.

"Yes, but a receipt book for Farini's eyes only."

I nodded, understanding his meaning. "Farini was blackmailing his fellow performers," I said.

"Precisely," Holmes replied. "He was supplementing his income. Which is perhaps why he could afford a more splendid caravan than the others."

"So one of these could have been Farini's killer?" Taylor said.

"Possibly, though they are rather small sums. Murder is usually a solution of last resort. But we must interview each of them. They are probably not aware that Farini kept such a record."

The ringmaster was not well pleased to learn that our investigation into Farini's death was incomplete.

"But it was obviously an accident," he protested. "I can't see what all the fuss is about. I do have a business to run."

"We are not satisfied that Farini's death was an accident," Holmes explained. "And, until we are, our investigations must continue. As for your business, we are not closing the circus. You can carry on performing as normal."

The ringmaster was somewhat relieved by this concession though he continued to complain about the inconvenience of having police officers on site. But eventually, the combination of Holmes's steeliness and charm persuaded him of the necessity of cooperating.

"We shall need a list of all your employees," Holmes said. "And the dates they joined the circus."

"Very well," he said. "But don't go upsetting them. I can't afford any more trouble."

"So much for the milk of human kindness," I said to Holmes as we came away.

"There's precious little room for sentiment in the world of public entertainment, Watson. That is the real tragedy here."

He turned to Taylor. "There's no more we can do today, Inspector. Watson and I will return tomorrow. But one last thing. Did Farini say anything before he died? I gather he was semi-conscious for a while."

"Nothing intelligible," Mr. Holmes. "The officer attending him said he repeated the word 'bute' several times, but he just seemed to be rambling."

"Do you make anything of that?" I asked Holmes as we sat in the cab returning to Baker Street.

"Bute is the first syllable in the word Butyrka," he replied. "It's the name of a notorious prison in Moscow."

The next morning I rose early with the drugged sensation of having slept heavily and dreamt badly. Even so, Holmes was up before me. I found him sitting in an armchair still in his dressing gown and the room resembling a London fog.

"Have you been up all night?" I asked, opening a window.

"More or less," he answered, laying down his pipe. "I am convinced Farini's murder is the work of Todorov. I am awaiting a telegram from Mycroft which will hopefully provide the missing link."

"In the meantime, Holmes, let us have some breakfast."

"By all means. There is some first-rate kedgeree."

I lifted the lid and surveyed the remains. "There was. You have clearly lost no time in finishing it off."

"My apologies, Watson. Try the eggs."

I was about to ask him the point of recommending something which no longer existed when Mrs. Hudson came in with a telegram. Holmes tore it open eagerly.

"Wonderful," he exclaimed. "I wired Mycroft earlier to ask if anything at all was known about Todorov before he became an agent. He has replied that Todorov is rumoured to have been a prison guard from where he was recruited to the Russian secret service. We have it, Watson."

"Presumably, Farini recognised Todorov and threatened to expose him," I said.

"That has to be our working hypothesis. Farini either knew or guessed that he was a spy. But one thing is certain, Watson, we shall have to be careful how we proceed. He will know we are hunting him."

Later that morning we returned to the circus and sought out the ringmaster who handed us a list of his employees. We had identified three sets of initials in Farini's notebook with various sums of money set against them: "L.S.," "E.M," and "R.D." Consulting the list, the first of these had to be "Lorenzo Sabatini," a clown; the second, "Emilia Morendo," a horse-riding acrobat; and the third, "Roland Dumas," an elephant trainer.

"None of these look like real names Holmes," I said.

"They are a trifle exotic," he replied. "Plainly, stage names, with the exception of the ringmaster. 'Gilbert Johnson' is hardly likely to be an invention."

Sabatini turned out to be a cheerful Londoner with a small yellow caravan on the edge of the complex.

"Mr. Sabatini?" Holmes asked as a head poked round the door.

"Who wants to know?"

Holmes introduced us briefly.

"Oh yeah. I heard you was about. You'd best come in."

The interior of the van was cram-full with the tools of his trade, brightly coloured wigs, false noses, jars of face paint, and boxes of giant-sized footwear.

"Excuse the mess gentlemen. Six changes of costume every night. It's a pain in the unmentionable!"

"But I'm sure the children love it," I said.

"It's kind of you to say so, sir."

"How well did you know Farini?" Holmes began.

"Not very well. He wasn't a particularly nice man to know, if you get my meaning?"

"There is reason to believe his death was not accidental," Holmes said.

"I'm not surprised. He was a bastard."

Holmes produced Farini's notebook. "You were paying him two shillings every week. Farini kept a record of it. What was the reason for that?"

Sabatini flushed. "There's no law says I can't. It's my money."

"We are not here to cause you trouble," Holmes said. "We are not the police. Farini was blackmailing you, wasn't he?"

Sabatini nodded. "I was sacked from me last job. They said I was thieving, but I never was. Farini found out. I didn't do for him though."

"Thank you," Holmes said. "That is all we wanted to know."

We got up to go. "Why 'Sabatini'?" I asked. "It's not your real name, is it?"

He smiled. "All the best clowns are Italian. Who'd come to watch 'Sid Smith'?"

"I can't see him as a ruthless killer Holmes," I said as we walked away.

"No, it would require a considerable leap of the imagination. Although the most cold-blooded murderer I ever knew was an old lady who cared for injured birds."

Emilia Morendo was self-evidently not an old lady. The diminutive form which answered our knock could not have been more than twenty and I had to suppress an impulse to ask if we could speak to her parents. We were both taken by the warm lilt of her Welsh voice as she invited us in. Despite her extreme youth, the brief account she gave us of her life made it clear she was not immune to the hardships of poverty, neglect, and ill-health. Like Sabatini, she readily admitted to being blackmailed by Farini.

"He was friendly to me when I first joined the circus. Then he found out I'd had an abortion. It was a couple of years ago. Anyway, Farini threatened to report me unless I paid him. He said he'd accept payment in kind, but I said I'd rather pay him the money."

"Thank you for being so frank with us Miss Morendo," Holmes replied. "Your secret is safe with us."

"I didn't kill him, sir. I'm glad he's dead, but it wasn't me."

"I'm beginning to think whoever killed Farini performed a service to the community, Holmes," I said afterwards.

"Indeed. We have yet to discover a single redeeming feature about him."

We found the last of the trio, Roland Dumas, busy rehearsing with his elephants in the circus tent. The huge creatures lumbered around the arena performing tricks, sitting on their haunches and catching objects with their trunks. I well remember the impression of nobility these creatures created when I had first seen them in Afghanistan some years before. To see them reduced now to objects of popular amusement, was dispiriting. But Dumas appeared kindly enough. A bluff Yorkshireman, he had studied his craft under mahouts in India and had learnt that elephants will perform better if treated well.

"Fine animals," I said as we approached.

"They are that," he replied.

"Is it true about their memory?" I asked.

"Well, it's a sight better than mine."

"You probably know why we are here Mr. Dumas," Holmes said.

"Ay, the whole circus does. Farini had it coming to him. I couldn't stand the fellow."

"Why was that?" Holmes asked.

"I'm sure you know," Dumas replied.

"We know you were being blackmailed."

"For the best part of three years. As to why, I'm not at liberty to say, gentlemen."

"Because it affects a third party?" I asked

He nodded. "And she's married. That's all I will say, except that although I hated Farini, I didn't kill him."

"Were you surprised that Farini performed that evening even though he was by all accounts not well?" Holmes asked.

"No, and neither would you be if you'd heard the argument between him and Johnson."

"The ringmaster told us he advised Farini not to perform," I said.

Dumas snorted. "Johnson told him to get his backside onto that platform or he could look for another job. I wouldn't call that advice, would you?"

"Do you think Dumas capable of murder Holmes," I asked as we left the arena.

"As much as the next man Watson. He certainly had motive enough, as did they all. But the obstacle here is the time they have been at the circus. If we are right in thinking this to be the work of Todorov then we are looking for someone who has only recently joined. Everyone on the ringmaster's list has been here for at least a year.

"And if Farini was blackmailing him, why is he not in the book?"

"As to that, the book is simply a record of payments. Presuming that Todorov decided not to pay, there would be no need for him to be in it. It is time we had another talk with Johnson."

The ringmaster and his wife were busy counting the takings from the previous night's performance when we encountered them in a makeshift office at the back of the arena. They both looked up as we entered.

"Receipts are down twenty percent, gentlemen," Johnson said. I hope you've come to tell me this charade is over, and the circus can now get back to normal."

"I am very much afraid I can't," Holmes replied.

"Why the devil not?"

"Because there is a murderer on the loose in your circus and unless we find him, I shall have to close you down until we do."

The ringmaster looked thunderstruck. "A murderer?"

"Yes, Mr. Johnson. Farini was murdered, deliberately and in cold blood. And I would remind you that obstructing our investigation could have serious consequences."

"What d'you mean?" he replied.

"This list of your employees," Holmes said flourishing the paper. "It's not complete."

"Of course, it is," Johnson protested.

"No dear," put in his wife. "Mr. Holmes is right. Remember we took on a new performer in Paris."

"Pyotr, yes, I'd forgotten him. Pyotr Ivanov, he stood in last week for Armstrong when he became sick. He's remained with us since. I haven't got around to updating the list."

"What does he do?" I asked.

"He's a knife thrower. Damned good one too. Much better than Armstrong ever was. Excellent English, even though he's Russian."

"And where can we find him?" Holmes asked.

"His caravan is on the far side, up by the animal enclosures."

"You were right Holmes," I said as we made our way outside. "How did you guess?"

"It was the only conclusion. If Todorov is here then he must have joined recently, which meant the list was incomplete. When you have eliminated the impossible, Watson…"

Ivanov's caravan was on the outer rim of the encampment amid a sprawl of wild animals. Here were the performing bears, high stepping horses, baboons, and lions of this travelling menagerie.

"I'm not sure I would like to sleep so close to this, Holmes."

"It's probably the safest part of the circus," he replied. "What thief would venture here after dark?"

The van door was opened by a dark-skinned man of about middle height who looked at us with an air of mild curiosity.

"Can I help you gentlemen?" he asked in slightly accented English.

"I am Sherlock Holmes, and this is my associate, Dr. Watson. We would like to ask you some questions about the death of Mr. Farini."

"I'm afraid I hardly knew him," Ivanov said. "I only joined the circus a week ago."

"Yes, we know," replied Holmes. "May we come in?"

Ivanov nodded and stepped aside to allow us through. Inside, the van was immaculate. Instead of the usual clutter, there were gleaming surfaces and carefully arranged personal items. The only concession to ornamentation was a set of icons on a small table, their vibrant colours and gold leaf irradiating the interior like a brilliant rainbow.

"These are beautiful Mr. Ivanov," I said. "Are you a collector?"

He shook his head. "No, they are memories of a former life."

"A former life?" Holmes said.

"I used to be a priest," he replied. "I lost my faith after a close friend died suddenly."

"When was this?"

"About ten years ago."

"Your present occupation would seem as far away from the priesthood as one could imagine," I said.

He smiled. "I had a talent for throwing as a young man, Doctor. It's a purely instinctive skill. When I left the priesthood, I decided to devote myself to the one thing I knew I was good at."

"And what made you join this circus?" Holmes asked.

"I had just finished a spell at the Cirque de Francais in Paris. Mr. Johnson saw me perform and asked me if I was free to replace their resident knife-thrower who had been taken ill suddenly."

"Would you have any objection to showing me your papers?"

"Of course not."

Ivanov opened a drawer and withdrew a leather wallet which he handed to Holmes.

"Thank you." Holmes spent the next fifteen minutes looking through the contents of the wallet.

"You have a Russian passport, Mr. Ivanov," Holmes said

"Yes, I was born in Moscow and lived there for the first thirty years of my life. I was a chaplain at Butyrka prison for several years."

"And when were you last in Russia?"

"I have not been back since I left."

After a few more questions, Holmes thanked Ivanov and we left the caravan.

"What do you think Holmes?" I asked as we made our way back past the animal pens.

"That our visit has raised more questions than it has answered. Ivanov is a pleasant enough fellow, and his story has the ring of truth, but then it is probably one he has told several times."

"And what of the coincidence of him working at Butyrka?"

"Which he freely owned to. It was either the act of someone with nothing to hide or one of deep cunning."

"I have to say I liked him, Holmes."

"Indeed. But then I also liked the old lady. And there was one other thing. Did you notice the smell of marijuana?"

I nodded.

"He is a user, Watson."

No sooner had he said this than I saw his eyes freeze as if in some hypnotic trance.

"Don't move," he hissed. "Stay completely still."

"What is it?" I whispered.

"Turn your head very slowly to the right."

I did as he bid me and saw about fifty yards away, a full-grown male lion, standing quite still, surveying us closely. I cannot adequately describe the sensation of fear which swept over me. The danger of our situation was immediately apparent. We were on open ground with the nearest shelter a good two hundred yards distant.

"If you have any lion-taming experience, Watson, now is the time to confess it."

"They only attack humans if they feel threatened or are hungry, so I'm told," I replied.

"Let us hope he knows that," Holmes said. "In the meantime, I suggest we do nothing to attract his attention. It may be that boredom will accomplish what resistance or flight clearly cannot."

It is generally the case that the more we are told not to do something the greater the desire to do it. After standing like a statue for ten minutes, I had an overwhelming urge to move my left foot. I carefully shifted my weight onto my right leg and allowed my left to slide forward a few inches. Instantly, the lion's ears began to twitch, and his body stiffened. Then he began slowly to pad towards us. Holmes gave me a pained look. After halving the distance between us the animal stopped and sniffed the air. I seemed to recall that lions could smell their prey from a great distance. But there was still nothing in his movements which indicated he was preparing to attack. I have no idea how long Holmes and I stood there trying to muffle our breathing and suppressing the instinct to flee. Probably only minutes, but it seemed like an eternity. Eventually, the lion turned his head away and appeared about to depart when, through sheer fatigue, I let my hand fall to my side. This was enough to settle the matter and the animal moved towards us in a more determined manner. Reaching me first, he lowered his head and began rubbing his nose against my ankle, before opening his mouth and licking my fingers with his warm leathery tongue. I felt my legs weaken and I was on the point of falling when suddenly Holmes let out an almighty sneeze. Immediately the lion gave a roar and rushed away from us like a scalded cat. We clung to each other in terror expecting the animal to turn again and attack, but it fled out of sight. At the same time, we heard a voice shouting, "Simba! Simba! Where the devil are you?" and saw the burly figure of the lion tamer striding towards us from the direction of the animal pens.

"Are you the lunatics who let him out?"

"Does that look likely to you?" Holmes replied. "We have been terrorised by the beast for the past quarter of an hour. The law requires you to keep your animals secure."

"Simba wouldn't hurt a fly, gentlemen," said the tamer, more respectfully. "Hasn't got a tooth in his head to bite you with. Now if it had been his partner, it might have been a different kettle of fish. She can turn nasty."

"Has he escaped before?" I asked.

"Never. He's short-sighted and can't see very clearly. Some bloody fool drew the bolt on his cage back. He'd better not let me get hold of him." With that, he hurried off in search of the lion.

"I have never been so frightened in my entire life, Holmes, as when you sneezed," I said. "It was a masterstroke."

"I've always been allergic to animal fur," he replied. "But I must admit it was rather spectacular."

"It probably woke up half of Surrey. If only the British army had had such a weapon in Afghanistan."

We both burst out into uncontrollable laughter. It was only when we were drying our eyes after several minutes of helplessness that we realised just how scared we both had been.

"This was no accident," Holmes said. "This was a warning."

"You think it was Todorov?"

"If I had any doubts before of his presence here, this has dispelled them. We are getting closer, Watson!"

Later that evening as we sat smoking in Baker Street, Holmes said,

"Tomorrow evening is the final performance of the circus. I have telegraphed Mycroft advising him again to dissuade the Nawab from attending, but if as I very much fear, he insists on it, there is little we can do to ensure his safety. Every instinct tells me that

Todorov will attempt something tomorrow, but as yet we have no definitive information about who he is nor how he intends to carry out the assassination."

"What can we do?" I asked.

"We need more time, Watson."

"But we don't have more time," I replied.

The following morning I rose later than usual. Holmes and I had talked well into the night discussing how we might protect the Nawab, but however we framed it, the task seemed impossible. Eventually, I retired to bed leaving Holmes to smoke yet another pipe. Even so, I found he was up before me and had departed early. He had left a note saying he had some arrangements to make and would explain later. I was just finishing my breakfast when Mrs. Hudson ushered in a bearded man dressed in a heavily patched cloth jacket, worn corduroy trousers, and carrying a bag.

"I'm sorry to disturb you, Doctor, but this is Joseph Gurney. He has a message for Mr. Holmes from the circus. I said perhaps he could speak to you."

"Thank you, Mrs. Hudson, that will be fine," I replied. "You are welcome, Mr. Gurney. If you will tell me your message I will see it gets to Mr. Holmes."

Gurney touched his forehead respectfully, "Beggin' yer pardon, sir, but I was told to give it to Mister Holmes himself."

"Well, I'm afraid he's not here, and I have no idea when he will return."

"Then, beggin' yer pardon, sir, I will wait."

"Very well, if you must. Take a seat."

I turned away from him not best pleased by his stubbornness and poured myself some more coffee.

"You might have the decency to offer me a cup too, Watson," a voice rang out.

I swivelled round and saw the beardless face of Holmes smiling triumphantly at me from the chair.

"Holmes!"

"Really, Watson, I am appalled at your treatment of our guests."

"What is the meaning of this? Why are you dressed in this fashion?"

"All in good time. I am pleased that you were not able to see through my disguise. It was important to know that. I wasn't so lucky with Mrs. Hudson, however. She knew me straightaway; something about the eyes."

"But why are you in disguise?"

Holmes got his pipe out and began filling it.

"After you had retired to bed last night, it occurred to me that if we were to have the slightest chance of stopping Todorov then we had to become like him – invisible. If we could blend in with the circus hands, we would be better able to detect anything out of the ordinary. So, early this morning I spoke to Mr. Dumas and asked him if we could assist him with his elephant act. I had to take him into my confidence a little. He agreed quite readily."

"Wait a minute, Holmes," I put in. "You said 'we'."

"Yes, I have a disguise for you too," he replied, pointing to his bag.

"No, definitely not," I said. "I am not dressing like a vagrant for anyone."

"I never knew you to be such a snob, Watson. It's for the good of your country."

"But how are we to assist Dumas? I know nothing of elephants."

"The duties are purely nominal. There will be other helpers there too. But in general, it means leading the animals into and out of the ring and clearing up any mess."

"Mess!"

"There is the occasional accident, Watson. But nothing of any significance. Remember that elephants are vegetarian."

"Good God, Holmes you are expecting me to shovel up elephant dung!"

He laughed heartily. "You might want to omit that detail when you compose your account of the case."

"And what will the forces of law and order be doing in the meantime?" I enquired.

"I have spoken to Inspector Taylor, and some of his men will be disguised as members of the public. The Nawab will have his own bodyguard and at the first sign of any disturbance, he will be hurried out of one of the emergency exits."

"If I might suggest something, Holmes," I said. "Ivanov is currently our chief suspect."

He nodded.

"So, one of us should be shadowing him throughout the performance."

"Excellent, Watson. I was about to suggest the same thing. Are you willing to assume that duty?"

"Anything rather than shovelling elephant faeces," I replied.

"One more thing," Holmes said. "Make sure you have your revolver. Todorov will stop at nothing to carry out his orders."

We spent the remainder of the day until early evening ensuring my disguise was as good as Holmes's. I baulked at wearing a beard, which I knew would irritate my skin, and decided to go clean-shaven. Accordingly, I bid farewell to my moustache and Mrs. Hudson assisted in discolouring my face so that I looked more swarthy. Gazing in the mirror I was shocked to see the difference.

"I hope you have informed Taylor of our disguises," I said. "I am in great danger of being arrested as a house-breaker."

"That is first-rate, Mrs. Hudson. I would not care to encounter you in a dark alley, Watson," Holmes replied.

"Thank you, sir," she said. "Please could you and the Doctor use the back entrance on leaving? I have my reputation to consider."

At about six o'clock we declared ourselves ready. Holmes looked at me, and I glimpsed in his face my own mixture of excitement and fear. We had reached the climax of the hunt. Everything was to play for. He seized my arm.

"The game's afoot, Watson," he said.

We arrived at the circus shortly before the commencement of the evening performance. All was noise and bustle. The ringmaster, resplendent in his top hat and coattails, was busy shouting at everyone while the various performers were limbering up or putting the last touches to their costumes. It was an extravaganza of colours, frills, and flounces as though some enormous fancy dress party were in preparation. It struck me how easy it would be for an assassin to conceal himself amidst such a pageant.

Out in the tent, every seat was taken. The Nawab and his party had arrived by a separate entrance and were in a cordoned-off area in the middle of the auditorium. Dumas had provided Holmes and me with colourful sashes which identified us as circus staff. With these, we were able to move freely around the circus complex without being challenged. We had decided that Holmes would stay as far as possible in the arena whilst I remained backstage. I found Ivanov at the rear of the tent dressed in the costume of a Cossack. He glanced at me briefly as I passed him and asked me to fetch him a glass of water.

He was busy inspecting an assortment of knives and giving some last-minute instructions to a young assistant who could not have been more than sixteen. I saw from the programme that he was due to perform just before the interval.

The first few acts passed off without incident. I glanced occasionally over at Holmes who was constantly in motion about the tent, helping to clear the arena for the next event or being the butt of the clown's practical jokes. I have always maintained that had Holmes not become a consulting detective he would have made a splendid actor. His facility at impersonation and gift for improvisation were remarkable. The climax of the first half was the knife-throwing act. After an impressive introduction by the ringmaster, Ivanov came bounding onto the stage followed by his assistant. It was immediately clear that he was exceptionally talented. He began by piercing the middle of a series of playing cards on a revolving wheel with pinpoint accuracy, moving backwards five paces every time till he was at the rim of the arena. I saw Holmes look anxiously at the Nawab's party, which at that point was about fifty feet away, still a considerable distance for most knife throwers. The high point of Ivanov's act involved him throwing twelve knives in quick succession around the body of his assistant, each one not more than an inch from her flesh. To the crowd's amazement, he proceeded to repeat the trick, only blindfolded. He was just about to throw the last knife when a large flap on the side of the tent opened, and a gust of wind blew into the auditorium. Immediately the candles lighting the arena began to flicker and in a matter of seconds, the tent was plunged into darkness. At that moment Ivanov turned towards the audience with the knife in his hand and ripped off his blindfold. Instinctively, I ran to where he was standing and threw myself on him. At the same time, I was aware of another body than mine hurtling from a different direction. There was pandemonium for about five minutes, by which time the flap had been secured and the candles relit. It quickly became apparent that the Nawab was safe and that nothing untoward had occurred. It also became apparent that Ivanov was furious. He turned to Holmes, his other assailant, and me and demanded an explanation. Fortunately, Inspector Taylor was at hand to calm matters down by explaining as simply as possible that the actions of Holmes and myself were simply precautionary due to the presence of the Nawab. Fortunately, too, the interval allowed tempers to cool and reason to prevail. But as Holmes was quick to point out our disguise had been penetrated.

"This may have been an accident," he said. "But we have revealed ourselves, Watson. I am not sure what good we will be able to do now."

The second half of the show consisted of the animal and high-wire acts. Holmes and I were kept busy assisting Dumas with his elephants which had become restive after the disturbance in the first half. It was difficult not to feel that we had failed in our task. Todorov would be fully alert to our presence and that of the police and less likely to risk an attempt in the arena. Which meant of course that the danger had merely been postponed, not eliminated. Towards the end of the show, Dumas approached us and thanked us for our assistance.

"If you are looking for employment in the future gentlemen, I could use two such handy assistants," he said, smiling.

"I rather think Watson and I have performed poorly this evening," Holmes replied. "We had hoped to apprehend a killer and have simply made ourselves look foolish."

"You suspected Ivanov?" Dumas said.

"The information we had from the ringmaster's wife inclined us to that view."

"Wife!" Dumas snorted. "That's not what I'd call her."

Holmes looked at him in surprise. "Are they not married?"

"The ringmaster has a 'wife' in every town we visit," replied Dumas. "They live with him until the circus moves on or they tire of each other. It's a convenient arrangement."

"Where did the present Mrs. Johnson come from?" I asked

Dumas shrugged his shoulders. "Probably some Parisian bordello. Though I must say she seems to have a bit more about her than some of the whores he picks up."

Holmes looked keenly at me. "We have been looking in the wrong direction, Watson. We must find her immediately."

"She usually stays in Johnson's caravan during the show," Dumas said.

It was beginning to rain as we emerged from the tent and raced across the compound to the ringmaster's van, the largest on the site. It was in complete darkness when we got there, and the door was locked. Holmes took out his revolver and shot into the lock. The door swung open, and we went inside. I lit an oil lamp hanging on the back of the door and shone it into the van. In the middle was a table with a figure slumped over it as if in sleep.

"It's Johnson," Holmes said as we approached. "Dressed in his underclothes."

"There's blood under his head," I said.

I swung the light over the body and a neat round hole became visible in the back of the ringmaster's head.

"This was an execution," said Holmes.

I lifted the lamp higher and in a far corner of the van, we saw a safe, the door wide open.

"We must get back to the circus Watson. Let's hope we are in time to prevent another death."

The music for the final grand parade had just started as we arrived back at the tent, soaking from the rain, now falling heavily. The entrance to the arena was heaving with performers waiting their turn to go round the ring and it took us several minutes to push our way to the front against the protests and abuse from the jugglers, acrobats, and high-wire artistes thronging the narrow passage. When we emerged into the glare of the arena, Dumas and his elephants were just parading round. In the centre of the ring was a figure that looked for all the world like the ringmaster, attired in his top hat and tails. In his hand was what appeared to be a long baton with which he was conducting the parade.

"That's not wood," Holmes shouted to me above the noise. "Look how the light catches it. It's a rifle."

As the elephants passed in front of the Nawab's enclosure, we saw the ringmaster raising the baton towards him.

"No," we yelled simultaneously and raced for dear life across the arena. The ringmaster saw us and turned in our direction. Holmes, always the fitter of us, was in front and almost upon him when I saw the baton jump and Holmes fall to the ground. Immediately it swung towards me. There was an almighty bang as we both fired together. I felt a bullet whistle past my right ear and saw the ringmaster clutch his stomach in pain and fall heavily. In the auditorium, there was absolute chaos. The elephants, frightened by the noise, were trumpeting loudly and threatening to rear up. As for the audience, terrified families were surging towards the exit trampling over each other in desperation. I rushed over to Holmes, who was crouching and holding his shoulder.

"Don't worry about me Watson," he said. "It's merely a flesh wound. Don't let Todorov escape."

When I got to the ringmaster it was clear there was no danger of that. She lay on her back with blood oozing from beneath her fingers. I knelt down beside her.

"Todorov?" I said.

She smiled grimly, "Todorova, Dr. Watson."

"Let me help you."

She shook her head. "It's too late."

I rolled up my jacket and put it under her head.

"How is Mr. Holmes?" she asked.

"He'll be all right," I replied. "Just a flesh wound."

She nodded. "I didn't want to kill him."

"And Johnson, Farini?"

"Bastards, both of them."

She began to shiver, and her eyes started to lose focus.

"I almost succeeded, didn't I?"

"Yes, you did."

"Pray for me," she said, and her head lolled sideways.

I have seen many people die in my career, but the moment itself has never ceased to leave me humbled and in awe. To see the light, disappear from someone's face as death asserts its supremacy is something to which only the most obdurate can be immune. I walked back to Holmes and helped him to his feet.

"She is dead, Holmes," I said.

"It's probably for the best," he replied. "The state would only have hanged her."

"So why do I feel sad?" I asked.

"Because you are a good man, Watson."

It was a few days later and Holmes and I were discussing the events of the past week. His shoulder was healing well, and we could now laugh at the error which almost cost us the case.

"How could the Diogenes Club make such a monumental mistake?" I asked.

Holmes smiled. "Sheer carelessness, Watson. It's proof that no one, not even brother Mycroft, is above making the most glorious of howlers. I have looked back through the case file on Todorov. It appears that the earliest mention is a letter from one of the club's Moscow agents. His handwriting was pretty appalling, but the name is clearly Todorova. Unfortunately, the scribe who compiled the file missed off the 'a' and thus a woman silently became a man."

"The Russians presumably knew we believed the agent to be male and were able to exploit that," I said.

"Yes, they laid a trap for Johnson. His penchant for a certain kind of woman was well-known. The only fly in the ointment was Farini who recognised Todorova from his time in Butyrka. But he made the fatal error of trying to blackmail her."

"What about Johnson?" I asked. Do you think she intended to kill him?

"Johnson was a swindler. He'd been defrauding the circus for years. I expect he intended to run off with the money and desert the woman. Only she outsmarted him. I imagine her plan after shooting the Nawab was to disappear in the mayhem with the money from the safe."

"I've been struggling to find one good thing to say about the circus, Holmes," I said. "Everything about it was false. Even the amazing Simba was toothless and short-sighted. As for Farini, the world is better off without him."

"And yet, Watson, if you had seen him perform you would have beheld one of the wonders of the world."

"That does not absolve him of being a vicious blackmailer."

"No, but perhaps when he performed, we witnessed the best of him. On that high wire, he could be everything he wasn't in real life, courageous, heroic, sublime."

I grunted. "Well, I don't think you will persuade Mrs. Hudson. I can't see her visiting the circus again next year."

Holmes laughed. "Five pounds says you are mistaken."

A knock on the door prevented me from taking up Holmes's challenge right away.

"Your brother is here to see you," said Mrs. Hudson.

We both looked up in surprise at this announcement. Mycroft was seldom seen away from the vicinity of his club or his office.

"Sherlock," he boomed, striding into the room. "Don't get up, dear boy. I wanted to come in person to thank you and Doctor Watson. The Nawab owes his life to you."

"I am glad we could be of service," Holmes replied.

"And as a token of the Emir's gratitude he has asked me to give you this," Mycroft said, handing a box to him.

Holmes opened the box and we stared in surprise at a diamond set in a surround of emeralds.

"They are from one of his mines in Afghanistan."

"Please convey my thanks to the Emir," Holmes replied. "I take it from this that the visit was successful, and that the protocol has been signed."

Mycroft hesitated, "Not exactly. Because of the incident, the Emir has decided to give fresh consideration to the terms."

Holmes gave him a bewildered look, "I don't understand," he said.

"The Russians have increased their offer," Mycroft replied.

"Forgive me Mycroft," I put in. "But didn't the Russians attempt to kill the Emir's emissary?"

"Indeed," he replied. "And had they succeeded, they would have started a coup and put the Emir's brother in power. But he is now in prison in Afghanistan awaiting trial. With the failure of their main plan, the Russians have now offered the Emir the mining rights to some of their territories. I have no doubt that the Emir's prevarication is simply a ploy for Britain to increase its offer, which no doubt we shall do. So, all will be well in the end."

We stared at him in amazement.

"You never cease to astound me, brother," said Holmes. "Watson and I could have been killed. Not to mention those who have actually lost their lives. And all for some game!"

Mycroft spread his hands disarmingly. "It's the 'great game,' dear boy."

After he had gone, Holmes turned to me, "I can't speak for you Watson, but I am not happy accepting the Emir's present. It has too much blood on it."

I nodded, "I agree Holmes. We should give it to some worthy cause."

A few days later Miss Emilia Morendo, (real name Doreen Jenkins), a horse-riding acrobat with the circus opened a package and read the following message:

"This is for the service you rendered Dr. Watson and myself in our investigation with the sincere wish that it will bring you some happiness,

Yours,
Sherlock Holmes and John Watson"

The Last Highwayman

My friend, Sherlock Holmes, could not be considered religious in the conventional sense of the word. That is to say, he never attended church, not even for the principal festivals, or declared himself a member of any particular faith. And yet he possessed a detailed knowledge of the Bible and a more than passing acquaintance with the seminal scriptures of other world religions. I often wondered why someone with such an enquiring mind appeared indifferent to the religious controversies of the moment. I tasked him with this one day, to which he replied,

"I have no interest in dogma, Watson. I have always found doubt more productive than faith. We are divided by our faiths but united by our doubts."

As to men of the cloth, he was always circumspect, holding that there was something unseemly in someone attempting to meddle with the soul of another. The one exception was the Reverend Matthew Hunter whom he exempted from the general proselytising inclination of his calling. We first encountered him during a short vacation in the West Country. Holmes had been working extremely hard on a case involving the embezzlement of a substantial amount of money from one of the larger banks. The case had dragged on for weeks, leaving him visibly exhausted. At the end, it became clear even to him that he needed to recuperate, and I managed to persuade him to lay aside his consulting practice and leave the city for the fresh air of Devon. So it was that we found ourselves at The Stag and Hounds, a small pub perched on the edge of Exmoor, within sound of the sea. For the first few days, we spent our time in long walks in the deep valleys and high tors of the moor, just emerging into full splendour after the bitter snows of the winter months. We ate fresh river trout and salmon, drank quantities of the local cider, and slept like newborn infants. By the end of the week, we both felt vigorous and refreshed, but it was evident that Holmes was already beginning to fret at the solitude and lack of mental stimulation.

"How long did you book the inn for?" he asked.

"You know very well, Holmes," I replied. "Three weeks."

"As long as that. Perhaps we should telegram Mrs. Hudson in case anyone has been enquiring for me."

"We are on vacation, Holmes. There is still much to do and explore here. We have the coast to walk yet, and there are several sites of archaeological interest to visit."

"Yes, indeed. But still, three weeks."

I continued pleading the many merits of the area for several minutes, but I could see that I was not going to prevail against his waning interest. It was at this point that we were interrupted in our discussion by the figure of a man approaching us from the taproom.

"Forgive me, gentlemen," he said. "My name is Matthew Hunter. I am the vicar of the local parish. I wonder if I might have a few minutes of your time."

Hunter was a tall lean man with a stoop and an anxious air. I guessed from his manner that he was not a frequenter of taverns.

"Certainly," replied Holmes. "I am Sherlock Holmes, and this is my friend, John Watson."

"Yes, I know who you are, gentlemen, which is why I have taken the liberty of addressing you."

"How may we be of assistance?" Holmes asked.

"It's a small matter," he began apologetically, "but it has been troubling me. It concerns a member of my flock."

"Reverend Hunter," I put in. "Holmes and I are on vacation. He is in need of rest and relaxation."

Holmes waved his hand dismissively, "Watson is a little over solicitous on my behalf. I am thoroughly well I assure you. Please continue."

"Thank you, sir. And let me say I understand the concern of Dr. Watson. A good friend is a balm to the soul."

"Quite," Holmes replied.

"I am the vicar of All Saints Church in Lower Barton," Hunter went on. "You may have seen it on your walks. It stands on a promontory overlooking the sea."

"Yes," I replied. "I remember remarking on it to Holmes. It seems perilously close to the cliff edge."

"Indeed, Doctor. The cliff is eroding several centimetres each year. I'm afraid the future of the church is in doubt. But the villagers continue to attend, though not in large numbers, I must confess."

"And what is the particular matter that concerns you?" Holmes asked.

"There is a woman who attends regularly. She is of advancing years but has never missed a service in the past twelve months, until the past three weeks, when she has been absent."

Holmes and I exchanged glances.

"Forgive me, Mr. Hunter," he replied. "But I fear an absentee parishioner is not something I am equipped to help you with."

"Might she not just be ill or otherwise indisposed?" I put in.

"She is absent from her home too, Doctor."

"Perhaps she has travelled to see a relative," I continued. "There are many reasons why someone might not be at home."

"Indeed sir, but the lady in question has certain…" Hunter hesitated momentarily, "eccentricities."

"Eccentricities?" we both said simultaneously.

"Yes," he replied. "Her name is Mary Selkirk."

"A Scottish name," I said.

He nodded. "I believe she is of Scottish descent though she has lived locally for a long time. She was here when I arrived five years ago."

"You have yet to mention anything remotely eccentric, Mr Hunter," Holmes reminded him.

"When I tell you that in all that time she has been living in a cave, gentlemen, perhaps you might understand."

"That is certainly unusual," Holmes replied. "There must surely be some more appropriate accommodation for her."

"Oh indeed," Hunter said. "But she is fiercely independent and resists all such offers. She has some deep and abiding mistrust of society, the cause of which is unknown to me."

"And yet she attends your church," I returned.

He nodded. "She has a liking for music and comes to hear the organ played and the hymns sung. I believe it is the only pleasure she has."

"How does this poor woman make a living?" Holmes enquired.

"She has some talents as a seamstress and goes from house to house seeking work. Unfortunately, there are those in the village who consider her an evil influence, and she is regularly abused."

"And you fear that she may have come to harm?" I asked.

"Her safety is a matter of concern, gentlemen," Hunter replied.

"You have presumably reported this to the local police," Holmes said.

"I'm afraid the police regard her as mentally unsound and there is no evidence of an actual crime."

"I regret that we can do little better," replied Holmes. "Without evidence, there is nothing to investigate."

"Naturally, gentlemen, and I would not be seeking your help if I did not have something to show you."

Hunter reached inside the pocket of his greatcoat and produced a small pouch which he proceeded to upend into his palm. We both stared in surprise as the most delicate golden filigree necklace and locket displayed itself on his hand.

"Mary gave this to me, the last time she attended church and asked me to keep it safe for her."

"Did she give a reason?" I asked.

"No," he replied.

Holmes stretched out his hand. "May I?"

"Of course," Hunter said, passing it to him.

Holmes drew out his magnifying glass and examined the necklace.

"The workmanship is extraordinary," he said at last. "The gold is of the finest quality. It was probably specially commissioned."

He opened the locket and a small piece of hair fell out. Engraved inside were the initials "A D".

"Have you any idea to whom the initials refer?" Holmes asked.

"No," replied Hunter. "I have not seen inside the locket till now"

Holmes replaced the hair and shut the locket. On the rear was a worn coat of arms with what looked like a Latin motto.

"It's too difficult to make out," Holmes said. "I shall need a stronger glass. It would be interesting to know how this came into her possession."

"She could have found it, I suppose," remarked Hunter. "I hesitate to suggest it was stolen, though that must also be a possibility."

"But if either were the case, I would have expected her to hand it in or exchange it for money. Why keep it? Unless its real value has to do with its origin," said Holmes. "One thing is clear. She gave it to you, Mr. Hunter, because she feared its loss. Watson and I will accompany you tomorrow to her cave. We will see what can be gleaned there."

"But our vacation Holmes!" I protested.

"Is merely temporarily suspended," he replied. "We shall have plenty of time for archaeology. The sites have existed this long, a few more days is of no consequence."

The following day was overcast with the threat of rain as we set out after an early breakfast to meet the Rev. Hunter. Holmes was alert and excited, the lethargy of the previous evening had vanished. A short walk brought us to a deep valley, heavily wooded and pitted with rocks. At the bottom, we saw Hunter blowing his hands in the mist, which still clung to the floor of the combe.

"It's a brisk day, gentlemen," he said in greeting us. "Thank you for coming."

Holmes waved his hand. "Watson and I are hardy warriors, Mr. Hunter. A little weather cannot deter us. Where is the cave?"

Hunter pointed up the far side of the valley. "Up there. It's a bit of a climb."

"Lead the way," Holmes replied.

We followed him closely as he threaded his way through the trees. A few minutes solid walking brought us to the end of the valley. Ahead of us rose a steep-sided hill strewn with boulders. I looked at Hunter in disbelief.

"Is this the only approach to the cave?" I asked.

"No," he replied. "It can be reached from above but that is rather perilous."

"The lady must have the legs of a mountain goat," I observed.

Hunter laughed. "Indeed, she's pretty nimble for a woman of her age."

"I think we can be certain that she did not have many visitors," added Holmes.

We climbed steadily for about five minutes when, rounding one of the larger boulders, Hunter pointed upwards. About twenty feet above us we saw the entrance to a large cave.

"It's probably been here since prehistoric times," commented Hunter.

Holmes clapped me on the shoulder. "You have been anxious to visit an archaeological site, Watson. Here we are."

A short haul found us standing at the outer rim of the cave staring into what appeared to be an open pit.

"How far back does it go?" I asked.

"No one knows for sure," Hunter replied. "Mary only inhabited the first part of it."

Holmes led the way into the cave holding aloft a lantern which we had borrowed from the innkeeper. There were clear signs of habitation with pieces of furniture and floor coverings scattered about.

"Where did these come from?" I enquired.

"I managed to salvage most of them from what people discarded. When I first arrived here, she was living very savagely," Hunter replied.

A small brazier just inside the entrance functioned as a source of heat and a means of cooking and, further back, items of clothing and footwear showed some concessions to the necessities of civilisation.

"Miss Selkirk was literate, I see," Holmes said, fingering a small pile of books.

"Yes, I believe she had a decent education," replied Hunter.

"Did you supply these also?"

"Over the years, yes."

"You are to be commended," Holmes went on. "Few people would have concerned themselves about such a woman."

"I have always considered our Lord's words 'inasmuch as you do it to one of the least of my people, you do it to me,' as an absolute injunction," he replied.

"You will oblige me by remaining as you are for the next ten minutes," Holmes said to both of us. "While I carry out a more detailed search of the cave." With that, he got down on his hands and knees and began exploring the floor of the cave with his magnifying glass.

"I take it Miss Selkirk does not smoke tobacco," Holmes said.

"Not to my knowledge, no," Hunter replied.

"In that case, she has had visitors. At least two, one smoked a pipe. There are clear signs of tobacco deposits. The other smoked cheroots, expensive ones."

"Might they have taken her away?" I asked.

"I think not," he said. "They were here for some time. Two cheroots were smoked. The bands have been trodden into the floor. They were waiting for her to return. Some of the furniture has been moved also. This chest for instance. The indentations on the rug indicate that it normally stood a few inches to the right of where it is now."

"What do you make of that, Holmes?"

"They were looking for something but did not succeed in finding it. They decided to wait for her return but eventually were obliged to leave empty-handed."

"Presumably, they were looking for the necklace," I said.

"That must be our working hypothesis," Holmes replied. "There is nothing more we can do here. Let us return to the inn."

That evening, back at The Stag and Hounds I observed Holmes over dinner fiddling with his food and tapping his fingers.

"Yes, I agree," I said.

He looked up.

"You were thinking that we should cut short our vacation and return to Baker Street," I continued.

He smiled. "Well done, Watson. It's the only way. I need to carry out some research into the necklace which Hunter has entrusted to me. The clue to Mary Selkirk's fate lies in its history. I am convinced of it."

I nodded and to tell the truth, I too was eager to pursue the case. So, the following morning found us on the morning train from Exeter to Waterloo. As we settled into the comfort of our first-class carriage I couldn't help reflecting on the privations and exigencies of the life we had just witnessed.

"What desperate circumstances would lead someone to embrace such an existence, Holmes?"

He shook his head, "There have been many hermits in our island's history. People who have shunned society either to commune with God or nature. But in this case, I sense a deep unhappiness, some tragic misfortune which has overwhelmed the poor woman's reason."

"You think she may be mad?"

"Who is to say what the borderline is between despair and madness?"

We passed the rest of the journey in silence and arrived at Baker Street late in the afternoon. Mrs. Hudson was surprised to see us back so early from our holiday. It was clear from her face as she opened the door that she had counted on us staying away longer.

"You'll find your rooms in a bit of a muddle at present," she said. "I've been giving things a good airing."

"Our rooms were perfectly fine as they were, Mrs. Hudson!" Holmes said

"Just a little spring cleaning," she replied. "To get rid of the smell of tobacco."

"She does this every time we go away, Watson," Holmes complained as we went upstairs. "It takes me weeks to find anything."

"She has a point, Holmes. The place was a complete mess."

He grunted, "Tidiness is much overrated. Can you name one important discovery which came from being tidy?"

"I once found a collar stud I thought I'd lost," I replied.

"Which has benefited mankind enormously," he commented drily.

Once inside, he regained his good humour and spent the remainder of the afternoon happily examining the necklace under his microscope. The surface of the locket was considerably scratched, but eventually, he succeeded in discerning the Latin text.

"As far as I can make out Watson, it reads, '*verba volant scripta manent*'."

"Words fly away, writings remain," I said. "And what about the family crest?"

"An eagle with its wings spread. It's not one I instantly recognise."

He stretched over to a pile of books underneath the dining table. "Thank goodness these have not fallen victim to Mrs. Hudson's obsession."

He pulled out a volume and after some minutes leafing through he let out a triumphant shout.

"Yes! I thought Golding's Register would have it. The crest and motto belong to the Drummond estate."

"Scotland again," I said. "If I remember rightly there was something about the Drummond family in the news a few weeks ago. Where are our back copies of *The Times*?"

"Mrs. Hudson," Holmes yelled. "What have you done with the newspapers?"

"I was about to throw them out," she said, appearing at the door with a pile of yellowing paper. "They're weeks old."

"Good," said Holmes. "That's how I prefer them."

After about ten minutes searching, I found the item I was looking for. *"Death of Sir Alistair Drummond at 93,"* the article read. *"Sir Alistair Drummond died at his Scottish estate of Castle Drummond yesterday. He leaves no direct heir, and it is likely his estate will pass to a distant relation."*

"What is the date of that announcement, Watson?"

"April 3," I replied.

"Roughly three weeks ago," he commented. "About the same time Mary Selkirk vanished. I think it's time to ruffle a few feathers."

The next morning Holmes was up early and off to the offices of *The Times* newspaper. He came back about midday looking very pleased with himself.

"What do you think, Watson? I have placed the following notice prominently in tomorrow's first edition."

He passed me a slip of paper on which I read: *"Information sought on the provenance of a valuable gold filigree necklace with locket inscribed 'A D'. Apply Sherlock Holmes 221B Baker Street."*

"We are likely to get every treasure hunter in London knocking on our door," I replied.

"Possibly, but we can instantly exclude any enquirer who is ignorant of the family crest and motto. We need to know who is looking for the necklace and why."

We waited the best part of a week, during which we were visited by an assortment of people claiming ownership of the necklace, which had either been lost or stolen from them, none of whom knew the details which Holmes had deliberately omitted from the notice. At the end of this time, we were beginning to think the strategy had failed when Mrs Hudson brought a heavily embossed calling card to us bearing the inscription *Sir Stanley Cartwright KCMG*. Holmes raised his eyebrows.

"Show the gentleman up if you please, Mrs. Hudson," he said.

A man in his mid-forties dressed in a fashionable frock coat and carrying a gold-topped cane was ushered into us. He glanced over at Holmes.

"Mr. Sherlock Holmes, I presume?"

"Indeed, and this is my friend and associate, John Watson. You are most welcome, sir. Please be seated."

"I have come about the notice you placed recently in *The Times*."

"You have some interest in the necklace?" Holmes enquired.

"Very much so. I am a friend of Sir Archibald Drummond, the new laird of the Drummond estate. The necklace you are in possession of is the property of the estate. May I ask how you came by it, sir?"

"I'm afraid you are mistaken in thinking I possess the necklace, Sir Stanley. I am acting for a client who must remain anonymous at the moment and wishes further information about the item. But can we confirm that we are talking about the same object?"

"Very well," Cartwright replied. "A gold filigree chain necklace with a locket containing a lock of hair and the initials 'A D'

– Anne Drummond. It also bears the Drummond crest and motto, '*verba volant scripta manent*'."

"Exactly so," Holmes said.

"If your client is willing to return the necklace to the rightful owner, then I shall be happy to reward them for recovering the item," Cartwright said.

"Indeed?"

"Yes, Sir Archibald is prepared to offer the sum of £50 for its safe delivery."

"That is very handsome," Holmes said. "May I enquire how it was lost in the first place?"

"If you think it necessary."

"I do," Holmes replied.

"Have you any objection to my smoking?"

Holmes waved his hand. "Not in the least."

Cartwright took out a cigar case and selected a long thin cheroot.

"Anne Drummond was the only child and heir of Sir Alistair Drummond," he began. "The necklace was specially made for her. It is her hair which is in the locket."

"Miss Drummond, I take it, is no longer alive," I said.

"No, she died tragically in an accident some fifty years ago. She was travelling in a stagecoach to London to stay with relatives when the coach overturned, killing the driver and the two passengers on board."

"Who was the other passenger?" I asked.

"A merchant returning to his business."

"And the necklace?" Holmes asked.

"Was missing. Anne always wore it, and it has not been seen since."

"How do you explain its disappearance?" Holmes asked.

128

"We believe the coach was robbed, probably by poachers, before the accident was discovered. According to the merchant's family, his gold fob watch was also missing."

"Presumably had Miss Drummond survived she would have inherited the estate on Sir Alistair's death," Holmes said.

"The title and estate are entailed on the male side," Cartwright replied. "But Sir Alistair had a large personal fortune of his own which was willed to her and her children in perpetuity."

"A sad story," I commented. "I can understand your desire to have such a memento returned to the family."

"Thank you, Doctor. And I hope, Mr. Holmes, that you will make your client see the necessity of returning it."

"Rest assured," said Holmes, "They will be fully informed of all you have said."

Cartwright nodded. "I need hardly add that in the last resort Sir Archibald will not hesitate to take legal action for the return of his property. Your client will not be able to hide behind anonymity then."

"I think we understand one another," Holmes replied.

"Then I bid you both good day. I hope to hear from you soon, sir."

Immediately he had departed Holmes pounced on the ashtray and began examining the remains of the cheroot.

"It's the same Watson, and so is the gold band."

"Cartwright visited the cave?"

"Yes. There's a lot more to this story than we have been told."

"Do you think he believed you about the client?" I asked.

Holmes shrugged his shoulders. "Who can say? But one thing is certain, Sir Archibald is desperate to get his hands on the necklace. Cartwright was barely civil."

"The account of the stagecoach accident can be checked I suppose."

"Indeed. It will mean a trip to the British Museum library. Even I don't possess newspapers that far back."

"Why would a young girl of her connections and wealth be travelling on her own such a distance?" I said. "No maid, no chaperone. It doesn't make sense."

"Precisely, Watson. You have it in a nutshell."

The following day Holmes left immediately after breakfast for the British Museum and did not return until early evening.

"Be so good as to pour me a brandy Watson," he said. collapsing into an armchair. "I have spent the entire day among the nearly dead. The average age of my fellow researchers must have been at least a hundred."

I laughed. "You exaggerate Holmes."

"Barely. There cannot be a greater collection of elderly clergymen than in the reading room of the British Museum. I had to wait two hours for access to the newspaper collection behind a rural dean and two vicars."

"What were they interested in?"

"Lord knows. They all fell asleep in the afternoon."

"But you found what you were looking for?"

"Eventually, yes," Holmes replied, becoming more animated. "There were several accounts of the accident and some interesting speculations as to the cause. Cartwright was correct about the basic details. There were only two passengers in the carriage, and it appears their deaths were a consequence of the horses bolting and overturning the coach. As to why seasoned animals should bolt there was some division of opinion. A couple of papers thought it was due to the inexperience and tiredness of the driver in whipping the horses too hard. It was only the second time he had driven a post chaise. But one paper speculated that it was the work of a highwayman."

"Really," I said. "But surely they disappeared years before."

"The last verified mounted attack on horseback was in 1831. But there is some suspicion that at least one highwayman may well have been active after then. The accident happened at Shooters Hill, a notorious site of such attacks. The horses have to slow down to descend the hill and coaches are more vulnerable."

"Well, it would explain the subsequent robbery more satisfactorily than Cartwright's version of events."

"Precisely," Holmes replied. "Let us suppose a highwayman attempts to halt the coach, is challenged by the driver, and pistols are fired. That would be sufficient to make the horses bolt."

"It certainly sounds feasible."

"Even more so," Holmes said. "When the name of one of the men thought to be still active was James Selkirk."

"A relative of Mary Selkirk, perhaps."

"We can assume so."

"Is anything known of Selkirk?" I asked.

"Very little. His grandfather was a Scottish gentleman who fought at the battle of Culloden in 1746. He was dispossessed of his estates after the defeat and took to the road, as did his son and grandson."

"Highway robbery became the family business?"

"Indeed. Unfortunately, Selkirk disappears from the public record after the accident. Except for one grim fact. He was hanged at Inverness, like his father and grandfather before him."

"Do you think Cartwright knows all this?"

"Almost certainly. He was also sparing with the truth about the laird's daughter. At the inquest into Anne Drummond's death, the coroner raised the same questions as did we about what she was doing travelling alone. A spokesman for Sir Alistair said there had been a falling out between them but declined to say why."

131

"I don't know about ruffling a few feathers, Holmes, but it seems to me you have dug up several skeletons."

"Exactly. We must be careful how we tread from now on. There are powerful forces ranged against us. I am sure I was followed today."

I went over to the window and twitched the curtain back.

"There's someone in the shadow of that doorway," I said. "Turn the light out, Holmes."

He did as I bid him and joined me at the window. A match flared in the darkness followed by several clouds of smoke.

"It's our friend with the pipe," Holmes said. "He'll need to be pretty nimble if he intends to pursue us tomorrow."

"Tomorrow?" I queried.

"I think a visit to Inverness is in order Watson. The gateway to the Highlands."

The overnight sleeper to Edinburgh was due to leave King's Cross at 3:15 p.m. At midday, we slipped out of 221B Baker Street into a hansom clutching our Gladstones and made our way across London to Waterloo station.

"There's a train to Exeter at 1:30 p.m.," Holmes said. "It will seem as though we are returning to Exmoor. But we shall alight just before it departs and make our way to King's Cross."

We went to the booking hall where we bought a couple of single tickets to the first station along the line and found the Exeter train. We sat down in the last carriage and waited. At half-past one precisely, the guard took a whistle out of his pocket and raised it to his lips.

"Now," Holmes said, opening the door and leaping out. The guard looked startled as we emerged from the carriage, but he continued blowing his whistle and the train began to move, increasing its speed until it was soon at the end of the platform.

"I'm sorry," Holmes said, picking himself up. "My friend got the wrong platform. We are supposed to be travelling to Bristol."

"You want platform seven for that," replied the guard. "You could have done yourselves an injury."

"Do you think it worked?" I asked as we made our way out of the station.

"I hope so Watson. I have ruined a perfectly good pair of trousers."

At King's Cross, we made the sleeper with half an hour to spare. As we settled into our compartment, I thought with pleasure of the comfort and safety of our train. The journey to Edinburgh would take eleven hours, including a stop at York for dinner. With a change onto a branch line, we should arrive at Inverness in time for breakfast the next morning.

"It's amazing, Holmes, to think how this journey has been transformed in a mere fifty years. It would have taken Anne Drummond several days to accomplish what we can do in a matter of hours."

He nodded. "We are fortunate to be living now, Watson. There have been more improvements to transport in the past half-century than in the preceding two hundred years."

Our opinion of modern travel was only slightly dented by the connecting train from Edinburgh to Inverness which wound interminably round all the small towns in-between rattling and shaking continuously like a child's toy. But finally, we arrived at our destination and immediately sought out a large inn close to the centre of the town where we took rooms and ordered breakfast. We discussed our plans over plates of eggs and bacon.

"I suppose the first thing is to see what we can learn about Selkirk from his prison record," I said.

"Yes, it should at least tell us where he lived in Scotland and who his immediate family were," Holmes replied.

"And what he did to deserve hanging."

"Indeed. Always supposing that the prison warden is cooperative, of course."

"I have thought of that, Holmes," I said. "I have brought with me an advance copy of *A Study in Scarlet*."

He laughed loudly. "Let us hope the warden is a man of such simple tastes."

"It amuses you to say so, Holmes, but my decision to enter the literary world has met with considerable interest," I bristled. "Even, I am told, from the Prime Minister."

"I rest my case," he replied.

Inverness prison lay at the centre of the small market town atop a steep hill. With its large turreted walls, it resembled a castle, except that it was a fortress built to keep people in, rather than out. The main entrance was an oak door with an iron grille through which visitors could communicate. We rang the bell, and the grille was opened by a turnkey who asked us our business. Holmes passed his calling card through and requested to speak to the warden. After a few minutes, the door swung open, and we were ushered into a long stone corridor which echoed loudly to the passage of our feet. At the end was a small room bearing the title "Mr. D. Campbell, Prison Warden." Inside we were greeted by a thickset man of about sixty with iron-grey hair wearing a smartly pressed blue serge uniform.

"Y'are welcome, gentlemen," he said with a soft Lowland lilt. "I dinna receive visitors withoot an appointment. But your reputation precedes ye, Mr. Holmes. The Scottish newspapers are full of your successes down south."

"Thank you, Mr. Campbell," he replied. "Dr. Watson and I are much obliged."

"How can I be of sairvice to ye. Is it a case y'are working on at the moment?"

Holmes nodded. "Indeed. We are seeking information about James Selkirk, who was a prisoner here about ten years ago."

"Aye, that's right. A wee bit before my time, but a sad case as I recall. He was hanged for murder."

"What were the particulars of his offence?" Holmes asked.

The Warden went over to a cabinet and rifled through some papers.

"Ah, here it is," he said, pulling out a file. "According to his record, he was hanged for killing a man in a dispute involving his daughter. He claimed the man was trying to abduct her, but the jury didna believe him. He had a record of violent behaviour, as did his father and grandfather. They all finished up at the end of a noose."

"Is there anything in the record about his children?"

"Just the one, a lassie named Mary born in 1835, but no mention of her mother. I'm afraid Selkirk was a wild fellow, sair. But if ye wish to know more aboot him, he had a smallholding in Galfries, a village on the edge of Loch Ness. I dessay someone will remember him."

"Thank you, Mr. Campbell," Holmes replied. "You have been extremely helpful. If anything, else occurs to you, we are staying at The Star and Garter."

"Glad to be of sairvice to ye. I see few people from beyond the border, especially such as yerselves."

"Well, I hope you will accept this from me," I said, handing a small packet to the Warden. "It's an account of one of Mr. Holmes's cases which will shortly be appearing in print."

"Vairy generous. Thankee Doctor. My wife will be pleased. She is the reader in the family."

"That was most enlightening Watson," Holmes said, as we stepped outside. "It may well shed some light on why Mary Selkirk felt it necessary to take such extreme measures to protect herself."

"Indeed," I said. "Thank goodness the Warden proved to be a man of such simple tastes after all."

"It is his wife who is the fan," he replied coolly.

We returned to our inn from where we hired a carriage to Galfries, a journey of about five miles. All around us, the land stretched away in purple folds of treeless heather, a vast unending prairie, broken only by a few spots of cultivated land. This was isolation, pure and simple.

"This is not unlike Exmoor Holmes," I said. "It seems endless."

He nodded. "Wildernesses are often beautiful, but they are seldom comforting. They put us in our place."

After about half an hour the landscape became hillier and we could see in the distance the mountains towering above Loch Ness. Galfries proved to be a small hamlet of a few turf-covered huts, a church and a low-slung timbered building which we recognised as an inn. I looked at the small coaching road along which we had come, disappearing into the stillness like a wisp of smoke.

"It's difficult to imagine living here," I said.

"Or to think of it as home," returned Holmes.

We made our way over to the inn, which at this time of day was deserted, except for a couple of elderly herdsmen in worn leather jerkins and tartan breeches sitting over tankards in a corner. We bid them good-day and approached the bar. The landlord, a tall, bearded man regarded us warily.

"Can I help ye?" He asked.

"Two glasses of your finest usquebaugh please, landlord," replied Holmes.

The landlord smiled, "Ye'll be wanting singles."

"Doubles, I think."

"It's muckle stronger than ye'll be getting in London, gentlemen."

"Doubles," repeated Holmes. "And please join us."

"As ye wish," said the landlord pouring our drinks. "What brings yous to this part of the world?"

"Curiosity. My friend and I are writing a book on famous highwaymen. I believe you have bred a few round here."

"Ye'll be meaning the Selkirks."

"Yes. Three generations, I understand."

"Ye heard right. But I'd advise yous to be careful. They were well-liked."

"But they robbed many coaches," I said. "You wouldn't deny that."

There was a stirring in the corner of the room as one of the herdsmen got to his feet.

"Sassenach coaches," he called out. "They ne'er touched a Scottish coach."

"That's the trewth," said the landlord. "They couldna' abide the English. Because of Culloden, ye'll mind."

"Even James Selkirk?" I asked.

"Aye, Jamie was a braw saucy lad by all accounts, but bitter."

"I believe he abandoned the highway some years before his death and settled back here?" said Holmes.

"So he did," replied the landlord.

"And lived on his own?"

"He had a lassie," put in the herdsman. "By a tavern wench."

The landlord nodded. "He wouldna' let any man near her. It caused a deel o' trouble."

"What happened to his daughter after the hanging?" I asked.

The landlord shrugged his shoulders, "Nobody knows. But y'are the second person to have asked me that."

"Was the other person well dressed and carrying a gold-topped cane?" Holmes enquired.

"Aye," replied the landlord. "I didna' laik the fellow."

Outside, the fresh air made us stumble as the full force of the whisky hit us.

"Perhaps we should have taken the landlord's advice," I said, clutching Holmes.

"I felt we had to uphold the honour of the English, Watson. I have no idea why. At least we can sleep it off on the journey back."

By the time we arrived back at the inn we had sobered up sufficiently to take stock of what we had learnt.

"The pieces are beginning to fall into place, Watson. The protectiveness of Mary's father no doubt produced in her a fear of ordinary society, which would only have been made worse by his death. But the question still remains why he behaved as he did. What was he protecting her from? We can speculate, but without evidence, we can prove nothing."

We were still mulling over what to do next, at dinner that evening when the landlord brought us a note from the prison. Holmes tore it open.

"It's from the Warden. He has found something further in the files. If we call on him tomorrow at 9 a.m., he will show it to us."

"Perhaps this is it, Holmes. The missing piece."

He nodded. "We deserve some good fortune, Watson."

Neither of us slept well that night, a combination of the whisky we had drunk and anticipation about what the next day might bring. We breakfasted early and at nine o'clock sharp presented ourselves at the prison entrance. The turnkey let us in and escorted us to the Warden's office where we found him pacing up and down.

"Ah gentlemen," he said. "I have found a wee paper which I think will be of interest. It fell oot the file."

He passed a document to Holmes, who scanned it quickly.

"It's a confession, Watson. Made on the day before Selkirk was hanged."

"Aye, that's right," said the Warden. "It seems he wished to clear his conscience at the last."

"What does it say?" I asked.

"Selkirk confesses to stopping a coach on Shooter's Hill on February 19th, 1835. There's an account of the horses bolting and everyone on board being killed. He admits to robbing a gentleman of a fob watch and a young girl of a gold necklace".

Holmes paused and looked triumphantly at me. "He also says that the lady had been nursing a young baby, which was thrown from the coach but had survived. He took pity on the child and brought it away with him to Galfries where he brought her up as his own daughter. The paper is signed by Selkirk and witnessed by the Warden and the prison chaplain. This is it, Watson. The missing piece."

He turned to the Warden. "Would you have any objection to my making a copy of this statement Mr. Campbell?"

"Not at all. My desk is at yer sairvice for the purpose."

Holmes sat down and made a transcript of the document whilst I shook the Warden's hand vigorously and expressed our gratitude.

"I have one last favour to ask of you, sir," Holmes said. "That you say nothing for the moment of this document. All will become clear in due course."

"As ye wish, Mr. Holmes."

We made our way back to the inn unable to believe our luck in having found evidence in Selkirk's own hand of Mary's true parentage.

"Do you think it will be enough?" I asked Holmes.

"It's a deathbed confession signed by two credible witnesses," he replied. "And it explains the circumstances better than anything else so far. Anne Drummond was on her own because she was fleeing from her father who one presumes was not happy with his young daughter having a child out of wedlock."

"Perhaps he was forcing her to have the baby adopted," I said.

"Possibly. We also have an explanation for what happened to the child. Highwaymen are not noted for their compassion. We can be thankful James Selkirk was an exception."

"He must have wondered why there wasn't an immediate hue and cry to rescue the child,"

"Indeed. He clearly led the rest of his life in fear of that possibility. He was not to know that it suited the Drummonds for the baby to disappear, until three weeks ago, when a distant relative inherited the estate together with the fortune and could not dispel his anxiety that another heir might still be living."

"Enter Sir Stanley Cartwright," I said.

He nodded. "Sir Archibald's friend and fixer."

"Do you think he intends her harm?"

"Let us just say I would not wish to see her dependent on his tender mercies."

Back at the inn we collected our bags and made our way to

the small station at Inverness. As the train rolled in, I thought how much we had learned in just two days. To all intents and purposes, the matter was resolved. All that was left now was to find Mary Selkirk and reveal her true identity. And if it were just a matter of pleading Mary's cause against ordinary opponents, I would have had no doubt of Holmes's success. But I knew enough about the power of wealth and privilege to be sure that Sir Archibald would prove a formidable antagonist. Holmes had not disclosed to me how he intended to proceed and, perhaps, on this occasion he was uncertain himself.

We arrived at Edinburgh in good time for the overnight sleeper and, as both of us were exhausted by our recent adventures, we retired early to our beds and did not arise until the train pulled into King's Cross the following morning. It was about five o'clock and the streets were still dark as the hansom conveyed us the short distance to Baker Street. The cabby dropped us at the corner of the street by one of the new gas lamps.

"It's better to alight here gentlemen," he said. "It's easy to miss your step. 221B is just over there." He pointed a few yards down the road.

We bid him good night and began walking the short distance. As we neared our door, three men emerged from the shadows and blocked our path.

"The travellers return at last," the leading man jeered. "We have some business with you, Mr. Holmes."

"My business hours begin at 9 o'clock," Holmes replied. "Perhaps you would like to make an appointment."

The man took a strip of metal out of his pocket and fixed it to the fingers of his right hand. "It's a little more urgent than that. You've been meddling in things that don't concern you. We're here to make sure you stop."

141

"I see," said Holmes. "This does not concern Dr. Watson. You can let him pass."

The man shook his head. "The message is for both of you."

"I am sorry to hear that," Holmes replied. "If it had just been me, I would willingly have tried my chances." He turned in my direction. "Have you got your friend with you, Watson?"

"Absolutely," I replied, drawing my service revolver from my overcoat pocket.

The effect on the men was remarkable. "You said nothing about shooters," one of them said.

"It's fully loaded, in case you're wondering," I said pointing the barrel at the leader.

"There's no need for this," the man said, backing away. "We just came to deliver a message."

"Well, I have one for you," Holmes replied. "Tell Cartwright that if he wishes to settle this he can come and see me tomorrow. Otherwise, I will immediately go public with what I know. Now, I suggest you scurry back to your holes before Watson puts a bullet in each of you."

"I think we have an answer to your earlier question, Watson," Holmes said after they had gone. "Our adversaries are plainly capable of anything. The sooner we end this madness the better."

Later that day, after a brief rest, Holmes sent a telegram to the Rev. Matthew Hunter asking him to be ready to come to London in the very near future.

"Do you think he has found Miss Selkirk?"

"In a manner of speaking," he replied.

"What do you mean, Holmes?"

"She was never lost in the first place," he continued.

I looked at him, mystified. "But Hunter told us she was missing," I protested. "We visited her cave."

Holmes shook his head. "He said she had been absent from church for three weeks. He never actually said she was missing."

"But what about the police? He reported her missing to them."

"No, no. If you recall, he said she was considered mad by the police and there was no evidence of a crime, both completely true statements, I am sure. But as soon as we returned, I asked Inspector Lestrade to make enquiries about what the local police had done and he confirmed that they knew nothing of the matter."

I shook my head. "I don't understand Holmes. What was the point of him asking us to investigate her disappearance if she had never disappeared in the first place?"

"Because it was the necklace he wanted us to investigate."

"So where is the lady then?"

"No doubt where she has been all along. In the vicarage."

He paused for a moment, relishing my confusion. It was one of those maddening moments where Holmes was several steps ahead of me.

"Think it through from the beginning, Watson. This all began a few weeks ago when Mary Selkirk had some unwelcome visitors to her cave. She probably came back after taking sewing to one of her customers and smelt the tobacco. We know one of these visitors to be Cartwright. I have no doubt he had known of her existence for some time, but it was of little importance while Sir Alistair was alive. Things changed once the new heir took over the estate, and the missing child and necklace became significant again. Mary quite probably panicked and abandoned her cave. But where was she to go? She knew no one apart from the vicar who had befriended her. He was the only person she could trust. What could be more natural than that she should seek him out and ask him to shelter her, probably telling him some, at least, of her story? Whether he believed her or not, we know enough about him to be sure he would not turn her away. Hearing we are in the area he obtained her permission to bring the necklace to us on the condition that he did not reveal her whereabouts."

"When you explain it like that it all seems so obvious Holmes"

"It's the only explanation which fits all the facts," he replied.

"But how can we be sure that Cartwright has not found her," I continued.

"Because he would not have set his thugs on us last night if that were the case. Once he has Mary, the game is over. The necklace on its own proves nothing."

"Nevertheless, Holmes, one does not expect deception from a man of the cloth."

"Agreed," he replied. But all things considered, he has gone up in my estimation."

It was growing dark, and I had begun to think that Cartwright did not intend visiting that day when a knock on the street door alerted us. A few moments later, Mrs. Hudson announced Sir Stanley and he strode in flushed and angry.

"I don't know what you're playing at, Holmes," he began. "But I don't take kindly to being summoned."

"Good evening, Sir Stanley," Holmes replied. "Won't you take a seat? I really think it would make things easier."

"Don't patronise me, sir. There is only one reason I am here and that is to receive Sir Archibald's property. Are you willing to hand it over?"

"I'm afraid there is some doubt as to whether it is his property," Holmes said.

"What are you talking about, of course, it is? I explained everything to you a week ago in this very room," Cartwright said.

"Not everything, Sir Stanley. I believe it to be the lawful property of Miss Mary Selkirk."

"Nonsense," he replied. "I warn you Holmes, those men who accosted you last night were just a foretaste of what you can expect if you continue to interfere in matters that do not concern you."

"Well, you have been blunt with me, Cartwright. Let me be equally blunt with you. I have information in my possession which casts doubt on the legitimacy of Sir Archibald's right to the Drummond fortune, and which would at the very least significantly embarrass him. This information will be released to the public and placed in the hands of the executors to the estate unless you agree here and now to my terms."

There was a heavy pause after Holmes finished speaking during which it was evident that Cartwright had not expected such a response. Holmes had obviously decided to throw caution to the wind and return like for like.

"You deserve a whipping, sir," Cartwright blustered.

"Perhaps so, but not by you. What is it to be?"

Cartwright wrestled with himself for a few moments and then we saw him wilt visibly.

"What are your terms?"

"This matter can only be resolved directly with Sir Archibald. No intermediaries."

"Out of the question. He will not get involved personally."

"Then I'm afraid the issue will have to be contested in public."

Cartwright breathed in heavily. "I will need to talk to him; maybe he will receive you at Drummond castle," he said.

Holmes shook his head. "You misunderstand me. The meeting must be on neutral ground."

Cartwright looked aghast. "Where for God's sake?"

"In London," Holmes replied. "I suggest a suite at the Dorchester."

"I hope you know what you're doing, Holmes. Sir Archibald is a very powerful man. He's broken better men than you," Cartwright said.

"I don't doubt it, Sir Stanley. But I am willing to take that risk. Are you?"

"You will hear from me within the week gentlemen. Good evening."

We listened to his footsteps as he hastened down the stairs, slamming the front door behind him. Holmes looked over at me, a glimmer of a smile edging his lips.

"There goes a very worried man, Watson," he said. "If I understand Sir Archibald aright, he will not take kindly to failure."

"You were magnificent Holmes!" I said. "The man positively buckled in front of us."

He laughed. "I was on form today, wasn't I? Like most bullies if you land one really good blow, they crumble. Sir Archibald, I fear, will prove a tougher opponent. We will need our full armoury if we are to bring him down."

It was the best part of a week before we heard again from Cartwright. Mrs. Hudson brought us in the briefest of notes which said that Sir Archibald would meet with us as requested on Thursday next at 1 p.m. precisely at the Dorchester Hotel, on which occasion he expected the matter to be fully resolved. Any precipitate action by Holmes prior to that would be met by the full weight of the law.

"It begins," said Holmes. "The final act."

"Do you honestly think we can win?" I asked.

"We'll have a damn good try, Watson! Mrs. Hudson, would you please see this telegram is sent to the Reverend Hunter straightaway?"

He looked pensively in my direction. "It is time we were introduced to the lady whose cause we are championing."

The morning of the meeting with Sir Archibald was bright and glorious. It was difficult to think anything bad could happen on such a day. Holmes had spent the previous week preparing for the meeting. Despite his optimism, I knew he was not sure of success. On paper, we appeared to have a strong hand, but Cartwright's warning was still ringing in our ears. We were due to meet the Rev. Hunter and Mary Selkirk mid-morning. Holmes had been right in his deduction about her whereabouts. Accordingly, at about 11 a.m. we heard the knocker on our street door, and a few minutes later they were both brought into us. Hunter looked older and more tired than when we last met and it was clear that the responsibility of hiding his companion had weighed heavily on him. He began immediately by apologising for the deception he had imposed on us, but Holmes cut him short.

"There is no need for any apology, my dear sir. You have performed your part admirably. Have you brought with you the package I requested?"

"Of course, Mr. Holmes," he said, handing him an envelope.

I looked quizzically at him.

"Later Watson," he said. "And this is the lady herself. Please be seated, Miss Selkirk. You are among friends here."

Mary Selkirk was a small, strong-featured woman with a weathered countenance dressed entirely in black. She bobbed briefly in our direction.

"Thank you, gentlemen," she replied in a quiet educated voice. "I am grateful for your endeavours on my behalf. I do not deserve such kindness."

Holmes waved his hand, "Think nothing of it. Watson and I are fortunate in being able to follow our inclinations. It is gratifying when these can be of service to others. But before our meeting with Sir Archibald, there are a couple of matters which I would like to clarify. Firstly, what do you wish from him?"

"To be acknowledged for who I am, Mr. Holmes."

"You mean the daughter of Anne Drummond and granddaughter of Sir Alistair," I said.

"Yes, she replied. "I am not interested in Sir Alistair's money. My life has been taken away from me, Dr. Watson. I would like it back."

"When did you first learn about your mother?" Holmes asked.

"The night before my father was executed," she said. "He sent for me and said he had something important to impart before he died. He told me then about the robbery and that he wasn't my real father."

"And you knew nothing before then?"

"No. My father was kind and good to me, but he would never talk about the past. I was brought up in total seclusion. He paid for me to be educated saying that one day it would stand me in good stead."

"It must have been distressing in the extreme, hearing all this on such a fateful occasion," I said.

She nodded, "Yes, Doctor. The day of my father's hanging was truly dreadful. It was as though a black pit had opened before me. The landlord evicted me from our cottage, and I had nowhere to go."

"It was then you decided to flee south," Holmes put in.

"Yes. I had a little money from my father. My plan was to go as far away as I could and take my own life."

"And you got as far as Exmoor?" I said.

"Yes. I walked along the cliff looking for somewhere suitably steep and I saw a cave high up in one of the hills. I decided to climb up to it and end things there."

"But you didn't die," I said.

"No, Doctor. I found the will to live. I don't know how or why."

"There's a destiny that shapes our ends, Miss Selkirk," said Holmes. "But it is time to beard the lion in his den. Watson, would you call up a cab? One last thing – Sir Archibald will no doubt do his best to antagonise us. It is important that we keep cool heads."

The journey to the Dorchester took about fifteen minutes, during which time we all remained silent, each preoccupied with their own thoughts. When we arrived at that imposing edifice a footman opened the carriage door and conveyed us through into a comfortable lounge area where we were met by the manager, who was clearly expecting us.

"Come this way please," he said. "Sir Archibald is waiting for you."

We were ushered into a large, carpeted suite with a high corniced ceiling and expensive furnishings. Inside were three men. At the centre was an imposing figure dressed in traditional highland costume. On his right was Sir Stanley and to his left a thin bespectacled man clutching a sheaf of papers.

"His lawyer, I'll be bound," Holmes whispered to me.

None of the men moved from the middle of the room where they stood in a dominating half-circle, forcing us to approach them deferentially.

"I am Sir Archibald Drummond," said the central figure. "Which one of you is Sherlock Holmes?"

"I am," replied Holmes. "And this is Dr. Watson, the Reverend Hunter, and Miss Mary Selkirk."

"I'm not interested in your companions, Holmes."

"As you wish Sir Archibald," Holmes replied.

"You have caused me a great deal of inconvenience and trouble. I am not accustomed to receiving ultimatums. However, I'm prepared to overlook it if you end this nonsense now and return my property to me. Otherwise, I can promise you a very unpleasant outcome."

"I take it you are referring to this pretty trinket," Holmes took out a pouch from his coat pocket and poured the necklace into his hand.

"I'm surprised you had the audacity to bring it, Holmes. I can tell you that officers of the law are standing by outside and if you attempt to leave with it, you will be apprehended."

"Then perhaps we had better proceed to business. We are agreed that it belonged to Anne Drummond and that it was taken from her person when she tragically died on the London-bound stagecoach on February 19th, 1835."

Sir Archibald glanced at the bespectacled man on his left who nodded.

"Yes, of course," replied Sir Archibald.

"And the accident which occurred to the stagecoach was a result of a robbery carried out by James Selkirk," Holmes continued.

"Most probably. The wretch robbed the girl as she lay dying. Come to the point Holmes!"

"We now know from a confession made by Selkirk the evening before his execution that he also took a young infant, the daughter of Miss Drummond, and brought her up as his own child. That daughter stands before you now, Mary Selkirk who is naturally the rightful owner of the necklace," Holmes said.

"Poppycock," Sir Archibald said.

"I have a copy of his confession here," replied Holmes.

"And so do I. My lawyer, Watkins, has it."

Holmes looked taken aback. This was our key piece of evidence.

Sir Archibald smiled at Holmes. "Did you really think the Warden would not alert me to its existence? He is a Campbell. The Campbell and Drummond clans have been allies for generations."

"Then you know the central allegation Selkirk made when he was virtually at the point of death," Holmes said.

"It's a fabrication. There was no child. The allegation is an invention." He turned to his lawyer. "Explain the legal situation to Holmes, Watkins."

"So-called death bed confessions are normally privileged in a court of law, Mr. Holmes," Watkins said. "Except when they are self-serving, as this plainly was. Selkirk saw an opportunity to advance the interests of his daughter after his death. He conceived an elaborate fraud in which she could lay claim to the Drummond fortune on the demise of Sir Alistair."

"The confession is worthless, Holmes. If you present it in a court of law it will be torn to pieces. You will be prosecuted for slander, and your client will be gaoled for fraud or possibly consigned to a lunatic asylum," said Sir Archibald.

"I must admit that outcome had not occurred to me," said Holmes quietly.

"I tried to warn you," Cartwright said. "Sir Archibald is nobody's fool."

"However, the offer I made earlier is still open to you," Sir Archibald said. "Return the necklace and cease this absurd nonsense and you can walk free from here."

"That is very considerate of you, Sir Archibald. But before I concede the field to you I have one further piece of evidence."

He paused and took out of his pocket the package which Hunter had given him earlier.

"On the morning of the day Anne Drummond boarded the London bound stagecoach, she performed one final duty. She was embarking on a long hazardous journey of several days, with a young baby of just a few weeks, in the middle of winter. So, before she went she visited the parish church and asked the vicar, the Reverend Samuel Ramsey to baptise the child and register the birth. I have a copy of it here. The original is in the parish register of St Mary the Virgin. It's dated February 16 and signed by the vicar. Perhaps your lawyer would care to see it."

Holmes handed the document to the lawyer who perused it closely. Sir Archibald looked angrily over at him.

"It looks genuine, Sir Archibald."

"It is," said Holmes

"But the child was still a bastard," retorted the laird

"You underestimate the lady," said Holmes. "She and the child's father were secretly married some time before the birth. That too is in the register."

"So why did I not know about this?" he demanded.

"Because Sir Alistair was a violent, tyrannical man," said Holmes. "The vicar knew this and kept quiet even when the child disappeared."

"And what will it take to keep *you* quiet, Holmes?"

"I want nothing for myself, Sir Archibald. But I have certain demands for my client."

"Demands!" Drummond exploded. "You are insolent sir. If you were my equal, I would call you out."

"Then let us be thankful I am not," replied Holmes. "Duelling is an offence punishable by law. But if you will allow me, Miss Selkirk's demands are more liberal than you might expect. In the first place, she is prepared to relinquish all title to the Drummond fortune."

Sir Archibald looked confused, wrong-footed by Holmes's unexpected concession.

"What does the wretched woman want then?"

"Justice," put in Miss Selkirk. "This wretched woman wants justice. I want to be acknowledged for who I am. The daughter of Anne Drummond and the granddaughter of Sir Alistair. And I want to be united with my natural father if he is still alive."

"And one thing more," Holmes added. "The sum of £1,000 to be paid annually to her for the remainder of her life."

Sir Archibald grunted. "You don't ask much, Holmes! Give me a moment."

He motioned to Watkins and Cartwright and conferred with them for several minutes.

"It will have to be put in writing," he said eventually.

"Naturally," Holmes replied. "I have prepared a memorandum for the purpose. I suggest both parties sign now, and it can be converted into a more binding agreement later."

"Let me make it clear, Holmes that if any of this becomes public you will have cause to regret it, as will your confederates. I can make life very difficult for you."

"As can I for you, Sir Archibald. But rest assured that we shall all take what has passed here today to our graves."

Holmes nodded to the laird, and we turned to leave the room.

"I underestimated you, Holmes," he said finally.

"And I, you," Holmes returned.

❖

Two weeks later, Holmes and I were relaxing in our sitting room at Baker Street reflecting on the case and its aftermath. Mary Selkirk had by then returned to Scotland and been united with her father, a local hill farmer, who was very much alive and overjoyed to meet a daughter he never knew he had. For her part, Miss Selkirk had sent Holmes a handsome cheque and dedicated herself to helping the Rev. Hunter secure his church against the threat of landslide. I wondered if she ever thought of the cave on Exmoor and the years of solitude she spent there. It seemed so much time wasted. I said as much to Holmes.

"I'm not so sure," he replied. "Miss Selkirk values what she has now more than she ever would have done. She has gained more than Sir Archibald with all his entitlements."

"But it was a close-run thing Holmes," I said. "If it had not been for the entries in the parish register the game would have been up."

"That was a gamble on my part. I put myself in Anne Drummond's situation and thought what I would do to protect my child. It seemed obvious to me that she would want to make a permanent record before embarking on such a journey. It was then a question of obtaining the information. I asked the Rev. Hunter to write to his colleague at the local parish church and search the records."

"What a wonderful irony Holmes, Sir Archibald caught out by the family motto."

Holmes threw me a puzzled look.

"*Verba volant, scripta manent*. Words fly away, writings remain."

"Excellent Watson!" He replied, laughing.

❖

Confession of James Selkirk made this day March 20, 1875

I hereby confess before God that this is a true and accurate record made the day before my execution. That I did, on February 19, 1735, hold up and rob the London coach at Shooter's Hill in the county of Kent on or about 8.35 in the evening. I had information that a fashionable lady was aboard and a wealthy merchant and had determined this should be my last robbery before returning to my home in Galfries.

I waited for the stage in a small wood halfway down the hill where the horses are slowed to walking pace. It was a cold fresh night with the threat of snow and the coach was late. I was on the point of abandoning the robbery when I heard the sound of the coach approaching. It came abreast of me and I rode out and bid the coachman "stand and deliver," but he drew his pistol. We fired together and the horses reared up and bolted down the hill. When I got to the coach it was on its side, the wheels spinning. The coachman had been thrown from his seat and lay deprived of life in a ditch. Inside the coach were two passengers, a well-dressed man in a serge coat and neckerchief and a young girl. The man was dead from a metal spring which had pierced his belly and the girl lay dying from a broken neck. I took a fob watch from the gentleman and a gold necklace from the girl. I saw her bodice was undone so I laced it up. I spoke gently to her, and her eyes opened. She tried to say something, but the effort was too great and she sank back. I covered her face with her cloak and left.

I mounted my horse and was about to ride away when I heard a cry coming from a wild hawthorn bush. I rode over, parted the bushes, and saw a small bundle of blankets resting in a web of foliage and twigs. I saw a tiny face with its mouth wide open, crying hard. I picked up the child and placed it with its mother in the coach and turned to go. But it bellowed louder. The weather had worsened, and it was beginning to snow so I took the infant and placed it inside my greatcoat and the wailing stopped.

I rode away with the baby and brought her back to Scotland with me. I named her Mary and have loved her dearly to this day.
May God forgive me for what I have done and have mercy on my soul.

James Selkirk

Witnessed: **Robert Thomas** (Prison Warden)
Oliver Trenchard (Prison Chaplain)

The Cathedral Cat

"Mrs. Hudson! Come quickly. I need your assistance."

Holmes's voice, several semitones higher than its normal pitch, rang through the house. A few seconds later, I heard our landlady running up the stairs, as I hastened from the bathroom where I was shaving. We burst into the sitting room at the same moment, expecting to see Holmes in mortal danger yet again from one of his many experiments. Only the previous week he had managed to ruin the ottoman after spilling sulphuric acid from a pipette. But we found him standing in the middle of the room, waving his walking stick like a conductor at next door's cat which was sitting serenely in the middle of a pile of papers.

"How many times have I asked you not to let that animal in here?" he said to Mrs. Hudson. "It causes havoc. Have the goodness to get rid of it."

"Och, it's only a wee cat," replied our landlady. "It doesn't mean any harm."

"It's a menace," he insisted. "I can't have it prowling around among my papers."

"It probably wants feeding," she said, scooping it up in her arms.

"No, Mrs. Hudson. It wants throwing out."

She disappeared down the stairs, muttering to herself.

"Was that really necessary Holmes? You've upset her yet again, and I've cut my chin."

"I'm sorry to say this," he replied. "But Mrs. Hudson is letting her standards slip. She is clearly encouraging that animal."

"What standards would they be?" I asked surveying the mess. "You will get us evicted, Holmes."

"Nonsense Mrs. Hudson depends on us."

"I overheard her sister the other day telling her she should give us notice and let the rooms to proper gentlemen."

"Tittle-tattle," he said. "She would never do it."

At that moment we heard Mrs. Hudson's footsteps on the stairs, followed by a sharp rap on the door. She came in holding a note.

"I should have given you this earlier, Mr. Holmes," she said, passing it to him.

"I told you," I said, once she had retreated to the kitchen. "You have tried her patience once too often."

I looked across at him as he perused the note.

"You are right, Watson," he acknowledged, his brow unusually furrowed. "We must leave. Read it."

I took it from him anxiously and read the following

"Dear Mr. Holmes," it began. *"I am in desperate need of your help. I have been arrested on a charge of murder and am in a cell at Scotland Yard. I beg you to come soon. Yours, Gilbert Worthington."*

I glanced up and saw him smiling at me, a triumphant gleam in his eyes.

"Most gratifying, Watson, don't you think? We have a case."

"Very well Holmes," I replied. "But you were worried for a minute. Admit it."

"I never doubted Mrs. Hudson for a second. But what do you make of the note?"

"An educated hand, polite, respectful, grammatically correct."

"And written with one of the newer fountain pens," added Holmes. "A professional man of some kind, possibly a clerk. If we make haste with breakfast, we can be there by 10 a.m. Call down to Mrs. Hudson, Watson. You are obviously her favourite at the moment."

The cells at Scotland Yard could hardly be considered commodious. A pallet bed and a bucket were the only conveniences most cells afforded, with the consequence that if the straw mattress did not keep the inmate awake then the smell certainly would. Not surprisingly, we found Mr. Worthington in a very despondent mood. Inspector Gregson informed us that he had been seized in the early hours of the morning with traces of the victim's blood on his clothes and no convincing explanation of how it got there.

"I'm afraid it's an open and shut case, Mr. Holmes," Gregson said. "Even your powers of detection won't be of much assistance to Worthington."

"Nevertheless, Inspector, he has requested my help, and I should like to hear what he has to say," Holmes declared.

"As you wish, I can allow you ten minutes," he said.

Gilbert Worthington was a fair-haired young man of about thirty, well-dressed and clean-shaven with an open countenance. His face was flushed and anxious and it was clear from his first words that he was extremely frightened.

"Thank you for coming Mr. Holmes," he said. "I am innocent. I didn't kill Elsie. You must believe me."

"I will do all I can to assist you," Holmes replied. "But you must be completely honest with me. If you attempt to deceive me, I can do nothing for you."

Worthington nodded. "I understand."

"Then please start by telling me who you are and what your connection to the victim is."

"I am Gilbert Worthington. I'm a clerk at a firm of accountants in the city and I live near London Bridge. A year ago, I started seeing Miss Elsie Turner and formed an attachment to her. That will probably surprise you, Mr. Holmes."

"Why so?" Holmes asked.

"Because she was a streetwalker."

"In other words, you were one of her clients," I put in.

"Yes, Doctor, though she was more to me than that," he replied. "I hoped one day to be in a position to marry her."

"But in the meantime, you were seeing her and paying for her services?" Holmes said.

He nodded. "I know how this must seem to you gentlemen. But Elsie did not choose her profession. She had been forced onto the streets by circumstance."

"We are not here to judge you, Mr. Worthington," Holmes replied. "Simply to understand what has led to your present situation. Tell me about the night in question."

"I met Elsie as usual about eight o'clock outside London Bridge station. We walked along the embankment to an inn called The Jolly Pigeon."

"That's the inn overlooking the Thames above Southwark, isn't it?" I said.

"Yes," he replied. "The landlord lets out rooms by the hour and no questions asked. We have been there many times before. I stayed until about nine and then left."

"And Miss Turner too?" Holmes said.

Worthington shook his head. "No, she stayed behind. I shall regret that decision for the rest of my life."

"And why did you leave her?" I asked.

"We had an argument, Doctor. I had planned that evening to propose to her. I've been offered a promotion at work and was sure I could afford for us to be together as man and wife."

"I take it your proposal was not well-received," Holmes said.

"She laughed at me and said although she was fond of me, she could never be a clerk's wife. She said she could earn twice as much on the streets and that when she married it would be to someone who was better able to keep her than I could."

"So you left and went straight home," Holmes said.

"Not immediately," he replied. "I called in at The Fox and Hounds for a couple of drinks."

"And how did you get blood on you?"

He shook his head. "I didn't know I had until the police arrested me this morning for Elsie's murder."

"One last question Mr. Worthington. You were not Miss Turner's only client. You can't have been comfortable with that," Holmes said.

"I wasn't. But once we were married that would have stopped," he replied.

"But it appears she wasn't ready to stop."

Worthington hung his head. "No. I realise that now."

"What do you think Holmes?" I asked as we left the cell.

"A guilty man wouldn't normally have gone home and waited for the police to come," he said.

"But the blood Holmes? What explanation can there be for that?"

"None at the moment. We must investigate further."

Inspector Gregson was waiting for us in his office at the front of the station.

"Well, gentlemen?" he said, raising his eyebrows.

"It is evident why you arrested him," Holmes replied. "But there are a few lines of enquiry. I have agreed to do what I can for him."

The inspector smiled. "As you wish Mr. Holmes. But I fear it is the hangman's noose for him."

Holmes nodded. "You may well be right, Inspector. How did Miss Turner die?"

"She was strangled with some sort of material. Quite brutally. Whatever was used drew blood."

"You don't have the item?"

"No."

"Curious," Holmes said. "May we see the body?"

Gregson called to his desk sergeant and instructed him to take us through to the mortuary. The body was laid out on a bare table and covered with a thin linen cloth. Holmes drew back the cloth and we looked in surprise at the fresh young face which met our gaze.

"She cannot have been more than eighteen, Holmes," I said.

"Indeed. Who would guess her trade from such a face?"

He pulled the cloth lower, and we saw a different story from her neck. I bent down to examine the bruising more closely.

"Considerable force was used, Holmes. The material has bitten into her neck and ruptured an artery."

Holmes drew out his magnifying glass and inspected the wound.

"There are flecks of colour here. Lend me your moustache tweezers, Watson."

I did as he asked, and he leant over and very gently removed several threads from the injury laying them carefully on his handkerchief.

"Silk, if I'm not mistaken," he said. "Possibly from a dressing gown cord or a scarf."

163

"But it wasn't found at the scene," I said.

"Apparently not. Observe here, Watson. Underneath her fingernails. She fought back."

"Thank you, Inspector," Holmes said after we had made our way back. "That was most instructive. I assume you have no objection if Watson and I visit the scene of the crime."

"None at all gentlemen. Though my men have searched the room thoroughly."

"I don't doubt it, Inspector. But you know my methods," Holmes said.

Gregson smiled. "I do. Though they're no substitute for good honest policing if you don't mind me saying so."

"Quite," Holmes replied. "One last question. How did you find Worthington when you arrested him this morning?"

"He was spark out on the bed, fully clothed. We had to break the door down to get in."

Outside the station, we hailed a cab and instructed the driver to take us to The Jolly Pigeon. On the way, I quizzed Holmes about the case. I knew him well enough to be sure he had formed some preliminary conclusions.

"Worthington clearly had motive and opportunity," he began. "He was infatuated with Miss Turner and angry at being rejected. And he had blood on his clothes which he cannot explain. It's the means which concern me. The killer must have removed the item from the scene. In addition to which, silk clothing is expensive and hardly normal wear for a clerk."

"And what of the situation in which the police found him? Why had he made no attempt to escape?" I asked.

"Because he was drunk, Watson. Worthington was a trifle economical with the truth in saying he had a couple of drinks at The Fox and Hounds. My guess is he was drinking himself into oblivion.

Trying to forget. But whether it was simply being jilted or committing murder is the question we must answer."

After a journey of about fifteen minutes, we arrived at a small timber-framed building on the south bank of the Thames. A bleached sign exhibiting an oversize fantail pigeon announced it to be our destination. As we alighted, the smell of the river at full flood swept over us.

"Not exactly a romantic location," I said.

"But private and out of the way, Watson."

We went through into a smoke-filled bar busy, even at mid-day, with an assorted scrum of bargees, trawlermen, and dockers. Our entrance caused a momentary lull in the conversation. Someone cracked a joke and there was laughter.

"Keep going," Holmes said, making for the bar.

The landlord, a hard-featured man with thickset shoulders, nodded to us and asked us what our pleasure was.

Holmes put a guinea on the bar. "Two whiskies landlord, and some information."

"Yer welcome to the whiskies gents but I can't say as I 'ave any information for yer," the man replied.

Holmes placed another guinea on the bar. The landlord stared hard at it and then scooped it up."

"Yer'd best come this way," he said.

He opened the bar and led us through to a snug at the back of the inn.

"I don't snitch on me clients," he announced. "If that's what yer after."

Holmes shook his head. "What can you tell me about the events of last night?"

"I told the p'lice all I know."

"Well tell me," said Holmes. "What time did Elsie Turner arrive?"

"About half-past eight."

"Was she a regular?"

"Every couple of weeks."

"With the same man?"

"Different fellas. But mostly one."

"Who?"

"The bloke what did it."

"Gilbert Worthington?"

"I never ask names."

"And he was with her last night?"

"Yeah, left about nine. Just 'im. In a bit of a state."

"What do you mean?"

"Shouting his mouth off. Wanted me to give 'im his money back. Said he paid fer two hours. I told him to shove it."

"Did he have any blood on him?"

"Didn't notice. It's dark in the bar at that time."

"Did anyone else go up to the room?"

"Not that I saw."

"And it was you that found the body."

He nodded. "About eleven. Stark naked, blood over the sheets. They'll never come clean."

"Thank you," said Holmes. "Would you mind if we saw the room?"

"Help yerselves. First on the left up the stairs. It's in a mess. I 'aven't 'ad time to tidy up."

"Excellent. One last thing. Did Miss Turner have any friends – female friends?"

"Try Maisie. Thick as thieves."

"Where can I find her?"

"Where they all are. Below London Bridge."

We made our way up a shallow flight of stairs and into a narrow unlit corridor with several rooms off it.

"What was your opinion of the landlord?" Holmes asked as we entered the first of the rooms.

"Blood out of a stone springs to mind," I replied. "I don't think he uttered a complete sentence."

"He's a worried man, Watson. He's virtually running a brothel. And he knows more than he is saying."

Inside, the bedroom reminded me of Worthington's cell, except there were some concessions to comfort in an armchair and a proper bed, across which lay a pair of crumpled blood-stained sheets. Holmes began exploring the room in his usual manner, face to the floor magnifying glass in hand. After about fifteen minutes he sat back on his heels and sighed in exasperation.

"This is useless Watson. The room hasn't been cleaned for weeks. There's nothing I can definitively say was made last night."

He got up and turned his attention to the bed. After a few minutes, he let out a cry.

"Smell that Watson!" he said, pointing to a dark stain on one of the pillows.

"I'd rather not Holmes if you don't mind," I replied.

"There's nothing to upset your delicate senses," he said, laughing. "Trust me."

I knelt over the bed and put my face close to the pillow.

"Snuff," I exclaimed in surprise. "Definitely snuff."

"And fresh too," Holmes added. "There are a few grains still there. If I can get them back to Baker Street, I should be able to identify the brand."

"Worthington doesn't look like a snuff taker to me, Holmes," I said.

"Nor me either," he replied. "And I think we can probably rule out Elsie Turner."

"But still no sign of what was used to strangle her?" I said.

"No. And there are very few places where it could be concealed."

"The killer must have taken it away with him," I continued.

"Which is surprising, considering it would have been covered in blood. We must assume it was too important to be left behind."

He looked round the room and I saw a faint smile form at the edge of his lips.

"What would you say is the best feature of this room, Watson?"

"Does it have one?"

"Certainly," he replied.

I followed his gaze. "The view!" I said. "There is a splendid view across the river."

"Precisely. Open the window and let us make a closer observation."

I lifted the latch, and the pungent smell of the river filled the room as the window swung open.

"There!" Holmes said, pointing to the wooden sill beneath the window. "It's blood. The killer threw it out of the window, resting it momentarily on the sill."

We stretched our heads out and looked at the dark swirling waters below.

"Then it's gone for good, Holmes," I said.

"Evidently so," he replied gloomily. "I think we have gleaned as much as we can here for the moment. Let us continue our survey of Bankside inns and walk down to The Fox and Hounds."

It took us about twenty minutes of solid walking to reach The Fox and Hounds, a more salubrious establishment than The Jolly Pigeon with a gabled exterior and an extensive courtyard.

"A coaching inn, Holmes," I said. "It's a pity Worthington didn't bring his lady friend here."

"More expensive, Watson, and far too public."

We went inside and were greeted in a jovial manner by the landlord.

"What can I get you, gentlemen? We have a fine Spanish brandy just the thing to keep out the cold."

"That will suit us nicely, landlord," said Holmes. "And please join us."

"That's very kind of you gentlemen. I don't mind if I do. I haven't seen you in these parts before. Are you new to the area?"

"In a manner of speaking. Your inn was recommended to us by a friend of ours who said it was the best inn in Southwark."

"And who might that be gentlemen?"

"Mr. Gilbert Worthington. I believe he called in here yesterday evening shortly after nine. A fair-haired man about…"

"There's no need to describe him," interrupted the landlord, his face darkening. "I know Mr. Worthington very well. He's a frequent customer. But I wish he'd stayed away last night."

"I'm surprised to hear that. I recall him as a rather decent fellow," Holmes said.

"Not last night," the landlord said. "He got very drunk and ended up in a fight with another customer, splitting his nose. There was blood everywhere. I had to throw him out."

"Indeed," Holmes replied. "I'm sorry to hear that."

"If you see him again tell him he's not welcome in my inn. Enjoy your drinks gentlemen. I'll bid you good day."

"Well, well," said Holmes rubbing his hands. "A bit more of the jigsaw falls into place."

We arrived back at Baker Street and Holmes immediately began trying to identify the small amount of snuff he had retrieved from the pillow. He pulled out a large loose leafed binder entitled *Upon the Distinction between the Ashes of the various Tobaccos*, and started looking through it.

"I'm certain I included a section on snuff in my monograph, Watson. Towards the back, I think."

He stopped suddenly, pointing animatedly at a paragraph at the top of the page.

"As I thought, it's a German mixture. They're moister and stronger in flavour than British varieties. In all probability, 'Berliner Rosengarten'."

"Delightful name," I said. "It certainly had an aromatic scent, though whether of roses I couldn't say."

"Distributed in London by 'The old Snuff House' in the Haymarket. I know the establishment. It's frequented by the nobility."

"These are murky waters, Holmes."

"Indeed. Our next step must be to seek out Maisie. Let us hope she can enlighten us about Miss Turner."

We waited till it grew dusk before venturing out again. A cab dropped us in Tooley Street, and we walked to the arches underneath London Bridge. There was a chill in the evening air, a sign that autumn was coming in. Here and there along the pavement were women, some singly, some in groups, dressed in gaily coloured outfits. As we approached, they glanced at us and asked whether we were "looking for business." On each occasion, Holmes replied, "Not this evening, ladies," tipping his hat politely, and enquiring if they knew Maisie. Some smirked at the formality of his address, but most answered in kind. I remarked on this to Holmes.

"Streetwalkers value civility like anyone else," he replied.

Despite our endeavours, however, it seemed that Maisie was unknown to any of the women, and we were on the point of abandoning our quest for the night when a solitary woman approached us.

"What's yer business with Maisie?" she said, a hint of defiance in her voice.

"We are investigating the death of Elsie Turner. I believe Maisie was a friend of hers," Holmes replied.

"Who are you?" the woman continued.

"I am Sherlock Holmes, and this is my friend Doctor Watson. May we know your name?"

"Maisie Belcher. It's me you want."

"We are not here to harm you, Miss Belcher. We just want to know a little more about Elsie," Holmes said.

"A shilling for fifteen minutes?" She said. "I've got a living to make."

Holmes put a coin in her outstretched palm

"She was a streetwalker, same as what I am," she continued. "Only prettier. The men liked her."

"How well did you know her?" I asked.

"She lived with me, back of Tooley Street. About a year since."

"And before that?" Holmes asked.

"A brothel in Stepney. But the owner beat her, so she ran away. She lived in mortal fear of him finding her."

"What was his name?" Holmes asked.

"Joe Sutton," she replied.

Holmes nodded. "I know the man Watson. He runs a gym in

the East End."

"That ain't all he runs neither," Maisie said.

"So I've heard," said Holmes. "He is a brute by all accounts."

"Did Elsie have many clients?" I asked

"She was good at it. She could have 'ad anyone she wanted."

"What did she do with the money?"

"Sent most of it home."

"Home?" Holmes queried.

"She come from the country. Cornhill, I think. Somewhere in Bedford."

"She was supporting her family?" Holmes said

"Yes, silly cow! Life's too short for that I said."

"What can you tell me about the night she died?" Holmes asked.

She shrugged her shoulders. "Same as usual. She was spending the evening with one of her reg'lars."

"Gilbert Worthington?"

"Yes, she'd decided to give him the shove."

"But he was in love with her, wasn't he?" I put in.

She laughed sourly. "He was at her night and day to marry him. What d'you want to marry a worthless clerk for, I said. You'll end up with six bawling kids and nothing to feed them with. For once she saw sense. Anyway, she said she'd got someone else in tow. Some rich toff who she was going to see later after she'd got rid of Gilbert."

"Did she say who he was?" Holmes asked.

"She shook her head. "Only that he was pretty gone on her and was going to set her up somewhere."

"What time did you last see her?"

"About eight. She'd only just left when Sutton turned up. Someone had snitched on Elsie. He was in a foul mood. Said she owed him rent and he was going to get it back."

"Did you tell him where Elsie was?" I enquired.

"He give me this," she said pointing to a bruised left eye. "And said there was plenty more where that come from. But I lied and said she was going to The Fox and Hounds. I was expecting him to come back. Then I heard that Elsie was dead."

"Thank you, Miss Belcher. You have been most helpful." Holmes said.

"Will Worthington hang?" she asked.

"If he's found guilty, yes," Holmes replied.

"Good, she didn't deserve that."

We decided to walk back to Baker Street. Along the Thames everywhere was bright with activity, evening revellers emerging from taverns and restaurants, couples strolling, and the endless passage of cabs and carriages.

"London is certainly bustling this evening Holmes," I said.

"Yes," he answered. "There is nothing like a great city to elevate the spirits."

"Or depress them," I returned.

"Indeed. But what mysteries are here, what adventures? London is like a great novel, Watson. Its alleys and passageways teem with life. Do you not feel it?"

"When I see it through your eyes, perhaps. But I am not a natural denizen of the city."

"Then we must have a change of scenery. Let us venture into the country tomorrow and see what we can discover of Cornhill."

I looked at him in surprise. "You intend to visit Miss Turner's family?"

He nodded. "We are at present at something of a standstill. There are three contenders for the role of murderer, Worthington, of course, now joined by Sutton, and the unknown member of the gentry. And while my instincts are to the last of these, there is at present a dearth of evidence. Maybe we can glean a little more about Elsie from her family.

The following day we caught the early morning train from King's Cross to the North. The tiny station of Cornhill was the second stop along the line, and we alighted there in little over an hour. All around us spread a vista of green fields and small copses, accompanied by the sound and smell of agriculture. It was the time of late harvest and there were labourers in the fields busy with wagons and horses. I breathed in deeply and looked at Holmes.

"This is more like it, Holmes. Better than all your alleys and passageways."

He laughed. "It is certainly beautiful," he replied. "And I fancy the air is cleaner. But it was still not enough to satisfy Miss Turner."

The local station master directed us to the family home, which lay in a gaggle of thatched cottages clustered around a small green.

"This is idyllic, Holmes."

"Charming," he murmured.

The Turner's cottage was in a row with a small, well-tended front garden and a low hedge of lilac bushes. Holmes knocked on the door and a homely woman of about middle age in a faded pinafore dress opened it. Her face fell as soon as she saw us.

"I'm sorry gentlemen. If you've come about the rent, I shall need a few more days."

"No, no, Mrs. Turner. We are not here about the rent," Holmes said. "We are here about your daughter."

"I haven't got no daughter. Not no more," she replied.

"We know," I put in. "Is it possible we could talk inside?"

"You'd best come through to the parlour," she said. "Please keep your voices down, gentlemen. My son's asleep upstairs."

She ushered us through to a room at the back of the house with a view of fields and distant hills.

"A lovely room," I said.

"Thank you," she replied. "It's a comfort to me. What is it you want?"

"My name is Sherlock Holmes, Mrs. Turner, and this is Doctor Watson," Holmes said. "We are investigating what happened to Elsie. Would you mind if we asked you a few questions?"

"The police have already been here," she replied.

"There are just a few loose ends," Holmes said. "We won't take up much of your time."

"What do you want to know?"

"When did Elsie leave for London?"

"About four years ago. Just after my husband took ill. He's a labourer on Sir James Hervey's estate. This is a tied cottage, Mr. Holmes. When he got ill, he couldn't work no more and we were behind with the rent. Sir James and his wife said they needed a maid in their London house, and Elsie could work there and pay off the rent. She was pleased as ninepence to be going. There's nothing for young girls round here."

"So she began in service to Sir James and Lady Hervey," I said.

"Yes, but a year later, she left. I don't know why. She said it didn't suit her. Anyway, she found another place soon after, or so we thought. The police told us she was working on the streets."

"But she still kept sending you money?" I continued.

She nodded. "As soon as my husband got better, Alfie, my eldest, took poorly. He's got consumption, gentlemen."

"I'm sorry to hear that," I said. "Is there nothing that can be done?"

"The doctors say he needs somewhere warm, but we don't have that sort of money. Elsie said she could get it for us. Her employers would lend it to her. We believed her, Mr. Holmes."

"From everything we have heard about your daughter Mrs. Turner, it is clear her family was important to her," Holmes remarked.

"But to go on the streets, with men. It doesn't bear thinking about," she burst out.

"And we must find the person who hurt her," Holmes said.

"But the police have, haven't they?"

"We just need to make sure."

"I have nothing much left of her. Only her last letter."

"May we read it?" I asked.

She reached into her pinafore pocket and took out a crumpled sheet of paper which she handed to us. *"Dear Mother,"* it began,

"I hope this finds you and father well. I know as how you are worried about Alfie. Mr. D. says he will lend me the money to send him away. I am earning ever so much now and can easily repay it. Please don't worry. Everything will be all right. Your loving daughter, Elsie.s"

"Thank you," I said, handing it back. "You have every reason to be proud of your daughter, despite everything."

"Bless you for saying so, sir."

The sound of coughing from upstairs brought a weary sigh from her.

"He's started again. You must excuse me, gentlemen. I'll bid you good day."

We thanked her again and left the cottage to the sound of her heavy steps as she hastened upstairs.

"A sad tale, Holmes," I said as we walked back to the station.

"Yes, but not uncommon," he replied.

"Presumably 'Mr. D' was a fiction."

He nodded. "But I think money is at the heart of this tragedy. It is what drove Elsie to the streets and what determined the course of action which resulted in her death."

We arrived back in London just after midday and decided to use the afternoon to seek out Joe Sutton.

"The East End is best visited in daylight, Watson, unless one is carrying a revolver," Holmes said. "Which I assume at present you are not."

"Not on this occasion, but it's a short step to Baker Street."

"That won't be necessary. I think Mr. Sutton will be compliant enough and we should be back before dusk."

We hailed a cab outside the station and made our way to Whitechapel. Passing through Aldgate the landscape of the city changed visibly. Respectable houses, roads, and gardens gave way to dense back-to-back houses and high tenements with narrow, unpaved streets and open drains.

"Good grief, Holmes. The smell is awful," I said, holding a scarf to my face.

"One gets used to it," he replied. "It's not one of the more salubrious areas of London."

Joe Sutton's gym was a squat one-storey building sandwiched between a pawnbroker's and an alehouse. Outside was a sign picturing two boxers squaring up to each other. We got out of the cab and asked the driver to wait for us.

"Fifteen minutes gents. No longer. It's not worth my while," he said.

We stepped over a small gully and went through into the gym. The floor was covered in sawdust and the air was heavy with the smell of sweat. Two boxing rings occupied the floor space in both of which men were busy sparring. A bare-chested man with a neck like a bulldog and a bloodied nose came over to us.

"Mr. Sutton?" Holmes asked.

"Who's askin'?" he replied.

"I am Sherlock Holmes, and this is my associate, Dr. Watson," Holmes said.

Sutton grunted. "Professional busybodies. What's yer business with me?"

"We are investigating the murder of Elsie Turner," Holmes replied.

"That little slut. I don't know nuffink about that," he said

"She lived in one of your houses I understand." Holmes went on.

"About a year ago. Left owing me rent."

"How long was she with you?" He asked.

"About two years. She was in service afore that. They chucked 'er out."

"Do you know why?"

He snorted. "That sort don't need a reason. 'Bad behaviour,' she said."

"And when did you last see her?"

"I told yer," Sutton said. "About a year ago."

"What about the night she died?" Holmes asked.

He shook his head. "You've bin talking to that tart Maisie, ain't yer?"

Holmes nodded. "She told us you were looking for Elsie. She has a black eye to show for it."

"I don't hit women as a rule," Sutton said. "But the bitch got cheeky."

"And is that what happened to Elsie?" I put in. "She got cheeky?"

"Now look 'ere. I admit she'd pissed me off right enough, but I never did fer 'er."

"How can we be sure of that?" Holmes asked.

"Because I got this didn't I?" He replied, pointing at his nose. "I went to The Fox and Hounds and some bloke glassed me."

Holmes and I exchanged glances. "You got into a fight with Gilbert Worthington?" Holmes said.

"I recognised 'im as one of Elsie's reg'lars. Off his head with drink. I asked 'im where Elsie was, and 'e smashed a glass in me face. I had to come 'ome. If I see him again, I'll 'ave 'im."

"That might not be for quite a while," Holmes replied. "But thank you for your help."

We left the gym and got back into the cab. The driver looked relieved to see us and whipped the horse into a trot.

"What do you think, Holmes?"

"The man's a bully but I don't think he's our killer."

"Unfortunately for Worthington," I said.

"Indeed, we are still woefully short of evidence. Unless our luck changes, I fear Worthington will hang."

We arrived back at Baker Street in sombre mood. I had never witnessed my friend at a standstill before. He did not like admitting defeat, especially in a case which he was convinced was by no means closed. He spent the next few days closeted in his bedroom smoking heavily. I could hear him in the early hours of the morning pacing up and down and feared that at some point he would ask for the syringe. As chance would have it, I spotted one morning a notice in *The Daily Courier* advertising a concert of baroque music that afternoon at

Southwark Cathedral. There was music by Charpentier and Couperin and a performance of Bach's sonatas and partitas for solo violin. I mentioned it to Holmes after breakfast and saw his face lighten.

"It will do you good, old chap," I said. "We could have a spot of dinner afterwards at Roussily's in Bond Street."

"Perhaps you are right, Watson. We have supped too full with horrors, as the bard has it."

So it was that just after midday, we found ourselves seated in the middle aisle of Southwark Cathedral, looking down the long nave to where a group of musicians were tuning their instruments. I looked at Holmes and saw him lounging contentedly in his chair awaiting the opening part of Charpentier's *Te Deum in D Major*. Once the concert started, he closed his eyes, and as the music soared up into the vaulted ceiling of the cathedral, his face seemed to soar with it. In the interval, it was evident that my device had worked. He turned to me and said.

"That was sublime, Watson. If anything could persuade me of the existence of the divine it would be Charpentier's *Te Deum*. And in this auditorium!"

During the second half, his interest waned a little with Couperin, whom I knew he considered graceful rather than sublime, but once the Bach began he was rapt in attention. These were compositions which he had spent many hours trying to master on his violin. It was towards the last of these works that something truly extraordinary occurred. Strolling down the aisle in a leisurely fashion came a cat. A quite beautiful animal, mostly white with some striking patches of ginger dotted along its body. The entire audience, including Holmes, looked at it with amusement. It seemed for all the world like a late member of the audience searching for his seat. Arriving at the rostrum it stopped for a moment in front of the solo violinist and looked up at him as if about to ask a question, before turning to the left and disappearing into a side chapel. The performance finished soon afterwards and once the clapping had stopped, I couldn't help laughing and saying,

"What a scene-stealer, Holmes. I thought for one second the violinist was going to stop."

"But did you observe what he had in his mouth?" He replied, a glimmer of excitement in his eyes. "He was carrying a tassel Watson, which unless I'm very much mistaken, had the look of silk."

I sighed wearily. "Holmes you must let this case go. There are some things which are beyond even your powers." But he was evidently set on ignoring me.

"We must speak to the verger," he continued. "Where is the fellow?"

He got out of his seat and turned round impatiently. To the right of the altar, a gowned figure was traversing the south transept heading for a door marked "vestry."

"There," he said, pointing. "Quickly, before he disappears."

We walked briskly up the aisle towards the altar, brushing past people still making their way out of the cathedral. I apologised as best I could while Holmes pushed single-mindedly on. Arriving at the vestry he rapped loudly on the door and an elderly man in a black gown opened it.

"Yes, gentlemen, how can I help you?" he said. "If it's about evensong, I'm afraid it's been cancelled tonight because of the concert."

"No," said Holmes. "It's about the cat."

The verger shook his head. "I'm sorry, gentlemen. I hope he didn't spoil your enjoyment of the concert. Humphrey is a law unto himself, I'm afraid. We usually feed him before a concert so that he sleeps through it. But the churchwarden forgot. I think he was protesting."

"He's a handsome creature," I said.

"Indeed," replied the verger. "He's been painted several times."

"You mean he belongs to the cathedral?" Holmes asked.

"The cathedral belongs to him, gentlemen," said the verger. "He adopted it for his home several years ago. Once we started feeding him there was no getting rid of him. But he earns his bed and board by keeping the mice under control."

"Might we see where he sleeps?" Holmes asked.

"If you wish to, sir. Are you particularly fond of cats?"

"Only this one verger," I replied.

The verger led the way back along the transept round the high altar and past a series of memorials until we came to the recumbent figure of Bishop Lancelot Andrewes. At the side of the tomb was a soft cushion covered in a blanket.

"We've tried his bed in several places, but he seems to prefer this corner," said the verger.

Holmes bent down and inspected the bed, sifting carefully through the cat's trophies, a few bits of bone, part of a lady's muff, and the bowl from a clay pipe.

"Here it is Watson," he said, at last, grasping a small bundle. "Definitely silk. And from a man's scarf, I should say." He straightened up and handed me the tassel.

"It smells a bit," I said. "Why is there so much mud on it."

The verger nodded. "Humphrey is an inveterate mudlark. The river is only a few hundred yards away."

"The question is, where is the rest of it?" Holmes said.

"Presumably still in the Thames," I replied. "Or somewhere along the shoreline."

We thanked the verger, whom we left shaking his head in bewilderment at our eccentricity and made our way outside. It was late in the afternoon but not yet dusk.

"There's just enough time to take a look for ourselves," Holmes said.

We crossed a small road, threaded through an alley, and within a few minutes were at a series of steps above London Bridge. Before us stretched the expanse of the Thames, shining in the low rays of the sun. Along the bank of the river lay a narrow ribbon of shale and mud running either side of the bridge. We clambered down and walked a few yards upriver. Here and there we saw debris washed up by the tide, glass bottles, bits of timber, and several corks.

"It's a pretty hopeless task Holmes," I said. "It's a pity Humphrey can't show us where he found it."

"Perhaps he can," Holmes said thoughtfully. "He just needs watching twenty-four hours of the day. Cats are creatures of habit. He must have his regular haunts."

"And who on earth is going to spend their time traipsing after a cat? I hope you're not suggesting we should!" I protested.

He laughed loudly. "Of course not, Watson. I know how much you are addicted to your bed. I was thinking it might be a job for the Irregulars."

"Do you think they could be trusted to undertake it seriously?"

"If we pay them enough," he said.

The Irregulars were not beloved of Mrs. Hudson, who made such a fuss about the mess they made of her carpet, that we had been forced to limit their presence in the house to Wiggins, their self-appointed leader. But despite being disorderly, they were fiercely loyal to Holmes and amazingly zealous in carrying out their tasks.

Accordingly, as soon as we returned to Baker Street, Holmes sent for Wiggins and instructed him to keep a watch on Humphrey.

"A bloomin' cat, Mister 'Olmes?"

"Yes, Wiggins. You must not let him out of your sight for a second. He forages along the banks of the Thames. Watch him like a hawk and if he finds the rest of this then bring it to me."

Holmes showed him the silk tassel. "I believe it to be from a scarf. I must have the rest of it. Do you understand?"

Wiggins nodded. "Usual rates, Mister 'Olmes?"

"A shilling a day for everyone and a guinea to the boy who finds it."

After he had gone, Holmes spent the rest of the day examining the tassel under a microscope.

"The weave matches the threads from Elsie's wound exactly," he said eventually. "And there are specks of blood which have survived the Thames. This has to be it. I'm sure of it."

The next few days passed like weeks. There was little to do but wait, with every likelihood that the remainder of the scarf was lost forever. Occasionally, we would take a cab to Southwark to check on the boys' progress and relieve the tedium of waiting. And a couple of times there was genuine excitement when it seemed one of them had found it and was eager to claim the prize. But in the first case it proved to be an item of silk underwear, and in the second, part of a dress.

"Really, Watson!" Holmes said despairingly. "The things people throw in the Thames. It has become the dustbin of the capital."

But on the fourth day, Wiggins appeared triumphantly at Baker Street holding aloft a muddy piece of fabric.

"Billy found it," he announced. "Just below London Bridge."

Holmes took the item from Wiggins and brushed off some of the mud which had since dried. It was plainly a scarf. He fetched the tassel and matched it against the item.

"See Watson," he said. "It fits perfectly with the others. They are a match."

He stretched the scarf out to its full extent. Despite the ravages of the Thames, the delicate red and blue pattern was plain to see, as were some darker stains, hidden in the folds of the garment."

"It's a beautiful scarf, Holmes," I said.

"And lethal too," he replied. "The perfect garotte. Well done, Wiggins. Give Billy this."

He handed the boy a gold coin.

"Thank you, Mister 'Olmes. But it wore the cat what led 'im there."

Holmes smiled. "The doctor and I will think of a suitable reward for Humphrey, never fear."

Wiggins disappeared and we began a closer scrutiny of the scarf. At one end was a raised circle with some heavier stitching.

"What do you make of this, Holmes?" I said.

He bent over it with a magnifying glass. "It's a monogram. There are some initials. "Possibly 'T' and 'M'. I can't be sure, there's been too much water damage."

"So it was handmade," I said.

He nodded. "Yes, no wonder the killer was anxious to get rid of it. Fortunately, the water has not destroyed the outfitter's label. Look."

He pointed to a small tag attached to the outer edge of the scarf.

"Bakers of Bond Street," he read out. "Our friend has excellent taste. We will pay the establishment a visit tomorrow and see what we can discover."

The following day we breakfasted early and made our way over to Bond Street. The thoroughfare was busy, even at that time, with suited men on their way to offices and women browsing the latest fashions in shop windows. Bakers was situated in a marble-fronted arcade with a high ceiling and a glass chandelier. It was the emporium of choice for the gentry with every type of clothing from opera outfits to hunting jackets and breeches. Once inside, we sought out an assistant and after announcing who we were, asked to see the manager. He gazed professionally at us. Fortunately, I had followed Holmes's advice and was wearing my smartest attire. "I have always found that a top hat and cane will open any door," he had said.

Having completed his survey, the assistant beckoned to us.

"If you will follow me gentlemen, I will see if Mr. Harris is available,"

We followed him up a staircase and along a corridor to a room with a brass plaque bearing the title, Robert Harris, General Manager. He knocked and went in, emerging almost immediately to usher us through.

The manager, a corpulent man sporting a handsome pair of side-whiskers, rose from his desk and came to meet us.

"How can I help you, gentlemen?" He said.

"Are you able to tell us anything about this item of clothing?" Holmes asked, producing the silk scarf.

The manager took the scarf from him, handling it with considerable circumspection.

"It's a bit the worse for wear, Mr. Holmes," he said.

"Indeed. It was washed up by the Thames. It's a trifle soiled, I'm afraid."

"Well," replied the manager putting it down on his desk. "It's one of ours. What else do you want to know?"

"Can you tell us to whom you supplied it?"

"Our client information is strictly confidential gentlemen," the manager returned.

"Let me be frank with you, Mr. Harris," Holmes said. "We are assisting the police in a murder enquiry. Any information you can give us will be treated with the utmost discretion."

The manager hesitated momentarily and then reached for a bell which he shook vigorously.

"Send Perkins up," he said to the attendant who appeared. "Perkins is head of gentlemen's outfitting, Mr. Holmes. He will know the answer to your questions."

A few minutes later, a small bespectacled man with a bald head knocked and came in.

The manager pushed the scarf towards him.

"Take a look at that Perkins," he said. "It's one of ours. Do you recognise it?"

"Yes sir, it's mulberry silk, our finest fabric."

"Can you tell us who the order was for?" Harris asked.

Perkins looked at the monogram. "The initials are heavily worn, but I know them, sir. 'J, H'. The scarf was made for Sir James Hervey. It's one of an order of six which was delivered to him a year ago."

"Thank you, Mr. Perkins," Holmes said. You have been most helpful. I would be obliged if you and Mr. Harris would keep this information to yourselves. Come, Watson, we have work to do. I bid you good day, gentlemen."

"This opens up a new avenue of enquiry, Watson," Holmes commented as we journeyed back to Baker Street. "If Sir James was Elsie's killer, it is probable the connection between them extends back to the period when she was in service to him and his wife."

"It would explain the sudden loss of her position, after only a year," I said.

"Indeed," he replied. "And why she resorted to prostitution. Supposing she was dismissed without a reference, any future employment would have been rendered impossible."

"Lady Hervey, as I recall, is a prominent member of The Women's Purity League," I said. "One can imagine she would not have taken kindly to anything of that kind occurring under her roof."

"And yet, if we are right, Sir James was still in pursuit of her years later," Holmes said.

"But why would he kill her?" I queried. "We don't have a motive."

"Don't forget that Elsie was in urgent need of money because of her brother's illness," Holmes replied. "Perhaps she was not above trying a little blackmail."

"Which would have been embarrassing given his wife's public position," I put in.

"Precisely," he said. "I think it's time we informed Inspector Gregson of our discoveries. He can hardly consider it an open and shut case now."

Once back at 221B Holmes dashed off a telegram to the inspector with a request for him to call on us when convenient. He arrived in a hurry, looking flustered.

"What is it, Holmes?" He said, "I'm due in court in half an hour. A stabbing in Dulwich."

"We won't detain you long, Inspector. We have made some progress in the murder of Elsie Turner," Holmes said.

He proceeded to bring Gregson up to date with our investigation, at the end of which the inspector shook his head in frustration.

"It's not enough, Holmes," he said. "I admit the evidence is compelling but if I go up against Sir James with this I'll be laughed out of court. He will just say he lost the scarf, or it was stolen. He's an important man."

"I'm not suggesting you should, at the moment, Inspector. If I am right about this man then we must box carefully. Might I suggest that you begin by interviewing the landlord of The Jolly Pigeon again?"

"For what purpose?" Gregson asked.

"He knows more than he has said. I am certain he saw someone visit Miss Turner after Worthington left. Just let him know that he is liable for prosecution for living on immoral earnings."

"All right, Holmes, but I don't know why you think Worthington is worth all this effort."

"I don't particularly, but Elsie Turner is. She deserves justice."

We had to wait until the following afternoon before seeing Gregson again. He returned at dusk, just as the first of the gas lamps was being lit.

"Well, you were right. Miss Turner did have another visitor," he said.

"I thought as much," replied Holmes. "Did the landlord supply a name?"

Gregson shook his head. "I had to threaten to arrest him to get that much. He said a man came about half an hour after Worthington, but the bottom half of his face was covered by a scarf. He didn't see him leave."

"Excellent, Inspector," Holmes said, rubbing his hands. "Our case is getting stronger."

"Perhaps so, but we still don't have enough to accuse Sir James," Gregson said.

"No, but there is enough to alarm him, and when people are alarmed, they make mistakes," Holmes replied.

"What are you proposing?"

"That you, Watson, and I visit Sir James for the purpose of making a routine enquiry. He can hardly deny knowing Miss Turner, nor owning the scarf. All we are seeking is an explanation of how it might have been used to murder her."

"I hope you are right about all this, Holmes. My job is on the line here. I cannot afford to antagonise someone like Sir James."

"Never fear, Inspector. We shall look like the innocent flower, but be the serpent under it."

Sir James and Lady Hervey resided in Portland Square, a small exclusive close of Georgian houses in Mayfair. It took a week for the inspector to be given a time to visit and then it was restricted to fifteen minutes.

"He is letting us know how important he is," Holmes commented. "To keep someone waiting is the privilege of the powerful."

But one weekday morning, at the stroke of eleven o'clock precisely, the inspector, Holmes, and myself presented ourselves at the top of the short flight of steps before Sir James's house. A footman answered the bell and showed us through into the library where we found Sir James Hervey and his wife seated around a small coffee table.

"I'm afraid we are expecting company very shortly, Inspector, so I must ask you to be brief. What is it you and your companions wish to ask me about?"

"Thank you for seeing us Sir James," the inspector began. "It's just a routine enquiry. You may have read recently of the murder of a young prostitute in Southwark."

"It's hardly my normal fare, Inspector. Who was she?"

"Her name was Elsie Turner. We believe you employed her some time ago as a maid," Gregson went on.

Sir James looked at his wife. "Do you remember her my dear?"

"Yes," she replied. "I am afraid she proved unsuitable. We had to dismiss her."

"Was there anything in particular?" Gregson asked.

"She behaved in a familiar way to my husband," Lady Hervey replied. "I am sorry she sank into prostitution, but I am not altogether surprised."

"Was there anything else, Inspector?" Sir James asked.

"Just one more thing, sir. Do you recognise this?" Gregson held up the silk scarf.

"What is it?"

"A silk scarf," Gregson replied. "I understand it has your monogram on it."

"Good God, so it does. Where the blazes did you find it?"

"It was washed up by the Thames. We have reason to believe it was used to murder Miss Turner."

"How awful," Sir James replied.

"My husband has several scarves like that, Inspector. I'm afraid he's always losing them."

"My wife is right. I probably lost it at the racecourse. Will that be all?" asked Sir James.

"Yes, sir. Thank you for seeing us."

The footman opened the door and we made to leave. As we did so, Holmes turned suddenly.

"Just one last question Sir James," he asked. "Have you ever visited The Jolly Pigeon? It's a public tavern in Southwark."

"Certainly not!" he replied angrily. "I am not in the habit of frequenting such places. My wife and I are both teetotallers. Show them out, Watkins."

"Did you have to ask that, Holmes?" The inspector said when we were outside. "There'll be hell to pay from the superintendent."

"He was just a little too smug," Holmes replied.

"You bowled him a googly Holmes," I said.

He laughed. "I did, didn't I?"

We took our leave of the inspector, who was still concerned about possible repercussions from the visit and hailed a hansom.

"I'm not at all sure of our next step, Watson, but if we are to maintain the pressure on Hervey we shall need the assistance of Maisie Belcher. She lives at the back of Tooley Street, as I recall."

We alighted near London Bridge and walked down a lane behind the station. A local market was in business, with stalls spread across the thoroughfare. We stopped at a fishmonger's and enquired about Miss Belcher. The stallholder smiled knowingly at us and directed us to a tenement building further down the street.

"Third-floor, gents. Just call out," he said.

"It's a bit of a climb," I said to Holmes as we went up the stairs. "I'm surprised that clients have enough energy for anything else after this."

The third floor was a veritable warren of rooms and we saw the wisdom of the instructions we'd been given. Holmes called out Maisie's name loudly and the second time a door opened, and a head appeared.

"There's no need to yell. I'm 'ere. What d'you want?"

"A word, if you please, Miss Belcher," Holmes said. "May we come in?"

She opened the door wider, and we went inside. The room was sparsely furnished with a couple of beds, divided by a thin curtain, a small sink, and two wooden chairs.

"Is this the room you shared with Elsie?" I asked.

She nodded. "Yes, I need to find someone else now she's gone."

Holmes produced a shilling and offered it to Maisie.

"What's that for?" she said.

"The price for fifteen minutes I believe. We need to talk further with you."

"I've told you all I know."

"It's about her killer," Holmes said.

"I thought it was the bloke what kept pestering her to marry him," she said.

"Gilbert Worthington is innocent," Holmes replied. "Do you recall Elsie mentioning a man named Hervey?"

She grunted, "Sir James? It was 'im that got her the sack. Tried to seduce her but Elsie wouldn't have it."

"I think he found her again," Holmes said.

"And did for her?" Maisie asked.

"Very probably."

"Well, I hope the bastard hangs. Forgive my language gentlemen."

"I'm afraid he may escape the noose, Miss Belcher. Unless we can get more evidence," Holmes said.

"I don't know how I can help," She replied.

"You may be able to," Holmes continued. "If Hervey thought you had evidence which could send him to the gallows, he might reveal himself."

"But I don't," she said.

"We only have to make him believe you do," he explained.

"And get myself murdered, too? You must think I'm simple-minded!" she burst out.

"We would make sure that didn't happen," Holmes replied. "The police, Watson, and myself would be close by all the time."

She shook her head violently. "No, I liked Elsie. She was my friend, but I'm not doing that! No!"

"I understand, Maisie," Holmes said. "I can't pretend there isn't a risk. You have every right to refuse. I'm sorry to have bothered you."

I looked at Holmes as we made our way out of the building.

"I know what you are going to say, Watson. But it was worth a try."

"You were asking the poor girl to take an unacceptable risk," I protested.

"Perhaps so," he sighed. "But it galls me to think Hervey will walk free from this."

"At least you have done enough to secure Worthington's freedom," I replied. "There must be some comfort in that."

"You are right, of course. And that is all I was hired to do."

Despite Holmes's admission, I feared the onset of one of his black moods. I knew that for him the case would go down in his estimation as a failure. The house was quiet for the best part of a week during which he threw himself into one of his chemical experiments. Conversation was minimal and I was beginning to wonder what I could do to shake him out of it when Mrs. Hudson appeared one day at breakfast with a letter for him. He tore it open unceremoniously and gazed at the contents. Suddenly his eyes brightened, and he let out a hoot of pleasure.

"She has agreed to do it, Watson. Listen: *"Dear Mr. Holmes, I haven't had no sleep thinking about what you said. It's not right he should get off. Elsie would've done the same by me. Tell me what I must do. Maisie"*

"I'm still not sure, Holmes," I said. "This doesn't change anything."

"I disagree," he replied. "It changes everything."

Four days later, on a damp Thursday night in mid-October, Holmes, Inspector Gregson and I waited under one of the arches of London Bridge. Gregson had been cajoled into the enterprise by being presented with a fait accompli by Holmes. He and Maisie had devised a letter saying simply that she knew Sir James had killed Elsie and would present her evidence to the police unless he paid her the sum of £30, to be left underneath a bench at the south end of the bridge by midnight on Thursday. Wiggins had hand-delivered the letter two days previously, and all that was left now was to see what would transpire.

"Do you think it will work Holmes?" I asked.

"It has a more than an even chance," he said. "Our visit to Hervey would have startled him if nothing else, and he has no reason to suspect a trap."

"I hope you're right Holmes," said the inspector. "I've got half the police force out tonight."

"Good. But no one must move before I say so."

A few minutes later our attention was caught by a figure speeding towards us. It was Wiggins.

"'E's left the 'ouse in a cab, Mister 'Olmes. Billy clocked 'im," he said

"Excellent," Holmes replied. "Tell the boys not to let the cab out of their sight. The Irregulars are tracking him, Watson. He should be here in about fifteen minutes."

We waited, trying to resist the temptation to blow into our fingers and stamp our feet as the temperature dropped. Eventually, after about half an hour we saw a small boy approach the bench carrying a parcel. He stooped down and placed it beneath the seat.

"Of course," Holmes said. "Hervey has employed a child to do the drop. But where is he?"

As if in answer, Wiggins suddenly appeared.

"We've lost 'im, Mister 'Olmes. E's vanished," he said

Holmes sighed. "Well find him again, Wiggins. And don't let yourself be seen."

The clock of Southwark Cathedral struck twelve. Maisie had been instructed to collect the package at half past the hour. Those thirty minutes were among the longest of my life. Longer even than waiting for the signal to advance at Maiwand. But at 12.30 a.m. precisely we saw the figure of Maisie pass the bench and stoop down quickly to pick up the parcel. She looked around her and then started back down the path to her home. We followed closely behind, taking advantage of late revellers along the bridge, as cover. In about ten minutes we had reached her home and saw her enter the building.

"Perhaps Hervey has just paid the money and returned home," I said.

"Perhaps," echoed Holmes. "Or, just possibly, he knows where she lives. Quick, let's follow her."

Holmes raced into the building and bounded up the stairs. As he did so, we heard a woman's scream echo round the staircase. On the third floor, the door to Maisie's room was open. Inside, Maisie lay on the floor writhing in pain. On top of her was the figure of a man with a garotte around her neck. Holmes picked up one of the chairs and smashed it over his head and the man fell to the ground. I took the garotte from around Maisie's neck. She had stopped breathing and her face was turning blue. I sat her up and compressed her chest from behind until she choked suddenly and began breathing again, in large deep gulps. Meanwhile, Holmes turned over her attacker. I saw him shake his head in shock.

"What's the meaning of this?" He said. "Where is Sir James?"

I glanced over at the body, just beginning to stir after Holmes's blow, and saw the face of Lady Hervey. She had difficulty focusing at first, but then consciousness came flooding back.

"Let me alone," she said. "I've nothing to say."

"But you almost killed her!" Holmes persisted.

"The slut's a blackmailer," she replied. "Like the other one."

"Elsie? But it was your husband who killed her," Holmes said.

She snorted derisively, "He hadn't the stomach for it! I followed him. I knew he was at her again. Just like before. She laughed at me, wanted money to stay quiet."

"So you killed her," Holmes said.

"I'm not saying anymore. Let me be!"

Holmes turned to the inspector. "You'd better take her away, Gregson. Perhaps she will say more at the station."

The inspector signalled to two constables, who helped Lady Hervey to her feet and led her downstairs.

"That's a turn up for the books, Holmes," Gregson said.

"Indeed. I did not anticipate that," Holmes replied.

"She killed to protect her reputation," I said.

"I fear so, Watson."

It was now past two o'clock in the morning and after making sure that Maisie had fully recovered, we returned home to Baker

Street. Neither of us was in any mood to sleep. Holmes was particularly affected by the case.

"I was wrong to expose Maisie in that manner, Watson," he said gravely. "She almost died."

I nodded. "It was a close-run thing. A minute later and she would have been gone."

"If ever I am tempted to do anything so foolhardy, you must remind me of this," he continued.

"I will Holmes, but your motives were good. You wanted justice for Elsie."

"I wonder. Reputation, Watson, my reputation."

Eventually, we retired to our beds. We slept heavily and late and were only woken by a knocking on our sitting-room door. Mrs. Hudson had a note for us from Inspector Gregson.

"Dear Holmes and Watson, if you care to visit the Yard today, the Superintendent would like to shake you both by the hand. As for the lady herself, she managed to give my men the slip last night. But I am confident we will recover her soon. There is nowhere for her to hide. Yours, Inspector Tobias Gregson, Scotland Yard."

"Shall we go, Holmes?" I asked.

"Not on this occasion Watson. I cannot yet rejoice in this case."

It was two days later and Holmes had begun to recover his usual equanimity, due in no small part to the success of his efforts in helping Miss Belcher to a more secure way of living. On discovering that Mrs. Hudson's sister was in need of a parlour maid, he had persuaded our landlady to recommend Maisie.

"She is a clever and resourceful girl," I heard him tell her. "Literate, willing to learn, and conscientious."

Mrs. Hudson gave him a fixed stare. "She is a prostitute, Mr. Holmes!"

"But not out of choice Mrs. Hudson. All she needs is a chance. If she disappoints, then you have my leave to disregard everything I say in the future."

"Well on those terms, I can hardly refuse. But my sister is not a soft touch. She will not make allowances. Not like me!"

Holmes also donated the whole of his fee from the case to Miss Belcher so that she might purchase suitable attire for her position, though this had not been without contention.

"Gilbert Worthington had the temerity to ask if I would discount my fee," he said. "I told him that I never varied my fees except when I remitted them altogether, which I did not think in his case was warranted. The cheek of the man!"

"It's good to see you have regained your spirits, Holmes. Things have turned out fairly in the end," I said.

"After a fashion, I suppose," he replied. "But there are many like Elsie Turner and Maisie Belcher. So much human misery, Watson!"

Towards evening, Inspector Gregson called. We had invited him round to share a drink with us and to hear what more remained of the case. It was evident from his demeanour that he had more bad news to impart.

"I'm afraid the case has been officially closed gentlemen," he informed us.

"Closed!" Exclaimed Holmes. "Explain yourself, Inspector."

"Lady Hervey's body was found this morning, washed up underneath London Bridge."

"Suicide?" I said.

"It would seem so, yes. There is no evidence of anything suspicious."

"Did you charge her before she absconded?" Holmes asked.

"No, it was an omission for which I will probably be disciplined, though I think the Chief Constable is not too displeased. Her trial would have caused a terrible public scandal. His own wife is a member of the same league. Lady Hervey was about to be made president."

"Miss Turner's death will be officially 'murder by person or persons unknown?'" I said.

"Yes," Gregson replied.

"Maybe it's for the best," Holmes commented. "The next worse thing to a murder is a trial for murder followed by a hanging."

After the inspector had gone, Holmes turned to me.

"We have one last duty to perform Watson before we can move on from this case. Please call Mrs. Hudson."

I opened our sitting-room door and called down to her. She appeared a few minutes later wiping her hands on a tea towel.

"Please give this to Wiggins, Mrs. Hudson, and ask him to deliver it to the verger at Southwark Cathedral."

He handed her a parcel.

"What is it" she enquired.

"A small gift for Humphrey, without whose invaluable assistance we would not have been able to solve this case."

"It smells a bit," she commented. "What's inside?"

"Oysters," replied Holmes. "Fresh from Billingsgate."

The Missing Heir

"How is your knowledge of the aristocracy, Watson," Holmes asked one morning as we were sitting smoking after breakfast.

"Patchy," I replied. "Do you have anyone particular in mind?"

"The Earl of Craigmouth. There's precious little in Debrett beyond the fact that his country seat is Craigmouth Castle in Hampshire, which has been in the family since the dawn of time. Burke adds several children and a second wife."

"He breeds racehorses I believe, Holmes. There have been a couple of Derby winners."

"That is not enormously instructive," he returned.

"I'm pretty sure there was something about him recently in the society column of *The Times*, too," I added.

I got up and walked over to a pile of papers heaped on the floor. "Yes," I said, picking up the previous Saturday's edition. *"The engagement is announced of Julia, only daughter of the Earl of Craigmouth to the Hon. Richard Cavendish, eldest son of the Duke of Devonshire."*

"Quite a coup for the Earl's daughter," Holmes commented. "The Duke is one of the richest men in the country. He owns most of Sussex."

"What is your interest in the Earl?"

"We are to get a visit from his equerry this morning on an urgent and highly confidential matter."

"Five pounds says it is something to do with the forthcoming nuptials," I said.

"Well, I hardly think he is coming to borrow money, Watson. That much is fairly predictable."

About eleven o'clock we heard a knock on the front door and a few minutes later Mrs. Hudson showed our visitor in. He was a well-built man of about middle-age dressed in a morning suit and flourishing an ivory-handled walking cane.

"Good morning gentlemen," he said. "I am Sir Jeffrey Marchmont. Which of you is Sherlock Holmes?"

"I am, Sir Jeffrey," Holmes replied. "And this is my friend and associate, Doctor Watson. Please be seated."

Marchmont frowned. "This is a matter of the utmost delicacy, Mr. Holmes. I did not anticipate anyone else being privy to our meeting."

"You may rely absolutely on Watson's discretion, Sir Jeffrey. I never undertake an investigation without him."

"Very well," he replied, sitting down. "But I should explain that his lordship is an extremely private person. He has a horror of publicity. I had considerable difficulty persuading him to allow me to consult you. It was only his fear for the safety of his child that enabled me to prevail."

"What has occasioned this fear?" enquired Holmes.

"Albert, his younger son is missing. His lordship believes he may have been abducted."

"You have naturally informed the police," Holmes said.

"No, the Earl has ordered everyone to keep the child's disappearance strictly within the family."

"Might I ask why?"

"Albert is not a normal child, Mr. Holmes. He is mentally defective. His lordship is concerned to protect him and the family from public exposure."

"What form does this defect take, Sir Jeffrey?" I asked.

"He is imbecilic, Doctor. Although now 16 years old he behaves like a child of seven or eight. His appearance is disturbing, and he has had to be kept out of polite society for much of his life."

"But he is not disabled?" I said.

"No, he has complete use of his limbs, but his face is flat and featureless resembling those of oriental origin, and he is unable to contain his tongue within his mouth so that it continually lolls open."

"Has he been like this from birth?" Holmes enquired.

"Yes. The Earl hoped he would improve but it soon became clear this was a lifelong affliction for which there was no cure. He could not be accommodated properly at Craigmouth, so arrangements were made for the child to be fostered. He lives in a cottage on the estate with a couple who are themselves childless."

"And the boy's mother was content with this arrangement?" Holmes continued.

"Sadly, she died during the birth," Marchmont replied.

"Are we to understand then, that the child's existence has been kept secret?"

"Out of the public eye, Mr. Holmes, would be a more accurate way of putting it," Marchmont said. "His lordship has not stinted on private tutors and carers for Albert, but it was not in Albert's interest or the family's for his situation to become a topic of common gossip."

"What are the circumstances surrounding the boy's disappearance?" Holmes asked.

"It occurred two days ago. Albert's movements are closely monitored. He has considerable freedom to roam the estate's grounds, but he is always accompanied. There was an occasion some years ago when he wandered off on his own and was lost for the best part of twenty-four hours."

"And how was he found?" I put in.

"One of the estate's gardeners came across him. He'd climbed a tree and was unable to get down," replied Marchmont.

"But you don't think that happened on this occasion," Holmes said.

"No. He went missing from the house, gentlemen. Mrs. Barker, Albert's foster mother, saw him to bed as usual on Wednesday evening and when she went to wake him the following morning he had vanished."

"Had the bed been slept in?" Holmes asked.

"Yes," Marchmont replied.

"And how easy would it be for an intruder to gain entry?"

"Not at all," Marchmont said. "The doors and windows are all securely locked at night."

"I shall need to visit the house and carry out my own inspection, Sir Jeffrey."

"Of course. I have told Mrs. Barker to expect you."

"Can you think of anyone who might wish to harm Albert?" Holmes went on.

"The Earl is not a wealthy man," Marchmont said. "But there may be those who might seek to gain from abducting him."

"But there has been no ransom note to date."

Marchmont shook his head.

"Does the Earl have enemies?" I asked. "Someone who perhaps wishes him ill?"

"Not everyone is happy about the engagement of Julia, the Earl's daughter, to the Duke of Devonshire's son," he replied. "The abduction of Albert could be extremely embarrassing in that respect."

"But it would surely not endanger the engagement?" I continued.

"Marriages between the nobility are all about blood, Watson. Am I not right, Sir Jeffrey?" Holmes said.

"The Duke is very proud of his ancestry," Marchmont returned. "The presence of mental instability in the Earl's lineage is not something he would regard favourably, and his lordship has always endeavoured to keep that knowledge within the family."

"But Albert is not insane," I protested.

"No, but there is a brain defect," Marchmont replied. "And Julia is his sister."

"Thank you for being frank with us," Holmes said. "There is just one more thing. Who is the heir to the estate?"

"Until six months ago it was Richard, the Earl's eldest son. Unfortunately, he was killed in a riding accident. The estate is entailed on the male line."

"So, Albert is now the heir?" I said.

"Yes, although his lordship intends to have his right to inherit set aside on grounds of mental unfitness, which means that his heir will now be Thomas, the Earl's stepson by his second wife."

"Well Watson," Holmes said after Sir Jeffrey had taken his leave. "It seems my services are being called upon to spare a few aristocratic blushes."

"I didn't detect any great anxiety about the fate of the boy himself," I replied.

"You recognised the condition of course?"

I nodded. "Mongolism. The plight of such children is not enviable. They are usually incarcerated in asylums and spend their lives in misery and neglect."

"Just so."

"I attended the lectures of Langdon Down recently at the Medical Society," I said. "A most enlightened man. He has achieved wonders with such children at Normansfield."

"So I have heard. But he is a voice crying in the wilderness, Watson."

"Have you formed any preliminary theories about the boy's disappearance?"

"I have formed precisely five possible explanations of which by far the most likely is that he simply absconded."

"But why? What reason would he have for running away?"

"No one likes being a prisoner, however comfortable the cage, least of all a young man in the prime of life," he replied.

The following morning we caught the early train from Waterloo to Ringwood, a small town deep in the New Forest. Alighting at the station we were met by a horse and carriage sent by Sir Jeffrey which took us the short journey to Craigmouth Castle. The way led through dense woodland with ancient elms and thick barrelled oaks. I couldn't help remarking to Holmes on its romantic aspect.

"We are in one of the few primaeval forests remaining in England," he replied. "These trees were probably saplings in the time of William the Conqueror."

After about half an hour we turned a bend in the track and the land fell away sharply to reveal a wide valley with lush heath and moorland, through which wound a river. In the middle, at a point where it bulged into a small lake, was an island. And at the centre, nestling like a crested bird lay a castle. Whoever had designed the scene understood exactly the right balance between artifice and nature.

"Magnificent!" I exclaimed. "Who would have expected such a gem? What a place to live."

"Idyllic, Watson. But only on the outside, I fear."

We descended the valley and crossed a narrow bridge which led into the castle courtyard. To our surprise we found it swarming with police. I looked at Holmes.

"It seems the Earl has changed his mind," I said. "Perhaps our services are no longer required."

"Possibly," he replied. "Though I rather think some new event is responsible for this extraordinary bustle."

We got down from our carriage and were immediately accosted by a thin, unshaven man in a loose-fitting gaberdine suit and worn bowler hat, who demanded to know who we were.

"I am Sherlock Holmes, and this is Doctor Watson. We are here at the invitation of the Earl," Holmes informed him. "May I ask what has occurred here?"

"You may, but I'm not at liberty to tell you," the man replied. "I am Inspector Butler of the Hampshire constabulary. I should be obliged if you would conduct your business as quickly as possible and without interfering with my officers. This is a crime scene."

At that moment we caught sight of the equerry standing in a distracted state at the entrance to the castle. Observing us he hurried over.

"It's all right, Inspector," he said. "His lordship has engaged the services of Mr. Holmes and Doctor Watson."

"Has he indeed!" replied the inspector. "I do not approve of the involvement of amateurs, Sir Jeffrey. In my experience, they are invariably a nuisance."

"Never fear, Inspector, we shall endeavour to keep out of your way," Holmes said. "If you have any concerns you might speak to Scotland Yard who have found my assistance helpful in the past."

"Scotland Yard is it?" repeated the inspector. "Very well, I will tell my officers to allow you access. But keep me informed about your activities."

"Willingly," Holmes said. "Watson will tell you that I have no interest in claiming the credit for any of my successes."

"That is absolutely true, Inspector," I said.

The inspector nodded. "Then I will bid you good day, gentlemen."

"It seems the reputation of Scotland Yard has preceded us even if ours has not, Watson," Holmes said, as we watched Butler hasten away.

"Yes," I replied. "I rather think he would have liked to arrest us."

Holmes turned to the equerry. "What has happened here, Sir Jeffrey? I thought the Earl had determined not to inform the police."

"A truly shocking event has occurred, Mr. Holmes," Marchmont replied. "His lordship's stepson has been killed. His body was found early this morning by the gamekeeper."

"Most distressing," Holmes said. "What was the cause of his death?"

"He appears to have fallen and hit his head on a tree stump," Marchmont replied.

"Has the body been removed?"

Marchmont shook his head.

"Then let us see for ourselves."

We followed the equerry a short distance to a copse at the rear of the castle where two constables stood sentry duty over a small tent. Inside, covered by a thin sheet lay the crumpled figure of a man. Holmes bent down and drew the sheet back. The body lay on its left side, its head pillowed on a large stump as if asleep. Holmes lifted the head, and a large wound became visible.

"This seems to be the cause of death," he said. "Take a look, Watson."

I knelt down and examined the wound. The bleeding had been extensive and covered the lower part of the stump.

"From the amount of coagulation and the condition of the body I would say death occurred at least twelve hours ago," I said.

"Late last night," Holmes commented. "What do you make of the angle of the body?"

"He appears to have fallen sideways rather than backwards or forwards as one would have expected from a trip. The arms are not extended. He made no attempt to save himself."

"He has been hit very forcefully and knocked sideways," Holmes said. "There is bruising to the side of the chin."

"Are you sure?" Marchmont put in. "Could his death not have been accidental?"

"He has been in a fight," Holmes replied. "Look at the ground around the body. The grass has been trampled."

"Mr. Holmes is right," a voice behind us said. We turned as the inspector entered the tent. "There are footsteps leaving the scene which indicate someone leaving in a hurry."

"Excellent, Inspector," Holmes said.

"I may not have the experience of Scotland Yard, but I consider myself just as thorough," Butler replied.

"Do you know why his lordship's stepson was outside at such an hour Sir Jeffrey?" Holmes asked.

"Thomas was greatly affected by the disappearance of Albert," replied Marchmont. "He spent many hours scouring the area for him. I assume he was doing that again last night."

"And yet he is not dressed as one would expect of someone intending to remain outdoors for a long while. There are no topcoat, scarf, or gloves and he is wearing indoor pumps. He has all the appearance of having stepped outside for a few moments from a drawing-room."

We watched as he got down on all fours and examined the area round the body more closely. He moved it slightly so that the ground underneath became visible.

"See here, Inspector," he said, picking up what looked like a charred piece of wood from underneath the left shoulder. "Did Thomas smoke, Sir Jeffrey?"

"Yes," Marchmont replied. "He was extremely fond of cigars."

"What is it, Holmes," I asked.

"A rather large cigar stump," he replied. "Thomas must have been smoking when he was hit. The blow knocked the cigar from his mouth. He landed on it when he fell, extinguishing it in the process. You can see that it is only half-smoked."

"So the blow took him by surprise," put in the inspector.

"Exactly," Holmes said.

"His hand is clenched, however," Butler went on, "suggesting he was intending to strike back."

"Possibly, though his other hand is not," Holmes replied. He lifted the fist clear of the ground and prised open the fingers. Inside was a ball of tightly squashed paper. Holmes unfolded it carefully, scanning its contents quickly.

"He was lured here, Inspector. See for yourself," he said.

Inspector Butler took the note and read it:

"Meet me tonight as soon as you can. Usual place."

"Thomas knew his killer," Holmes said. "This was an assignation of some kind and not the first."

Butler nodded. "This note is of material value, Mr. Holmes. I am indebted to your vigilance."

"Thank you, Inspector. May I suggest we work together on this case in future? And now, Sir Jeffrey, if you will be so kind as to point us in the direction of the Barkers' residence Watson and I will continue our investigation there."

The way to the cottage lay along a small well-trodden path. We followed it through overhanging silver birch and thickets of bracken. As we walked, I observed to Holmes on the singular misfortunes that had befallen the Earl's family.

"The poor man has lost two of his children, and possibly a third, in the space of one year, Holmes. It's a tragedy worthy of the Greek theatre."

"Indeed," he replied. "If I were a superstitious man, I would say the Earl's family was cursed."

"Do you believe this death and the disappearance of Albert are connected?"

"It's difficult not to think otherwise. But we must avoid speculating in advance of the facts."

After half an hour of stiff walking, we arrived at a large house, which resembled the home of one of the better-off farmers, with the luxury of a slate, instead of a thatched roof, and a pretty apron of manicured lawn facing the front door. An elderly woman answered our knock, thin-faced and with lips pursed in frozen civility. Holmes was about to introduce us when she cut in.

"You'll be Mr. Holmes and friend," she said. "I was told to expect you."

"Yes, ma'am," Holmes began.

"There's no need to ma'am me, Mr. Holmes. I'm just a servant of his lordship. You'd best come inside."

She led the way into a small hallway, at the end of which was a good-sized sitting room with high French windows opening onto an expanse of woodland.

"Enchanting," I exclaimed.

"It is indeed, sir," a voice replied from the middle of the room. A sturdy, open-featured man of about sixty, rose from an armchair and came to greet us.

"Walter Barker, at your service gentlemen, and this is my wife, Doris."

We shook his hand, and something in the firmness of his grasp and the mien of the man stirred a distant memory.

"Are you by any chance a military man, Mr. Barker?" I asked.

"I was sir," he replied. "I served in the Northumberland fusiliers many years ago."

I snapped my fingers, "I thought as much. John Watson, assistant surgeon. I was out in Afghanistan during the first war."

"Good God!" he said. "You were invalided home after Maiwand."

"Indeed, I was. The shoulder still bothers me. You were in charge of the ordnance as I recall."

"Yes, Doctor, but the battle did for me too. My lungs have never been the same."

He turned to his wife, "You see Doris. I told you there was nothing to worry about. Doctor Watson and I are old comrades. And I daresay Mr. Holmes is decent too."

Holmes smiled. "Thank you, though I cannot claim the merit of having served my country with distinction."

Barker shook his head. "Very little distinction about it, sir. It was mostly hell. I was glad to get out."

"Anyone who risks his life so that I don't have to is deserving of merit, I believe," Holmes replied.

Barker's face flushed suddenly, and he fell silent.

"But I'm sorry if your wife has been concerned about our visit," Holmes continued. "Our only purpose is to ascertain for ourselves the circumstances of Albert's disappearance."

"That's all well and good sir," replied Mrs. Barker, "But we know his lordship blames us for that."

"Has he indicated as much?" Holmes asked.

"Not in so many words," she replied. "But he was very angry. Nobody understands how difficult it's been for me and Walter. Albert has a mind of his own. You can't keep a boy like that cooped up forever. He needs to be with other children."

"Does he see no one at all?" I asked.

"He was allowed to play with some children from the village once a week. But that stopped once he reached thirteen. Thomas, the Earl's stepson, has taken an interest in him. He takes him to visit the Earl's horses whenever he can," she replied.

"Albert loves horses, Mr. Holmes," Barker put in. "He'd live in the stables if he could."

"You've heard of course what has happened to the Earl's stepson?" Holmes said.

They both nodded. "I don't know what the world's coming to," Doris said. "So many bad things."

"On the night Albert disappeared," said Holmes. "Did you notice anything different about him?"

"He was a bit restless, fidgety," Barker replied. "Though he could get like that sometimes."

"Had anything happened in particular which might have caused that?" I asked.

Barker looked at his wife.

"He may have heard Doris and me talking in the kitchen," he said. "We'd heard a rumour that his lordship was intending to place Albert in a home with other children like him."

213

"It would be a wicked thing to do, Mr. Holmes," Doris said. "Albert is our family. He's all we've got."

"Why do you think he would do such a thing?" I continued.

Barker snorted. "His daughter's getting married to the Duke of Devonshire's son, isn't she? It's a case of out of sight out of mind."

"Supposing that Albert did overhear you, perhaps he decided to take matters into his own hands and run away," Holmes said.

Doris shook her head vehemently. "I don't believe he would do that. Where would he go? He doesn't know anybody."

"As far as you know then," Holmes went on. "Albert went to bed last Wednesday evening and when you went to wake him the next morning he had disappeared?"

"Yes," she said. "I saw him into bed as usual."

"What time was that?"

"About nine o'clock."

"And neither of you heard anything at all during the night?" Holmes asked.

"We're both heavy sleepers," Barker said. "And it had been a tiring day. We're not getting any younger, Mr. Holmes. More's the pity."

"Might we see Albert's room? If it's not too much trouble," Holmes asked.

"Of course," Barker said. "It's the first on the right at the top of the stairs. We haven't touched anything since that night."

"Excellent," Holmes replied. "And your room is close by?"

"Just across the landing, Mr. Holmes."

We made our way up a flight of creaky wooden steps to the floor above. It struck me that it would be well-nigh impossible to descend such a staircase in the dark, silently. I could see that the same thought had struck Holmes.

"What do you make of the Barkers?" I asked.

214

"They are troubled by guilt," he replied. "Though of what I am not sure."

"But you cannot think they had anything to do with Albert's disappearance?" I said. "They clearly loved the boy."

"That in itself could be a motive. Put yourself in their situation for a moment. They hear of the Earl's plan to remove the boy from their care and place him in a home. What are they to do? They know what such institutions are like. What could be more natural than to spirit the boy away themselves, to a relative, or friend, anywhere out of the Earl's power? Having done so, they then concoct the story of an abduction as a smokescreen."

"I hadn't thought of that, Holmes. It fits perfectly," I said.

"Yet my instincts are against it. I have little doubt that the Barkers are capable of deception, but there is a degree of subterfuge entailed by this explanation which I am inclined to think is beyond them."

Albert's room overlooked the rear of the house with a clear view to the edge of the forest. The window was secured by bolts which allowed it to be opened sufficiently to let in air, and nothing more. But in any event, there was a sheer drop to the ground below.

The centre of the room was dominated by a large single bed with the top sheet thrown back as if someone had just arisen from it.

"This bed has not been slept in," Holmes commented. "There is no depression in the pillow and the bottom sheet has no sign of disturbance."

"What significance do you attach to that?" I asked.

"Albert may have been taken from this room, but he was not asleep in bed as we have been led to suppose."

Next to the bed was a table with a few personal items. A musical box containing a bird's feather, some marbles, and a compass. And beside the box, a small leather-bound book. Holmes picked it up.

"A diary, Watson," he said, leafing through. "There is something for almost every day."

I looked over his shoulder at the unsteady handwriting which flowed across the pages. There were frequent references to "Elsa" and "Erin" and stroking their heads with "T".

"The Earl's horses, I imagine," Holmes said. "Presumably 'T' is Thomas"

"But there are no entries for the past nine days," I replied.

"Indeed. Something happened to stop him writing."

He looked about the room. "What strikes you about this room, Watson?"

"There's no mess," I answered. "It doesn't resemble any boy's room that I know."

"Precisely. Let's see how secure the rest of the house is."

Holmes took out his magnifying glass and spent a good hour inspecting the doors and windows on both floors of the house, at the end of which we returned to the sitting room where Mr. and Mrs. Barker were waiting expectantly for us.

"Have you been able to discover anything, Mr. Holmes? What is your opinion?" Barker asked.

"That you have not been entirely frank with us," Holmes replied.

"We've told you the truth, sir," Barker protested.

"Perhaps, but not all of it," Holmes said. "What you have described is an impossibility. You wish us to believe that Albert was taken from a house that is more securely locked against intruders than a royal palace, and with no sign of any break-in. Watson and I are not the police. I am willing to help you all I can, but you must be completely honest with me."

Barker glanced at his wife who nodded briefly at him. "We never meant any harm, Mr. Holmes," he said. "When we discovered that Albert was missing it scared us, I don't mind telling you. The Earl is not a very forgiving man. He has always impressed upon us the importance of keeping Albert secure."

"And to be perfectly clear," Holmes put in. "we are not talking about three nights ago."

"No," Barker replied. "Albert disappeared over a week ago."

"As I thought. His room showed no sign of recent occupancy," Holmes said.

"I spent the first four days searching for him, hoping that he had just wandered off, but there was no sign of him."

"You presumably held off from informing the Earl, fearing his reaction," Holmes commented.

Barker nodded. "But in the end, I had no choice. We heard that his equerry was intending to visit to discuss Albert's future with us."

"So you announced the disappearance bringing forward the date on which he went missing,"

"What else could we do Mr. Holmes?" said Doris. "Walter and me can't afford to lose our places. We're too old to find employment elsewhere. The rest was as we said."

"And what explanation do you have for the disappearance itself?" Holmes said.

"We have a barn at the side of the house, where we keep chickens," Barker replied. "We've lost several to foxes over the past month and I've begun checking on them last thing at night and laying traps. It usually takes no more than half an hour, but during that time, the side door to the house is unlocked. If someone was watching the house they could easily have entered."

"Albert has a very trusting nature, Mr. Holmes," said Doris. "He would go with anyone."

"Perhaps," Holmes said. "Although it is equally possible that he simply ran away."

"Yes, but it's hard for us to accept that he might do that," Barker replied.

The afternoon was closing in by the time we arrived back at the castle. Sir Jeffrey had arranged rooms for us at The White Hart, in the nearby village of Holtby in case we missed the last train back to London. It was fortunate that we had had the foresight to bring our Gladstones in case of such an eventuality.

"In other circumstances, you could have stayed at the castle," the equerry said. "But his lordship has been greatly affected by the loss of his stepson."

"The White Hart will suit us perfectly," Holmes replied. "Watson and I are habitues of village inns. But I should like to speak to the Earl at his earliest convenience."

"I will talk to him tomorrow morning and see what can be arranged."

"His lordship has clearly abandoned any attempt at privacy," I remarked to Holmes as the carriage conveyed us the short journey to the inn. "There are few places more conspicuous than a village tavern."

"And few people more given to gossip than village innkeepers," he replied. "Let us hope the landlord of The White Hart is no exception."

The White Hart was an old coaching inn situated round a large pond and facing an imposing Norman church, which together, dominated the small village of Holtby. The landlord was expecting us and ushered us to a couple of rooms at the back of the inn with fine views of the church spire. It wasn't until I got into the room that I realised how weary I was. I sat down on the bed and the next thing I knew Holmes was knocking on the door two hours later with the news that dinner was being served.

"I couldn't let you sleep any longer, Watson," he said. "The smell of roast beef is just too wonderful."

I followed him down to the snug where a table had been set up for us. From the adjoining public bar, the noise of early evening drinkers drifted through.

"Is this your first time in the area gentlemen?" the landlord asked, setting our drinks down.

"Yes," Holmes replied. "We have never had occasion to visit before but the views are quite remarkable. And within such easy reach of London."

"I'm pleased you think so sir," said the landlord. "We get forgotten about down here, but I like to think we have as much to offer as more fashionable places."

"Indeed you do," I put in. "There can be few places to compare with Craigmouth Castle which we were fortunate enough to see today."

The landlord nodded. "True enough sir. It will be a sad day when that changes hands."

"A remote prospect surely," said Holmes.

The landlord shrugged his shoulders. "It's no secret gentlemen that the estate is heavily in debt."

"You surprise me," Holmes replied. "It would seem to have every natural advantage. There is ample land for agriculture and the production of timber."

"The estate is profitable enough, sir, but I take it you do not know the Earl."

"We haven't had the pleasure of meeting him yet," he said.

"He's a fine old gentleman and I'll not have a word said against him," the landlord continued. "He comes into my inn sometimes and is as free and easy as you like. But he's a man of the turf if you take my meaning."

"Perfectly," I said. "I enjoy the sport of kings myself."

"Yes sir, but I venture that you are more circumspect in your pleasures. The Earl has incurred some heavy losses recently. Creditors are impatient people, as I know myself."

I looked at Holmes when the landlord had gone.

"A lot is resting on the marriage of the Earl's daughter, Holmes," I said.

"That much is clear," he replied. "None of which reassures me about Albert's safety."

As the evening wore on, the tavern filled with yet more customers and the atmosphere became increasingly rowdier. Having finished our dinner, a loud burst of laughter made us move into the bar to see what entertainment there might be. Standing at the counter was a large bull-necked man with a flushed countenance who was amusing customers with his imitation of an excessively genteel gentleman. I recognised in his mockery the mincing tones of the Earl's equerry.

"So he said, 'I'll inform his lordship of the matter.' And I said inform my arse. His bleeding stepson has knocked up my daughter, and I want to know what he's going to do about it."

A couple of voices in the gathering told him to "steady on" and reminded him that the stepson had been killed last night but this goaded him still further.

"Good, the bugger had it coming to him. What is a bloody equerry anyway?"

He looked round enquiringly until his gaze fell on Holmes.

"You!" He called out, poking his finger at him. "What's a bloody equerry?"

"A senior officer in the household of a nobleman," Holmes replied coolly.

"Wrong! He's a bleeding toff!" he jeered.

At that moment the landlord, alerted by the growing aggression of the man entered the bar.

"Come on Joe," he said, "putting his hand on his arm. "You should go home and sleep it off."

The man pushed his hand away and began swearing loudly at the landlord who redoubled his efforts to get him out of the bar. Suddenly, he grabbed hold of a bottle, smashed it against the counter, and swung round. Everyone immediately fell back.

"Come on then," he said. "What yer waiting for?"

"Be so good as to hold my coat, Watson," Holmes said handing me his jacket and stepping forward.

The man turned to face him. "I'll cut yer," he said.

Holmes beckoned to him to come closer, taunting him. The man moved his arm swiftly to one side and swung at him. Holmes swayed back and the glass passed within an inch of his mouth. At the same time, he turned his body sideways, stretching his right leg to its full extent, and hit the man powerfully in the chest. The force was enough to send him sprawling and several customers immediately overpowered him.

The speed and agility of Holmes's attack stunned the whole room until someone started clapping and then everyone burst into applause.

"You never cease to amaze me, Holmes," I said as he took his coat from me.

He smiled, "It's just something I acquired," he replied. "It's a Japanese form of boxing involving the whole body."

The landlord came over and shook Holmes's hand.

"Thank you, sir. I haven't seen a display like that since Tom Allen floored Bob Simpson."

"In the first round, as I recall," Holmes said.

"You must forgive Joe Parker," the landlord continued. "He's not normally like that."

"He mentioned something about his daughter," I put in.

"Alice," he replied. "She's pregnant and saying the father is Thomas, the Earl's stepson."

"Is that likely?" I asked.

The landlord grimaced knowingly. "He has a bit of a reputation, I'm afraid."

The next morning, we were up early and after a quick breakfast were soon on our way back to the castle. Holmes was bristling with energy, and I could see that he was in no mood to accept any more delay.

"This case has been bedevilled by evasion, Watson. It's time for some action."

We were met in the courtyard by Sir Jeffrey who greeted us in an agitated manner.

"There has been a development, Mr. Holmes," he said. "The inspector has made an arrest."

"Has he?" Holmes replied. "Then he would appear to have made more progress than Watson and I."

The equerry led us through the hallway of the castle and into a large library. Inside, seated on a divan was a frail, elderly man in a dark frock coat and matching waistcoat with a younger woman in a black crepe mourning dress by his side. Standing in front, facing them was the inspector. He turned as we entered,

"Ah, Holmes," he said. "I was just informing his lordship that we have made an arrest."

"So I have heard, Inspector," Holmes replied. "You are to be congratulated on acting with such rapidity."

"It proved to be a fairly straightforward case in the end," Butler said.

"May I know who it is you have arrested?" Holmes asked.

"Joseph Parker," Butler replied.

Holmes nodded. "Has he confessed to the murder?"

"No. But he admits to having a violent altercation with the Earl's stepson on the evening in question and there are bloodstains on his clothing," said Butler.

"And the note?" asked Holmes.

"Written by his daughter and used by Parker to lure Thomas outside," replied Butler

"His intention presumably being to confront him about the situation of his daughter," Holmes said.

"I am certain my son was completely innocent of the whole thing," put in the lady. "Thomas would never dishonour his family by forming such a connection."

"Have you charged Parker, Inspector?" Holmes went on

"Not yet," Butler replied

"Then I would advise against doing so. He could not have killed the Earl's stepson."

"Do you have evidence to the contrary?" Butler asked

"The blow to Thomas's face was inflicted to his right jaw by a left-handed man. Parker is right-handed."

Butler looked stunned. "That may be, Holmes, but he has no alibi and all the evidence points in his direction."

"Nevertheless, Inspector, I advise you to inspect the injury again," Holmes said.

"Very well," Butler replied. "But I shall take some convincing."

"And what of Albert, Inspector. Have you had any success there?" put in the Earl.

"Not yet, Your Lordship. We are continuing to search outbuildings and countryside within a radius of ten miles. I don't doubt we shall find him soon. With your permission, I will return to the search."

The Earl waved his hand airily and the inspector left the room, nodding briefly in our direction.

"And you, Mr. Holmes," the Earl continued. "Do you share the inspector's optimism?"

"I think it likely that Albert disappeared of his own volition, Your Lordship," he answered. "Although, it is too soon to be sure where he went."

"But what reason would he have for absconding?" the Earl asked. "He has not been ill-treated."

"May I ask whether you have planned any change in his care?"

"What do you mean?" returned the Earl.

"It is possible that Albert believed you were intending to remove him from the care of Mr. and Mrs. Barker and place him in an institution," Holmes said

"Absolute nonsense," the Earl burst out. "Albert is happy with the Barkers. They have been like a mother and father to him. Do you know anything of this my dear?"

The Earl's wife placed her hand on her husband's. "We did discuss it, dearest, if you remember. The Barkers are getting elderly, and Albert is no longer a child. They are finding him hard to control. Thomas and I wondered whether he might be happier with other people like himself."

The Earl shook his head. "Perhaps we did, my memory is not what it used to be. But I could never place Albert in an asylum. He is my son."

"And also, I believe, your heir," Holmes said.

"Yes, although I fear he would be unable to run an estate like Craigmouth."

"Had Thomas not been so brutally murdered, Mr. Holmes, it was our intention that he should inherit the estate," said his wife.

"You were intending to alter your will to that effect?" Holmes said.

The Earl nodded. "But now Craigmouth will pass out of my family to strangers."

We took our leave of the Earl and his wife and made our way out through the Hall. As we did so we were met by a young girl in a riding habit. It was evident from her glowing cheeks and windswept hair that she had been exercising vigorously. Holmes tipped his hat and bid her good day

"Are you Mr. Holmes?" she enquired. "My father said you would be calling. And you must be Doctor Watson. My name is Julia." She extended her hand to us in a friendly manner.

"Have you found my brother yet?" She went on.

"Albert?" said Holmes. "No, I'm afraid we haven't."

"Don't believe all they tell you about him," she said. "They think he's stupid. But he's not. He can ride much better than me."

"They?" Holmes queried.

"My father and his wife. I don't see Albert much. I'm not allowed to. But please find him."

"Watson and I will do our best."

"Thank you," she replied.

"And congratulations," I put in.

She gave me a puzzled look.

"On your engagement."

"Oh that. Yes, I suppose one does have to get married."

She vanished into the house leaving us smiling absurdly,

"What a breath of fresh air," I said. "It's a pity the estate is entailed on the male line. The Earl could do much worse than leave it to her."

We walked round to the stables, situated a few hundred yards from the castle entrance. If we were to believe Walter Barker, it was here that Albert had felt most at home. As we entered the timbered building our senses were immediately assailed by the heady aroma of hay and horseflesh. Holmes breathed deeply.

"If only one could find a tobacco that tasted of this," he said. "It is quite a narcotic."

I laughed. "I'm not sure Mrs. Hudson would agree with you, Holmes. She complains as it is about Old London Shag."

Inside was a series of stalls, four of which were occupied by fine-looking horses that pricked up their ears and whinnied as we approached.

"Can I help you, gentlemen?" A voice behind us asked.

We turned and saw a stocky, fresh-faced man in rough worsted breeches and an open-necked shirt studying us.

"Good morning," Holmes said. "I am Sherlock Holmes, and this is Doctor Watson. We are assisting the Earl in the recovery of his son, Albert."

"Then you are welcome, sirs. I was sorry to hear he was missing. I'm Jonas Williams, his lordship's groom," he replied.

"Albert was a frequent visitor here, I understand," Holmes said.

"Reg'lar as ninepence. Every week and sometimes twice. There wasn't nothing he wouldn't do. Mucking out, grooming, feeding."

"And riding too, so we've been told," I put in.

Jonas nodded. "Took to it like a duck to water. He'd have made a fair jockey. I told his lordship, but he wouldn't hear of it."

"He mentions Elsa and Erin in his diary. They are two of your horses I take it?" Holmes asked.

"Standing behind you sir. That's Elsa with the white star on her forehead and the other one's Erin. They've won a few cups in their time, but not no more. Elsa was injured in her last race. Still gets panicked. Albert was the only one could calm her down."

"Does the Earl still race his horses?" I asked.

Jonas shook his head. "There used to be more'n twelve horses at one time in here, but the Earl's been winding things down. It's mainly leisure riding now."

"That's a pity," I said. "I remember him winning the Derby last year."

Jonas smiled. "Yes, that was Erin. Won by two furlongs. His lordship hasn't been well this past year. Had a stroke about six months ago after the death of Richard, his eldest. He hasn't been the same since."

"I believe that Albert was accompanied on his visits by the Earl's stepson, Thomas," Holmes said.

"Yes, some years ago Albert wandered off and got lost so he has to be accompanied everywhere. I've told the Earl he's older and more responsible, but now this has happened it makes you wonder."

"And did Thomas share Albert's love of horses?" I asked.

"Hardly. He hated it here. Used to complain about wasting his youth buried in the country and having to mind a simpleton."

"Was Albert ever allowed off the estate?" Holmes asked

"The only time I can recall recently was when the circus came to Holtby," Jonas replied.

"When was that?"

"About a month ago. Albert came in one day very excited. He'd seen a leaflet about it. I think it was the animals that interested him. Anyway, Thomas said it might be amusing and offered to take him. Albert was full of it for days afterwards."

"Thank you, Mr. Williams," Holmes said. "You have been most helpful. One last thing, can you recall the name of the circus by any chance?"

"Culpeper's Touring Circus," he replied

"Are you thinking the same as me, Holmes," I said, as we walked back to the castle.

He nodded. "Yes, we have just stumbled across our first solid clue."

"Do you suppose it possible Albert ran off to join the circus?"

"Yes, though he couldn't have managed it on his own," he replied. "Nevertheless, I believe we have enough to frame a reasonable hypothesis. Let us imagine that Thomas had been planning to rid himself of Albert for some time. Probably since the death of Richard. He finds the task of minding him irksome. But beyond that, Albert is a hindrance to his ambitions. With the assistance of his mother, he has been working on the Earl to declare his son mentally unfit and have him committed to an asylum so that he can be declared heir to the title."

"But his lordship resists having his only child committed," I put in.

"Precisely," Holmes said. "At the same time, he is not a well man and could conceivably die at any moment. If he is to change his will, he needs to do it soon. It occurs to Thomas that if Albert were to disappear, his path to the title would become easier."

"Surely the best option then would have been to kill him," I said.

"Yes, but it is also the riskiest," Holmes replied. "The shadow of the gallows hangs over it. Much simpler and more convenient to persuade Albert to vanish of his own volition. And then along comes the circus. It must have seemed a godsend. He has already planted the seed in Albert's mind that the Earl is planning to send him away. All that is required is to offer to help him escape to the circus, where he could work with the animals."

"But how could he be sure the circus would take him?" I asked.

"Many circuses have freak shows, Watson. Albert would be considered an asset. If we are to recover him, we must return to Baker Street now."

Arriving back at the castle we sought out the equerry and informed him of our intention to return to London

"Have you made some progress, Mr. Holmes?" He enquired.

"I believe so Sir Jeffrey, but I need to investigate further before I can be sure. At all events, we have finished here for the time being. Before we leave, do you by chance have a likeness of Albert?"

"His lordship had a miniature done of him two years ago. Will that suffice?" Marchmont said.

"Perfectly," Holmes replied.

An hour later we were reclining in a first-class carriage on our way to Waterloo. I could see from Holmes's face that he was not entirely easy at the sudden turn of events.

"A penny for your thoughts, Holmes," I said

He removed his pipe from his mouth and looked earnestly at me.

"You have heard of Culpeper's Touring circus, I take it?"

I shook my head. "I can't say I have."

"It is an American circus," he went on. "It must be on tour in England."

"So, it will be returning to America at some point."

"Exactly. Indeed, it may already have done so. In which case it will be the devil's own job to find Albert."

It was mid-afternoon before we arrived back at Baker Street and Holmes immediately set to work to trace the whereabouts of the circus. He went out for several hours returning weary and dispirited.

"Ah Watson," he said. "If only I had been called in earlier. The Barkers did a great disservice in hiding his disappearance."

"You mean we're too late?"

He spread his hands, "The circus is in Liverpool, one of the crossing points for liners to America. The next ship is due to leave tomorrow at midday."

I jumped up and took down the railway timetable for the northwest of the country. There's a train from Kings Cross at six tomorrow morning," I said.

He nodded. "Arrives at eleven o'clock. I've looked Watson. But I doubt we would make it to the docks in time."

"We haven't come this far to fail now," I replied. "We don't know for sure that the circus is booked on the next crossing."

"Ever the optimist, Watson. But you are right. We have to try. Be so kind as to ask Mrs. Hudson to arrange a cab for five-thirty. There is time for a few hours rest, I think."

At a quarter to six the next morning we boarded the express to Liverpool. Despite the early hour, the train was full of travellers journeying north, among them several families with young children in tow and quantities of baggage. I wondered how many were intending to try their fortune across the seas. The popular press was full of tales of success in the Americas and every day brought forth a fresh account of someone who had started a farm in Arizona or begun a business in New York.

"Humanity is on the move, Holmes," I said.

"Indeed," he murmured. "T'is not too late to seek a newer world."

The train was a quarter of an hour late arriving at Liverpool station and it took us a further fifteen minutes to make our way through the scrum of people on the station concourse. Once outside we hailed a hansom and asked to be taken to the dockside, a large sprawling area of ships, tugs, and cargo, where we arrived shortly after midday. We looked at the jumble in dismay. Our task seemed impossible.

"Let's try the shipping office, Watson," Holmes said. "Otherwise, we'll never find it."

The office lay in the middle of the docks, but any hope of accessing it was immediately dashed by the sight of a huge crowd surrounding the door, all waving tickets.

"What's going on?" Holmes asked a passer-by

"All sailings are cancelled for today. There's bad weather in the Atlantic," he replied.

"What about the 'Queen of the North' bound for New York?"

The man pointed to a sign which we had missed in our haste. It read: "New York sailing delayed. Time of departure Friday 12 noon."

"That's two days away, Holmes," I said. "We're in time!"

We stared at each other, unable to believe our luck. We had both secretly been resigned to failing. Further enquiries from the crowd brought the information that Culpeper's Touring Circus was camped in Stanley Park, a sizeable arena near the centre of the city. We found a cab and travelled the short distance to the park. On arriving we saw a large poster at the entrance advertising the circus, and across it, in bold lettering, the words "Final performance today at 2 p.m." All around us lay a sea of tents and caravans. Many were already in the process of being dismantled and being packed onto carts.

"They are preparing to leave," I said.

"But the big tent is still standing," he replied. "Look at the queue waiting for admission."

We threaded our way through the tangle of tents and joined the throng snaking round the ground. At a few minutes to 2 p.m., we finally entered the arena and took our seats towards the back of the tent. A fanfare of trumpets announced the commencement of the performance followed by a glittering parade of costumed entertainers and animals round the ring. It was not difficult to imagine what effect such a display would have had on a boy whose life had been as sheltered as Albert's. The first half of the show consisted of various acrobatic and tumbling acts all of which amazed by their skill and daring. After the interval, it was the turn of the animals, sleek horses with their glossy manes, and lumbering elephants performing incredible feats of agility and balance. With each act, we scanned the arena hoping to catch a glimpse of Albert, but we had not reckoned on the scale and pace of the show. Spotting him in such an extravaganza was next to impossible. We had begun to reconcile ourselves to waiting until later when our attention was caught by a huge roar of laughter from the audience. Bounding into the arena came the clowns, four of them, in outlandish costumes and with the usual accompaniment of large noses, heavily rouged cheeks, and brightly coloured hair. In the front was what seemed like a small child about three feet high but which on closer attention proved to be a fully formed adult who amused the crowd by haranguing them in a shrill piping voice. Next to him was a woman covered from head to toe in hair and following her a man with no legs, swinging himself along by his arms like a monkey.

"My God, Holmes," I said. "They are all deformed."

"Yes," he replied. "And cast your eye on the one at the end."

I followed his gaze and saw a lanky young man dressed as a scarecrow milling around with outstretched arms, spilling straw over those in the front row.

"It's Albert," Holmes muttered. "Observe his face."

The troupe entertained the audience with their antics for about a quarter of an hour, during which time the scarecrow managed to throw several buckets of water over the hairy lady and trip over the disabled man innumerable times. It was difficult to know whether to laugh or cry. It seemed we had finally found the Earl's son, but in circumstances that were appalling. After the performance had ended, we made our way to the rear of the tent to where the larger caravans were parked. Holmes pointed to one decked out in the colours of the American flag and displaying a sign saying, "Circus Manager's Office". He knocked sharply with his cane and the door was opened by a thick-set moustachioed man in shirt sleeves smoking a cigar.

"Mr. Culpeper?" Holmes enquired.

"That's me. How can I help you, gentlemen?" The man replied.

"I am Sherlock Holmes, and this is Doctor Watson. May we come inside?"

Culpeper gave us a surprised look and removed the cigar from his mouth.

"Jumpin' Jehosophat! Look who it is Ruthie. Sherlock Holmes in person! I'm a big fan of yours, Mr. Holmes."

A buxom woman with an exceptionally broad smile came to the door.

"You're truly welcome gentlemen, please step inside," she said.

We followed her into a small chamber furnished like a saloon bar from the Wild West with polished oak surfaces and an array of pistols and rifles decorating the walls.

"What an original room, Mrs. Culpeper," I said.

"Ruth, please. Thank you, sir. It reminds us of back home."

"Did you see the show, gentlemen?" Culpeper asked.

Yes, we did," Holmes replied. "In fact, it is one of your performers who is the reason for our visit."

"Which one, sir?"

"One of your clowns. He was dressed as a scarecrow."

"Ah, Bertie. Joined us recently. Still learning the ropes but he's a good lad. What's your interest in him? Not been up to anything he shouldn't, I hope."

"No, nothing of that kind," replied Holmes. "Watson and I have been hired by the Earl of Craigmouth to find his son, Albert, who went missing from his home three weeks ago."

"And you think it could be Bertie?" Culpeper said.

Holmes nodded. "How did he come to work for you?"

"He was brought by his brother, as I recall. Said he was Bertie's guardian."

"How much did you pay for him?" I asked.

Culpeper flashed me a look. "I don't need to buy performers, Doctor. I hire the best and pay them well."

"But you were aware that Albert is underage, Mr. Culpeper?" Holmes said. "He is still a child and under the care and protection of his father."

"I didn't know that, no. He looks older. But his brother gave me a signed statement agreeing to the transfer. I can show it you".

He opened a drawer and shuffled around some papers, eventually handing Holmes a sheet of paper. Holmes scanned it quickly.

"This is not a legal document," he said. "Albert is not the property of his brother, to be traded as he wishes. Kidnapping is a serious offence, Mr. Culpeper, to which you have become an accomplice."

"Now look here," Culpeper replied. "I know nothing of any kidnap. I was just doing him a favour. He said Bertie was mad about circuses and would I take him. He was willing to do anything. As it happened, I needed another clown, and I could see that he would do."

"You mean, you saw an opportunity to exploit his disability by putting him on show," I put in.

"None of my performers is exploited, sir," rejoined Culpeper angrily. "Far from it. I expect you noticed the midget leading the clowns. We call him Colonel Titch. Have a guess at how much that man is worth."

"I have no idea," I said.

"A cool million dollars. He owns two houses in the States and a steam yacht. A few weeks ago, he met the Prince of Wales. If that's exploitation, I'll eat my hat."

"But for that, he has to endure the mockery and humiliation of the crowd," I said.

"The crowd loves him," he replied. "They can't get enough of him. The Colonel wouldn't thank you for seeing him as a victim. True, he had the misfortune to be born abnormally small, but he's turned that to his advantage. Where's the harm in that? That's what life is all about. It's the American way."

"Nevertheless," returned Holmes, "your continued detention of Albert is in breach of British law and this piece of paper will not protect you should the Earl wish to prosecute."

"As to that, gentlemen, I am more than happy to return Bertie to his family. I am not and never have been a kidnapper. But you may find that he is less than happy to go. He belongs here."

Culpeper gave us instructions where to find Albert and we got up to leave. But just as we were departing, he addressed himself to Holmes,

"Have you ever considered entering the world of entertainment yourself, Mr. Holmes? I am about to extend my business to include short dramas. Your presence at such events could command a lot of money. Mr. Dickens made a fortune from his dramatic readings in the USA."

"They also, as I recall, contributed greatly to his demise," said Holmes. "Which is something for which no amount of money can provide adequate recompence. Good day, sir."

We found Albert sitting outside a tent a short distance away from the manager's van. He looked up as we approached, his frank open gaze resting first on Holmes then on me.

"Let me speak to him Holmes," I said.

"Very well," he replied.

We stopped in front of him, and I smiled down.

"Hello, Albert."

"My name's Bertie."

"Of course, Bertie."

"Are you my friends?"

"Yes, we are. We are also friends of Walter and Doris."

His face became heavy, and he looked away.

"They miss you," I went on.

"I miss them too."

"They want to know when you are coming home."

He shook his head.

"I can't," he said. "This is my home."

"They are very sad, Bertie."

"But I can't leave my friends!"

At that moment, the bearded lady and the disabled man emerged from the tent.

"This is Mary," Albert said, pointing at the lady. "And this is Daniel. They're my friends."

I nodded. "And where's Colonel Titch?"

Albert pointed at a caravan a few hundred yards away.

"He has his own quarters," Daniel explained.

"Have you come to take Bertie away?" Mary asked.

"His family misses him," I said. "They would like him to come home."

"But I don't want to go!" Albert protested loudly.

Mary bent down until she was level with his face.

"Bertie," she said. "I like it here too, but I would rather be with a family. They love you."

"Mary's right," said Daniel. "We're you friends but having someone who loves you is different."

"You should go, Albert," urged Mary.

Albert lifted his face and there were tears in his eyes.

An hour later we were sitting in the London express to Kings Cross with Albert hunched in a corner fast asleep.

"Did we do the right thing, Holmes," I asked.

"I believe we did," he replied.

"I keep thinking of what Culpeper said. Could this have been an opportunity for Albert?"

"Culpeper is a businessman and an American as well, Watson. For him, life and opportunity are the same thing. But what would happen if Albert were to fall ill? Who would be there to help him once his usefulness had gone? Not Culpeper, I think. That's the purpose of families."

"It's an invigorating outlook nonetheless," I said.

"Agreed," he replied. "And one thing we have learned from this is that Albert deserves more freedom, not less."

It was almost midnight by the time we returned to Baker Street. Mrs. Hudson greeted us in surprise as we entered with Albert. Holmes briefly explained things to her, and she took in the situation immediately.

"He can sleep in my rooms, Mr. Holmes. It will be much more comfortable for him than sleeping with you and the doctor," she said.

"Thank you, Mrs. Hudson," Holmes replied. "It will only be for one night. Tomorrow we shall take him home."

Despite our tiredness, neither of us slept well and we rose early the next morning, the events of the previous day still fresh in our minds.

"I shall not be unhappy to return Albert and finish this case, Watson," Holmes said. "There are matters here beyond my powers."

At about 8 o'clock, Mrs. Hudson brought in our breakfast accompanied by Albert who was cradling next door's cat.

He looked up at us, smiling.

"You have found a friend," I said to him.

"Yes," he replied. "I gave him some of my food."

"We shall never be rid of the creature now, Mrs. Hudson," Holmes complained.

"He's called Marmaduke," Albert informed us.

"You have to hand it to Albert, Holmes," I said. "He's found out more about the animal in five minutes than either of us have in five years."

He grunted. "Remarkable Watson! But I see you have something in your hand, Mrs Hudson. Is that for me?"

"Yes, Mr. Holmes. It came just now." She passed Holmes a small package. "Come with me, Albert. Let's go downstairs and see if Marmaduke wants some water."

"It's from Mycroft," Holmes said in excitement. "I went to see him before we left for Liverpool."

"What on earth for?" I asked.

"The Duke of Devonshire is a member of the Diogenes Club," he replied.

"And how is that important?"

"It means that he is known to, and known by, Mycroft."

"I still don't understand," I said.

"The Earl is worried the Duke might break off his son's engagement over Albert, which is why he has been so secretive about him."

"And also, why he is considering disinheriting him," I added.

"Precisely, so I suggested to Mycroft that he use his talent for diplomacy and talk to the Duke."

"Was that wise, Holmes?" I said. "We have been given strict instructions to be discreet."

"There has been too much discretion in this case already," Holmes replied. "The Earl is in poor health. If a stranger takes over the estate what will Albert's fate be then? He could still end his days in an institution."

"What did you learn about the Duke?" I asked.

"He is not quite the dinosaur which the equerry would have us believe. He's an educated man, a trustee of the British Museum, and a founding member of the Royal Agricultural College."

"I recognise that gleam in your eye, Holmes," I said. "You have a plan."

"It's really very simple," he replied. "Albert should be allowed to inherit the title, while the Duke's son and the Earl's daughter become his guardians and manage the estate. This would secure Albert's future and give control of the estate to the Devonshires. Everyone benefits."

"And Walter and Doris Barker?" I asked.

"They can continue providing his day-to-day care," he said.

"Do you think the Duke will agree?"

Holmes waved the letter aloft. "This tells me that he has. He intends to speak to the Earl immediately."

"There is just one fly in that particular ointment Holmes," I said. "According to the landlord of The White Hart, the Earl is virtually ruined. There may be nothing to inherit."

"Fortunately, the landlord does not know everything," Holmes replied. "There are some gambling losses, but they have been acquired by the Earl's stepson, using his father's money. He is well-known around the racecourses of the country for his profligacy, in which I don't doubt he has been aided and abetted by his mother. It was clearly his intention once he inherited the estate to sell it and cover his debts. But these have now been cancelled by his death. Fortune is beginning to shine on us, Watson."

It was midday before the train to Ringwood pulled out of Waterloo, puffing steam into a cloudless autumnal sky. Holmes had wired ahead to the Earl's equerry informing him of our success in finding Albert and saying we would be returning with him. For the first time, we felt the strain of the case begin to slip away. All that was left was to sink back into the leather upholstery of our carriage and smoke quietly while Albert sat glued to the window watching the countryside of southern England flash past in an endless kaleidoscope of woods and green fields. My thoughts were suddenly interrupted by Holmes who said completely out of the blue.

"Yes, Watson, I think you should remarry."

I looked up in complete bewilderment.

"What the blazes do you mean, Holmes?"

"I have been observing you closely. For the past ten minutes, you have not taken your eyes off Albert, smiling when he pointed at the horses in the field, frowning when he was bothered by a wasp. And when your gaze slipped and you took the pipe out of your mouth, I knew you were thinking of the pleasures of being a father. At which point you sighed."

I laughed. "You're the devil of a fellow for reading one's thoughts," I said.

"You would make an excellent father, Watson. You have a nurturing quality in your nature, which I do not."

"Nonsense, Holmes. You pretend indifference, but I know otherwise."

"I am not like you," he continued. "I am not a family man. I belong to the Robinson Crusoes of this world. You do not."

"Well. First of all, I would have to find the right person," I said.

"Or she would have to find you," he replied.

We were met at the station by a pony and trap which carried us the short distance to Craigmouth Castle. In the autumnal shadows, it seemed even more like something from a fairy tale than the first time we had seen it. Albert's face, as we crossed the bridge, lit up excitedly.

"Can I see Elsie and Erin?" he said.

"Soon," I replied.

Sir Jeffrey was waiting in the courtyard and greeted us warmly as we descended from the cart.

"Congratulations, Mr. Holmes. The Earl was delighted to hear of your success. He is waiting to receive you in the library."

We followed the equerry into the room where we had first met the Earl. He rose now to meet us as we entered, with his wife and daughter by his side.

"Welcome, Mr. Holmes and Doctor Watson. You have rendered an old man an invaluable service and I thank you for it," he said

He took our hands briefly in his, the fingers thin and trembling. He seemed frailer and more infirm than before.

"I have not been well of late, gentlemen, but I could not be more pleased to see Albert safely returned."

"Watson and I are happy to have brought this matter to a successful conclusion," Holmes replied.

"Can I see Erin and Elsie?" Albert broke in suddenly. "They're my friends."

"Yes, my boy," said the Earl.

"I'll take him," said his daughter, coming forward and taking his hand. She led him out, laughing at his impatience.

"Was it a difficult task Mr. Holmes?" the Earl asked once they had gone. "Where did you find my son?"

"I think a narration of the facts might wait until another occasion," Holmes replied. "I fear it would weary, Your Lordship."

"As you wish, sir," the Earl replied.

"I'm afraid events have taken their toll on my husband, Mr. Holmes. We are still grieving for the death of Thomas," his wife said.

"Of course," Holmes replied. "Have the police made any progress?"

She shook her head. "They have released Parker for lack of evidence. The inspector seems to think poachers might have been responsible. They have been a great nuisance recently."

We took our leave of the Earl and his wife and went outside to the stables. Albert was talking to the horses, watched by Julia.

"It hasn't taken him long to make himself at home," I said.

"No," she replied. "Innocence is a great gift."

Holmes nodded. "He is none the worse for his adventures. Has your father made any decision about his future?"

"What do you mean?" she asked.

"I understand that His Grace, the Duke of Devonshire has proposals for the estate which he urgently wishes to discuss with the Earl," Holmes said.

"You're too late, Mr. Holmes," Julia replied. "My fiancé, the Duke's son, visited us this morning. Everything has been agreed between us. Albert is to inherit when my father dies. He will move into the castle with the Barkers as his principal carers. And Richard and I will manage the estate. I love my brother, Mr. Holmes. Albert will be safe with me."

"Excellent!" Said Holmes. "That is most gratifying news."

"And if I might advise, Lady Julia," I put in. "Write to John Langdon Down at Normansfield. He is the foremost authority on your brother's condition and the best person to ask about caring for him."

"Thank you, Doctor Watson. I will," she said.

"The old order changeth, Holmes, yielding place to new", I quoted as we walked away.

"Let us hope so," he replied. "But there is still unfinished business. We must call on the Barkers."

We found Walter and Doris Barker working in the kitchen of their cottage as we entered. News of our arrival with Albert had already filtered through to them and they were eagerly awaiting his return.

"I've baked some of his favourite biscuits, Mr. Holmes. Is he coming soon?" Doris enquired.

"Yes," Holmes said. "He's in the stables at the moment."

"Those horses!" said Walter Barker. "I swear he prefers them to people. Where did you find him in the end?"

"In a circus. He was lured away, as you rightly suspected, Mr. Barker."

"A circus. Good God! Who took him?" Barker asked.

"Thomas, the Earl's son. But you knew that already, didn't you?" Holmes replied.

Barker stared at him, "How could I possibly know that?"

"Because you found the note," said Holmes.

"What note?" protested Barker.

"The one Thomas was holding in his hand when he died – "Meet me tonight as soon as you can. Usual place". We thought it was written by Thomas's killer to lure him to his death, whereas it was in fact written by Thomas himself. The handwriting is identical to this transfer note which Thomas gave the circus owner."

Holmes flourished a sheet of paper before us. One glance at the swirling, looping style made it clear the handwriting was the same.

"You found the note when you were going through Albert's things and recognised who it was from," Holmes said.

Barker hesitated.

"Be honest with me, Mr. Barker, otherwise, I cannot help you."

"You're right Mr. Holmes," said Barker. "I knew it was from Thomas. He must have given it to Albert the afternoon before he disappeared when he was at the stables. Thomas knew I was in the habit of checking the barn last thing at night and leaving the door unlocked. All Albert had to do was wait his opportunity and then slip out unseen."

"And when you found the note you decided to confront Thomas about it," Holmes said.

"Yes. But not to injure him. I just wanted to find out where he'd taken Albert. I knew he was in the habit of meeting that girl from the village at night in the grounds so I waited for him. I could tell he'd been drinking. I showed him the note. He didn't deny anything. He just said Albert was better off without us and I would never find him. I begged him to tell me, but he just laughed and screwed up the note. I saw red, Mr. Holmes. God forgive me, I hit him. Just one punch and he fell hitting his head on the stump. I panicked and ran home."

"What will happen to Walter, Mr. Holmes?" His wife asked. "Will he be sent to prison?"

"As I told you earlier, Mrs. Barker, I am not the police. I cannot answer for what they may do," replied Holmes. "At present, they have not charged anyone, and I am not about to do their job for them. But if an innocent man were to be prosecuted, I could not remain silent."

"Thank you," said Mrs. Barker. "My husband lost his temper. We must live with the consequences of that."

"If it's any consolation," Holmes replied. "I do not expect the police to make any more progress in their enquiries."

Later, as we sat in the train returning to London, I quizzed Holmes on his leniency towards Barker.

"It is not like you to frustrate the law Holmes," I said. "What made you do it? After all, he did attack and kill another man."

"In circumstances of extreme provocation," he replied. "And I do not believe he intended to kill him."

"Surely that is for a jury to decide," I said.

"Agreed. But what would be achieved by sending Barker to prison, or possibly the gallows? He is of much more use to society looking after Albert, whom I have no doubt he loves."

"I see that, Holmes, but he has escaped justice. That cannot be right," I said.

"No, Watson. He has escaped the eye of the law, but not the eye of heaven. Walter Barker will have to answer for his actions one day, as will I."

Six months later, Holmes and I were sitting over a late breakfast. I was busy writing and Holmes was buried in that day's issue of *The Times* when he suddenly let out a cry.

"What is it?" I said. "Another crisis in the Indian sub-continent?"

"Page three," he replied, passing me the paper. "Right-hand column."

I took it from him and scanned the page. There in heavy black lettering I read, *"The death has been announced of James Morton, 4th Earl of Craigmouth. The Earl died peacefully in his sleep on Tuesday night after a short illness. He had been fortunate to attend the wedding of his only daughter, Julia, to the honourable Richard Cavendish, son of the Duke of Devonshire, a month before. The Earl is succeeded by his son, Albert, who will assume the title of 5th Earl of Craigmouth under the guardianship of his sister and her husband. The funeral will take place at St Botolph's church in the Strand. Attendance by invitation only."*

"Another death," I said. "That family is due some better luck."

"Let's hope the daughter's glittering marriage is the beginning of it," he replied. "And for Albert too."

"I believe the Devonshires are into horse racing, like the Earl," I said. "Perhaps we shall yet see Albert in the Grand National."

"Perhaps," he said, picking up my manuscript and leafing through it idly.

"What are you working on?"

"Something new, I haven't decided what to do with it," I replied. "It's experimental at the moment."

"I can see that," he said "What is the significance of the highlighted chunks?"

"I have been thinking about what Culpeper, the circus owner said. What if I were to give dramatized readings of your best cases? Tour the country with them. Think of it, Holmes. It would make you a household name and us a lot of money."

There was a deathly silence after which he said, "That is, without doubt, the worst idea you have ever had, Watson. As you value our friendship, I beg you to abandon it."

"My dear fellow," I said. "of course, if you wish it."

"I do. Now, if you will excuse me, I shall retire to my room."

"But it's only eleven o'clock in the morning," I protested, as he closed his door.

A few minutes later, the silence of the morning was broken by the melancholy sound of his violin.

The Archaeopteryx

It was a foggy November evening, towards the end of 1886, when I looked up from a book I had been reading and saw Holmes gazing at me with the kind of idle curiosity which a man usually bestows on a foreign object that has just strayed across his field of vision.

"What is it?" I asked, apprehensively.

"You have been reading that book for the past half hour, Watson, but have yet to turn the page. The matter is either very dull or your mind is elsewhere. When I compare that with the way you devoured the sporting pages of *The Times* this morning, I can only conclude you have had a not insignificant loss."

I cast the book aside. "Three horses, Holmes. Three! All of them completely useless. One fell at the first hurdle, the second threw its rider and the third was so slow the winning horse lapped it."

He laughed loudly. "Your addiction to gambling has always been a mystery to me. No one would suspect it. It is quite out of character."

"I owe it to the army," I replied. "Everyone gambled in Afghanistan. It was one of the more innocent distractions. It was that or the brothel."

"And yet you chose it as a career."

"I have no regrets about that. One joins the army for the camaraderie, Holmes. Nothing can compare with it. Friendships forged under fire last a lifetime. If I had not been wounded, I would happily have remained until retirement."

"Well, I, for one, am glad you did not," he replied.

"You have been fortunate in finding your ideal purpose in life. The role of consulting detective was designed for you."

"Perhaps," he said. "But it was not my first choice of profession."

I looked at him in surprise. "And what was that?"

"Paleontology. As a young man, Owen, Cuvier, and Marsh were my heroes. To attempt the reconstruction of the entire history of life on earth from fossilised remains seemed a noble and magnificent enterprise."

"Then why did you not pursue it?"

"Money," he replied. "Paleontologists are usually men of private means. Expeditions are costly, and there is little commercial interest in the study of old bones. I used my investigative powers in the service of the living rather than the dead."

"And I, for one, am glad you did," I said.

He smiled. "Touché, Watson. However, there is one thing about which I have no regrets. The life of the paleontologist is spent in rancour and dispute. It is a great irony that men of science are among the least rational of human beings."

I was reminded of this conversation, a few months later, when Mrs. Hudson brought in a note for Holmes shortly after breakfast one day.

"We are to receive a visit this morning from Inspector Lestrade," he announced. "Accompanied by Mr. William Flower."

"Who is he?" I asked.

"Flower is the director of the Natural History Museum," Holmes replied. "He replaced Sir Richard Owen on his retirement a few years ago. He has made quite a name for himself in the field of comparative anatomy."

"What in the world can he want from us?"

He shrugged his shoulders. "Nowhere is exempt from crime, Watson. But we have only a brief time to remain in ignorance. They arrive within the hour."

Half an hour later Mrs. Hudson ushered in the two men. Lestrade nodded briskly to Holmes.

"Thank you for seeing us, Holmes. This is William Flower, director of the Natural History Museum. I take it you are acquainted with him."

"By reputation only I'm afraid, Lestrade. But you are most welcome sir. This is my friend and associate, John Watson."

Flower bowed briefly. He was a tall imposing figure with a flowing beard and whiskers which gave him a stately, venerable air.

"We have an urgent case which I think should interest you," Lestrade continued.

"Please be seated, gentlemen," Holmes said. "Watson and I are all ears."

"Thank you, sir. I am greatly obliged for your time in this matter," Flower began. "You are familiar I assume with the archaeopteryx?"

"Indeed," said Holmes. "Probably the museum's most valuable fossil."

"Precisely," Flower returned. "It was discovered over twenty years ago and bought by my predecessor Richard Owen for the museum. There is only one other in the world. It is quite frankly irreplaceable."

"Are we to understand some mishap has occurred?" I said.

Flower nodded. "It has been stolen, gentlemen. During the night."

"How was the theft committed?" Holmes asked.

"The fossil was on public display in the zoology gallery. It consists of two medium-sized cases containing the limestone originals, displayed on a stand. Because of its rarity and value, a member of the museum staff is permanently on guard in the gallery. When the museum was opened this morning, the fossil had vanished as had the guard. A search was carried out immediately with no sign of either."

"What is known about the guard?" Holmes asked.

Flower hesitated. "His name is Martin Berry. His father is an acquaintance of mine."

"You mean you hired him as a favour," I put in.

Flower nodded. "A favour I now deeply regret."

"The point is Mr. Holmes, Berry has a record with the police," Lestrade said. "Seven years ago, he served six months for attempting to steal some goods from a shop."

"That is no doubt an embarrassment," Holmes replied. "Nevertheless, this is a crime of a very different order."

"What would be the point in stealing such a well-known object?" I asked. "Most museums and dealers would presumably recognise it immediately."

"Yes, Doctor. But some private collectors might purchase such an item and no questions asked," Flower said.

"It is likely then that the person or persons responsible for the theft were well-versed in the fossil trade," Holmes commented.

"Yes. It could well be that it was stolen to order," Flower went on. "My greatest fear is that it is already abroad and beyond recovery."

"Other possibilities do suggest themselves, however," said Holmes. "The thief or thieves may intend to hold the fossil to ransom. I imagine the museum would pay for its recovery."

"Yes," replied Flower. "Though its resources are not extensive."

"Perhaps the purpose of the theft was not financial," I said. "From what one reads in the popular press there are those who consider fossils to be fakes."

"Excellent, Watson," put in Holmes. "I intended to make the same point."

"It is a possibility," acknowledged Flower. "I receive letters every week claiming fossils are the work of the devil and demanding I remove them from public display."

"Though it does not appear there was any attempt to damage or destroy the archaeopteryx," Holmes said.

"Thank God. That eventuality does not bear contemplating, gentlemen," Flower replied.

"Have you considered offering a reward?" Holmes asked. "A crime such as this will be known. Someone will have information."

"The museum may be forced to if there is no progress soon," Flower said.

"In the meantime, Holmes, my opinion is that the key to this lies in finding the guard," put in Lestrade.

Holmes nodded. "You may well be right, Inspector. I suggest you devote your efforts to that, while Watson and I visit the scene of the crime and see what can be gleaned there."

"Thank you, sir," Flower said. "I must confess I am at my wit's end. Anything you can do to recover the archaeopteryx will be of enormous assistance not just to the museum but to me."

"There goes a very worried man, Holmes," I said after Mrs. Hudson had shown our visitors out.

"He has every need to be," he replied. "The archaeopteryx is the jewel in the museum's crown. He will not easily be forgiven for its loss and certainly not by Owen. The two men are bitter rivals."

"What is the reason for that?"

"Pride, Watson. Owen has long aspired to be the scientific genius of the age, which for many years he was widely considered to be. Unfortunately for him, along came a better candidate."

"You mean William Flower?"

"I mean Charles Darwin," he continued. "Owen has loathed Darwin ever since *The Origin of Species*. Flower is an ardent Darwinian. Soon after succeeding Owen, he erected a statue of Darwin near the entrance to the museum.

"Do you think it possible the theft might have a personal motive then?"

He nodded. "I do. Owen and Flower are both brilliant men. But brilliant men make enemies."

The late winter sun was sinking below a bank of clouds as Holmes and I mounted the steps and entered the large swing doors of the Natural History Museum. The director had closed the museum to visitors an hour earlier to allow us to work undisturbed. Entering the huge interior with its magnificent arches, decorative pillars and soaring ceiling, one could have been forgiven for thinking it the entrance to a great medieval cathedral or basilica. And at the top of a flight of stairs looking down on this, like some modern-day high priest, was the white marble figure of Darwin. We made our way swiftly up the stairs and into the first of several large galleries where we found a short, stout uniformed man in early middle age waiting for us.

"Good evening, gentlemen," he said, extending his hand to us in turn. "I am Samuel Jackson, the keeper of zoology. The director told me to expect you. How may I help you?"

Holmes smiled briefly. "Thank you, Mr. Jackson. You could start by telling us what you know of this affair."

"I was the first to discover the theft, Mr. Holmes. I start work early at around 6 a.m. This morning I arrived as usual and found the staff entrance open. That is unusual. The guard, Martin Berry, is told to keep the doors locked whilst he is on duty inside."

"Does he have his own set of keys?"

"He has a duplicate set which I give to him when he starts work and take from him when he finishes," Jackson said. "I ran up to the zoology section and found the cases containing the archaeopteryx missing and no sign of Berry. I searched quickly round the other galleries and then locked up and went to inform Mr. Flower. The rest I believe you know, Mr. Holmes."

"Indeed," replied Holmes. "Did you see anyone else in the building or notice anything out of the ordinary?"

"Nothing, sir."

"How many people have keys to the building?"

"Just myself as head keeper and the director. I also have the duplicate set which other staff borrow from me as required."

"I see. And this set is now missing, I presume?"

"Yes, Mr. Holmes, which has already caused a deal of inconvenience."

"Quite," Holmes replied. "Perhaps you could show us the site of the robbery."

We followed Jackson down the gallery to a small stand set apart from the other displays.

"The cases containing the fossil were fixed to this stand gentlemen," Jackson explained. "They were locked in place by a small padlock and the stand bolted to the floor."

Holmes examined the padlock closely. "There is no sign the lock has been picked or the mechanism forced. It was clearly opened with a key."

A few feet away from the stand was a small wooden chair. Holmes pointed at it. "Has that been moved here since the theft?"

"The room is exactly as I found it this morning," Jackson replied. "The chair is normally in the corner. It's used by the gallery attendant to keep an eye on visitors."

"Curious," said Holmes. He got out his magnifying glass and bent down. After a few minutes, he straightened up holding a few threads.

"Hemp, if I'm not mistaken, Watson. On the frame of the chair, and marks of abrasion on the wood. Someone has been tied here and has struggled to free himself. There are spots of blood underneath the chair."

"So it would appear Berry was acting under duress," I said.

He nodded. "Though where he is now, and the rope used to restrain him remain a mystery." He turned to the keeper. "What was your opinion of Martin Berry as an employee, Mr. Jackson? Did you consider him reliable, trustworthy?"

"I had no complaint about his work, Mr. Holmes. He could be moody and a bit free with his opinions at times, but he was conscientious enough. Though I wouldn't have taken him on, not as a guard, had I known he'd been in prison."

"Is there a particular colleague in whom he might have confided?" Holmes asked.

"Stephen Jewsbury, an attendant here, probably knew him better than anyone. I'll ask him to speak to you."

"Thank you. In the meantime, I would like to look around the other galleries."

"Of course. There are two more in this section devoted to the fossil record and one on dinosaurs," Jackson said.

Holmes strode off and for the best part of an hour, I watched him, magnifying glass in hand, prowling around the display cases like some hunter seeking his prey. I glanced quizzically at him as he returned with a noticeable gleam in his eye.

"There are more cases that have been tampered with, Watson. Items have been moved. There are none missing, but they do not always match their labels."

"It could be simple carelessness I suppose, Holmes," I said.

"Possibly, though it affects only certain fossils," he replied. "However, it looks as though the keeper has succeeded in finding Mr. Jewsbury for us."

A young man somewhere in his twenties was coming towards us. He was smartly dressed in the uniform of the museum and approached us with a confident, open manner.

"I'm Stephen Jewsbury gentlemen," he began. "The keeper said you wished to talk to me."

"Yes," Holmes replied. "I gather you are a friend of Martin Berry."

"Of sorts, sir. Martin and I are both attendants. The job can be a bit dull at times, so we get to talking to each other."

"Do you talk of anything in particular?"

"Mostly about things we'd like to do. Martin wants to travel. He doesn't like England much and wants to go abroad," Jewsbury said.

"Is he a single man?" I asked.

"No sir. He's married but they don't get on, so he told me."

"And what about the job?" Holmes asked. "Does he get on with that?"

"Mostly. But he doesn't like working at night. Says it's spooky. He fancies he can hear someone moving about," Jewsbury said.

"What did you say to that?" I asked. "Could it be true?"

"The place is all locked up, sir. I told him it was just his imagination."

"Thank you, Mr. Jewsbury. You have been most helpful," Holmes replied.

A few minutes later as we were descending the staircase into the main hall, the keeper hailed us, waving a scroll.

"I meant to give you this, gentlemen. It's a scale drawing of the archaeopteryx. It might be helpful to you in your enquiries."

"Thank you, Mr. Jackson," Holmes said, taking the scroll. "One final thing. Did Berry ever tell you that he thought someone was moving about in the museum at night?"

"No, Mr. Holmes, and I wouldn't have given it much credence if he had?"

"Why not?"

"Because others have said the same thing. The museum is rumoured to be haunted. Complete nonsense in my opinion. But the mind can play strange tricks."

"So, there would appear to be two mysteries, Holmes," I said, as we journeyed back to Baker Street. "Do you think they are connected?"

"I am inclined to think not," he replied. "Whoever has been opening the fossil cases has access to a set of keys and would not seem to be bent on theft. There are also tallow droppings which indicate a nocturnal activity."

"A member of the museum staff then. Berry himself, perhaps," I said.

"Possibly, though the account of his nervousness at being alone in the gallery at night has the ring of truth."

"What do you think has happened to him?"

"If my deductions are right, and he resisted the thieves, then I fear for his safety. We must assume that he managed to free himself and went in pursuit."

"Let's hope Lestrade has had some success in tracing him," I said.

Later that evening, over supper, Holmes spread out the scroll given him by the keeper. Before us was a striking pen and ink drawing of a spiny skeleton belonging to a creature, about the size of a raven, spreadeagled on a limestone base.

"What species is it?" I asked.

"Careers have been made and lost debating that issue," Holmes replied. "To some, it is a small dinosaur. Observe the lizard-like tail, the talons, and teeth. To others, it is a bird. Witness the feathered wings and body. For disciples of Darwin, it is the holy grail of paleontology, a transitional species between dinosaur and bird, proof positive of the transmutation of species."

"The missing link," I commented.

He nodded. "Precisely. More important even than the bird of paradise, or the fabled phoenix. We are looking at something 150 million years old. It is quite simply, priceless."

"Though to be honest, Holmes, it seems a poor scrap of a thing. What is your opinion, Mrs. Hudson?" I said as she entered the room to clear away our plates. "We are examining a valuable fossil of something which resembles a giant mosquito with claws."

"I know nothing of such matters, Doctor, but my father would have considered it unnatural, a fiend or demon."

"He wasn't a believer in the new science?"

"He was a true man of the kirk," she replied. "The Bible was the only book he needed. There were those in the congregation who thought differently, though."

"What happened to them?" I asked.

"They left. A few lost their faith. One poor soul took his life. There are some things it is better not to know, Doctor."

After she had gone, I looked at Holmes. "I wonder how many think the same."

"The tree of knowledge bears bitter fruit," he replied. "There is often a price to pay for progress."

We went to bed early, sobered by our landlady's words, but sleep did not come easily to me. I tossed and turned, troubled by dreams of winged creatures, pursuit, and death. I was woken early by the sound of Holmes knocking on my door.

"Watson," he called out. "Get dressed quickly. We have a summons from Inspector Lestrade."

I threw on some clothes and opened the door.

"There is news of Berry. We are to meet Lestrade at the Royal Brompton Hospital"

"Hospital?" I echoed

He nodded. "My thoughts exactly, but we must hope for the best."

We hailed a hansom and arrived at the Brompton within the hour. Lestrade was waiting outside for us.

"Grim news I'm afraid, gentlemen," he said. "Martin Berry was brought here early yesterday morning. He'd been hit by a carriage and four in Pelham Street. He died without regaining consciousness."

"Who brought him here?" Holmes asked.

"The coachman," Lestrade replied. "He said Berry just seemed to fall in front of the horses."

"May we see the body?"

"Of course. It's in the mortuary."

The mortuary was in the basement of the hospital, a dark subterranean jumble of passageways and cold, uncongenial rooms. Lestrade led us into the first of these where we saw a table with a body covered by a loose, thin cloth.

"Are you sure this is Berry?" Holmes asked.

The inspector nodded. "His wife identified him yesterday evening."

Holmes pulled back the sheet and we saw the face of a man of about thirty, clean-shaven with sunken eyes and pallid cheeks.

"This man shows signs of drug addiction, Holmes," I said.

"He has also been in a fight recently," he replied. "There is bruising to the right jaw and his lower lip has been split."

"We are treating his death as suspicious," Lestrade replied.

Holmes rolled the cloth down further revealing the full extent of the wounds inflicted on the body. Berry had quite literally been smashed by the horses' hooves and the carriage wheels.

"It's a mercy he died," I said. "If he had survived, he would have been crippled for life."

Holmes took out his magnifying glass and inspected the body more closely.

"There are signs of chafing to his wrists and ankles Lestrade," he said. "Consistent with being tied."

"Yes," the inspector replied. "Everything seems to support your interpretation of events, Holmes, apart from one thing. We found £100 in his coat pocket."

Holmes looked up in surprise.

"Payment of some kind?" I said.

"Did you also find the keys to the museum?" Holmes enquired.

"No," Lestrade replied. "There was no sign of them."

"What do you think, Holmes?" I asked as we came away from the hospital.

"There is manifestly a piece of the puzzle missing," he replied. "What we have at present does not fit together. I think a visit to the widow is in order."

Gladys Berry lived in a small terraced cottage a few streets behind the Natural History Museum. When she came to the door, it was immediately apparent she had been crying.

"Mrs. Berry?" Holmes asked.

"Yes, what do you want gentlemen?"

"I am Sherlock Holmes, and this is Doctor Watson. We are assisting the police in their enquiries into the death of your husband. May we come in."

She looked blankly at us for a moment and then her lower lip began to quiver.

"Don't upset yourself, Mrs. Berry," I said. "We are not here to cause you further distress. Mr. Holmes and I simply wish to talk about Martin but if it is inconvenient, we can return at another time."

She hesitated and I thought she was going to refuse, but then she seemed to change her mind.

"No, I would like to talk about him. You may come in. Please don't mind the mess. I haven't felt like doing anything."

"That's understandable," I said as we made our way through to a small parlour at the rear of the house.

"When did you first become concerned about your husband?" Holmes asked.

"When he didn't come home from his shift the night before last. I went to the museum and spoke to Mr. Jackson. He told me a valuable fossil had been stolen and Martin was missing. I could see he thought Martin had done it. But he wouldn't do anything like that, Mr. Holmes."

"No," Holmes replied. "And if it's any comfort, we don't think he was responsible."

"And neither do the police," I put in.

Her face relaxed instantly. It was clear that her chief worry, after the death of her husband, was that he was guilty of the theft.

"How long had Martin been working at the museum, Mrs. Berry?" I enquired.

"Five years, this Christmas, sir."

"And was he happy there?"

She paused and looked down at her hands. "Martin was a good man, Doctor, but he wasn't what I would call a happy person," she said.

"I'm sorry to hear that," I returned. "Life can be hard sometimes."

"I was with child when we married. I think Martin felt trapped. He always wanted to travel."

"So, you have a child then?"

"I did. He died when he was two. Martin thought it was a judgment on us. He started going to church, a Baptist chapel in Southwark."

"The Zion Tabernacle?" Holmes asked.

"Yes sir," she replied.

"Do you know it, Holmes?" I said.

"It's the stamping ground of the reverend Philip Easterbrook, a popular evangelical preacher. He regularly has hundreds in his congregation. He is no friend of the Natural History Museum, however, which he claims teaches atheism."

"Did you attend the church with your husband?" I asked.

"At first, but I didn't feel comfortable there. Martin liked it, though it changed him," she said. "He became quick-tempered and started to hate his job, particularly when he was working nights."

"Did he say anything about hearing noises in the museum at night?" Holmes asked.

"All the time," she replied. "He was convinced someone was watching him."

"He didn't say who?" I said.

She shook her head.

"Did you know he was taking laudanum?"

"I did wonder, Doctor," she said. "But he always denied it."

"The police found a large sum of money in his pocket," said Holmes. "Have you any idea how he might have acquired it."

"No sir. We didn't talk much lately. We'd become strangers." Her lip began to tremble again.

"I have to say, Holmes," I said, as we came away, "that if someone presented at a surgery of mine with those symptoms, I would diagnose him as mentally unwell."

"I agree. He seems to have been near breaking point."

"But we are no further forward in reconciling his bravery and loyalty to the museum with the payment in his pocket," I commented.

"Men at the end of their tether are rarely consistent in their behaviour, Watson," he replied. "Perhaps we have been approaching this wrongly. Let us suppose that Berry, a depressed and paranoid individual is worked on by someone to facilitate the theft of the fossil. It involves him admitting the culprit to the museum and allowing himself to be tied up. For these services, he is paid a significant sum of money. But for some reason, as yet unknown to us, he has a sudden change of heart, manages to free himself and pursue the thief."

"It fits the facts," I said. "Though it means assuming the thief was known to Berry."

"And if so, then the more we discover about the guard the closer we will be to our quarry. Let us see if the Reverend Easterbrook can shed any light on the matter."

It took us about twenty minutes by cab to travel across the river to Southwark High Street, to where the Zion Tabernacle stood in all its red brick glory. It was set back from the main thoroughfare by a well-trimmed sward of grass and could have been mistaken for a town hall or small manufacturing concern except that the outside was festooned with notices announcing forthcoming services. To the right of the building was a modest two-storey house with a wooden plaque telling us it was the manse. Holmes knocked on the door. It was answered by a maid, who bobbed and took his card requesting an interview with Reverend Easterbrook. She went away, returning a few minutes later to usher us into a well-furnished drawing-room. A soberly dressed man sporting a bow tie and side-whiskers rose from behind a desk to meet us.

"Good morning, Mr. Holmes," he began. "I am Philip Easterbrook."

"Thank you for seeing us, Mr. Easterbrook. My companion and I are enquiring about Martin Berry, an attendant at the Natural History Museum. I believe you knew him," Holmes said.

"I still do, Mr. Holmes," he replied. "He is a member of my congregation, though he has been absent from services for a while. I trust no misfortune has befallen him."

"I regret to say that he had an accident two nights ago and died from his injuries," Holmes said.

"I'm most sorry to hear that. How did it occur?" asked Easterbrook.

"He fell in front of a coach and horses. Death was almost instantaneous," Holmes replied.

Easterbrook winced. "There is no doubt it was an accident, I suppose?"

"Is there any reason you might think otherwise?"

"Martin Berry was a troubled soul, Mr. Holmes," Easterbrook said. "When he first joined the Tabernacle a few years ago he had recently suffered a bereavement which he took very badly. He felt he was being punished."

"Punished for what?" I asked.

"For immorality. His parents were god-fearing people, but when Martin arrived at manhood, he fell into loose living. He got a woman with child and was obliged to marry her. Then came stealing and time in prison. It's a familiar story, gentlemen. One evening he wandered into the church when I was preaching and was converted. Things improved for a time. He and his wife both started attending regularly but after a while, she stopped coming and his attendance became more intermittent. He seemed to be oppressed with a new burden. He told me he felt there was something evil loose in the museum, that he was being watched when he was alone at night. I told him to remember that the museum was a temple to godlessness and human pride and that perhaps God was speaking to him to seek a new occupation."

"And do you sincerely believe that about the museum?" I asked.

"I do," he replied. "It is a monument to heresy. Who do we see set on high when entering the building but a statue of the perpetrator of that heresy? It is the great lie, gentlemen. That we are

265

not made in the image of God but the image of an ape. Darwinism is idolatrous, sirs, and no good will come of it."

"And how did Martin respond to your advice?" Holmes asked.

"I think it struck a chord with him. He believed there were forces at work in the museum which are not of this world."

"Were you aware that he had begun taking laudanum?" I put in.

"I confess, I suspected as much. When I last saw him there was a vacancy about his gaze which I have witnessed before on the faces of addicts. I very much feared that he was becoming unreachable, though I continued to pray fervently for him."

"Heaven preserve us from well-meaning men," said Holmes as we returned across Southwark Bridge. "If Berry was not deranged before speaking with the Reverend Easterbrook, he certainly would have been afterwards."

"Is it possible a member of the Tabernacle was responsible for the theft?" I asked.

"The same thought has occurred to me, Watson, but let us hope not. It would make the task of finding the thief and Berry's killer infinitely more difficult."

We arrived back at Baker Street having made little progress in our enquiries and feeling deflated at our lack of success. Holmes took to smoking his pipe vigorously whilst I made a pretence of reading *The Times*. When Mrs. Hudson came in, just as it was getting dark, she found the room thick with smoke and both of us sitting silently. She immediately began coughing and rushed to open a window.

"For mercy's sake, gentlemen. I thought the house was on fire. Did you not hear me knocking? I have a letter for you, Mr. Holmes."

Holmes stretched out his hand languidly and took the envelope from her. One glance at the contents roused him from his torpor. He sat bolt upright and waved the letter at Mrs. Hudson.

"When did this arrive?"

"Earlier this afternoon," she replied.

"And you waited until now to give it to me?"

"I was busy, Mr. Holmes. It slipped my mind."

"What is it, Holmes?" I asked.

"It's a note from Sir Richard Owen," he replied. He wishes to see us. He has been unwell; otherwise, he would have called on us. He begs us to wait on him at our earliest convenience. If this had been delivered to us when it arrived, we could have gone today, but now it will have to wait until tomorrow."

"I'm sorry, I'm sure, sir. I didn't realise it was urgent," Mrs. Hudson said.

"It isn't, Mrs. Hudson," I replied. "Don't concern yourself. We've had a trying day."

"Very well, Doctor. I'll bring your supper up directly," she said.

"I know what you are going to say, Watson," Holmes said after she had gone. "I am too sharp with her."

"Yes," I remonstrated. "And she takes it to heart. You know how she looks up to you."

"But it is most annoying. I have been waiting to hear from Owen. I suspect he knows more of this business than he has said."

"By all accounts, he is not the easiest of people to deal with," I commented.

"He does not suffer fools gladly, that's certain. We should be on our guard tomorrow."

Sheen Lodge, the home of Sir Richard Owen, was an elegant Georgian house set in the pastoral surroundings of Richmond Park. Approaching it on a bright morning in winter, it seemed redolent of comfort, leisure and success. Our hansom skirted a large pond bordered by willows before stopping at the midpoint of a semi-circular drive.

"This is charming, Holmes," I said.

"It's a grace and favour house in the gift of the sovereign. Sir Richard's social credentials are of the highest," he replied.

We were met at the door by a footman who said Sir Richard was expecting us and took us through to a high-ceilinged library where we found a tall elderly man stooping over a microscope. He straightened up as we entered and came towards us. He had a large forehead with receding hair and protruding eyes which gave him a stern, headmasterly appearance. But his manner when he greeted us was courteous and hospitable.

"Good day, gentlemen," he said. "I am greatly obliged to you for coming so expeditiously. I have a touch of rheumatism, otherwise, I would have called on you myself at Baker Street."

"It is no matter," Holmes replied. "Watson and I are happy to be of service."

"Most kind. Please be seated," he said, waving a tremulous hand in the direction of a large divan. "I asked to see you," he went on, "because I am anxious to know whether any progress has been made towards recovering the archaeopteryx."

"Have the police not communicated with you?" Holmes asked.

A derisory look crossed Sir Richard's face. "I have little faith in the powers of the police. It is you, sir, I wish to hear from. I know of your reputation."

"Might I ask how you learned about the theft? It has not been made public as yet."

"I have my sources, Mr. Holmes. I may no longer be the director, but I make it my business to know what goes on in the museum."

"Perhaps on this occasion," replied Holmes. "You visited the museum yourself and found it missing."

"I fear I am no longer fit enough to go traipsing around museum galleries. And for what purpose?"

"As to the purpose, I am hoping you can enlighten us," Holmes said. "But I am certain you have been visiting it."

"This is absurd. What are you accusing me of?" Owen replied.

"Let me be frank with you, Sir Richard," Holmes said. "Someone has been visiting the galleries regularly over the past few weeks at night when the museum is closed. I believe that person to be you."

"Preposterous. The museum is securely locked at night," Owen protested.

"You could easily have had a spare set of keys made before you retired," answered Holmes.

"And why should I do that?"

"At a guess, to keep an eye on the collection and the work of your successor, in particular," Holmes replied. "Cases have been opened and exhibits moved and by someone with an unsteady hand. Scratch marks on the locks and tallow droppings from a candle indicate as much. A case of Baltic amber shows evidence of having been examined repeatedly. The person responsible knows what they are searching for. I put it to you, Sir Richard, that the person is you. I suspected it from the beginning but when I saw that you suffer from tremor, I became convinced of it."

Sir Richard shook his head. "I see your reputation is deserved, Mr. Holmes. You are right. I own it. But I was fully justified in my actions. Let me show you something."

He got up and led the way over to a desk. Opening one of the drawers he took out two pieces of amber and handed them to Holmes.

"These are flies fossilised in amber dating from around 38 million years ago," he said. "But one is a fake. The question is, which, Mr. Holmes?"

Holmes took out his magnifying glass and examined them closely.

"This one has been interfered with," he said at last. "It has a slight fissure indicating an attempt to cut the amber and then conceal it. Undetectable by the naked eye, however."

"Bravo, Mr. Holmes. The amber has been cut in two, a small hollow created, and a fly inserted inside. Once resealed it is practically invisible."

"What alerted you to it?" I asked.

"The flies, Doctor. The genuine fossil contains an extinct crane fly from the Eocene era. The other has a latrine fly, very common today, but unlikely to have been in existence when the amber was formed."

"I assume the purpose of your nocturnal visits to the museum was to look for similar fakes," Holmes said.

"Just so," Owen replied. "I'm afraid Flower has allowed standards to slip gentlemen. There are several forgeries which he has allowed into the museum. I am making an inventory which I intend to present to the trustees of the museum in due course."

"But was it necessary to gain illegal entry to the museum to conduct the inventory?" Holmes said. "It could surely have been done just as well in daylight and with the cooperation of the director."

"William Flower is not to be relied on, Mr. Holmes. He should never have been given the directorship. It is due to his laxity that the archaeopteryx has been stolen."

"Were you not concerned about being caught by the guard?" I asked.

"To apprehend someone, you have first to be awake, Doctor. A state that Martin Berry was very seldom in. He glimpsed me briefly once but took to his heels immediately as if he'd seen a ghost,"

"I take it you were not there two nights ago when the fossil was stolen," Holmes said.

"No sir, and it's as well for the thief I wasn't. There is much I would lose rather than the archaeopteryx be taken. Securing it for the museum was the great triumph of my career, gentlemen. I was the first to describe and classify it."

"Do you consider it to be the missing link?" I asked.

"I do not. That is nonsense disseminated by the supporters of Darwin. In my view, it is an early species of bird."

"Have you any idea who might want to steal it?" asked Holmes.

"The fossil trade is extremely lucrative, Mr. Holmes. Which is why there are so many forgeries. You can ask Berry when you find him. Presumably, he is the person responsible. Another absurd decision of Flower's. The man had already been in prison for theft."

"Mr. Berry was killed shortly after the disappearance of the archaeopteryx. It is likely he died trying to recover it," Holmes said.

"I see," replied Sir Richard. "As I explained earlier, I have had little communication with the police."

"But you have plainly had communication from someone," commented Holmes, pointing at a small pile of letters, their contents strewn across the desk."

"I have another reason for asking you to call, Mr. Holmes. Someone has been writing to me anonymously. I have received such letters before in my career, usually objecting to something I have said or written. But these are more personal and more abusive."

"What do they allege?" Holmes asked.

"That I am a thief, have stolen the work of others, and am responsible for ruining lives and careers. See for yourself."

He handed Holmes a small packet of letters which he began scanning quickly.

"They are all in the same hand, written on cheap notepaper and composed in haste," Holmes said. "There are numerous errors and crossings out, but the style is educated, if repetitious. They threaten some terrible retribution unless you make a public apology. Have you any idea, Sir Richard, what is being referred to?"

"None, whatsoever," Owen replied. "A man in my position makes enemies. I can only think it is someone who harbours some grudge because I rebuffed his opinion publicly."

"This one refers to a wrong done to 'a Great Man'," Holmes said.

"Everyone considers himself to be that," Owen replied. "It is the disease of the age. But my question is, Mr. Holmes, whether I should take these threats seriously or whether they are the harmless ravings of a lunatic."

"The purpose of the letters is clearly to allow the writer to vent his fury," Holmes said. "That much is evident from their style and manner. The problem arises when that is no longer sufficient to satisfy him. He will then be faced with a choice either to abandon his harassment of you altogether or move on to something more threatening."

"Which do you think he is likely to choose?" Asked Owen.

"I fear the latter, Sir Richard. My advice is to be completely honest and think who might bear you such a grudge. The writer assumes you know."

"I'm afraid he has the better of me, Mr. Holmes. I am a strict man, some would say severe, but my honours have been fairly earned."

"Then all I can advise you is to be on your guard, Sir Richard."

"Do you think he is in danger, Holmes?" I asked as we left the house.

"The venom in those letters was real enough," he replied. "He would be wise to take heed."

"At least I assume he will now end his nocturnal visits to the museum," I said.

"One must hope so, Watson, but we are dealing with a stubborn man. I believe he knew what the sender was referring to."

"Could it be relevant to the disappearance of the archaeopteryx?"

"It presents a new avenue for our inquiry. My instinct from the beginning has been that the theft is personal. Remember too, Watson, that the thief still has keys to the museum. We may not have seen the end to his activities."

Arriving back at Baker Street, we found a note waiting for us from Inspector Lestrade. Holmes read it quickly and smote his head in despair.

"There is still no sign of the fossil, Watson, and Lestrade writes that he fears the trail has gone cold. The director is intending to announce a reward tomorrow of fifty pounds for information leading to the safe return of the archaeopteryx."

"That might tempt someone to come forward," I said.

"Yes," he returned. "But it will also tell the world how little we know. We must act quickly, Watson. I am going to revisit the museum. You could assist me, if you will, by searching through my collection of press cuttings and seeing what you can discover about Sir Richard Owen."

Of course, Holmes. Am I looking for something in particular?"

"Anything which might tell us why someone might bear him a grudge," he replied.

He disappeared, and I spent the remainder of the day with several volumes of Holmes's extensive collection of news cuttings strewn around the floor. When Mrs. Hudson came in mid-afternoon bearing some refreshment she looked in horror at me seated, like some latter-day Canute, amid an ocean of papers.

"If I didn't know better, Doctor," she said. "I would think you'd taken leave of your senses. This is some doing of Mr. Holmes, I'll be bound."

"Indeed," I replied. "He has nominated me as his research assistant for the day. But don't concern yourself, Mrs. Hudson, I will make sure everything is tidied away."

"I'd be obliged If you could tidy it away into a bin. It's the bane of my life, Doctor. Such a pile of rubbish."

I spread my hands in a gesture of despair and she left the room muttering to herself. Her annoyance was not without warrant. Although Holmes was a man of science, he was not orderly in his habits. His manner of storing material was to put it in whatever space presented itself at the time, with the consequence that the room bulged with documents and papers in varying stages of preservation.

Human nature being what it is I wandered down several blind alleys learning about the Fenian dynamite campaign of 1883 and the repairs to the London sewage system before settling methodically to my task. Richard Owen, I discovered, was one of those people who is loved and loathed in equal measure. A resumé of his achievements left one in no doubt of his exceptional talent. Hunterian professor of anatomy at the age of 32, Fullerian professor at the Royal Institution, winner of the Royal Medal, founder of the Natural History Museum, Knight of the order of the Bath, the list simply went on and on. As did the mounting numbers of his peers who considered him vindictive and treacherous. Terms such as "odious", "deceitful", and "contemptible" were just a few of the epithets thrown at him by contemporaries such as Huxley, Flower, and Darwin. If Holmes wanted a list of people with a grudge against him, there were plenty to choose from.

Holmes returned in the early evening, tired but animated. It was evident from his demeanour that he had made a discovery but although I taxed him about it, he refused to be drawn.

"It's too early to speculate, Watson, but I believe our thief has been active in the museum again."

"You mean something else has been stolen?" I said in surprise.

"No, something has been added."

I was about to press him further when Mrs. Hudson informed us that a woman had just called and wished to see us.

"I told her you were not in the habit of receiving visits from strangers at this late hour and that I was about to serve dinner, but she was most insistent."

"Watson and I can wait for dinner, Mrs. Hudson," Holmes said. "Please show her up."

"Very well, Mr. Holmes. But it won't stay hot for long"

She retreated downstairs and returned a few minutes later followed by Gladys Berry in a state of confusion.

"I'm sorry to disturb you, gentlemen," she began. "I know it's not convenient to call at this time, but I've had a letter which has worried me to death."

"Don't upset yourself, dear lady," Holmes said. "Doctor Watson and I are not engaged in anything particular at the moment. Please sit down and take your time."

"Thank you, sir," she said, holding out an envelope. "I had this sympathy card, first thing today. I've had several recently, but not like this."

Holmes took the envelope. Inside was a black-edged card containing a short message.

"Dear Mrs. Berry," Holmes read. *"I'm sorry for your loss. Martin was a decent man and didn't deserve his death. I want you to know that everything will be made right, and I hope you will accept the enclosed."*

"What does it mean, Mr. Holmes? What's going to be put right?"

"It's unsigned," said Holmes. "I take it you have no idea who sent it?"

"No sir, none at all, nor why he should give me money."

"How much was enclosed?" I asked.

"Fifty pounds," she replied. "I've never had so much money in my life. What will people think? I had nothing to do with the robbery, you must believe me."

"I do," said Holmes. And so will the police. You were completely right to bring this to me. All I ask is that you say nothing to anyone about it."

"But what about the money? What shall I do with it."

"Keep it," replied Holmes. "It's not against the law to retain money sent anonymously."

"Thank you, sir. You've taken a weight off my mind."

"What do you make of it, Holmes?" I asked after she had gone.

"Look at the handwriting," he replied. "Imagine it written in haste on cheap notepaper and with corrections."

I nodded. "I see what you mean."

"Mrs. Berry's correspondent and Sir Richard's are one and the same. Did you find anything of importance this afternoon?"

"Sir Richard seems to have offended most of the scientific community at one time or another," I replied. "Fortunately for our enquiry, most of them are dead. I have made a list of those still living who might wish him harm."

"Thank you, Watson," he said scanning the list. "First thing tomorrow we shall call on William Flower. It's time we flushed our quarry from his hiding place."

The following morning, we rose early and breakfasted lightly before setting off to the Natural History Museum. From the gleam in Holmes's eye, it was clear he had formulated a plan of action. He had already sent messages to Lestrade and Flower requesting a meeting at the museum and when we arrived at the director's office shortly after eight, we found Lestrade waiting.

"What's so devilishly important, Holmes, that it couldn't wait until a more civilised time of the day?"

"Never fear, Inspector, it will be worth your while. If all goes well, I hope to be able to deliver our thief into your hands by the end of the week," he replied.

"Do you mean you know who is responsible," Flower asked.

"I believe so, but I prefer to say nothing until there is more evidence, though I think it is clear why we have heard nothing about the archaeopteryx. No whisperings from traders who must by now all be on the alert for it. No offer of a ransom."

"Why, Mr. Holmes?" said Flower.

"Because it was not stolen for financial gain."

"What was it stolen for then?" asked Lestrade.

"We must wait a little longer to determine that," replied Holmes. "But I can tell you that the thief is still active in the museum."

"Impossible," Flower said. "We have taken the utmost care since then."

"Remember that he still has keys to everything," Holmes said.

Flower rose from his chair abruptly. "My God! Of course. I will have the locks changed immediately."

"No sir. I would advise the opposite course of action. Give him the free run of the museum. Make it known that this weekend the museum will be closed for important maintenance work. I suggest an advertisement in the newspaper. Send the entire staff home on Friday evening with instructions not to return until Monday morning."

"For what purpose, Mr. Holmes?"

"The thief will suspect that you intend to change the locks over the weekend. He will know that he has one last chance of unfettered access to the museum. Friday night it will be locked and empty. If he has unfinished business this will be his opportunity to return and we, gentlemen, will be waiting for him."

"It sounds like a long shot, Holmes," Lestrade said.

"I couldn't agree more, Inspector," he replied. "I may have misjudged my man. But it's worth a try."

"And if it fails"? Flower asked.

"Then I fear for the safety of the archaeopteryx," Holmes said.

"Then by all means let's do it, sir."

❖

Friday evening, February 17, was the coldest night of the year. The temperature had slumped to minus fourteen degrees Fahrenheit, with snow forecast for midnight. The prospect of spending many hours in the cold, dark recesses of the Natural History Museum was not an inviting one. Mrs. Hudson had prepared some sandwiches for us, and I took the precaution of packing a flask of brandy.

"It's utter folly, Doctor," she said, shaking her head in bewilderment. "You'll both catch your deaths."

"Very possibly. But you know what Holmes is like once his mind is made up. He's impervious to reason," I replied.

"Then make sure you wear two of everything. Tell Mr. Holmes."

I nodded, but I had seen little of Holmes in the days leading up to our adventure. He had spent the intervening time buried in the national records office at Somerset House and resisted any attempt to discover what he was doing.

"All in good time, Watson," was all he would say in his maddeningly inscrutable manner.

So it was that at six o'clock when we would normally have been looking forward to a hot supper in front of a roaring fire, we sat heavily mummified in winter clothing in a hansom cab bound for South Kensington.

"How do you rate our chances of success?" I asked.

"Forty to sixty," he replied.

"As low as that?"

"I'm afraid so. And I apologise in advance for ruining your evening."

"Then I propose a wager to enliven matters. Five pounds says we are successful."

He laughed loudly. "You are incorrigible, Watson. Very well, five pounds it is."

When we arrived at the museum, Lestrade and Flower were waiting for us by a side entrance. We nodded quickly to them and Flower opened the door. Inside it was dark and musty, with a smell of old bones and ancient stones like a church crypt. We seemed to be in the bowels of the museum. Holmes put his finger to his lips, and we followed him up several staircases to the galleries above. As we passed the seated figure of Darwin, I put my hand on the ghostly white marble and felt its profound coldness like a current of electricity through my fingers. Reaching the first gallery where the larger fossils were displayed Holmes assigned each of us to a position instructing us to conceal ourselves on the floor behind a display case and remain silent. If the thief appeared, we should stay hidden until a signal from him.

Flower locked the gallery door and we settled down. I have waited on many occasions in my life with Holmes for something eventful to begin and have always been amazed how much stamina is needed in doing nothing. Every impulse to cough, scratch or move one's limbs has to be unnaturally controlled. The sheer effort of it is excruciating until, with a kind of saving grace, tiredness envelops the senses, and one begins to drowse. And also, unfortunately, to snore. The first I knew of this was a hissing noise from Holmes.

"Watson, for God's sake, wake up."

I came to with a start, "What is it? Is he here?"

"No," he replied. "And he's not likely to come with your infernal noise."

"Sorry, Holmes. What time is it?"

"Almost midnight. Now be quiet."

I got my brandy flask out and took a quick draught. Never was alcohol so welcome. The liquid fire burnt in my throat and I felt instantly alert.

"Sssh," came Holmes's voice again. "Listen!"

I strained my ears against the dark and heard, as if from afar, the scraping sound of metal on metal. Someone was attempting to unlock the gallery door. After a couple of minutes, the door swung open and the light from a lantern pierced the darkness. I huddled down further into my greatcoat as the beam swept over me followed by the echo of footsteps advancing cautiously down the aisle of the gallery. Midway down, they stopped, and I heard the noise of something being moved. This continued for several minutes until a sigh signalled its completion and our visitor began moving back down the aisle. Suddenly, Holmes sprang from his hiding place and slammed the gallery door shut. The figure stopped abruptly and looked around him, startled.

"It's no good," said Holmes. "There are too many of us."

Flower and Lestrade both stood up. Flower stared uncomprehendingly at the figure of the slight young man standing before us.

"Jewsbury!" he said. "What in God's name is the meaning of this?"

"I have returned the archeopteryx, sir," the man replied. "It's completely unharmed."

We stared down the aisle to where he had been working and saw the stand on which the fossil had rested, with the display cases re-attached. The director took the lamp from Jewsbury and rushed over to them. He stood for a moment, head bowed, and then said, "Thank God for that. The archeopteryx appears to be intact, Mr. Holmes."

"You are Gideon Mantell's grandson, are you not?" Holmes said addressing the young man.

"Yes, sir, though I don't know how you know that," he replied.

Inspector Lestrade stepped forward and put a hand on his shoulder.

"Stephen Jewsbury," he said. "I arrest you for theft and for the murder of Martin Berry."

Jewsbury shook his head. "No, I admit to stealing the archaeopteryx, but Martin's death was an accident."

"Inspector," Holmes put in. "Before you arrest him might I suggest that we return to Baker Street where we can be more comfortable and allow Jewsbury to give his account of things. I for one would like to hear what he has to say."

"It's highly irregular," Lestrade said.

"So is the situation," Holmes replied. "You can arrest him just as well at Baker Street."

"I suppose there's no harm. But I must take him to the station immediately afterwards."

"Then let us return to a warm fire and a glass of whisky," said Holmes.

Half an hour later we were all seated in Baker Street where we thawed out around a good fire, and Mrs. Hudson performed one of her miraculous feats of conjuring up some hot food out of thin air.

"Now, Lestrade," Holmes began. "It will probably take me about three-quarters of an hour to smoke a bowlful of tobacco. I suggest we allow Jewsbury that time to explain to us why he decided to steal and then return the most famous fossil in England."

"Very well, Holmes" Lestrade replied. "I could do with another dram of your fine whisky, though."

"Help yourself, Inspector. How about you, Jewsbury?

He shook his head.

"Then please begin by telling us exactly who you are."

"I am the only child of Geraldine Jewsbury and Walter Mantell, the son of Gideon Mantell."

"The paleontologist," put in Holmes.

"Yes, sir. My father emigrated to New Zealand before I was born. So, I was raised by my mother. It was from her that I learned the story of my grandfather. How he found the fossilised remains of an iguanodon, one of the first dinosaurs to be discovered in England, and how his career as a paleontologist was ruined by Richard Owen."

"Why would Owen do that?" I asked.

"He was a young professor at the Royal Society at the time, a rising star in paleontology. He saw my grandfather as a rival and determined to destroy his reputation. He had many of his research papers rejected by the Society and claimed the discovery of the iguanodon for himself."

"But surely," I said. "Your grandfather can't have been entirely without friends?"

"He was a poor country doctor, sir, whereas Owen was well connected and had influence. But that wasn't the end of it. In 1841 he had a serious accident. He fell from the seat of a carriage crossing Clapham Common and was pulled by the reins underneath the horses' hooves. He was crippled for the rest of his life."

"My God, how awful," I said.

"But Owen didn't stop. He continued to attack his work publicly and did his best to prevent it being published. Eventually, in 1851, my grandfather took his own life."

A silence fell on the company. Jewsbury's narrative was darker and more painful than we had expected.

"And it was this which prompted you to steal the archaeopteryx?" Holmes said.

"My mother died of cancer, sir, a few years ago, shortly before Sir Richard became the director of the Natural History Museum. The thought of that man enjoying the fruits of success and public acclaim was too much to bear. I promised on my mother's grave, to seek justice for my grandfather. She was a wealthy woman and left me well provided for, so I had no need to work for a living, but I took a job at the Natural History Museum. I wrote several letters anonymously to Owen, threatening to expose him unless he publicly acknowledged my grandfather's discovery of the iguanodon."

"You tried to blackmail him, in fact," Lestrade interjected.

Holmes raised his hand. "Let us hear him out, Inspector."

"Thank you, sir," Jewsbury said. "In any event, my efforts were futile. Owen was hardened against such threats and too powerful to be troubled by them. So I decided on more serious action. I had become friendly with another attendant, Martin Berry. It was his job to guard the more valuable of the museum's exhibits, one of which was the archaeopteryx. I knew Owen considered the purchase and description of this to be his finest achievement. I determined to steal the fossil with the help of Berry and dispose of it abroad unless Sir Richard published a true account of Gideon Mantell's discovery in the newspapers. After that, I would see the fossil returned. I offered Martin £100 to help me. With that, he could afford to give up his post, which he had come to hate, and start a new life away from London, with his wife."

Jewsbury paused in his narrative. "Perhaps I could have that drink now, Mr. Holmes."

Holmes got up and poured him a shot of whisky. "What went wrong?" He asked. "It sounds a simple enough plan."

"I reckoned without Martin's conscience," he replied. "We agreed that he would let me into the museum after dark and help me dismantle the display cases, after which I would tie him to a chair to give the appearance that he had been overpowered by an assailant. At his insistence, I agreed to hit him on the jaw. But the more I brooded on the wrong done to my grandfather, the more it seemed to me unlikely that my course of action would get justice from Owen. If I wanted that, I would have to exact it myself. I decided I would destroy the archaeopteryx and send it back to Sir Richard, to hurt him, as he'd hurt my grandfather. After I had tied Martin up, I told him of my change of plan. That was my mistake. He was appalled and begged me not to do it and when I said my mind was made up, he began wrestling with his ropes to get free. I put the money I had agreed to give him in his pocket and left the museum taking his keys with me. But in my hurry to escape I forgot to lock the outer door behind me and when I reached Pelham Street, I saw he was pursuing me. He came abreast of me and tried to secure my arms with the rope. I was desperate to get free and pushed him as hard as I could away from me. What happened next has haunted me ever since."

He paused and wiped the beads of sweat which had appeared on his brow.

"Martin fell back into the street, in front of a carriage. I didn't mean him to die, Mr. Holmes. I tried to hold onto him, but I couldn't. He screamed as he went under the horses' hooves. I can still hear it."

"What did you do?" I asked.

He looked up at us, his face ashen. "I ran," he said. "God forgive me. I ran, as fast as I could. But after that, gentlemen, I had no appetite for revenge. It fell completely away from me. I had inflicted on Martin the same injuries my grandfather had suffered all those years ago. And for what purpose? The more I looked at the fossil the more I realised I couldn't destroy it just to wreak revenge on an old man. The only honourable course of action was to return the archaeopteryx unharmed. And if you hadn't caught me, Mr. Holmes, I would have surrendered myself to the police."

285

The first light of dawn had begun to filter through the curtains by the time Jewsbury had finished his story. Lestrade put a pair of handcuffs on him and, after formally charging him, led him away. Flower followed soon after having thanked Holmes profusely for rescuing the archaeopteryx. And then we were alone, I looked at Holmes and wondered if he felt the same as I. Normally, on completion of a case, there was a feeling of satisfaction at the successful conclusion. But not on this occasion.

"A tragic tale," I said. "A young life destroyed and one ruined."

"Indeed," he replied. "There can be no good ending where revenge is the matter."

"What made you suspect him?"

"Do you remember our first visit to the museum? I spent some time looking at the fossil collection. There was an iguanodon in an adjacent gallery. A magnificent specimen. Beside it was a card attributing its discovery to Richard Owen. When I paid my second visit a few days ago, there was a different card attributing it to Gideon Mantell."

"The thing that was added?"

"Yes. I was certain then that the motive for the theft had to be personal. I knew a little of Mantell, but he had died many years ago and his son had settled in New Zealand. If this were the work of a relative, it was likely to be of the next generation along, someone who by now would be well into his twenties. There were only three people at the museum of that age, one of whom was Jewsbury. The morning I spent in Somerset House I was searching for their birth certificates. Jewsbury's gave his father as Walter Mantell."

"A wonderful piece of detection Holmes."

"And one which has cost me £5," he said, holding out a note.

I laughed. "Which is exactly the amount I lost on that horse several days ago."

"And which you will no doubt lose again, before long."

"I wonder what made Martin Berry so determined to save the archaeopteryx," I said. "Why should he care, after all, he had been paid?"

"People are always surprising us," he replied. "I suspect Berry's wife was right about him. He was not a happy man, but he was basically a good one. While he could countenance the fossil being sold, the thought of its wanton destruction was just too much."

"What do you think will happen to Jewsbury?" I asked.

"With a good lawyer, which he can obviously afford, he should be free in a few years. He can claim the death of Berry as self-defence, and he will gain some credit for returning the archaeopteryx unharmed."

"Meanwhile, Sir Richard Owen escapes with his reputation intact."

"Perhaps, but I have no doubt that Jewsbury will have his day in court, where he will tell his story again."

Two weeks later we received an invitation from William Flower to the Natural History Museum where a small celebration was being held for the safe return of the archaeopteryx. Though Holmes was not usually interested in such events, on this occasion, he decided to go. It was a brief affair consisting of a speech by the director and several glasses of champagne. Afterwards, we stood in front of the display cases contemplating the fossil.

"You know, Holmes. The copy which we were given does not do it justice," I said. "It is quite beautiful."

"Yes, Watson," he returned. "Observe the delicate outline of the wings etched into the limestone like gossamer, and the limbs, looking as though they are about to leap into life again. Whoever, or whatever, was responsible for such a thing, it is a miracle of nature even in death. I regard myself as a man of science but there is something here beyond a simple artefact."

I looked at him in surprise and saw that he was moved more than I had known him to be before.

"What do you mean, Holmes?"

"Several decades ago, a young poet, a man not much younger than Jewsbury, stood in the British Museum contemplating an object of exquisite beauty from the ancient world, an object which he knew would survive him, but which brought him a message of consolation: 'Beauty is truth, truth beauty. That is all ye know on earth and all ye need to know'."

The Dunwich Ghost

The summer of 1898 was excessively hot. A dry spell had set in at the beginning of June and by July temperatures had soared into the nineties, with uncomfortably humid nights and sweltering days. I had taken a couple of consulting rooms in Paddington and begun practising again. My army pension, which was barely sufficient at the best of times, had become sorely depleted as a consequence of a run of bad luck at the tables, and I reluctantly decided that it was time to abandon the life of comfortable idleness to which I had become accustomed and render myself useful once more to the general public. Thus it was that five mornings a week, I sat behind a desk in my consulting room ministering to the sick of Westminster, with the windows flung wide open. I hadn't seen Holmes in several weeks, not since he'd travelled to Amsterdam on a case involving the disappearance of Wilhelmina, the young Queen of the Netherlands. It was the first time we had lived apart from one another since I had returned to 221B Baker Street some years before and I had begun to realise how much I missed his company. The day after he left, Mrs. Hudson took it upon herself to tidy our rooms, a duty she embarked on with extraordinary Scottish zeal.

"Never fear doctor," she said. "I'll soon have everything shipshape."

I nodded cheerily, but in my heart, I wished she would leave things as they were. Holmes's untidiness was legendary, but it spoke of his presence. As the days rolled on, I became used to dining alone and going to bed early. During the day, I had my practice to distract me, but time weighed heavily. I received the occasional letter from

Holmes narrating the latest developments in the case, but they were dry and dull by comparison with his conversation. However extraordinary his talents, Holmes was no correspondent. So, it was with unexpected pleasure that one morning, before I left for my surgery, I received an invitation from an old army friend of mine, to dine with him at the Regimental Club in Pall Mall.

Colonel Gerald Wainwright was a few years older than I and also my senior in rank, but we had struck up a close friendship during my time in Afghanistan. He was a long-serving soldier with a veritable chest of campaign medals and had taken me under his wing when I arrived in the Middle East. In turn, I was fortunate in being able to do him a singular service by extracting venom from a snake bite dangerously near a major artery, a procedure which undoubtedly saved his life, and which he had never forgotten. But I had heard nothing from him since his retirement, which occurred ten years or so after I was invalided home. All I knew was that he had an estate on the Suffolk coast, and I imagined him happily ensconced there with his wife.

The Colonel's letter said very little beyond the fact that he was coming up to town on some business concerning his estate and knowing of my address from the regimental office, would be delighted if we could renew our acquaintance. I replied immediately, accepting his invitation and, accordingly, two days later, as dusk began to descend on the city, I set off for Pall Mall in my regimental dress suit. The club was a handsome building in early Regency style with classical porticos and wrought-iron balconies. My own membership had lapsed long since, a victim of the economies forced on me in recent years, and in truth, I had only entered its portals on one occasion before. This was not the case with the Colonel, however, whose name gained me instant admission. I was escorted upstairs to a large, carpeted lounge with deep armchairs and heavily draped, tall windows. Around the room, groups of men were smoking and drinking. The busy hum paused briefly as I entered, and then resumed. I was led over to the far side of a room to where a tall, bearded man was sitting solemnly over a brandy glass. He looked up as I approached, and I saw the light of recognition in his eyes.

"Watson," he said getting up and stretching out his hand. "It's good to see you."

"Colonel," I replied, taking his hand. "I was extremely glad to get your letter."

He beckoned towards an armchair and we sat down.

"I was concerned you might think it an imposition," he went on. "After all, it's been quite some time."

"Not at all," I replied. "I look back on those years with fondness. Apart from my wound, of course."

"Does it still trouble you?"

"From time to time. But one gets used to such things. Others suffered much worse than I."

"Indeed. Are you still in touch with anyone?"

"Unfortunately not. Which is why your letter was so welcome. It's my own fault of course. I have discovered a streak of slothfulness since leaving the service."

He smiled. "I find that hard to believe."

"I live with someone who has enough energy for an entire battalion."

"Mr. Holmes?"

"Precisely."

"My wife and I enjoyed reading about his exploits. Tell me. Are they all true?"

"Holmes would say I embellish them. And perhaps I do. But were he to write them, nobody would read them. It's a constant bone of contention between us."

The Colonel looked down at his brandy glass and I had a sense that the conversation was effortful for him.

"How is your wife?" I asked. "Well, I trust."

He hesitated briefly before replying. "She died last year, Watson."

"I am very sorry to hear that," I said. "Had she been ill?"

He shook his head. "It was an accident, though I blame myself for it. She drowned."

"Drowned!" I echoed. The word fell heavily between us.

"We were out in the bay in our sailing boat and a freak wave caught her."

"How dreadful, but you cannot be to blame for that."

"It was my decision to go out that day. Martha didn't want to. She said there had been a weather warning. I ignored her."

A waiter appeared at that moment and informed us that our dining table was ready, and we followed him into an adjoining oak-panelled room decorated with regimental insignia, reminiscent of an officer's mess.

"You do not object to eating here?" the Colonel asked.

"Not in the slightest," I replied. "I was pleased to find that my dress suit still fits me."

"I have always considered the regiment as a kind of family," he continued. "A sentimental notion, I know, but I'm accepted here, with no fuss. Whenever I have occasion to come up to London, I make a point of staying here."

"I can understand that. Do you miss Afghanistan?"

"I do. I have probably lived too much abroad ever to feel truly at home in England. Most of us dream of retiring here, but the country of our youth is never the country of our old age."

"But you have a comfortable house and estate on the Suffolk coast I believe. Most men would envy you that."

"Indeed. And you are right to remind me of it. I did not invite you to dinner to complain about my lot. Tell me about your adventures and those of your friend, Sherlock Holmes."

The waiter came over with baked partridges in a Madeira sauce and I spent the next two hours regaling the Colonel with some of the more eventful of our cases. I was rewarded by seeing his eyes regain their animation. He was particularly taken with the fate of Major Bartholomew in the "Sicilian Defence." He had known Bartholomew and read with surprise about his sudden death in the Dolomites. At the end of my story, he shook his head sadly,

"He was a fine soldier," he said.

"Holmes always regarded the case as one of his failures," I replied. "Wrongly, in my view."

With the conclusion of my narrative, we fell silent again. We had each drunk a considerable amount of brandy, which was beginning to take its effect, and had reached that part of the evening where both parties realise the need to separate but neither wishes to initiate it. I was about to get up when the Colonel put his hand on my arm.

"I can't tell you how much I have enjoyed this evening," he said. "My circle of friends is limited these days. Martha was always the sociable one."

"These things take time, Colonel. A year is not very long. I miss Holmes, although it's only been a few weeks."

He glanced keenly at me. "Have you ever been to Suffolk?"

"No," I replied. "The closest is Lincolnshire."

"Then come and stay with me. It's beautiful at this time of year. And Dunwich is a fascinating place. I can promise you an interesting time."

"I am sorry. It's tempting but I have my practice to take care of."

"Are you sure?" he said. "I have an excellent wine cellar."

Two days later as I sat by the window on the morning train from Liverpool Street to Ipswich, I thought of the Colonel's invitation. It occurred to me that it had really been the purpose of the entire evening. He had waited till I was at my most relaxed and pliable before planting the seed in my mind, rightly calculating that I was not too enamoured of my practice and pretty much at a loose end now that Holmes had gone. I could recognise loneliness when I saw it. His wife, as I remember her, had been a lively, outgoing woman. It was not difficult to see that he was lost without her. As for my patients, it was fortunate that I had a locum who was available to stand in for me, so I could afford to take some time off. In any event, I told myself I was due a holiday and settled back into the leather upholstery to enjoy the journey.

It was another sunny, cloudless day and the countryside, as it flashed by, seemed stunned by the heat. Herds of stationary cattle, and empty hamlets huddled around a spire, appeared and disappeared like apparitions. Lulled by the motion of the train and the warmth and comfort of the carriage I soon succumbed to sleep and awoke with a start three hours later to find that we were already pulling into Ipswich station. I changed onto a branch line which meandered its way northwards along the coast towards Lowestoft and got out at Darsham, a small village a few miles from my destination. Stepping out of the carriage onto the single platform I was struck by the difference from the metropolis. The hugeness of London seemed as nothing to the immensity of the sky and the broad sweep of heath and moorland enveloping the station, and as the train disappeared from view, I was immersed in a quiet so profound, I fancied I could hear my heart beat.

I had declined the Colonel's offer to send a trap, saying my luggage was light and the walk, which was across open countryside, would do me good. The path to Dunwich ran from behind the station, through a wicket gate, and across a large water meadow with cattle grazing. I lifted the latch and the cows looked at me lazily as I made my way past them, mounted a bank at the other side, and entered a small wood. Emerging from this I was met by a grassy landscape, crisscrossed by low hedges, and dense thickets of gorse. My route, such as it was, threaded its spidery way over this expanse. I breathed deeply and felt more alive than I had in months. After an hour of walking, I began to perspire quite heavily and wished I had had the sense to pack some water. Above me, a buzzard was circling in the cool blue of the sky and I looked up enviously at the effortlessness with which he floated like a huge leaf. Dunwich was still about a further half-hour of walking, but I was close enough to catch the faintest of breezes and the salty taste of the sea in my throat.

So busy was I with my exertions that I didn't notice her at first. But a flash of blue at the corner of my eye made me turn my head to the right, expecting to see a jay, or perhaps a kingfisher. But it was a woman, about two hundred yards away, dressed in blue. She seemed to be signalling to me. However, looking closer, I saw she was pulling fiercely at her dress which was caught on a thorn bush. I hesitated, unsure whether to offer assistance, but then she cried out in frustration, "Help me, please." I made my way towards her as quickly as I could. Between us lay a ditch with a stream running through it, which it was clear I would have to wade through. I clambered down the bank, sliding the last few steps, and felt the water suddenly rise to my knees. It took just a few seconds to wade the short distance across and then I was up the other side and looking around me. To my utter astonishment, the woman had vanished. There was no sign of her in any direction. I ran over to the bush thinking there would be traces of her dress on the thorns. But there was nothing. The nearest cover was some distance away, and impossible for anyone to reach in the time. I called out "hallo" loudly and was rewarded by a few partridges springing up in front of me. I was completely alone. I decided to walk a little further, towards a distant copse to see if perhaps she had fainted and was lying injured somewhere. But after ten minutes of strenuous walking, I gave up. She had evidently disappeared in a landscape in which it seemed impossible.

It was also evident that I had become hopelessly lost. The small track I had been following was now completely invisible and I had only the vaguest of ideas of the direction in which I had been travelling. But I reasoned that the sea breezes I had been feeling were coming from straight ahead of me and, therefore, Dunwich must lie that way. I set off once more, wishing now that I had taken up the Colonel's offer. After half an hour, I was no longer sure in which direction I was going. The breeze had shifted and what was worse, I could hear the rumble of thunder. I looked up anxiously at the dark bank of clouds which had replaced the sun. And then the rain fell. Heavy penetrating drops which quickly soaked my summer clothing.

Two hours later, I finally made my way into Dunwich, looking like the survivor of a shipwreck. The rain had ceased, and the heat was building again causing my body to emit clouds of steam in the silent air. It was this sodden vision which entered the bar of The Ship Inn on the outskirts of the village, causing the few drinkers within to observe me wryly.

"Good evening," said the landlord. "You look in need of a drink sir."

"Indeed landlord," I replied. "A whisky, if you please. Make it a double."

"Would you like some water with that?"

I glanced at him, but he remained poker-faced as he passed me the glass.

"You got caught in the storm just now then?" he said.

"Yes. I walked over from Darsham. It was fine when I set out."

"You can never count on the weather in these parts. Comes straight off the North Sea. It's as well to be prepared."

"So I've discovered," I replied. "I thought I saw a woman out walking on the heath."

"A woman!" he said in surprise.

"Yes, a lady. Dressed in blue. She was on her own."

The landlord shook his head. "That's not likely, sir. Respectable women don't walk there. Not on their own. You must have been mistaken."

"Yes, perhaps. I was rather fatigued."

"Might I ask where you're going?"

"To Colonel Wainwright's house. I am staying with him."

"A fine old gentleman, if you don't mind me saying. Though we don't see much of him since the accident. The Grange is about half a mile away down by the coast. I'll get my boy to run you there in the cart."

I thanked him for his assistance, and a few minutes later I was being driven down the long curving drive to the Colonel's house. No sooner had I stepped down from the cart than he came out to greet me.

"Watson, I was beginning to think you might have changed your mind," he said, shaking my hand.

"My journey has not exactly been straightforward, Colonel."

I followed him into the house where, after a hot bath, some fresh clothes and another whisky, I gave him an edited version of my escapade, omitting my encounter with the vanishing lady, about whom I felt embarrassed enough, and attributing my predicament to heat exhaustion.

After I had finished, he smiled knowingly at me. "You made a simple mistake."

"Yes, I realise that now. It was stupid of me to attempt that walk in the heat."

"No, not that one," he replied.

"What do you mean?"

"You should not have called in at The Ship. The landlord is a great gossip. The entire village will be ringing with your exploits by tomorrow, suitably embroidered no doubt."

Later that evening, as I lay in bed, listening to the movement of the sea in the distance, I wondered what permutations my encounter with the woman in blue would go through in the retelling. I imagined myself forever memorialised in some bit of local folklore. Cursing my naivete, I fell into a deep slumber.

I awoke the next day refreshed, after the soundest night's sleep I had had in a long time. I drew back the curtains and looked out on the manicured gardens of the house, bathed in morning sunlight, and beyond them, the sea, at peace beneath the blue of the sky. It seemed idyllic. A point I remarked on to my host over scrambled eggs and coffee.

"Appearances can be deceptive," he replied. "We will take a stroll out after breakfast, and I'll show you the estate."

The sun was almost at its zenith as we walked back down the drive and across a patch of grass edged with a line of willows towards the sea. It was difficult to think anything could disturb the tranquillity of such a scene. As we emerged from the trees, Gerald grasped my arm suddenly.

"Careful," he said. "It ends here."

I looked down and to my astonishment saw that we were on top of a cliff. About forty feet below us was a shingle beach and then the sea, as far as the eye could reach. Either side of me was a jagged edge as though a giant had taken a bite out of the land.

"Good God!" I exclaimed. "Why is there no barrier here?"

"There was," he replied. "Until a month ago. You can just see it below."

I peered over. At the bottom of the cliff in a scattered heap lay some wooden fence panels and the roots of a tree.

"We have had exceptionally high tides recently," Gerald continued. "The cliff is mostly sandstone it can't withstand the force of the ocean. Every few months more disappears."

"What about the village? Surely it can be protected?"

He pointed out to sea. "Do you see that marker buoy?"

"Just about," I replied, screwing my eyes up against the sun.

"It's three miles away. It marks where the coastline used to be several hundred years ago. Out there lie the remains of a city. Twelve churches, hundreds of houses, and scores of taverns."

"And the people?" I asked.

"Most retreated inland. As will those who are still here. In time, the Grange will have disappeared beneath the waves. It is of no consequence to me, of course. I shall not be here, and I have no children."

"But it's still enormously sad," I said.

"Perhaps, though I find it comforting. Just where we are looking now my wife drowned. She was never found, and in my mind, she lies with the other dead souls who never retreated. When my time comes, I intend to be buried there too."

"But that may not be for many years. Martha would not want you to spend your days grieving."

He didn't answer me but pointed instead to some higher ground to the right of where we were standing.

"Let me show you her favourite part of the estate. It's close by."

We followed a path to the top of a small barrel-shaped hill surrounded by bushes, in the middle of which was a bench that commanded views along the coast.

"We often sat here. You can see in every direction, but it's completely sheltered and totally private. Since her death, I come here sometimes and talk to her."

"Talk to her?"

"I know it sounds foolish, but I feel her close by."

"It's not as unusual as you may think," I said. "I have had several patients in a similar situation who do the same. But at some point, you have to accept that she has gone."

He shook his head. "Not yet, Watson. The local archaeological society has asked permission to dig here. It's a Neolithic tumulus. But I have said no. I won't let it be disturbed."

We made our way back to the house through a copse of oak trees, their gnarled and twisted branches flung against the sky like a large web.

"These are the oldest things on the estate," the Colonel said. "They were planted by my great-great-grandfather who bought the house and gardens at the end of the Civil War in 1651."

"Your family has lived here ever since?"

"Yes, I am almost the last of the line."

"Almost?" I queried.

He smiled. "I have a younger brother. A widower who lives nearby. You will meet him this evening. I have invited him to dinner. He is eager to meet the author of 'The Red-Headed-League'."

Roland Wainwright was not as I expected him. In place of the older brother's rather stiff, old-fashioned courtesy, he was free and easy in his manner and something of a bon viveur. The signs of middle-aged indulgence were clearly visible on his frame as he greeted me. It was easy to guess that he was not a military man, like his brother. A fact he confirmed soon after I had been introduced to him.

"You are another soldier, I understand, Doctor," he said shaking my hand firmly.

"Well, I did not do much fighting. I patched people up," I replied.

"So they could kill more people," he remarked.

"So they did not die," I said.

"Now then Roland," put in Gerald. "I am sorry, Watson. My brother is rather outspoken, especially on the subject of the army."

"It's no matter," I replied. "But I assumed you came from a military family."

"He does," said Roland. "I am the black sheep. Never could understand the attraction of parading around in fancy costume with the possibility of being shot at for my pains."

"My friend Sherlock Holmes would probably agree with you," I said. "Though his dislike of the army comes more from a general disinclination to taking orders."

"Sensible fellow," Roland replied. "It's a pity he was not able to accompany you. I should have loved to meet him. He is by all accounts a remarkable man."

"You would probably have been disappointed," I said. "He is not sociable. His preferred way of spending the evening is with a microscope, a test tube, and a bunsen burner. How we have escaped incineration, the Lord only knows."

Roland shook his head. "That is something I can't understand. A man with the intelligence and ability of your friend could make a fortune in the City. Yet he chooses to spend his time on such petty pursuits. It seems a waste."

"My brother was a banker," Gerald explained. "And a very successful one."

I nodded. "Holmes regards detection as an art. Just as a painter must paint and a sculptor must sculpt so he must detect. He is never more alive than when puzzling over a problem and never so depressed as when he has solved it."

"Well, each to his own, I suppose," Roland replied. "And I must say the stories make capital reading. But between friends now, they're mostly made up, I assume."

I bristled at this. "Then you assume wrong, sir. If anything, I have omitted some of the more sensational details."

"So there really was a Red-Headed League?" He said.

"Indeed. And there are stories more outré than that," I replied. "The world has yet to hear of the giant rat of Sumatra."

"Amazing! Let me fill your glass, doctor, and you must tell me more."

Roland took my glass and went over to a tray of drinks on a side cabinet. His brother looked despairingly at me.

"I apologise, Watson. I should have warned you about Roland. He does not mean to offend."

"Do not concern yourself, Colonel. I think I can amuse your brother, though I may lay a few false trails in the process."

For the remainder of the evening, I entertained the company with some of the more lurid achievements of the Sumatran rat. It was fortunate that Holmes was absent, otherwise, he would have been startled to hear that it had single-handedly torn the throat out of several villagers and attacked a bishop.

After dinner, the conversation began to flag and the Colonel went to the cellar to look for another bottle of claret. As soon as he had gone, Roland turned to me with a sombre look on his face.

"I am glad you are here, Doctor," he said. "I have been worried about my brother. How do you find him?"

"He is lonely," I replied. "He is still grieving for his wife. Which is entirely natural. It will take time, but he will be all right. He is a soldier. He is tough underneath."

"I wish I could be so sure. He is acting very strangely. He sometimes talks as if Martha were still alive. A few days ago, I asked him if he had made any decisions about the house, and he replied that he would talk to her about it. When I reminded him that she was no longer here, he said she was upstairs."

"Accepting the death of someone we love is hard," I said. "Harder even than accepting one's own. But I will keep an eye on him."

"Thank you. I am worried the house is no longer safe for him with the cliff edge so close. I have been trying to persuade him to move but to no avail."

"He is obviously attached to it and worried about its future."

"It doesn't have a future, doctor. It's practically worthless now. Gerald had to remortgage some years back. It will eventually have to be sold to cover the debt."

"Who inherits it?"

"It's been willed to a charity, who will probably auction it off."

At that moment his brother returned and we resumed our earlier conversation, but later, after Roland had gone, I began wondering about his concern. It seemed genuine. He was evidently anxious about his brother's safety. And without saying as much was worried in case he did anything desperate. But though I considered the Colonel depressed, I did not think him suicidal. Not then at any rate.

It was in this state of mind that I finally retired to bed at about midnight. I slept fitfully at first but then fell into a deep slumber, from which I was woken in the early hours of the morning by the tolling of a bell. I assumed it was the village clock but then remembered there wasn't one. I slipped out of bed and went over to the window, drawing back the curtain. The sound seemed to be coming from the direction of the sea. As I stood there, I heard a noise in the corridor. I opened my door and peered out. Further down, a figure emerged from the Colonel's room and made his way towards the stairs. I quickly put on some clothes and followed him to the head of the staircase. The figure descended to the front door of the house where he drew back the bolts and exited onto the drive. I ran down, anxious not to lose him. Outside the air was fresh and the tolling had become louder. Ahead of me, Gerald was moving at a steady pace towards the sea. I hurried as fast as I could, taking advantage of every bit of cover in case he should turn round. Reaching the cliff, he turned to the left and followed a narrow path onto the beach below. I watched from on top as he stood for a moment looking out to the horizon. It occurred to me that he was waiting for someone. Then, suddenly, the tolling stopped, and he returned up the path. I guessed where he was heading. At the top he turned right, passing by me where I lay crouching behind a thicket of gorse, and began climbing the mound. I waited a few minutes and moved closer. The hushed tones of someone talking rapidly floated towards me on the night air. I moved to within a few feet expecting to see two people. But Gerald was sitting all alone on the bench, staring into the surrounding dark. After about ten minutes, he got up and began retracing his steps to the house. I managed to get ahead of him, and once inside, I went up to my room and peered through the door until I saw him appear in the corridor and re-enter his room.

The experience left me shaken and alarmed. I had confidently asserted to Roland that I did not think his brother was in any danger, and now this had happened. I knew that bouts of somnambulism were often triggered by intense grief and that sleepwalkers should not under any circumstances be awakened during an episode. But awake or not there was a very great risk of injury. The cliff was hazardous at the best of times but, during the dark, a slip could be fatal. The next morning when I came down to breakfast, Gerald was already before me, sipping coffee and scanning the pages of the local newspaper. He greeted me heartily and I began to wonder whether I had exaggerated my concerns. He asked me how I had slept, to which I replied, "Fine, though I was disturbed in the night by a bell. It continued for about half an hour."

"Ah! I meant to warn you about that," the Colonel said. "It doesn't happen frequently, but it can be bothersome."

"What is it? Some form of warning bell for ships?"

He shrugged his shoulders. "No one knows. The locals believe it comes from a church bell out in the bay, disturbed by a shift in the current."

"That is impossible," I said.

"Perhaps, but there isn't anything in the village which could cause it."

"I couldn't help noticing that you were disturbed by it too."

He replaced his coffee cup. "You heard me. I wondered if you had."

"I saw you go outside," I replied. "You were gone for a long while."

He paused and appeared to be debating with himself how to reply. At length, he looked directly at me.

"Do you believe the dead ever return to us?" he said.

"You mean, do I believe in ghosts?"

He nodded. "Yes."

"It's not something I have ever experienced. I know people claim to have seen them but, frankly, I have always thought them deluded."

"My wife appears to me, Watson. I know she is dead. I saw her die. But I see her."

"The mind can play all sorts of tricks on us, Colonel. You see her because you are desperate for her to be alive."

"I see her as clearly as I see you now, though farther away. It is not an illusion. It started a few weeks ago. It is always accompanied by the sound of the bell."

"And what is she doing when you see her?"

"She is beckoning to me as though she wants to say something. She is wearing her favourite blue dress."

I started. "Blue dress?"

"Yes, I bought it as a present for our last wedding anniversary."

"And did she appear last night?" I asked.

"No," he replied. "She didn't. I am worried she might not appear again."

"I think perhaps you need to get away from here for a while, Colonel. Take a holiday."

A look of exasperation crossed his brow.

"That's Roland's opinion too. He wants me to sell up and move away. But I will never do that. Martha wishes me to stay. I am convinced of it."

He pushed the newspaper towards me.

"What do you think of that?" he asked, pointing at an item on the second page. I picked up the paper:

"Mrs. Elizabeth Fox, the celebrated medium and spiritual psychic will be visiting Suffolk next month. Available for private consultations or group sessions." A brief biography and account of her many successes as a medium followed.

"I have asked her to conduct a séance here," he said.

"Was that wise?" I returned. "The reputation of such people is questionable, to say the least."

He shook his head. "You have heard of spiritualism, Watson."

"Of course," I said.

"There is a small group of us in the village. We meet occasionally. All have lost loved ones."

"Who are they?"

"George Haskins, the local archaeologist; Timothy Evans, the village doctor; and Edward Carter, a retired solicitor. All highly respected men."

"But not the vicar," I said wryly.

"No, though he is not unsympathetic."

"And when will this event take place?"

"In a week's time. I would like you to be there too."

"Me?" I said in surprise. "I don't know about that. If I came, I would be a dissenting voice."

"Good. If Mrs. Fox can persuade you, then I will know she is genuine."

"Very well," I replied. "If it will please you."

"Thank you. And not a word to Roland. He already believes my mind is disordered."

I retired to my room after breakfast saying I needed to attend to some correspondence, though in truth the conversation with Gerald had thrown me into turmoil. Could it be just a coincidence that the woman I saw on the heath had been wearing a blue dress? She had been calling to me, too. And what did it say about his mental condition that he was so ready to believe it was his wife? Above all, what would Holmes make of it? I tried to think it through in the same manner as he would but ended up in a muddle. If it was a hoax, it was rather an elaborate one. And to what purpose? Why would anyone wish the Colonel harm? He had no money, and the estate was worthless. After wrestling for a while with these paradoxes, I took a sheet of paper from my bureau and began writing: *"My dear Holmes, I should be grateful if you could find the leisure to peruse this letter and give me your advice on how I should proceed....."*

I wrote for a full hour, then sealed the contents in an envelope, addressed to 221B Baker Street, and went in search of the gardener's boy to take it to the village post office.

I kept a close watch on the Colonel during the following week but nothing out of the ordinary occurred. If anything, he seemed more relaxed and content than I had known him in days. We took several walks together and reminisced happily about our time in Afghanistan. On the morning of the séance, he was up early preparing the room. The five of us were to sit around an oval table, in the centre of which was a branched candelabra with three lit candles. The curtains were drawn sending deep shadows across the room and bathing everything in a sepulchral glow. Haskins, Evans, and Carter arrived together about midday, dressed soberly in dark suits and waistcoats. Haskins was the most striking of the three, a handsome fellow of about forty, sporting a carefully manicured moustache and beard. Evans and Carter were older, and hung back nervously, as if uncertain what to expect. We were ushered into the room and sat in silence around the table. After a few minutes, Gerald came in, escorting a diminutive lady, heavily veiled and wearing a full-skirted black dress. It was impossible not to feel that we were about to witness something unusual.

Mrs. Fox lowered her head for a few minutes seemingly in prayer. Then she stretched out her hands either side of her. The Colonel, who was seated on her right, took one hand, Haskins, who was on the left, took the other. The rest of us followed suit until all our hands were joined. The medium looked straight ahead of her and then whispered as if to someone standing at her side.

"Martha, are you present? Speak to me."

We waited for about ten minutes while the medium repeated the question several times. But to no avail.

"We need something to summon her," she said. "Have you a favourite item of hers Colonel?"

"Yes, excuse me one moment," Gerald replied. He got up and left the room, returning almost immediately clutching a bright blue dress. Mrs. Fox took it from him and draped it carefully over the table. Then she repeated the question.

At first, everything was as before. But then the temperature suddenly dropped, and a breeze blew through the room causing the candles to gutter. The medium's head shot back, and a moaning noise issued from her lips.

"Who calls me?"

I looked across at Gerald whose attention was transfixed on the medium, his mouth open, his eyes staring.

"I do," he said. "Is it you, Martha?"

"I was called so when I was alive."

"Forgive me, dearest. My life is empty without you."

There was a pause during which the medium seemed to be struggling to breathe and then she spoke again in the same low voice.

"Do not grieve for me. Death is nothing at all."

"But how can I live now that you are gone?"

"I cannot answer that. I am at peace now."

"Shall I come to you, my dear?"

"When it is your time."

The medium's head fell forward suddenly as if in a swoon. After a few minutes, she looked up and resuming her normal voice enquired,

"Did she come?"

"Yes," replied Gerald. "It was her voice exactly."

Mrs. Fox nodded sagely and said more spirits were trying to "come through," but she needed to re-energise. We fell silent for a time while she lowered her head again. After a few minutes, I saw her lips move as if she were corresponding with an invisible presence and then she spoke.

"There's a young person, a girl, I think".

Carter, the solicitor sat bolt upright. "My daughter," he replied.

"She is worried about you," the medium said. "Be careful about your health."

Carter confirmed that he had not been well of late and after a few more messages the medium spoke to other spirits one of whom was discovered to be the doctor's wife and another who was Haskins' sister. In each case, her method was to begin tentatively and wait for some response from her audience. If none were forthcoming, she would move swiftly on until some sign of recognition from us indicated a match. It was a simple but strikingly successful technique.

"There was much energy in the room today," said Mrs. Fox, eventually. "Thank you, gentlemen, for attending."

We released each other's hands and began preparing to get up from the table when I turned to the medium.

"Have the spirits no message for me, Mrs. Fox?"

She looked sharply in my direction.

"Has a member of your family passed over?" she enquired.

"Forgive me, I thought you might know that already."

"I know only what the spirits tell me. I cannot command them, sir."

"But you can contact the dead?"

"I prefer to call them 'the departed'."

"Very well," I said. "Could you contact them for me please?"

"I will try. But they are not always responsive to negative energy."

She closed her eyes and lowered her head, and the room became completely quiet. I could sense the eyes of the company on me. I had dared to question something to which they all gave credence.

"There is a lady here," the medium said, at last. "She knows you, I think. She is called 'pretty Polly'. Does that mean anything?"

I gasped perceptibly. This had been the pet name of my mother who had died thirty years ago.

"Yes," I heard myself saying. "It was my mother's name."

"She wants you to know how much she loves you."

I shook my head in disbelief. It was not possible. No one alive knew my mother was known as "pretty Polly." There had to be a rational explanation, but I could not think of one. I saw Gerald smiling at me and guessed my attendance at the séance had served its purpose for him.

"You looked rather shocked in there, Doctor," said George Haskins, as we were sipping sherry later in the library. "Is this your first experience of a séance?"

"Yes," I replied. "I'm afraid I am naturally sceptical of such events."

"I was too, in the beginning," he continued. "You and I are both men of science, but the longer I live the more I am convinced there is more to existence than science can explain."

"I readily concede that, but there has to be an explanation, and one which consorts with reason," I said.

"Why must it? Who knows what we might understand if only we could suspend our disbelief?"

"And who knows what credulous delusions we would fall victim to if we did," I protested.

"Is love a credulous delusion, Doctor?"

"No, of course not."

"Yet it often defies explanation. That is why you will never convince the Colonel that his wife has not spoken to him today. When you do, he will have ceased to love her."

"I must confess I had not considered it in that light."

"My sister was very dear to me, and I know what Gerald is experiencing."

"You are the custodian of the village museum, I believe."

"For my sins, yes," he answered. "And you would be most welcome to visit it. There are some very interesting artefacts of the history of the village which I could show you. Come tomorrow, if you are free."

I thanked him and went outside for some much-needed fresh air. The late afternoon sun was warm, but a breeze was freshening from off the sea. I walked towards it pondering on the events of the day. Perhaps I had been too ready to dismiss the manifestations of Martha. After all, what did we really know about the afterlife, the "bourne" from which "no traveller returns" as Shakespeare put it? Could it be that Shakespeare was wrong and some people do return? Though why would Martha appear to me? With reflections like these revolving in my mind, I reached the tumulus and sat down on the bench. It was then I realised that I was not alone. Someone was moving on the edge of the barrow, alternately stooping and scanning the ground, before concealing himself behind the next clump of gorse.

"Hey," I shouted out. "This is private land. What are you doing?"

The figure stood up. "That's a fine way to treat a friend," he said. "Especially one who has travelled halfway across Europe to see you."

"Holmes," I said. "What the devil! What are you doing here?"

He climbed up the bank and sat down beside me. "It was clear from your letter that you were making an absolute mess of things. So I decided the only course of action was to come in person."

"That is a little harsh, Holmes," I said.

"On the contrary," he replied. "You have been here the best part of two weeks and have discovered nothing material about this case. Whereas I arrived today and have already ascertained several important facts

"Which are?"

"Firstly, the mound is not a Neolithic tumulus. Which you would know if you had bothered to inspect it properly."

"How can you be so sure?"

"Because they are made of earth, stones, and clay, not brick."

"Brick!" I exclaimed.

"There are fragments here and there in the bushes where the soil has eroded sufficiently to expose it, and because someone has been digging. There are at least two places where a spade has been used to dislodge soil."

"But for what purpose?" I asked.

"That remains for us to discover. But someone knows more than we do. And what is more, they ride a bicycle. I found fresh tracks of a Dunlop tyre at the base of the mound."

I laughed loudly. "I can't tell you how good it is to see you again," I said. "I was beginning to doubt my own reason. I only wish you had been at the séance."

"I have seen Mrs. Fox perform before," he replied. "Did she impress?"

"She convinced Gerald he was in contact with his wife. And what is more, she knew my mother was called 'pretty Polly,' something which is known only to me. How could she have discovered that?"

"These people are professionals, Watson. They do their homework thoroughly. She would have expected a list of all those present."

"But that still does not explain how she knew my mother's name. Would you have known it?

He shook his head. "I confess, I have no answer to that."

"And secondly? You said several important facts," I reminded him

"Secondly, The Ship Inn does a remarkably fine lobster mornay. The crustaceans are brought in fresh every day from Lowestoft."

"Well as to that, I am sure the Colonel will happily accommodate you at the Grange when I tell him you are here."

"No, Watson. It is better that I remain independent of you for the time being. Besides the landlord is a veritable mine of information. He tells a good story about the gentleman from London who thought he saw a ghost."

"Hmmph. I bet he does. What is our next step?"

"We should pay a call on the archaeological society and see what they can tell us about the area."

"The society is run by George Haskins. I met him today at the séance. He invited me to visit the museum tomorrow."

"Excellent, Watson. We shall go together."

Dunwich museum was a small one-storey building in the centre of the village, a few yards from The Ship Inn. In times past it had served as the local school, but this had closed a few years before and children now had to walk to Darsham. Since then, the building had doubled as the village library and museum. I met Holmes on the porch of the building about ten in the morning and together we surveyed the yellowing notices pinned to the inner wall. Someone had a wheelbarrow for sale, another was offering his services as a gardener.

"I wonder what success I would have were I to offer my services here," Holmes said.

"Interesting question Holmes," I replied. "Which is more useful to a village on the verge of extinction, a consulting detective or a wheelbarrow?"

He threw his head back and roared, and it was in this state of mutual good humour that we entered the building. To the right of the corridor was a door which announced itself to be the entrance to the museum. Inside we saw Haskins busy moving an exhibit from one side of the room to another. He looked up as we entered.

"Good morning, Doctor," he said. "I am extremely pleased you decided to come."

"Well, I have been meaning to learn a bit more about the village, so your invitation was very welcome. Allow me to introduce my friend, Sherlock Holmes."

"Mr. Holmes," Haskins said, extending his hand. "This is a surprise. I understood you were engaged on an exciting case abroad. Dunwich will seem very dull by comparison."

"On the contrary," Holmes replied. "It is often in the forgotten corners of the world that the most extraordinary things happen."

"That is well-observed, sir. Dunwich does have the most amazing history as you can see for yourself. It's a small exhibition at the moment but it is expanding all the time. The sea still gives up its treasures. During the last storm, it yielded up a very nice altar cup. It is on display over there." He pointed to a glass cabinet in the middle of the room.

"Fascinating," murmured Holmes. "Is there a map of the village showing the incursions made by the sea?"

"Indeed," Haskins replied. "Though it is a little out of date now. But it will give you a good idea of how much has been lost."

He led the way into an adjoining room dominated by a large round table on which was spread a map of the area.

"As you can see, gentlemen, what is now a village was once a significant town and port dating back to Anglo-Saxon times. It flourished up until the late Middle Ages when a prolonged period of heavy storms followed by coastal erosion destroyed much of it."

We surveyed the litter of churches, monastic buildings, towers, and manor houses listed as sunk beneath the waves.

"England's very own Atlantis," I mused.

"Yes," Haskins said. "One day, far in the future, the sea may yield up its secrets. But we lack the means to venture that far down."

Holmes took out his magnifying glass and began examining the map more closely.

"The Grange, I take it would be somewhere about here," he said, pointing to an area towards the bottom left-hand corner of the map.

"Yes", Haskins replied. "But the sea is much nearer now than appears on the map."

"And the area marked 'NT' is presumably the Neolithic tumulus."

"That's right. I asked the Colonel for permission to excavate it, but he refused. Not that it is of great significance; the whole area is littered with tumuli. Dunwich is a place of the dead, Mr. Holmes."

"Quite," Holmes replied. "You have a collection of coins, I see," he continued, glancing over at a large display running the length of the room.

"We have some very early Roman coins from when Dunwich was a Roman Fort and a few Merovingian deniers dating from the 8th century when the town was a trading centre. They still turn up from time to time."

"And a couple of gold dinars," Holmes said. "Of Mediterranean origin. They are very rare, I believe."

"Indeed. They were found washed up by the old port area."

"Might I examine them?" Holmes asked.

Haskins looked at him in surprise, "Are you a student of numismatics Mr. Holmes?"

Holmes smiled thinly. "I have a passing interest in the subject," he replied.

Haskins opened the cabinet took out the coins and handed them to Holmes who observed them closely through his magnifying glass.

"Exquisitely fashioned," he said at length. "Arabic in origin. See the Islamic inscription, Watson."

"How odd," I said. "Moslem coins in Christian Britain."

"Commerce knows no boundaries, religious or otherwise," said Holmes. "Am I right in thinking these medieval?"

"Yes," replied Haskins. "Probably brought back from the Crusades when Christians and Moslems were at war."

"Who found them?" I asked.

"I did. I was out cycling down by the harbour and saw them glinting."

"Most fortuitous," said Holmes. "Thank you for showing us round. Watson and I won't take up any more of your time."

We made our way back through the museum. Through the half-open door of another room, I caught a glimpse of a large bronze bell. Haskins saw me looking.

"That is probably the most modern object in the museum, Doctor. A ship's bell from the SS Aphrodite. It was wrecked off the coast during a storm three years ago."

"Is it still in working order?" I asked.

"I wouldn't know," he replied. "I have not had occasion to try it."

Once outside Holmes turned to me, smiling broadly. "Bravo, Watson. That was inspired. Did you observe his expression?"

"Yes. He appeared a trifle disconcerted."

"You took him off-guard. I think we may have started a few hares this morning."

"He wasn't expecting you to be there, that was evident. Why did you question him about the dinars?"

"Do you remember my list of important facts last night?
I nodded.

"I didn't get to number three," he said.

Holmes reached inside his pocket and handed me a coin. "I found this while I was investigating the mound."

"A dinar," I replied. "The same as the others."

"Precisely. But unlike Haskins, I didn't find it down by the harbour. It was lying in the undergrowth round the mound where the soil had been disturbed."

"What do you make of that?" I asked.

"Haskins is either concealing something from us or he is not a very good archaeologist."

"And we know he possesses a bicycle," I added

"That too," Holmes replied. "Let us return to the mound and continue our investigation."

We walked briskly back along the coast towards the Grange. The tides had been rather high during the past week and all along the beach were signs of the sea's recent depredations. Groynes damaged and in danger of being breached, banks and shoals becoming ever larger.

"When I was a boy, I used to dream of living by the sea," I said. "But it is a merciless foe."

"The battle between land and water is the most ancient struggle of all," replied Holmes. "If the truth be known, we are all on temporary licence."

Arriving at the Colonel's estate we began searching the area thoroughly. Holmes showed me the evidence he had found of stonework around the base of the mound where erosion had been at its fiercest. It was also evident that despite the Colonel's prohibition someone had been digging in the more concealed parts of the hillock. But though we searched for above two hours there were no more coins to be found. At length, we paused in our efforts. It was clear that further investigation would involve more invasive disturbance. Holmes raised his head and surveyed the open countryside.

"Those are very fine oaks," he said, looking in the direction of the house.

"Aren't they just?" I replied. "Apparently, they are the oldest things on the estate. 1651, I believe Gerald said."

"And they are inhabited," he went on.

I followed his gaze and saw what looked like a colony of rooks.

"Yes, noisy beggars. I can't say rooks are my favourite birds," I said.

"But they are not rooks, Watson. Unless my eyesight betrays me, they are jackdaws. We should take a closer look."

"Whatever for?"

"They are known collectors of metal objects."

"It's a bit of a long shot, Holmes. And besides their nests are out of reach."

"You disappoint me, Watson. Where is your sense of adventure? Did you never climb a tree as a boy?"

"Yes, and I fell out of several too."

We walked the hundred yards or so to the copse. High above us several birds were circling, chattering noisily like small black gulls.

"They are definitely jackdaws," said Holmes. "Observe the distinctive grey nape."

"And observe the height of the nests, too," I replied. "It would be sheer madness to try to reach them."

"They are not all high. This smaller oak has a few within reach."

He pointed to a tree on the outer edge of the copse with hanging branches and half a dozen muddy clumps of twigs perched precariously about thirty feet above our heads.

"If you were standing on a crane perhaps," I said.

"No, No, that is perfectly climbable. I just need some assistance to reach the first branch."

I knew Holmes when he was in this mood. Once he was convinced of something, nothing on earth could persuade him otherwise. It was just my misfortune that "some assistance" meant me kneeling whilst he stood on my shoulders and launched himself upwards. The consequence of this manoeuvre was that I was sent sprawling whilst Holmes stretched out for the lowest branch like a drowning man reaching for the hands of his rescuers, leaving me cursing on my back, hoping to God he would not fall down again. However, to my surprise he made it. And after a few seconds of frantic scrambling, he glanced down in triumph.

"Now you see the benefits of attending the gymnasium regularly, Watson."

"Possibly. But how do you propose getting down?"

"Pooh," he said, waving his hands dismissively. "That is a trifle."

For the next fifteen minutes, I watched while he climbed further up the tree. He reached the lowest of the nests fairly easily and I saw him look inside and shake his head disappointedly. This happened twice more, and I shouted up to him not to take any more risks and come down. He hesitated for a moment and held up his index finger.

"Just one more," he mouthed.

The remaining nests were slightly higher and farther away from the main trunk. Holmes laid himself along a slender-looking branch and stretched out his arm tentatively until he was able to feel inside the nearest of them. At first, it seemed no different, but then I saw the edges of his lips curl as he withdrew his fist and raised it excitedly. It was as he was inching his way backwards along the branch that I heard the ominous sound of something snapping. I looked up to see him falling like a stone, crashing through the dense canopy of the tree towards what seemed certain doom. Directly beneath him at a distance of about ten feet lay a primary branch. I shouted to him in desperation to grab it and almost immediately heard a thud as he smashed into it. Somehow, he managed to grasp the branch with his right hand and steady himself sufficiently to get both arms round it. For several perilous seconds he hung there, legs flailing, and then he swung his feet up and crawled like an upended turtle towards the trunk. Once there he descended quickly to the lowest fork, still about ten feet from the ground.

"I shall have to jump, Watson."

"You will break an ankle," I replied. "Let me get help."

"That will alert everyone to our presence here. I can manage."

He turned to face the trunk and slid his feet downwards, holding onto the fork with his fingertips. I heard a sharp intake of breath and then he pushed away from the tree, twisting his body round to face me. Hitting the ground, he let his legs go limp and rolled head over heels forward. I rushed over but he was already sitting up and smiling.

"You had me worried, Holmes. That was foolhardy."

"I trained once with the Turkish army. Toughest soldiers in the world. I have seen men jump twice as far completely unharmed. It's all a matter of weight distribution."

"If it had not been for that branch you would have been well and truly distributed. I hope it was worth it."

He reached into his coat pocket and pulled out three coins.

"I would say it was, Watson. Gold dinars. And I should be surprised if there were not more up there."

"You are not proposing to go back up?"

"No, I am proposing we retire to The Ship Inn. I don't know about you, but I am in need of a brandy."

An hour later, we were sitting in the snug at The Ship nursing our third round of drinks.

"So Holmes, are you going to tell me?" I said. "I know that look. You have formed a theory."

He smiled and put his glass down. "What do you know of the Knights Templar?"

"Only what is commonly known," I replied. "They were an order of warrior Catholic priests who were very powerful in the Middle Ages."

"Yes, though they are mostly remembered for their financial, rather than their military, achievements. Many historians consider them the world's first bankers."

"That does not sound a very priestly activity," I commented.

"They were formed after the capture of Jerusalem during the First Crusade," Holmes went on. "Their job was to protect the pilgrims, who flocked to Palestine to see the holy places, from robbers and local warlords."

"A pretty hopeless task, I would have thought."

"Precisely. But their solution was absolutely inspired. Instead of pilgrims taking their money with them, they were able to give it for safekeeping to the Knights. In return, they received a letter of credit which would enable them to be reimbursed once they arrived at their destination."

"A service for which the Knights were presumably handsomely remunerated," I put in.

Holmes nodded. "They soon became immensely wealthy. But, as with all things, success brought its own problems. What to do with the money? Some they lent out, but much of it they hid in caves and vaults or buried in the ground."

"I see what you are driving at, Holmes. But what evidence other than a few coins is there that the mound contains Templar money?"

"Two things, Watson. Firstly, the dinar was ubiquitous throughout the Middle East. It was the Templar's chosen currency. Secondly, there was a Templar church in Dunwich until Tudor times. I did a little research of my own in the British Museum before travelling here. It was destroyed by Cromwell at the dissolution of the monasteries, no doubt hoping to find treasure. It was thought the remains were subsequently washed away in the sea. But what if the foundations are still here, on the Colonel's land?"

"Well, then he could be extremely wealthy?"

"Exactly, let us suppose that Haskins, originally assumed the mound was Neolithic. And despite the Colonel's prohibition, did a little surreptitious investigation of his own, soon discovering his error. Once he found the dinars it would not take him long to arrive at the same conclusion as us. But the problem was, if there was Templar gold in the mound how to get his hands on it, without alerting the Colonel. Retrieving it would involve excavation which could hardly be done secretly. So, he devised a plan to convince Roland that his brother was mentally unsound and needed to be removed from the property for his own safety."

"It sounds plausible," I said. "Though I must confess I like Haskins. He seems a decent fellow, despite everything."

"I am inclined to agree," Holmes replied. "But it's a workable hypothesis, nonetheless."

"Should we tell the Colonel what we have discovered?"

"No. I am not convinced he would be out of danger. There is a ruthlessness here, which concerns me. We must be patient and keep our counsel until we have searched this matter to the bottom."

"Well, at least you can now remove to the Grange. Gerald has been asking after you."

"It's better I remain at The Ship. Invent something if you must. Tell him I am not fond of society."

"That hardly qualifies as an invention, Holmes. Besides, he is already aware of that."

❖

The following day, the heatwave, which had enveloped the country since early June, finally broke. A series of thunderstorms set in which confined the Colonel and me to the Grange until the middle of the week. I saw nothing of Holmes and most of my time was spent reading and smoking too much. Since the séance, a change had come over Gerald. He was convinced that Martha had spoken through the medium and that a message was concealed in her words.

"She said death is nothing. She did not want me to fear it. I believe she is waiting for me," he said.

"But when you asked her if you should come to her, she said, when it is your time," I replied.

"But maybe it is my time now. Don't you see? She was preparing me."

Try as I would, I could not deflect him from a pathological conviction that his wife wanted him to join her in death. I wished sincerely that Holmes had not decided to stay at The Ship. I felt in need of his wisdom more than ever. By Wednesday, the worst of the storms had subsided, and the weather became more settled. I gave silent thanks for this and looked forward to speaking with Holmes again. But around ten in the morning, I received a note from him saying that Inspector Taylor from Scotland Yard had wired asking his assistance with a murder at Wapping. He would be catching the morning train to London but expected to be back the next day. He exhorted me to keep a close watch on Gerald and make sure he did not venture out unaccompanied. I couldn't help cursing Holmes. He clearly considered the Colonel to be in danger, so why the devil was he rushing off to London? Scotland Yard could surely wait. As it happened, however, Gerald showed no appetite for the outdoors and spent the day on correspondence, appearing only for lunch and dinner. In the evening we relaxed over a very fine port from his cellar, and I began to think my fears had been exaggerated. We retired to bed around midnight having consumed most of the decanter between us, and I fell into a heavy slumber.

I was woken in the early hours of the morning by the sound of a bell tolling. I jumped out of bed, instantly alert. There was no knowing how long it had been ringing or whether Gerald had heard it. I dressed quickly and went along the corridor to his room. To my alarm the door was open. I looked inside and instantly took in the empty bed and rumpled sheets. How could I have been so stupid as to drink myself insensible? I hastened downstairs. The front door was unlocked, and the bolts drawn back. Stepping outside, I shivered momentarily in the fresh air. The Colonel was nowhere to be seen. I ran down the drive towards the sea and crossed over the lane at the bottom onto the grassy sward. I turned right in the direction of the mound, reckoning that he would probably have gone there. Reaching the top, I soon saw that the bench was empty. I stood on it and surveyed the cliff edge below me. It seemed nearer than when I had first viewed it. Then, I saw him. He was standing about twenty yards away to the left of me staring down at the beach below. I followed his gaze and saw the figure of a woman dressed in a full-length skirt facing towards the cliff. As I watched she raised her arm in a beckoning gesture. Gerald acknowledged the signal and began to move forward. He couldn't have been more than a couple of yards at most from the edge. I called to him loudly and raced down the mound. But even as I did so, I knew I would never make it in time. I was still at least ten yards from him when I saw him lift his foot and step out onto thin air. Suddenly, from nowhere, a figure hurtled out of the darkness towards him, catching him sideways and pulling him to the ground. They rolled backwards in a jumble of flailing legs and arms. I heard Gerald shout in pain and then a familiar voice I knew well.

"Don't be alarmed, Colonel. You are safe."

"Holmes," I called out. "Thank God! I would never have reached him."

"We must get further back from the edge, Watson. It could give way at any moment."

Together we helped Gerald up and moved several yards away from the cliff. Not a moment too soon. With a rumble of thunder, an avalanche of soil and rocks broke away from the side of the mound and poured over the edge taking a sizeable portion of the cliff with it. I heard a clatter as it hit the beach, followed by a scream.

"Quick, Watson. Go and see what you can do. I will stay with the Colonel. Be careful!"

I made my way cautiously down the cliff path. At the bottom lay a huge pile of rubble. Anyone standing underneath would have been buried instantly. For the best part of an hour, I tore at the debris with my bare hands and was on the point of giving up when I glimpsed a hand. After a little more scraping and digging, I uncovered the body of a woman wearing a blue dress, face down. I turned her over gently and looked down in absolute amazement at the countenance of Roland Wainwright. He was clearly dead. A large gash on the side of his head indicated that he had probably died quickly. At his side was a portion of the bench from the mound. As I pushed it aside, something glinted in the early dawn light. I picked it up and saw I was holding in my hand, a gold dinar.

By the time I returned to the top of the cliff, the Colonel had recovered sufficiently to be able to stand and walk. With our assistance, he made it back to the house where I gave him a sedative and saw him into bed. Over a stiff brandy I filled Holmes in on what I had discovered, but I could see from his face that he wasn't surprised.

"It's a dark business, Watson," he said. Brother against brother."

"But why, Holmes? As I understand it Roland was wealthy."

Holmes grunted. "It suited his purpose to be thought so, but he has lost heavily on some investments recently."

"So, he set out to murder his own brother and enrich himself. Presumably intending to buy the estate cheaply at auction."

"Exactly."

"But how did he know about the mound?"

"Because he had an accomplice. This is the work of more than one person."

"Haskins?" I said.

"I fear so. Haskins must have told him what he had discovered about the mound and together they hatched a plan to get the gold for themselves. At first, Roland probably hoped to get his brother committed to an asylum. But time was running out. It was distinctly possible that the cliff would erode further and either reveal its treasures for all to see or, worse still, disappear into the sea. So he moved to the endgame. He decided to lure Gerald to his death. But he needed to be sure the coast was clear. That is why I broadcast to the landlord and his customers at The Ship Inn that I had suddenly been recalled to London, whereas I remained here all the time."

"I am extremely glad you did, Holmes. But you might have told me."

"I am sorry, Watson. I didn't want to take the risk. It was important to tempt Roland to reveal himself. He had already been scared off the first time when you unexpectedly followed Gerald."

"But what was the point of him appearing to me on the heath?"

"You were meant to confirm to the Colonel that the ghost was real. Only you stayed silent."

"So how the devil did he disappear? I found no trace of him."

Holmes smiled. "The ditch, Watson. You recall you had to clamber across it? I spent a couple of hours this morning retracing your footsteps. The stream doubles back on itself after about twenty yards. At ground level, it's practically invisible to the naked eye. All Roland had to do was wait till you were temporarily out of sight and then duck down into it."

"It all sounds so simple when you explain it," I said.

Holmes got up and went to the window, drawing back the curtain.

"It's almost daylight," he said. "Are you up to walking into the village? We need to confront Haskins."

We instructed one of the servants to take the trap and inform the sergeant at Darsham of Roland's death and then set off for the village. The sun was shining by the time we reached the outskirts and there was the promise of a fine day after the dismal weather earlier in the week. Arriving at the museum we saw Haskins' bicycle resting against the outside of the building. We tried the front door and finding it open, went inside. Haskins was sitting at his desk a half-empty bottle of whisky by his side.

"We have some unwelcome news for you, Haskins," Holmes began. "Your accomplice is dead."

He looked at us uncomprehendingly. "Dead! I do not understand, gentlemen. Who is my accomplice?"

"Well, I would have thought that could hardly be clearer," Holmes went on. "Roland Wainwright, your partner in this wicked crime, is dead."

"I don't know what crime you are alluding to, and I am sorry to hear Roland is dead, but I am not his partner," Haskins replied.

"Come, sir," Holmes said. "I would advise you to be straight with me. There is nothing to be gained from deceit now. Do you deny knowing that the Neolithic tumulus, as you called it, is nothing of the kind?"

Haskins breathed deeply. "I acknowledge that I was less than honest about its origins."

"This simply will not do," Holmes protested. "You knew that in all probability it housed the last remains of the church of the Knights Templar, and instead of being just another empty Neolithic burial site, it could be a site of immense wealth. It is where you found the gold dinars. Not down by the harbour as you would have us believe. Is that not so?"

He nodded. "Yes, I confess that you are right. But it was never my intention to deceive the Colonel."

"Then tell us the truth. Hold nothing back, if you want my help. What do you know of this matter?"

Haskins poured himself another drink. He spoke slowly at first, choosing his words carefully.

"I first became interested in the tumulus three months ago when I was carrying out a new survey of the area. I thought then that it was Neolithic and asked the Colonel for permission to excavate it. He refused, as you know, but he did allow me to carry out an external examination of the mound. It was then I discovered its true provenance. I went immediately to the Grange to tell the Colonel. I was sure this new intelligence would persuade him to allow me to excavate. However, he was away in London, so I told his brother, who was staying with him at the time. Roland was extremely agitated by the news and said he would inform Gerald on his return. But he made me promise not to say anything to him myself or anyone else about the discovery. I was to continue the pretence of it being a Neolithic site."

"A demand which I hope you refused as completely unprincipled," I said.

"I did protest, Doctor, but I was eventually obliged to agree," Haskins said.

Holmes looked keenly at him. "Because he knew something about you which would be embarrassing if it became public knowledge?"

"Yes," Haskins replied. "When I applied for the post of county archaeologist, several years ago, I claimed to have a degree from Oxford University. That was not true. I left the university without graduating because I could no longer afford the fees. I don't know how, but Roland found out. He seemed to find it rather amusing, and I thought he had forgotten about it. But plainly, he had not."

"In other words, he was blackmailing you," I said.

Haskins nodded. "If the truth were to come out, I would lose my post and possibly be liable to prosecution. Roland said he would keep my secret if I would keep his. A few weeks later he came to me and said he required me to do something extra for him. I was to ring the ship's bell, which you saw, at certain times that he would specify. I asked him why, but he refused to say, and I never enquired again."

"So, you were not aware that he was planning to kill his brother and that you were part of the deception?" Holmes asked.

"Good God!" Haskins replied. "No, I was not."

"Fortunately, we were able to prevent it," said Holmes. "But that does not excuse you. Willing or unwilling, you were an accessory to attempted murder."

"Gentlemen. I acknowledge that I am not a good man. I have been weak and foolish. But I am no killer. Do with me what you will."

"Thankfully, your fate will be in the hands of the Colonel, not mine," Holmes replied. "I will have to inform him of your actions. He may decide to hand you over to the police or he may overlook it. But you should count yourself lucky that Roland did not succeed."

331

"You let him off," I said to Holmes once we were outside. "You could report him to the police yourself."

"I think justice has been served by Roland's death," he replied. "And I am not about to do the police's job for them."

Six months later Holmes and I were in 221B Baker Street relaxing after a splendid breakfast of freshly caught Lowestoft herring.
"You know, Holmes, once in a while Mrs. Hudson excels herself. The fish this morning was superb."

"Indeed," he replied. "It seems next door's cat agrees with you. He has found enough on the bones to keep him nibbling for the past hour."

He came away from the window where he had been gazing languidly out into the street. There had been little to occupy him since the end of the case and he was already showing signs of that restlessness which was his eternal enemy.

"I shall have to write and thank the Colonel for sending them," I said.

"Perhaps you could also let him know that London is not entirely lacking in produce of its own."

I laughed. Ever since the case, we had been bombarded with weekly hampers of food from Suffolk.

"You should be pleased that he is such a completely changed man," I replied. "When I met him at the club a few weeks ago he was unrecognisable. He has begun regenerating the village, erecting new flood defences, and building a school."

This was all true. The "Templar hoard" as it quickly became known in the newspapers was one of the largest ever discovered. Six amphorae were found buried beneath the foundations, each containing a thousand gold pieces. Gerald decided that he was going to use the money on promoting the health, happiness, and well-being of the village. Despite an initial disappointment at the cruel hoax worked on him by his brother, he saw a happy coincidence in the fact that the mound, which he associated most closely with his wife, had yielded such benefits.

"I was right in believing Martha was trying to tell me something," he said. "I was just not listening. I thought the message was about death. But it wasn't."

When I reported this to Holmes, he said, "I think the Colonel missed his way for a while. He lost his compass. He has now recovered it."

We also received a letter from George Haskins. The Colonel had not reported him to the police but had obliged him to give up his post as county archaeologist whilst he returned to Oxford to finish his degree.

"And what have you gained out of this case, Watson?" Holmes asked. "I know it has affected you more than usual."

"I still think about the séance, Holmes," I replied. "The message from my mother. Could it have been true?"

He went over to the bookcase and reached down a volume of Baker's *Military Register*. Opening it at a specific page, he passed it to me.

"I was debating whether or not to show you this," he said.

I looked at a section in red which he had marked for me to read:

"Doctor John Watson, only son of Nancy Pollyanna Dixon and Doctor Herbert Watson of Shrewsbury, Shropshire. A serving physician in the Northumberland fusiliers 1879-1880."

"Your mother's middle name is there for all to see," Holmes said. "Pollyanna, or Polly."

"And there cannot be a Polly in the land who doesn't get called 'pretty Polly'," I added.

He nodded.

"I suppose you're right, Holmes."

"But you're disappointed, nonetheless."

"Well, you must admit it would be nice if the dead could communicate with us."

"And if they could, what do you think they would say? What do you think your mother would tell you?"

I thought for a moment, "to carry on living and value what I have."

"Precisely. A sentiment with which I'm sure Gerald would agree."